T0013441

HIGH PRIESTESS
AND EMPRESS

BOOK TWO, ARCANA ORACLE SERIES

HIGH PRIESTESS AND EMPRESS

SUSAN WANDS

Copyright © 2024 Susan Wands

All rights reserved. No part of this publication may be reproduced, distributed, or transmitted in any form or by any means, including photocopying, recording, digital scanning, or other electronic or mechanical methods, without the prior written permission of the publisher, except in the case of brief quotations embodied in critical reviews and certain other noncommercial uses permitted by copyright law. For permission requests, please address SparkPress.

Published by SparkPress, a BookSparks imprint,
A division of SparkPoint Studio, LLC
Phoenix, Arizona, USA, 85007
www.gosparkpress.com

Published 2024
Printed in the United States of America
Print ISBN: 978-1-68463-234-3
E-ISBN: 978-1-68463-235-0
Library of Congress Control Number: 2023919350

Interior design by Tabitha Lahr

All company and/or product names may be trade names, logos, trademarks, and/or registered trademarks and are the property of their respective owners.

This is a work of fiction. Names, characters, places, and incidents either are the product of the author's imagination or are used fictitiously. Any resemblance to actual persons, living or dead, is entirely coincidental.

NO AI TRAINING: Without in any way limiting the author's [and publisher's] exclusive rights under copyright, any use of this publication to "train" generative artificial intelligence (AI) technologies to generate text is expressly prohibited. The author reserves all rights to license uses of this work for generative AI training and development of machine learning language models.

For Robert Petkoff, for continuing to believe in me

CONTENTS

PART 1—BUILDING AN ARMY

PART 2—RETALIATION RESOURCES

Part 3—Battle of the Cards

PART I

BUILDING
AN ARMY

CHAPTER ONE

Flames in Snow

"I brought snow with me from America," Pamela said, pressing her smiling face against the cold glass windowpane of the carriage.

Ellen leaned to look out at the London street filling with snow, miniature albino comets streaking by. In the seat across from them, Bram Stoker leaned forward as well, the smoke of his cigar infusing the air. The slushy ruts in the street were deepening, and the three passengers clung to their seats as the horses' charge swerved the carriage back and forth.

"Ah! There's my darling!" cried Ellen, pointing a gloved finger at the back window. Pamela twisted around to peer out.

Two houses back, a small Jack Russell terrier leapt from the curb into the snow-sodden street, giving merry chase to their carriage, biting at snowflakes. Big Ben rang out, each ring reverberating midnight's toll in the cold air, and clumsy partygoers piled into the street. Exuberant and chatty, guests wrangled hats and scarves as they stalked their carriages. *Happy New Year!* Pamela and her friends were lucky to have caught this cab just before the witching hour. Uncle Brammie and Ellen had traveled to Belgravia after the Lyceum theatre performance to pick up Pamela at her job reciting folktales, an exhausting venture after arriving that morning from a transatlantic voyage. A long day for all.

After a hard turn at the corner, Pamela stared out the window. No black-and-white dog raced alongside them. What if he was hit by another carriage?

"Oh no, I think we lost him," Pamela said, scrambling to keep from lurching against Ellen's side at another jolt.

Ellen just laughed, her strawberry blonde hair escaping her purple velvet hat. She was the beauty of the age, a profile featured in all the popular magazines and cabinet cards. In her prime, the actress was as gay and youthful as she was twenty years ago. Many aspired to be in her company; Pamela knew how lucky she was to be in her orbit.

Surrendering to the comfort of nestling against her, Pamela said, "No, Miss Ellen, truly—I think we've lost him."

Ellen chortled, "You'll see, Pixie."

Pixie. No one called Pamela that except Ellen, and sometimes Ellen's daughter, Edy, a long time ago.

Pamela smiled at Uncle Brammie, who winked at her. Six feet tall, he barely cleared the roof of the carriage. In his mid-forties, he dressed like an expertly tailored banker, reinforcing his status as the manager of the Lyceum Theatre. Pamela still wore her Gelukiezanger costume from that afternoon's performance: a crow-feather turban and a thickly pleated pink cashmere dress under her coat.

"How did your performance go tonight, Miss Smith?" Uncle Brammie asked. She was never Pixie to him.

"It was a mixed bag, Uncle Brammie," Pamela said. "I introduced myself to the mistress of the house as Gelukiezanger, the Jamaican folktale storyteller. She asked me what sort of name that was."

"I can understand her confusion," Uncle Brammie said.

"Gelukiezanger is Dutch for happy vocalist," Pamela said, trying not to be belligerent as she saw Ellen and Uncle Brammie exchange a smile. "I think it's a perfect stage name. At any rate, she asked if I was going to perform Dutch singing, instead of the West Indies stories."

"Dutch singing?" Ellen asked. "For a young girl's birthday party?"

"Exactly, Miss Terry," Pamela said. "Then, she asked if I was Jamaican. I reassured her I was born here in London to American parents but would be performing the Jamaican folktales taught by my nanny in St. Andrews."

This was not the first time there was confusion over Pamela's lineage. Pamela heard Ellen once claim she was Japanese, others whispered she was Black, still more said she was from India. She was short, round, with unruly hair and "vulgar" clothes, and her loud laugh and ability to see fairies defined her as American to her English friends.

"So, you bring us snow from New York City," Uncle Brammie said. "How are people to go out in this weather?"

"It snowed the night of my Stieglitz exhibition, too," Pamela said, wiping condensation off the windowpane.

"And how was the reception, Pamela?" Uncle Brammie asked. "Was Manhattan as you remembered?"

"Yes, was your artwork a raving success?" Ellen chimed in. "How could it not be when you're exhibited at the Macbeth Gallery?"

Her carefree tone and toss of her head caused Pamela's stomach to sour. Pamela's family had helped her arrange the gallery show, hoping to get Mr. Stieglitz interested in her work. She knew she was lucky at twenty years of age to have this opportunity. But then she had ruined it; no one had warned her that performing her Jamaican folktales with her paintings would be so disastrous. Maybe Aleister Crowley's curse was in full effect. If only that would-be magician would stop stalking her.

The carriage hit a pothole, and for a moment the entire left side lifted in the air before coming down hard with a crash. All three cried out, and as they righted themselves, laughed in surprised barks. When the driver called back with apologies, Uncle Brammie answered with a few curse words flavored by his Irish accent.

Good. Maybe Pamela would not need to tell them about the reception. If she could just keep the news from Edy—Ellen's critical daughter. Edy gave her enough criticism about going to New York before the exhibit disaster.

"My trunk is still there," Pamela said looking back to make sure it wasn't in the street. Albert, her stuffed alligator, was in the valise at her feet. Arriving at the dock that morning, clearing customs, shoving through the hoards to find her trunks, getting a cab, making sure she had what she needed for tonight's show. What madness to perform the day she'd arrived.

A dog's bark brought her back. The terrier was charging down the middle of the street. Wobbling lights of a new contraption, an automobile, beamed onto the charging animal. Pamela's palms hit the window as the dog rushed to confront the car, leaping in the arc of headlights, stretching out in full flight as he soared. The car skidded sideways to miss him, car horn blaring. Once it came to a standstill, the dog rushed to try to bite its tires.

"Ho, there, dog!" the carriage driver called out. Their carriage came to a jerky stop.

Ellen tugged off one glove and cracked open the door. She whistled between two fingers, sharp and loud, and the dog's head snapped up. He dashed toward the carriage, giving little yelps of joy. Once Ellen patted him on his head, the terrier bolted away to challenge the horses.

The cabman cried, "Look out!" as they jolted forward.

Uncle Brammie's eyebrows went up. "You will lose him one day."

Pamela loved hearing Uncle Brammie's Dublin accent, even if he insisted it was "Trinity Oxford," not Irish. It was the voice of Celtic fairy tales and monster stories.

Ellen laughed. "Oh, no! Mussie follows my carriage everywhere, day or night, going to the theatre or leaving it, strange town or otherwise. Especially since I have this." She motioned to the floor where a small square piece of patterned carpet lay at their feet. "That is his magic carpet. He lies on it in my dressing room. Sometimes, just as we are leaving for the theatre, my maid pretends to forget it and Mussie will dart back up and drag it back to the carriage door. He looks for it when we arrive and insists on bringing it to my dressing room."

Uncle Brammie sighed. "And now every extra and walk-on thinks they're entitled to keep a goat, pig, or monkey in their dressing room."

Ellen playfully swatted him with her gloves. "Now, Ma,"— Ellen's nickname for him—"both Pixie and I have had a very long day performing. If we need a dog or an alligator to be guardian angels, let it be."

The difference between Ellen's performance and Pamela's was that the Lyceum Theatre held two thousand seats while the parlor for the debutante's birthday party was crowded with just sixty guests. Uncle Brammie had arranged this private performance with the parents, patrons of the Lyceum, and the townhouse rooms were packed with upper-class dilettantes and dandies. Coming into the room to perform, Pamela was struck by a sudden memory of her mother boasting of being a "parlor actress" to her high-society, Brooklyn family. And here she was, her daughter, performing in a London parlor.

Right through the blood.

Her mother had died in Jamaica when Pamela was fifteen and attending art school in Brooklyn. Settling back on the uncomfortable carriage seat, she tried to remember her mother's face from a decade ago. She conjured up the only photograph of her: a stern, delicate woman looking beyond her, not at her. Would she have approved of Pamela performing Nana's folktales?

That afternoon she had staged her show as usual: sitting cross-legged before three lit candles, with her stuffed baby alligator, Albert, by her side. Pamela had Albert as a pet, but he had expired at a young age, preserved now as her good luck talisman.

"Careful, he be full of good and bad luck," Nana had said.

Nana would have been proud of today's storytelling. Even if the Jamaican patois Pamela used during her recital in New York was so thick some said they couldn't understand her. But the performance today was a success, from the opening sing-song onward, she felt it. The captivated crowd sat spellbound during her story of the spider and the fish. When she reached the moment where the spider, Annancy, dressed in a coat of tails, tricked old Grannie Fish into thinking he was a doctor, even the dour men standing in the back of the room laughed. Unlike in New York, where Mark Twain was the only one to guffaw, this afternoon's performance elicited chuckles as well as clucks of the tongue. Afterward, guests initially recoiled at the after-supper seating arrangements, where Albert had his own seat at the table. Soon, several young men tried to buy the stuffed alligator off Pamela, but she just laughed and taught them how to call an alligator. Their attempts to make the *chumpf* sound took up her attention until Ellen and Uncle Brammie arrived.

Pamela had jumped up from her seat when she saw them, relieved to be free from the constant gaze of strangers. If only Edy had been there, like in the old days of the Lyceum Theatre tours. Before all the bad blood spilled between them.

Now the dog leapt ahead of them as they passed elegant townhouses and settled back into their seats. They were almost down Embassy Row, where elegant doors marked with wreaths and candles glimmered in upper story windows. The cream of society clamored amongst themselves, street sparrows appearing by their sides. They were local boys working as hired guides, leading stumbling passengers, dangling coal lamps, and encouraging their charges to their carriages. Curbside hansom cabs dotted with snow queued up to stately homes.

The carriage jerked again, causing the trio to smash against one another. Bram's top hat, Pamela's turban, and Ellen's flowered hat all flew off. Pamela's hair sprang out around her head like an unruly halo. She had to pull it back with both hands so she could see. After sorting themselves out, Ellen picked up Pamela's feathered turban and placed it on Bram's large head. With his full, red beard and mustache, he was an Irish genie.

Feeling inspired, Pamela took Ellen's hat and perched it backwards on her own head, while Bram placed his top hat on Ellen, tilting it sideways.

The three imitated one another with elaborate poses; Uncle Brammie wiggled his fingers as "Pamela the sorcerer," and Ellen wagged her finger as "Bram the nagging manager." Pamela performed Ellen's neat trick at curtain call of shaking her head and clutching her heart while signaling with the other hand to the audience to stand for an ovation. Uncle Brammie and Ellen burst out laughing. Pamela's heart skipped a few beats. Her surrogate parents. *Don't scare them by telling them how much you want this moment to last.*

Staying with Ellen at her home in Barkston Gardens was a fleeting privilege. Ellen had a maid, a cook, and a number of bedrooms perfect for company, but there was always a queue for the next guest. Pamela was no longer employed by the Lyceum Theatre and had no idea how long this job with the Golden Dawn designing tarot cards would last. She needed housing.

Last year, Uncle Brammie put her on payroll at the Lyceum Theatre, designing theatre programs and playing extra roles. But when the promise of designing sets or costumes faded, she asked to be introduced to the Golden Dawn, a society dedicated to the study of magic. In London in 1898, the worlds of magic and science were combining forces to see what was fact and what was fiction. The President of the Golden Dawn decided to develop a tarot deck that would serve as a study source for magical skills. Pamela had been hired to cocreate it, and she was to illustrate the first twenty-two cards of a seventy-eight-card deck. So far, she and a Mr. Waite had only collaborated on the first two, the Magician and the Fool. It had been a fraught partnership. And dangerous.

Uncle Brammie adjusted her feathered turban so that it looked even more ridiculous, cheering any thoughts of danger away. Pamela dipped Ellen's wide-brimmed hat down on her head so it obscured her eyes.

"Perhaps I could earn a living staging *tableau vivants*," Pamela said. "No more storytelling or drawing, I'll just costume scenes for parties."

Bram took off her turban and handed it back to Pamela with a flourish. "So, child, speaking of earning a living, when are you going to finish the tarot deck job?"

Ellen stretched her tall, lithe frame, and draped her arm around Pamela's shoulder. "Yes, I loved your first two tarot cards, Pixie."

Ellen's reassuring gesture only reminded Pamela that Ellen didn't know much about the war between Pamela and the black magicians. How the Golden Dawn chiefs fought over her appointment to create the cards, how Aleister waged a war against her, how her tarot muses showed signs of magical powers. She couldn't explain all that to Ellen. Pamela wiggled out of Ellen's arm to sit against the door.

Uncle Brammie squinted. "I know you had a rough time of it with some of the magicians with the Golden Dawn but . . ."

But one of them tried to kill me.

He continued, "But your two first cards are brilliant. This week, Mrs. Horniman has asked me when you intend to finish the tarot deck. You know this project with the Golden Dawn will pay you much better than a theatre job, Pamela. Is working backstage at the Lyceum Theatre or performing parlor shows making full use of your talents? Designing costumes and scenery for other theatres without being credited for it? Is this your future?"

Ouch. Uncle Brammie, always direct. He never had any qualms expressing what Pamela should do next, and right now that was to continue to design tarot cards with A. E. Waite. The funds came from Annie Horniman, the richest heiress in England and president of the Golden Dawn. Just today, on the carriage ride to Belgravia, Pamela had seen Horniman's Tea adverts outside Victoria Station. But there had been such angst and dark magic in the creation of her Fool and Magician—just the beginning of her twenty-two-card deck.

A student of the dark arts, the magician Aleister Crowley had been dead set against Pamela being chosen as the artist, threatening her with demons and terrifying monsters until finally trying to kill her in the Vault, the Golden Dawn's magical chamber. Until that point, the members of the Golden Dawn had no idea how much danger Pamela was in while creating the tarot deck. Aleister had threatened to harm the incarnates she had chosen for her muses. Henry Irving, theatre star and manager, her Magician, and William Terriss, matinee star, her Fool, were targeted by the black magic he conjured.

Pamela was about to answer Uncle Brammie when Mussie barked again. This time he was yapping in front of a great bonfire raging in the middle of the street ahead of them. The huge bonfire created a massive traffic jam, blocking the street. The horses reared, whinnying, and the carriage bumped backwards. The fantastical colors of the bonfire were of vivid yellows and blues; a familiar scent she could not place came over her.

"Uncle Brammie, I have to see this, please."

His dark eyes flashing, Uncle Brammie was about to refuse when Ellen handed him his hat and took her own from Pamela.

"Let's have an adventure, yes, Ma?" she asked.

Who could refuse Ellen Terry?

Uncle Brammie pounded the roof with his hands. "We'll come out for a look," he said.

The driver calmed the horses and shouted down. "If you do, steady on. It's treacherous."

Pamela jumped down first, not waiting for the small step unit from the driver, and landed off-balance. Being barely five feet tall, ladders and chairs usually presented a challenge. Ellen, on the other hand, waited for Bram to help her gingerly down into the sloppy mess of snow.

A small crowd of passengers from the stalled carriages milled around the bonfire, the street completely cut off by the blaze. A tightness gripped Pamela's chest. Mussie approached the fire with caution, tail drooping, head jutting forward, ears folded back. Pamela looked back at Uncle Brammie and Ellen conversing by the carriage.

A pop exploded in the center of the fire. As the blaze whirled, Pamela pulled forward as if a rope was jerking her toward the flames. Like the lure of Pandora's box, something deep in the heart of the bonfire called to her. A dark form emerged from the flames, an outline of a large box. An oversized coffin. It grew and twisted until it loomed, an eight-foot-tall casket, pulsing in the inferno.

She moved closer. She knew this spell; this was magic from her Nana's bonfires on the beach in Jamaica. Her caretaker may not have been blood, but Pamela was still taught the signs when witches, dupies, the bat woman, and the loogaroo were near.

The casket wasn't burning, the fire rolled right over it. But the energy rolling off the coffin snapped around her waist, jerking her nearer the roiling bonfire, the flickering tongues of flames waving overhead like outstretched arms. Where had she seen this casket in fire before?

Dread filled her mouth, then a dry, acid taste. It was the seven-sided crypt, the Vault, from the Golden Dawn headquarters. The chamber where Aleister had appeared as a devil.

As she looked closer into the flames, the Vault opened, claws grasping at the side of the panel before a pair of gleaming arms flailed out. A body floated outside the Vault: a slim, dark man with winged feet, claws, a mask for a face, and a disc on his head. Mercury, god of thieves and tricksters. Naked, he was exactly like the statue at the British Museum: eyes a ghostly white, and holding a short staff entwined by two serpents.

From far away, Mussie barked and snatches of conversation from carriages floated in. But those sounds died away as a loud hum began in her head. She couldn't move. The terrible white eyes in Mercury's mask glowed as he directed the snakes from his staff. The snakes thrust forward, gliding on the smoky air, threading their bodies on the backs of drifting tufts of charred wood smoke. They wended their way toward Pamela, swimming on an invisible river.

A scream rose in her throat. She swung at the flying snakes and batted them away.

"Your Magician and Fool will protect you." A deep bass voice echoed in her ear. Only one person spoke like that—Henry Irving, her Magician.

Pamela shut her eyes. In the blackness, her Magician and Fool appeared. Her Fool, leaping off a cliff, her Magician, summoning forces. Within herself she shouted, *I have magic and I will use it!*

The bonfire dimmed, consuming all of the Vault and Mercury except for his gleaming, alabaster eyes. As Mercury turned into smoke, he writhed upwards into the dark night sky. When the ribbon of fumes was almost gone, two white eyes fell into the pit of red coals. The eyeballs sat in the flames, fantastically blinking.

"Ownership has Responsibilities," the deep voice said.

She rushed to the edge of the dying bonfire and kicked snow at the charred remains. Mussie and Uncle Brammie were at her side, helping to bury the embers. They kicked and hoisted mounds of soft snow into the remains of the yellow flames.

Other spectators began to throw snowballs, scooping up snow from the outer ridges of the fire. A frenzied jostling of swinging arms, accompanied by grunts and groans filled the air as the blaze finally drowned in snow.

After one last kick at the coals, Uncle Brammie walked Pamela back to the carriage.

"Did you see him? Mercury?" she asked. "It was Aleister, wasn't it? Did you hear me call out?"

Uncle Brammie held her arm, steadying her faltering steps, "We'll talk of this later. For now, not a word to Miss Terry."

Back in the carriage, Pamela concentrated on removing the icy clumps in Mussie's fur. A lump in her throat made swallowing difficult. Almost giving way to tears, she rested her head against Ellen's shoulder. Mr. Irving's voice echoed in her head. *Ownership has Responsibilities.* She didn't ask for ownership of her second sight. Maybe he was talking about her art, how she couldn't seem to finish most of her projects. Or when she did, few people took them seriously. The horses settled to a slow clip-clop.

All right, Aleister, I'm back. And I will claim ownership of my tarot cards.

Mussie's yip brought her around. His paw on her lap, his eager face looking outside the window. The dark interior of the cab swayed. Uncle Brammie and Ellen comforted her with kind and soothing words. She looked out the window where Mussie was gazing. Inky swirls pulsed midair in the snow until they formed a beautiful woman's face undulating right outside the glass. It was the ghostly form of Maud Gonne, her childhood infatuation, floating alongside the carriage, escorting her home.

CHAPTER TWO

WATKINS BOOKS

~⌒◞❧◟⌒~

Aleister Crowley frequented Watkins Books, the quaint bookstore on Charing Cross Road, at least once a week. The young magician's ritual consisted of looking up at the three bearded gargoyles flanking the doorway and extending his middle finger while bowing. It was this gesture to dons at Cambridge that had led to his early departure from the university. Now it was a fitting greeting to the gargoyles since they were said to be modeled on the Golden Dawn chiefs.

The center ghoul, fashioned after Dr. Felkin, received the brunt of his animosity. The treacherous Golden Dawn chief, with his well-groomed beard and bushy eyebrows, peered down at him. Felkin had been the main one on the committee excommunicating him. Aleister exhaled puffs of the frosty January air and opened the door with so much force it banged against the wall.

Inside, the afternoon light came in through the bookshop's front window. A small fire puffed away in the fireplace against the wall, smoke dancing with dusty motes in the slanting sunlight. Only four bookshelves ran the length of the room, the scent of old leather perfumed with inked parchment permeated the air. To fill out a sparse inventory, art books were splayed open between stacks of jewel-toned tomes, their gilt titles facing out.

Most of the books were products of John Watkins's printing. The printing press in the basement provided the main source of John's income. A recent review in the *Theosophist* claimed Watkins's published books were: "of paper, printing, and binding, all excellent." Nothing was mentioned about the contents of the book. Aleister was just one of many struggling authors. Since he was part of the University of Rejected Sciences, finding someone willing to publish his work was difficult.

Walking in the center of the room, Aleister saw himself in the ornate mirror on the wall above the cash register. He patted his thick, dark hair. How astute Watkins was to place another mirror on the opposite wall. It channeled magical energy and the means to catch sticky hands stealing books. He approached two men lounging at the register's counter.

John Watkins was a solid plug of a man. His shiny, bald head and bespectacled, blue eyes made him look much older than twenty-three-year-old Aleister, even though there was only ten years' difference between them. Next to him draped the limp, posturing William Butler Yeats. Yeats, a mousey-looking Irishman, also wore spectacles and could have been any number of Irish bank clerks working in London at the time. He drummed his fingertips, stained by his ever-present cigarette.

Aleister spotted the display table next to the counter and Watkins stood straight up. Yeats's framed photograph, a prized cabinet card given to rising stars of the literary world, was next to a stack of his latest poetry, *The Wind among the Reed.* A placard engraved with "1899 Royal Academy Prize for Best Book of Poems" perched on top.

Goddammit, Watkins, you're stocking The Wind instead of Jephthah?

Jephthah, Aleister's book, was proposed to several publishers, to no avail. After visiting Watkins several times to try to butter him up to print and publish his writing, it was gutting to see Yeats gloating over a poetry prize. Wasn't it enough that this dreary Irishman continued to be an exalted member of their joint club, the Golden Dawn, without this damn *Wind* poetry being published to high praise?

Aleister stood apart from the men for a moment and collected his thoughts, concentrating on the phrase that had been bringing him comfort these past lonely months of exile.

The key to the Hermetic Order of the Golden Dawn will be mine, as master, not member.

"Count Vladimir Svareff!" Watkins said, the corners of his mouth twitching. That was the name Aleister used on his first visit here. It had seemed a good idea at the time, but now Watkins teased him with it each time they met.

Aleister sauntered over and rested an elbow on the counter, ignoring Yeats. "Watkins, any new listings in your catalog for me to look over?" Then he turned to Yeats and feigned surprise, clasping his shoulder with a firm hand. "Yeats? How is my old club, the Spookical Research Society, doing? Have you skyred over to magical Maud lately?"

William Butler Yeats was known as one of the most talented magicians in the Golden Dawn. His ability to astral travel, or skyr, long distances to commune with the object of his obsession, Maud Gonne, was legendary. Still, even though Yeats was madly in love with Maud, she had turned down all three of his marriage proposals, skyring ability or not.

Yeats shrugged off Aleister's hand and blew cigarette smoke into his face. "Miss Gonne has more magic in her pinky than you will ever have, despite your congress with demons."

Aleister laughed. "Ah, the manly women of the Golden Dawn will unsex us all. Really, Yeats, do you know how to play the man's role? Miss Gonne has often told you to desist, so now you float to her, like devil to angel. I, on the other hand, can play both angel and devil, as one must in order to heal the rift with heaven."

He plucked the cigarette from Yeats's hand and brought it to his lips, taking a long draw. Handing the cigarette back, Yeats crushed it out in the metal ashtray on the counter.

Watkins waved his hands. "Now, now, let's not have you two in a quarrel."

Aleister crumbled the traces of tobacco clinging to his fingers and flung the pulverized crumbs onto Yeats's face. The whirling crumbs became stinging gnats, biting his nose and cheeks.

With a flick of his forefingers, Yeats blew the gnats back to Aleister, stippling his face with dots of bleeding ink.

The magician turned away and shook his head, sending the blots of ink flying. He took out his handkerchief and wiped his face with care. He faced Yeats, maintaining his neutral expression. "Of course, you have ink congealed in your veins, not blood. Is this one of your Golden Dawn tricks? Or are you saving your cheap theatrics for your tarot cards?"

Yeats adjusted his glasses. "Our tarot cards will be a journey of enlightenment beyond your imagination. All you've revealed is your desire to overthrow an organization you have no business leading. Typical anarchist."

"But this mutt-of-a-child you've hired for the tarot cards is capable of tapping into the reserves of magic? Is her path dotted with fairies and unicorns and the dreary music of your singing poetry?"

Watkins hurried out from behind the counter and positioned himself between them. "Now, you two, enough of this."

Aleister waved his smudged handkerchief as dabs of ink ran together. He held the cloth taut and two small images appeared: Pamela's Magician and Fool. With a shake of Aleister's wrist, Yeats's cabinet card image appeared to take over the tarot images. As Aleister handed the handkerchief to Yeats, smoke ate away at the corners of the fabric. In seconds, the cloth was in full flame. The image of Yeats's head in the center burned, distorted and twisted, turning into charred remains raining onto the counter.

The cloth's ashes flew up, covering Yeats's spectacles. "The holes in your head will burn through all your abilities."

Yeats's brown eyes held a steady gaze as he cleaned his glasses. "You don't scare me."

"Oh, I'm not intending to scare you, only warn you that if this Miss Smith doesn't discontinue the tarot cards, her safety will be in question," Aleister replied.

He felt Watkin's hand on his shoulder.

"Mr. Crowley or Count Svareff, let's have no threats here," Watkins said.

"Ah, John, I didn't come here to threaten anyone," Aleister replied, "but to offer you the opportunity to publish some real poetry—my *Jephthah*. It is a lofty and subtle tragedy written by a gentleman of the University of Cambridge, with poetry and invocations set in the dialogue of a play."

Yeats walked away from them, bending down to investigate a bookshelf's contents.

Aleister called out to him, "*Jephthah* has real Magick in it, Yeats. Magick and poetry, only I can manage."

Yeats snorted. "Is that like the sex Magick that got you kicked out of the Golden Dawn?"

"The Golden Dawn has missed an opportunity to disturb the sleep of the world," Aleister replied. "We could have been leaders instead of royal sheep to the malignant Queen."

Yeats stood tall. "I may be Irish but I'm still a loyal subject of the Queen."

"Yes," Aleister said. "Loyal to a decrepit Queen, peopling the thrones of the world with her offspring, insisting we create by their rules. I've found a spirit who knows the way to battle the Queen's censorship. It will be done with the magic of a newfound science."

"You've found a portal of demons," Yeats replied. "Inspiring you to thoughts of anarchy, nothing more."

Aleister closed his eyes and crossed his arms. "'And of those demons that are found / In fire, air, flood or underground/ Whose power hath a true consent / With Planet or Element/ Sometime let gorgeous tragedy / In sceptr'd Pall come sweeping by.'"

Yeats grunted. "From your *Jephthah*, no doubt. You see war coming. Not very original."

Just as Aleister was about to reply, something smacked him on the back of his head. He cradled his skull, as a sensation of typed words made their way through his cranium. The fiery ulcer emblazoned a pathway to his eyes, taking over his sight until he could only see the letters forming: *Royal Academy Prize—Yeats*.

Yeats had embedded the phrase inside his skull. Aleister's blood pumped faster, the pounding sensation stronger.

Lifting up his right hand, he walked before the four rows of bookshelves. He shook his fist to each shelf. The wind in the chimney moaned, and the complete inventory of books disappeared until all that was left were empty shelves etched with dusty outlines of books. A graveyard of cherished tomes.

Watkins shouted.

Yeats yelped as his glasses fell off his face, but he caught them at the last second. When they were back on his face, the lenses filled with the typewritten words of *Jephthah*. He snatched them off and shook them, the lettering still filling the glass.

Aleister slapped his thigh and howled with laughter. "Just imagine what I can do to Miss Smith if she continues the tarot cards."

Watkins held up his hand. "I'm lost here, Mr. Crowley. What do you care if the girl makes tarot cards?"

Of course, John knew nothing about the properties of magic. He didn't know magic wasn't a boundless ocean of energy just waiting to be transformed. It was a limited resource to be mined only by just the right psychic with access into both worlds, the seen and unseen. Pamela's first two cards had siphoned off most of the lake's magical reserve Aleister had allocated for himself. He would need a lot of magic for his magical reign, and the idiot child's tarot cards were gulping it down.

"You see, Watkins," Aleister said, "she's an idiot savant who shouldn't be in charge of anything with magical text."

Yeats crossed his arms, "She's just a confused artist. Leave her alone."

Aleister stood in front of Yeats and leaned down to whisper in his ear, "If you think she is addled now, just wait!"

He walked to the door, shouting over his shoulder. "Yeats will pay for all your disappeared books."

"You chronic rotter!" Watkins roared. "I will snake you out until you pay for each and every one of my missing books!"

Aleister threw open the front doors, and after walking through them, slammed them shut with such a force that Yeats's framed photograph fell off the counter and smashed. Saluting the gargoyles as he passed, he glanced in the front window. Someone was moving.

Yeats ambled to the center of the aisles. With a lift of the poet's open palms, all the books appeared and flew through the air: art books, atlases, periodicals, poetry compilations, novels, anthologies—their spines, the backbones of birds; their pages, wings. They swooped and dipped through the air, buzzing past one another until they settled back in place. Only the outlines in dust were smudged as books lined up back in order.

Royal Academy Prize—Yeats throbbed in the back of Aleister's skull as he made his way down Charing Cross Road.

CHAPTER THREE

EARMARKED

Waite giggled and wiped his walrus mustache. "Ah, German fountain pens, sixteen hundreds with two quills! Exquisite."

Pamela watched Waite wander over to another display case. How was she to get through designing the next seventy-six tarot cards with him? So far, there had been only two meetings since she was back in London, but already her patience was strained. Who could she go to for help with him? The first night back when Maude astral traveled next to her carriage gave her hope she was being watched over. But that was over a month ago with no reoccurrence.

She tapped her foot, thinking of his nickname, "Wait for It Waite." But even as he moved at a snail's pace, she felt the vibration from him all the Golden Dawn chiefs had: a dark frantic clawing. Metallic. Powdery.

You would never know it to look him, a balding, middle-aged man looking at the fountain pens in the NEWLY ACQUIRED glass showcase at the British Museum. He moved on to timepieces.

I am going to explode. Standing next to her, Ahmed Pascal Kamal, director of new acquisitions, emitted a low hum. In his diplomat style coat and his Egyptian fez, the forty-two-year-old Ahmed was a combination of Cairo and London.

He raised his eyebrows as she turned to him. "Mr. Waite is aware we have a noon reservation?" he asked.

"Yes, Mr. Kamal," Pamela replied. She walked over to Waite just as he was starting for another display case. "Mr. Waite, please, we can't keep Mr. Irving and Mr. Terriss waiting."

"Rightly so, Miss Smith." His faded blue eyes and red splotches on his cheeks belied his dark energy. "How fortuitous you are to have a rendezvous with Mr. Irving. Lifetime fan, I am." He trotted over to her and offered his bent arm. Looking to Ahmed, she saw him shake his head and look away.

Rather than take Waite's arm, she leaned in closer to him, looking at his elbow. "No, I don't see any lint, Mr. Waite." She blew on his bent elbow nonetheless, as if to help dispense imaginary fluff. Transparent strands of otherworldly fuzz flew off his coat and flew back at her transformed as powder puffs, hitting her face. She should know better; magic doesn't understand a dumb show. Waite and Ahmed looked blankly at her; they had seen nothing.

"There we are. Shall we go?" Pamela said, charging ahead through the Great Court.

A young boy did a double take seeing Ahmed's fez. Her own exotic, black-crow-feather collar got no response. Usually she was the odd one in a crowd.

It was a fifteen-minute walk from the museum to the Savoy Hotel. Today, in the frigid January cold, it took thirty as Waite talked nonstop about publishing houses and bookstores. They finally arrived in the foyer of the Savoy restaurant. It was an impressive setting: red carpets, marble columns lining the room, gaslit chandeliers. As she prepared to go into the restaurant, Waite pressed a small book into her hands.

"Please give my poems to Mr. Irving with my compliments," he said with a plaintive urgency. "Until our next meeting, Miss Smith." He turned and shuffled away.

He had let it be known all morning in the research room that he wanted to be invited along to this luncheon. Wasn't he the main collaborator on their tarot cards? Pamela had to reassure him this was a Lyceum Theatre reunion with Mr. Irving and William Terriss. Still, that didn't explain to him why Ahmed Kamal was invited.

At the Savoy restaurant reservation desk, the maître d' greeted every society woman with the solicitude of a butler and charm of a Frenchman. They were handled with brusque politeness and shown to Mr. Irving's table.

Once seated, Ahmed and Pamela watched the aristocratic women in full regalia rustle behind their tables like preening birds competing for the title of tallest hairstyle, tiniest corseted waist, or most elaborate skirt. Perhaps her coat's crow-feather collar and Ahmed's fez were not so out of place.

She was accustomed to the world of dining room etiquette from time with her Brooklyn family and touring with the Lyceum Theatre. Ahmed's rigid posture, blinking eyes, and the smoothing of his goatee showed he was not. This was a very different Ahmed from the cool authority she worked side by side with at the British Museum.

"Fascinating crowd here, isn't it, Mr. Kamal?" Pamela asked, sitting straight up. Even though her feet barely brushed the ground, she did not want to be mistaken for a child, which happened during her last transatlantic dining.

"If by fascinating, you mean that it is relaxing to dine among strangers—men and women—we have had very different upbringings," Ahmed answered, relaxing his hands on the table. Ahmed's English had a slight Parisian lilt. Egyptian, French, English, he was a hybrid, like herself.

Pamela watched him as Lady Glizzard entered. Accompanied by two Irish wolfhounds, she was escorted to her table by three wait staff, the maître d' paving the way. Once seated, a waiter presented a bowl of pate on the floor for the giant canines. Straddling the bowl, and with much grunting, the hounds devoured the contents in seconds.

"For example, dogs should not eat in the same room, much less before us. Your family allowed dogs at the table?" Ahmed asked, a small glimmer of a smile cracking.

Pamela smiled back. "No, but John Jacob Astor's dog, named Kitty, was allowed at eat at every banquet he attended."

"This Mr. Astor is an important man?" Ahmed asked.

She didn't know how to answer him. On her father's side, her grandfather, Cyrus P. Smith, was the mayor of Brooklyn. Smith Street in Brooklyn Heights was supposedly named after him, and there were many nights in restaurants where the Smith family name was celebrated. On her mother's side, the Colman side, the lineage of publishers, painters, and artists went back to the 1600s. Her American family was anchored alongside Mr. Astor and Mrs. Astor's network of blue bloods. How could she explain to him the world of New York social registry — top families qualified by industry fortunes, not titles?

"Yes, Mr. Astor has many streets and buildings named after him," Pamela answered.

Ahmed often helped Pamela's research requests at the British Museum. Every day she had questions only he could answer. *Where were the Sola Busca tarot cards? What does an Egyptian Horos crown look like?* Sometimes, when Waite insisted she use an image she disagreed with, pounding music filled her head and her mouth was full of wood shavings. To shake her out of this mood, Ahmed would find books or scrolls she was looking for, often off-limits to the general public. As curator to the Egyptian exhibits, he had personal access to artifacts unexamined or unpacked. A few times, after hours, he had even given her private access to steles and mosaics still in crates.

There was a quick bark from the dogs as Lady Glizzard tossed them a morsel. Her oversized hat, the size of a lampshade, held a tableau of a white dove bedding in cherries. As her dogs finished licking their chops, they sat in front of her. They focused on her hat's embalmed dove, their great heads following every movement her hat made as she talked to her dining companions.

Ahmed's eyes sparkled. "What is that phrase you use here?" he asked. "Birds may rest in my bones?"

"Birds may roost in my bonnet, not bones," Pamela answered. Ahmed shook his head in puzzlement. "It's a sort of self-praise, proclaiming you are such a good person that birds, carrying messages from heaven, feel at home in your hat."

"Well," Ahmed answered, "I hope the dove in that hat over there does not take it into her head to fly over here and take on your crow feathers," Ahmed teased. "What are your crows' feathers telling you? What to order for lunch?"

Pamela's loud laughter spilled out into the room, causing a few heads to turn in their direction. "Oh, my crow feathers are telling me 'Birds of a feather flock together.'"

"Ah. Miss Smith," Ahmed replied, "perhaps I have seen one too many a hawk take on a hapless bird to believe they all roost together."

As silence fell between them, glances were thrown their way. The British Empire's new restaurants may have many nationalities dining in proximity to one another, but it was unusual to see a young woman with a man wearing a fez. Pamela could tell by his renewed fidgeting he was anxious for the men to arrive.

Tea arrived, and after being poured, his lips pursed. He hated English tea.

"Do you often dine in restaurants with your family in Egypt, Mr. Kamal?" she asked.

Ahmed looked down at his plate. "When I am in Egypt, I am served at our home or in the homes of others. We do not dine out."

Pamela asked, "Did the women in your family have meals at other families' homes?"

"My mother and aunt came from a good family. They mostly entertained at home."

"Did they speak French and English too?"

"The women in my family spoke Arabic, but they did not read nor write."

"They did not read or write? In the country where the oldest library in the world was founded by a woman?" she asked.

Ahmed sat back in his chair. "Ah, your favorite subject, women and learning. So, you have heard of Al Quaraouiyine in Fez, then?"

He would lecture her, especially anything to do with Egypt, with a combination of humor and exasperation. Pamela toyed with the crow feathers at her jaw. She knew his banter well.

"The library of Al Quaraouiyine was founded in the eight hundreds by a Turkish woman named Fatima," Pamela said. "Was it Fatima...." She faltered, her fingers motionless in the collar's feathers.

"El-Fihriya, not Fatima," Ahmed said, sipping his tea. "And she was Tunisian, not Turkish."

"Well, the library was world-famous for all Egyptians," she retorted.

"Except Fez is in Morocco, Miss Smith, not Egypt, and there is a world of difference between Morocco and my city, Cairo."

"How is it that a woman once owned a massive library in your family's part of the world," Pamela asked, "and yet now most Egyptian women cannot read nor write?"

"Such concerns for my region of the world, from Egypt to Morocco," Ahmed answered, his condescension almost brotherly.

She almost playfully kicked him under the table but checked herself. She knew he would see such an act as being disrespectful to him in public. It had been enough of a struggle to get him to accept this luncheon date. Uncle Brammie's vague invitation only said they had a "number of subjects to discuss." Undoubtedly, Mr. Irving and Mr. Terriss would talk about theatre and Uncle Brammie, the Golden Dawn.

Ahmed's face relaxed. "Did Mr. Irving teach you about Al Quaraouiyine when he was teaching you hieroglyphics?"

"No, Miss Farr taught me that during her Golden Dawn course."

She knew Ahmed was impressed by Miss Florence Farr. Florence, an actress, belonged to the Golden Dawn and often visited the British Museum Egyptian rooms, much to his distraction. In Florence's presence, he blushed and became tongue-tied, not at all the assertive historian he was with Pamela.

The room hushed as a woman in the corner began to play the harp.

"Mr. Kamal, do you believe, like Miss Farr, that mummies can speak?"

He smiled. "I believe many things try to communicate," he answered. "A casket, a coffin may ring with past vibrations of sorrow. A crown may echo with a crowd's joy or a murderer's cry. How you hear it is in the paint, in the secret clues echoed within to send a message. With all the forces following you, Miss Smith, I would not be surprised to learn that many things speak to you."

Pamela saw he was not teasing her about her gifts, as some of the Golden Dawn members did. "And what do you think these forces are saying to me?" she asked.

He smiled. "'What can we do to help this girl with this insatiable curiosity? This girl who is not afraid to research Egyptian symbols and curses?'"

A cooing at the entrance set several heads and hats swiveling. Uncle Brammie was in the lead, behind him the taller figure of Henry Irving and spry William Terriss. Uncle Brammie saw her and gave his signature two-fingered salute. He had greeted her that way ever since she had drawn a picture of him as a ship's captain wearing a hat with "SS *Dracula*" inscribed on the brim.

The dapper trio made their way in between tables, a chorus of oohs and ahs followed by a round of applause. As they arrived at the table, Henry took off his hat and made a courteous bow to the room, escalating the applause. People leapt up from their chairs.

"Bravo, Irving!"

"Bravo, Terriss!"

Terriss took his seat, knowing his employer should have the last bow. The headwaiter pulled out a chair. Henry joined the table and pulled a white handkerchief from his sleeve, waving it to his adoring public. A renewed burst of energy greeted the familiar gesture, made famous at the end of *The Corsican Brothers* duel when he killed Terriss's character. Finally, the clapping stilled and people resumed their conversation.

Looking around the dining room, Henry conspiratorially whispered to her, "Well, Miss Smith, our public seems to have remembered *The Corsican Brothers* duel."

Blood rushed to her face. Henry Irving, her magician and mentor, included her in this aside. Her heart felt an extra squeeze as it pumped faster.

Terriss half-smiled, "They enjoyed my death scene, at least." Then, he winked at her. The handsome and virile Terriss was the only one who could tease Henry Irving. Terriss, a matinee idol who worked extra jobs training horses so he could provide for his sick wife and children, was also a major childhood crush for Pamela.

Henry smiled and motioned the waiter over to the table, his pencil poised over his pad as though receiving military maneuvers.

The order was given for the table by Henry's rumbling voice, afterward adding, "Please see to it that we are not to be disturbed for the next half hour."

Uncle Brammie moved his chair closer to Pamela, saying, "I'm still waiting to hear how your gallery show in New York City went."

Pamela felt the veins in her temple pound. She hadn't seen him since they were last in the carriage New Year's Eve. How

to explain to him that her reception was a catastrophe. She especially did not want to talk about it in front of Henry Irving or
William Terriss. Ahmed had heard the story already; he knew
enough to look away.

"Miss Smith is humble and doesn't wish to boast," Henry
said. "Let's leave banging the drum for another time."

Uncle Brammie lifted his shoulders and replied, "You're
right, Mr. Irving." He looked at Pamela and smiled gently.
"Later, Miss Smith?"

Terriss said, "Ah, lass, I'll take any chance I have to talk
about my misfortunes. It's what made me. Failed cowboy, sailor,
farmer, explorer. Perfect material for an actor. That's why you
picked me as muse for your Fool, I'm sure."

She almost blurted out the story of William diving off a
bridge to save her as child, but she caught sight of Henry's half-
closed eyes and set mouth. This was Henry's luncheon.

Henry cleared his throat. "Well, I will say Miss Smith's cast-
ing of her tarot cards seems right; she could not have found a better
subject for the fool," he teased. "Being cast as the Magician—"

"Miss Pamela," Ahmed said, "has applied herself most
diligently in creating her first two tarot cards. She will surpass
all your expectations."

The other men at the table turned to Ahmed as his serious
tone resonated. Uncle Brammie rested his elbows on the table.
"I'm sure we will be proud of her when all of Miss Smith's work
is revealed. After all, I was the first to recognize her artistic merits.
And now she is like family to my wife and I and little Noel."

It was true. When she was but fifteen, with her father's help,
she had submitted her portfolio to Bram Stoker, general manager
at the Lyceum Theatre. After he had hired her to create postcard
watercolors of Sir Henry and Ellen to use in marketing the theatre's American tours, she was promoted to company member.
But her aspirations to be hired as a set designer were met with
stony silences by Henry. She was just eighteen when she first

asked to be considered. And even though she had attended art school in Brooklyn and had a portfolio of numerous projects, she was "not qualified."

"Oh, Uncle Brammie, I so wish to make you all proud of me," Pamela replied.

Uncle Brammie mumbled, "Mr. Stoker. Not Uncle Brammie."

Terriss took a butter knife off the table and playfully held it to his breast.

"Ah, woe is me! The mad school-girl crush of Miss Pamela, gone, gone, gone! I may have saved her life years ago, but her artistic triumphs have blotted all that out."

Ahmed knit his eyebrows together. "You saved her life, Mr. Terriss? Is this a play on words?"

Brammie grunted. "No, Mr. Kamal. The short story is: I introduced Miss Smith's family to the scenic painters at the Lyceum Theatre. Afterward we walked across the Waterloo Bridge. This one"—Bram gestured to Pamela—"leaned over to grab her hat that had fallen off, and she went after it. Terriss happened to be there and jumped in after her to save her. It nearly killed both of them."

Pamela glanced around the room, taking in the women giving fawning looks. She was the envy of the dining room. Here were the idols of her youth: Henry Irving, her mentor and father figure; Bram Stoker, her artistic lifeline; William Terriss, her heroic matinee idol; and Ahmed Kamal, her equal and supporter. To be in the company of these men all at once was thrilling.

Ahmed cocked his head at Bram. "I see. She is like a cat with many lives. Is this why she is creating these cards?"

"Mr. Kamal, Pamela being hired for the tarot cards is the reason for our luncheon." Uncle Brammie took a deep breath and continued. "We believe she may be in great danger. The Golden Dawn and Lyceum Theatre have agreed to join resources to protect her. We'd like to ask the British Museum to also pledge their support."

So, Uncle Brammie does believe Aleister appeared in the bonfire.

The waiter arrived to serve, but Henry waved him away. "Mr. Kamal, we believe Pamela may be in great danger creating these tarot cards. When Miss Smith first returned to London, Aleister seemed to present himself to her in fire, as he has done previously. Mr. Stoker was with her to witness it. Terriss and I have also been approached by otherworldly entities. We think the creation of her first two cards, the Magician and the Fool, may have unleashed — something."

Henry and Terriss simultaneously touched their right earlobes. A slight welt began to appear, then a white series of lines emerged.

The letters P, C, and S combined together into a faint symbol.

My first sigil. At the Pratt Institute of Art in Brooklyn, she had fallen in love with the Japanese style of calligraphy and had worked for hours on her signature. Once she perfected it, she worked the symbol of her three initials into the design of almost everything she drew. From an ancient grimoire, she found a spell that could imbue her symbol with magical intent. Her intent had been to always own her artistic creation while setting it free. She had never shared her intent of the symbol, as sigil spell required. She only knew from the spellbook that her magical symbol could be used as a gateway. She just didn't know which gateway or how to use it.

Uncle Brammie took out a pencil and pad from his vest pocket and quickly sketched something on a piece of paper. He handed the pencil to Pamela and slid the pad over to her. "Miss Smith, I've seen something like this on Mr. Irving's and Mr. Terriss's ears. Perhaps you can tell us what it means."

She saw in his eye a request and a command. She took his pencil slowly and wrote three letters. PCS. Artfully she drew them in an interlocking column.

Ahmed was the first to speak, "Pamela Colman Smith. PCS. I see it now, the symbol of your cojoined initials."

Henry asked, "Is this just a signature, Miss Smith? Or is it something else?"

The harp in the corner of the room played louder and the letters on the pad throbbed in different colors. Pamela looked at Henry and Mr. Terriss, the gray-blue tattoo on each of their earlobes vibrating. She could taste the tattoo's color, dry and chalky. Her face burned with excitement and embarrassment. *Do Henry and Terriss hate having my initials marked on them? Do they think I am stalking and harassing them?*

She looked at the three men staring at her, and she stared back. The mashed-up symbol was plain to see on their ears.

Ahmed leaned forward staring at Terriss. He softly said, "I see them. Her symbols."

Uncle Brammie replied, "I also see them at the theatre. On occasion."

Pamela lowered her voice. "It is true that I created a symbol of my initials, but I never intended it to be marked on anyone."

Terriss laughed. "So, why are they on our ears? And why only at certain times?"

She took a deep breath. "I researched what a sigil is, the emblem of a magician, when I was creating the Magician tarot card. I decided to create my own sigil."

"And what did you conjure while creating this sigil?" Uncle Brammie asked.

Pamela replied, "If my initials were a real sigil, I could not tell you its meaning. I always ask for protection and guidance for all my muses and my creations. I ask that my art be used for good."

"Do you think your tarot cards could be used for evil?" Henry asked.

The waiter came back with wine goblets on an oval, black metal tray and placed the crystal glasses on the table. He bowed and turned to go when Henry took hold of his arm. On the underside of the man's tray was a painted advert. It was the symbol for Crowley's Ale—a large, black crow, adorned with the same crow feathers as Pamela's coat collar.

"A crow for Crowley Ale. How interesting," Henry said, releasing the waiter's arm, who then moved away. "Miss Smith, what sort of feathers are those in your collar? Crow?"

"These feathers are from my Nana in Jamaica," Pamela replied. "I've had them since I was ten years old."

Folding his hands together, Henry asked, "Miss Smith, is this a coincidence that you are wearing crow feathers, or are you signaling Aleister's magic?"

"No, I want nothing to do with Mr. Crowley or his magic!" Pamela replied.

"My dear Miss Smith," Uncle Brammie said, looking at the other men. "We are concerned you may be playing with the dark arts unaware. Aleister may try to channel Egyptian magic, Thoth magic, to create his own deck to combat yours. We want to be sure you are not unconsciously calling in his bad magic."

Ahmed lowered his eyes. "Mr. Crowley has access to Thoth magic? What is this Golden Dawn group?"

"It is a collective of educated men and women exploring the world of magic, Mr. Kamal," Uncle Brammie answered, puffing his chest out.

Terriss grinned at Ahmed. "I'm a plain man, Mr. Kamal. I feel the same way about this group gathering to study magic. A bunch of hooey if you ask me."

Ahmed might understand second sight and magic. Mr. Terriss never will.

Uncle Brammie shifted in his seat. "As a proper young lady, your background may not have prepared you for someone like Mr. Crowley."

Pamela was accustomed to his advice: "Don't let the married men on tour escort you back to the hotel," "Keep out of the men's dressing room." Fatherly warnings, even though she had never been romantically pursued by anyone at the theatre. Short, round, and outspoken, the opposite of Ellen Terry, Florence Farr, and Maud Gonne, the professional beauties of the day, she was the "character" in every group. And as the character, she was the confidant. Whispered confessions to her late at night revealed sordid stories from the Lyceum's ingénues and Golden Dawn neophytes. Assaults during auditions in rival theatres green rooms. Aleister trying to rape young recruits in the Vault before his ejection from the group.

Henry placed his hand over hers on the table. "We received word Mr. Crowley is out for vengeance against those who exiled him from the Golden Dawn, especially the women. We want to make sure we take every precaution to look out for you and for whoever may be your next muses."

"Miss Smith, who or what is your next card?" Uncle Brammie asked.

"Mr. Waite wants it to be the High Priestess. We are negotiating who she is," Pamela replied.

"We ask that when you choose your next muse," Henry said, "you let us know so that we may protect them. And you."

Ahmed shook his head. "Signs. Like seeing a crow on a serving tray? I do not wish to mock you, gentlemen, but you can imagine signs everywhere."

"Possibly, but Mr. Kamal, we suspect Mr. Crowley may show up at the British Museum to harass Miss Smith," Uncle Brammie said. "Could you make sure she is safe there?"

"Of course," Ahmed replied. "But in my country, we would handle this very differently. Women would not be unescorted in public places."

Henry answered, "But since you work alongside Miss Smith at the museum, we are asking you to be diligent on her behalf."

Uncle Brammie placed both palms on the table. "You must promise that Mr. Crowley does not get access to Thoth magic materials."

"I cannot promise things I cannot guarantee, Mr. Stoker. But I will try my best," Ahmed answered.

Uncle Brammie's face flushed. "You owe it to Miss Smith to make every attempt."

Why is he being so overbearing? This isn't like him.

Ahmed suddenly looked at Henry and Terriss. "Well, gentlemen, the tattoos on your ears are gone! They've disappeared!"

Sir Henry and Terriss both massaged their earlobes, and Terriss held up a silver knife to see his earlobe.

"Hell's Bells," he said, tilting the knife back and forth. "Whatever marking was there is now gone." He laughed and hit the table with a quick slap. "Miss Smith, we pledge to do our best to protect you. Only say the word. And keep off bridges."

How did Mr. Terriss know bridges were crossroads where magic traveled?

"What say you, Mr. Kamal?" Uncle Brammie asked. "Will you be our liaison at the museum?"

Ahmed kept his eyes on Pamela as he said, "I will continue to be of service to my friend."

Henry replied, "Excellent. It is agreed, we will all have our guard up and report any unnatural doings."

Unnatural doings. My daily fare.

After an uncomfortable moment as Pamela coughed in embarrassment, the sure-footed maître d' appeared with a line of servers behind him. Pointing his white-gloved finger, he cued the waiters to waltz to the table and set a plate with a large silver dome in front of each guest. Then the staff lifted every cover off together. Every conceivable space on the table was then filled with hot-house asparagus, quail, potatoes, jellies, roasted glazed carrots, and Sir Henry's favorite: beefsteak, the blood running into pools on the plate.

The men settled in to feast as Pamela snuck a look at the actors' ears. PCS was still etched plainly on Henry and Terriss.

Why am I the only one to see they are still earmarked?

As she picked up her fork, her eye caught movement at the table across the room. It was the dove in Lady Glizzard's hat. It had come alive and was now shifting about, thrashing in a circle, knocking off the artificial cherries. The dove wiggled, flapped its wings, and took off in a faltering arc. Once firmly aloft, it transformed into an enormous raven, black wings swooping past the diners' tables as it flew straight toward Pamela, claws aiming directly for her eyes. Hands up in defense, dropping her fork with a clatter, she shut her eyes, and braced for the attack.

Feeling only a passing wind, she opened her eyes. On Lady Glizzard's hat, the remains of the dove were splayed out—burrowed in a bed of blood-red cherries. Lady Glizzard stared back at her as though she were quite rude. The heads of the dogs trained on the hat as though they were loaded with pate as Lady Glizzard returned to her conversation with her friends.

She heard a voice deep within. A voice whispering just to her.

A curse on you and your tarot cards.

CHAPTER FOUR

Mutemmenu, Dancing Girl

~⌒⌒~

Pamela took the train from Earl's Court, looking out for a crow to dive-bomb her or a mysterious fire to break out on the railway track. Neither event happened, but by the time she entered the Golden Dawn Headquarters she was spent. If Mrs. Horniman were to ask for new drawings, she would have nothing to show. She'd been unable to sketch anything since her luncheon at the Savoy.

Entering the lecture hall, she saw the meeting had started without her. Keeping track of time is such a bother. She sat in the back, quietly placing her satchel of art supplies on the chair next to her. The three rows down to the dais were filled. The Golden Dawn chiefs' monthly meeting at the Mark Mason Hall had more members ever since Annie Horniman had pledged next year's rent.

"Her intentions are as I dictate!" Waite said, almost shaking the podium. "I am the one establishing the contents of the tarot cards. Miss Smith is merely following my instructions!"

Pamela squeezed her hands together to quell the typewriter keys pounding inside her head. His claims stung. Her artwork was not an empty vessel filling up with Waite's dictates, but he wanted her to be inspired from the Sola Busca and Marseille decks, and not to create original tarot cards.

"Aleister Crowley has a different impression," a man in the front answered. It was Dr. Felkin, the society doctor. "When Crowley materialized last year threatening us, he came for the girl, not you, Waite. Obviously, the girl is channeling something powerful, or Mr. Crowley would not have used his black magic trying to prevent her."

The Golden Dawn chiefs fidgeted. The few women guests drummed their fingers on the arms of their chairs, men pulling on their beards. Waite may have been named cocreator by a donation from Annie Horniman, but it had not bought the group's respect.

There were now two dozen upholstered chairs around a small stage instead of cane chairs and a single desk. Antique mahogany sideboards lined the walls, full of artifacts from her parent's worldwide travels. Miss Horniman had no trouble claiming ownership.

Last year in the Vault, the magical chamber was available only to the few Golden Dawn chiefs. It was there that Aleister had transformed himself into a terrifying deity. Goat, dragon, monster. It had reared up and threatened Pamela before flying out a window. Witnessed by only a few members, all here at this meeting, the transformation was legendary. If members of the Golden Dawn had heard Nana's stories of Jamaican duppies and monsters, they would have been prepared to meet this devil. But instead, they recognized it only as their version of a church devil, ignorant of the world's darker demons. Since the incident, the Vault had been moved to a secret location.

"Aleister targeted the weakness in the project, which is Miss Smith," Waite answered. "The tarot is all that is necessary for the Golden Dawn's higher degree of study. It will unlock the keys of power through symbolic vibrations."

"There are no shortcuts to knowledge," Dr. Westcott said, stretching his legs. "You experience knowledge. You cannot cram it in your head or glean it off a tarot card flashed in front of you. Knowledge is not processed that way. What is it that these tarot cards will do?"

Waite's voice rose higher. "Just as the Italian Sola-Busca exhibit of tarot cards is rumored to contain a new language, so will mine."

His cards, his ideas. Typewriter keys tapped inside her skull. When Waite lectured, this sensation usually appeared, most recently when he droned on about the history of pomegranates in art.

Dr. Felkin fussed with his monocle. "Mr. Waite, your idea of cocreating these tarot cards with Miss Smith seems foolhardy."

Uncle Brammie and Annie Horniman shifted in their seats.

"Miss Smith is merely an artist on commission," Dr. Felkin continued, "and only on Mr. Stoker's recommendation."

Uncle Brammie slyly eyed her and pretended to become mock enraged. Giggles bubbled upside her.

"But I need her gifts," Waite answered. "Miss Smith is a profound psychic and able to see through to other vibrations."

"So can my dog on a windy night," Dr. Westcott shot back.

Uncle Brammie whispered something to Miss Horniman who lifted a gloved finger signaling silence.

"Yes, Miss Smith is able to see beyond the veil," Mr. Waite replied, "but I am the one who can understand and interpret them." He dabbed his watering eyes with his handkerchief.

"Mr. Waite, I know you hope these cards will be your legacy," Dr. Westcott said, "but neither Miss Smith nor you have completed even the second degree of study with the Golden Dawn. How can they be used as part of our agenda when you don't even know what it is?"

True, she hadn't completed the first degree of the Golden Dawn studies. Boring. Dull. Too much math and science, as well as endless drawings of the Tree of Life. She'd known there would be trouble when she'd picked her motto to resistance at her Introductory Ceremony. *Whatever you would have done unto thee, do unto others.* Dr. Felkin reminded her this was not a Christian study group.

Samuel Mathers stood. The polyglot who spoke different languages and in tongues when the ritual was right.

"W-we . . . we've seen Mis Smith's first two cr-cr-creations, Magician and Fool. Now she is on to the High Priestess and Empress." Mathers turned around, spotting Pamela. "Why not let her create the first four cards and see what power these cards have? I believe she has the best of intentions, and the magic is strong in her cards. She is Jamaican, after all, and able to tap into voodoo magic."

This is the limit. Pamela took off her hat, shaking her head until her wild hair flew out like coiled springs erupting from a basket. The audience rustled as she trotted down the stairs.

"Doctors, Golden Dawn chiefs, ladies and gentlemen," Pamela said, facing them. "Let me just clarify: I was born here in London to American parents. I spent some of my childhood in Jamaica, but I do not practice voodoo."

Disappointed grunts came from the Chiefs.

A calm Irish brogue came from the back. "But you've seen magic in your tarot cards?" Uncle Brammie asked.

"Oh, yes."

"And you were recently threatened to stop creating them?" he continued.

"Yes."

Miss Horniman stood.

"I expect the chiefs to protect Miss Smith and my project or my funds will cease." She looked down at Pamela. "Now, I believe Miss Smith has some research to do at the museum?"

"Yes, ma'am."

"Carry on."

Seeing the sullen looks of the doctors and chiefs, Pamela spiritedly climbed the lecture room stairs. Uncle Brammie winked as she picked up her satchel and sailed out the door.

An hour later, she approached the threshold of her "purple room" in the Egyptian Antiquities wing of the British Museum. The lilting sounds of chanting and harp strings drifted from inside, followed by a man's gruff tones, "I declare before creation you are an idiot!"

Pamela stood on the other side of the doorway, peering inside. A woman playing small harp was seated in front of a mummy coffin while a tall, red-haired man in knickers loomed over her. Pamela felt a knot in her stomach. It was George Bernard Shaw, the notorious critic famous for his cleverness and cycling knickers. She had often seen him swaggering down the aisles on opening nights at the Lyceum Theatre, settling in just as the curtain lifted.

Florence Farr, the actress, looked like an angel playing a small harp. In a low, throaty voice she chanted: "The blind eyes can see more than other eyes."

Pamela broke out in a cold sweat. William Butler Yeats's poetry. The next phrase she knew by heart: "Because the soul always believes in these, the cell, the wilderness shall never be long empty."

At her New York art gallery opening, she recited this poetry after her Jamaican folktales started scaring people away. Yeats's poems cleared out the place in a heartbeat.

Shaw clapped slowly when Florence took a pause. Pamela peeked further around the doorframe and saw Florence get up, her combination toga and flowing peignoir floating around her as she packed up.

Pamela had helped Florence get permission from Ahmed to perform for the mummies here. He seemed captivated by her but later said he was "more amused than offended by her singing."

"Your performance should be hired as crowd control," George jeered.

Florence stood up to the glowering giant and uncrossed George's locked arms. "George, my mummy channeling makes more sense than most of your plays."

"Florence, I insist you stop this mumbo jumbo!"

Pamela guffawed, causing them both to turn and discover her. Sheepishly, she gathered her satchel and entered. As she walked in, orange vibrations in the room swirled around her: a bittersweet smell of dust, varnish, lemons. A fantasia, her friends would call it, a fantasy manifestation.

Pamela embraced Florence, who quickly hugged her back as though to get it over with. Pamela took in the theatre critic. Tall as Mr. Irving, over six feet, and his long, bony face with a ginger-colored beard and strawberry blond hair. With his protruding ears, curled mustache, and pointy beard, he looked like an Irish devil.

He curtly dismissed her, waving his hand.

Florence took Pamela's hand and presented her to him.

"George, this is Miss Pamela Colman Smith, a true aesthetic and artist. Miss Smith, this is George Bernard Shaw, writer, playwright, and troublemaker."

The bittersweet lemon smell intensified.

He grunted. "Miss Farr, you are seriously damaging your credibility with this Golden Dawn nonsense."

"Let us discontinue this useless conversation," Florence answered.

The two continued to bark at one another in staccato whispers as Pamela walked to her favorite bench against the wall. Her purple dress with the orange sash shone back at her from every glass case she wandered past. Usually wearing purple in this room was inspirational—she was an elegant vine of grapes, a swirling cloud at twilight—but today she felt more eggplant than grape.

Once at her bench, she took out her sketchbook.

"George, this is Mutemmenu," Florence said motioning to a casket. "She is the dancing girl of the temple. Through her connection to the universe, we can become Osiris, the Perfected One."

"Mother of God," George muttered.

Florence sat on the floor next to Mutemmenu with her palms turned upright.

Pamela grabbed her sketchbook. A shutter clicked. An image appeared. *The pose for the High Priestess.*

"George, you don't miss my acting," Florence said. "What do you want?"

"Annie Horniman, coleader of your Golden Dawn, is a theatre producer," George answered. "She is skulking around Henry Irving and Bram Stoker to produce something with them. You must get her to read my script, *Caesar and Cleopatra.*"

Florence looked off in the distance, "You want me to solicit the Lyceum for *Caesar and Cleopatra*? I've told you; you must delete your stage directions first, they are endless."

"Endless? Where?" George asked.

"In all your plays. Unless you intend to bore people, Mr. Shaw? That can't be your heart's desire," Florence said.

"There are two tragedies in life, Miss Farr. One is not to get your heart's desire. The other is to get it."

Pamela sighed.

"You disagree, Miss Smith?" George asked.

Pamela looked up at him bending over her. His sneer had a gray hue to it. Pride was his weakness. He would never win over Mr. Irving. He was a broken-hearted cynic who could find no joy, trying to rob it from others.

"To get your heart's desire, Mr. Shaw, is not a tragedy," Pamela answered. "But if you propose *Caesar and Cleopatra*, Miss Farr would be an excellent Cleopatra."

George's eyes widened. "What? Cleopatra? No. Too old. She could possibly play Ftatateeta, Cleopatra's handmaid."

Pamela went back to sketching. "Ftatateeta. Well, it's at least a better name than Shakespeare's 'Charmian,' but still not a very Egyptian name, is it, Mr. Shaw? And what happens to Ftatateeta?"

"Her throat is slit on the throne room floor."

"And that's historically correct?" Pamela asked.

George looked away. "History belongs to the victors."

Florence laughed. "Well done, George. Did you write that?"

"I did. In a manner of speaking. After reading something like it attributed to Napoleon."

Ahmed entered the room, followed by workmen pushing a cart. His thick, glossy hair was pulled back, no fez worn. His workman's hours clothes. He spotted Pamela, giving her a friendly nod and then, seeing the others, stopped in his tracks. Recognizing Florence, he smiled and grimaced at the same time.

"Miss Farr, I thought you had left the museum already," Ahmed said.

"I would have, Mr. Kamal, but my friends appeared," Florence said motioning to George and Pamela.

George stepped forward and energetically shook Ahmed's hands. "Mr. Bernard Shaw, at your service."

George's polite manners with Ahmed did not surprise Pamela. She had seen men like him before: gorgons to women but courteous to men.

Pamela felt dizzy. Waves of ropey energy buzzed around her head. Swinging orbs floated right and left, intensifying the pressure in the top of her head. She saw faint purple smoke begin to ooze out of Ahmed's ears. Purple, the color of seventh chakra, the meeting of body and infinite. Florence was a wavering, yellow flame before him.

"Miss Farr has mentioned you are the foremost authority on Egypt, Mr. Kamal," George said, his furry eyebrows moving up and down. "And that you are her guide in communicating with long-dead Egyptians."

"Miss Farr has no need of a guide. She is an intrepid researcher," Ahmed replied. Then, eyeing George's fluttering brows, he added, "You must excuse me, Mr. Shaw. I need to set up a display."

Ahmed turned away and as he passed Pamela, he wiggled his eyebrows up and down in imitation of George's. Pamela let loose a short laugh and immediately tried to turn it into the sounds of a cough.

"Ah, Miss Smith, you are all right?" Ahmed asked, with a new teasing inflection.

"Yes, Mr. Kamal, thank you for asking," she replied, giving him a teasing look back. His eyes twinkled in response.

He motioned to the workmen, and they wheeled in a long box covered by a sheet. Pamela moved nearer to watch them unload. She had never attended an unveiling before. Could she sketch it all before Ahmed stopped her?

Ahmed spoke an unfamiliar language to the men and removed the sheet.

Pamela gasped.

It was a floating coffin, the lid of which had been painted with a beautiful, reclining, open-eyed woman. Her heavily lined eyes conveyed a starkness of expression, and her long, plaited hair was secured by a red band across her forehead. An elaborate necklace draped across her chest, and her two palms were splayed open, her fingernails painted a reddish-black color. She seemed to glower up at the ceiling in her new location.

Florence rushed forward to take in the casket, while George slowly trailed behind.

The men lifted the casket off the cart and shuffled it over to where it was to be placed. They grunted, shifting as they shouldered the heavy load. Ahmed whistled and clicked his tongue, guiding them to the exact spot. They lifted the straps up to a uniform level and, guided by more clicks and whistles, gingerly lowered the casket precisely to its destination. The floating lid bobbled slightly as it settled with a thud. A polite round of applause from Florence and Pamela rewarded the winded workers. Ahmed beamed with relief as he stroked his beard with satisfaction.

A glass level was handed to Ahmed, and he set it on top of the coffin. Once the level's bead stabilized, Ahmed dismissed the workers and began taking tools out of a box.

"I am also an enthusiast of dialectology, Mr. Kamal. What language were you speaking to your men?" George had sidled next to Ahmed with a small notebook and pencil in hand.

Ahmed took in the squiggles George was drawing. "Coptic. The language of rural Egypt," Ahmed answered.

Not making eye contact as he wrote, George continued, "So, you're a regular Greek scholar."

"An Egyptian scholar, Mr. Shaw."

Pamela came over to stand by Ahmed's side as he examined the painted lid.

"Mr. Kamal, is this a mummy?" Pamela asked.

"No, this is a mummy board, or coffin liner. The lid would have covered another container with the mummy of a young woman of royalty. Or perhaps a serving girl from the Temple of Amen-Ra. It is the most recent donation."

"A recent donation?" Florence asked, walking around the case as though hypnotized.

"Yes, we believe this is from the collection of Amen-Ra's court. There has been an increase of donations ever since Dr. Woodman's death," Ahmed replied.

George perked up at the sound of Dr. Woodman's name. "Yes, Dr. Woodman. He was quite excited about the donation of Esquire Kennard's mummy. Too bad he died before he could study it. I understand Earl Ashburnham is donating a load of mummies from his Wales estate. Any credence, Mr. Kamal, to the belief that mummies are cursed?"

"Mr. Shaw," Ahmed replied, choosing his words carefully, "rumors of cursed mummies have been with the museum since the first donation almost two hundred years ago. The mummy curse is a common rumor, especially right after a donor's death."

George snorted.

"The recent donations of mummies and artifacts are mostly from guilty, amateur archeologists who looted while on vacation," Ahmed replied, selecting several brushes from the toolkit. "If the gods of Egypt could avenge stolen property, the Rosetta Stone here would have evoked at least one major disaster."

Florence looked up at Ahmed from her crouched position near the coffin. "Well, Mr. Kamal, it is possible there will be an upcoming disaster. It may be natural or not, but there are magical curses now unleashed in this time and place because of these thefts."

Pamela asked, "Where in time and place?"

Florence looked at her. "In London. Don't you feel the curses around us?"

Pamela felt a vibration. The yellow shading around Florence shimmered.

George snorted. "You must pardon Miss Farr's irrational interest in magical curses. Her father named her after Florence Nightingale, and she has been struggling to live up to that name ever since."

Florence just stood and shook her head.

"Florence Nightingale . . ." Ahmed repeated, stepping back to take full measure of George.

Florence cut in, "Mr. Shaw, really, for an authority on everything, you know very little about me, except that I was once married to a bully. But Mrs. Emory is no more, and Miss Farr won't respond to bullying."

George blushed the color of his ginger beard and shook his head. "Properly chastised, Miss Farr. I shall take my bad manners with me and hope some good opinion of me shall remain. Miss Smith, Mr. Kamal. Good day."

Florence waited until he left, his footsteps echoing along

the marble hallways, before throwing up hands. "Oh, he can be such a bore."

Ahmed exhaled. Florence smiled at him, but he turned away, settling his attention on his array of tools, brushes, knives, and small bottles of paint.

"Miss Farr, I didn't know you were formerly Mrs. Emory," Pamela ventured, taking Florence's hand. Florence did not shake her off.

"I've had several names, Pamela," Florence answered. "Married names, stage names, birth names I wasn't allowed to use."

"Well, I love your birth name. Miss Florence Farr," Pamela said. "It's very poetical. Ellen Terry also uses her mother's family name, Terry, just as I use my mother's name Colman."

Florence let go of Pamela's hand at the mention of Ellen Terry. Even though Florence was chief officer with the Golden Dawn, a former mistress of George Bernard Shaw and an actress herself, Pamela sensed jealousy.

"Ah, the Grand Dame Ellen Terry," Florence said. "She is the master of beautiful affectations. Now, I will come back to play music for Mutemmenu another day. Pamela, we will talk of your tarot cards later in the week. Mr. Kamal, good afternoon."

As Pamela watched her retrieve the hand harp's case and lock up her instrument, the yellow aura around her faded.

Once she was gone, Ahmed looked at Pamela with a sigh of relief, silently dusting every crevice of the casket. Pamela inspected the painted handmaiden on the lid. *How annoying that Ahmed becomes so unsocial in front of my friends.* She sketched the casket lid. The sounds of his swooshing brush and the scratching of her pencil eased the familiarity between them. Pamela stopped drawing to crouch down next to the painted inner coffin lid as he dusted the sides.

"Is this Amen-Ra's coffin?" Pamela asked.

"The hieroglyphs on the side and the top painting show this is from one of Amen-Ra's handmaidens."

"May I touch it?" she asked.

"No, Miss Smith," Ahmed answered.

She playfully stamped her foot. He ignored her. He knew she would touch it respectfully. Why was he being so persnickety.

"Why did they mummify a handmaiden? Was that a usual process?" she asked as he continued to brush.

"Likely, she came from a wealthy family or had unusual skills that benefitted the temple. That is why she might have been a mummy. And if she was a handmaiden to Amen-Ra, she would be groomed to be a High Priestess."

"A High Priestess . . ." Pamela deliberated.

The swishing of his brush was hypnotic and steady as Ahmed worked his way over the painting of the elaborate braided hair on her head, then her expression, unsettled and fierce. Her dark-rimmed eyes had an intense glare, almost resentful. *Swish, swish, swish.*

"Yes, she would be a High Priestess," he answered at last. "That is your next tarot card?"

Shyly, Pamela tilted her sketchbook in his direction to show him. A woman in a toga sat between two pillars, the Roman numeral two at the top. Across her chest she held a scroll with "Tora" written on it, and at her feet, a crescent nestled among flowers.

"She is very evocative," Ahmed said. "Not Egyptian though. Roman? Greek?"

Pamela sighed. "Mr. Waite is quite insistent that the High Priestess is Isis and must have a cobra on her head as a crown."

"And you disagree? Isis is very powerful and known for her magic." He looked at her and blew on his brushes. "She brought Osiris back to life."

"I see the High Priestess as life, temperament. She could be like our Virgin Mary but only with more joy. Singing. Dancing. Beer."

"Then it is Hathor you should be using. Hathor liked beer. And singing and dancing."

"Isn't she the cow goddess?"

Ahmed laughed. "Her crown is drawn as two horns between the sun disk, and she has, on occasion, turned into a cow, but she is not the cow goddess."

"What does her crown look like?"

Ahmed put his brushes down and walked to a mummy case across from them, pointing at the hieroglyphics on its side. "Here, Miss Smith. Here is your crown of Hathor."

Pamela inspected the crown embedded in the symbols on the mummy case.

"Oh! The very thing!"

She sketched the crown furiously, adding the Roman numeral two.

"Miss Smith, I thought this was your third tarot card," Ahmed said. "Why is number two at the top of this card?"

"The first card, the Fool, has no number," Pamela answered.

"Fool, then Magician. But why is your High Priestess the third card?" Ahmed asked.

"First, there is the folly of man—the Fool—followed by the gifts of the divine Magician. Now, with the High Priestess comes the desire to be whole. She is the manifestation of the Magician's desires. But, lately . . ."

Pamela flipped the pages and closed her sketchbook, hugging it to her chest.

"I don't see the signals."

"Signals?"

"When I draw, I hear a click. Like a shutter opening, a hole appears before me, and when I look through it, there is my drawing. But, ever since our restaurant luncheon, when I heard a voice say the tarot cards have cursed me, I don't see it."

"Ah." Ahmed walked back to his Amen-Ra coffin and continued to brush. "Miss Smith, so you have heard of mummies' curses. Would you like to hear the curse on this casket?"

Pamela nodded as Ahmed crouched and went back. Of course, he knew she would.

"Thomas Murray, who found this in Egypt, had to have an arm amputated right after he discovered it and two of the servants who touched it when it arrived in England died within a year. And Mrs. Hunt, who donated Amen-Ra to the museum, lost all her money. Over twenty people have been afflicted since coming in contact with this handmaiden."

Seeing he was trying to scare her, she grinned. "Do you believe in the curse?"

"Do I believe bad things happened to those who touched the casket? Possibly. Do I believe bad things would have happened anyway if they did not touch it? Probably."

"Aren't you worried you will be next, Mr. Kamal?"

"No, because I ask for permission and guidance from all my artifacts. But I will ask for my spirits to pressure this Earl Ashburnham to bring in all his mummies right away, cursed or uncursed. But, first, I will ask for permission from my guide."

He stood and closed his eyes, his brushes still clenched in both hands. As he took a deep breath, his eyelids quivered. When he exhaled, he emitted purple wisps.

A tiny screeching noise began to reverberate in the room, echoing against the glass cases. The sound was emanating from the coffin—a strange cooing, growing louder. It sounded like a baby falcon inside an egg, calling to its mother.

Pamela's pulse quickened. Though it was a sound that she could not logically place, her very bones knew it. Hot palms with pinpricks on the insides of her hands. Eyes twitching. Heart racing. The cooing escalated. Was it a bird? Or something else?

"Mr. Kamal, do you hear that?" she whispered.

"Indeed, I do," he said, opening his eyes.

"What do you think it is?"

"It is the High Priestess saying yes to my request for guidance. For both of us."

CHAPTER FIVE

ROYAL POMEGRANATES

⁓⦿⦿⦿⁓

When Pamela returned to Ellen's house after the long day at the museum, a note was under her bedroom door.

Pixie! Carriage tomorrow, 10 a.m., trip to the Cabbage.
A surprise awaits! Love, Ellen

The Cabbage was slang for the Savoy Theatre in Covent Garden, five miles away. It would take an hour by carriage. At least with the promise of Ahmed's priestess looking after her, traveling through the streets of London should be safer.

The next morning, the cook informed her at breakfast that Ellen had already left, although the absence of Mussie told her the same. Living in Ellen's house was like living in a hotel: maids cleaning bedrooms, meals waiting in buffet on the side table, and any number of temporary guests slamming doors late at night. She and her hostess's paths rarely crossed.

Unusually mindful of the time, Pamela made sure to step through the front door at 10 a.m. sharp. Three horses with a Unicorn cabman were hitched in tandem, waiting patiently in front of Barkston Gardens. *Let's see if fiery Aleister shows up in the street this time.*

Working as Ellen's assistant, sometimes she would have to arrange for a cab to take Mussie home. Newspaper headlines about Ellen Terry's Jack Russell terrier were legend. *Vendor feeds dog pie through the open window. Dog's play session in Hyde Park. Dog visits Mistress at Lyceum Theatre.*

Arriving at the Savoy Theatre in less than an hour, she hurried into the lobby, where a clerk hunched over a list in front of the auditorium. Once inside, a group of women circled around Helen Carte onstage. The wife of the Savoy producer, Richard D'Oyly Carte, was lecturing in her Scottish accent. Snippets drifted to the back row—"Gilbert and Sullivan," "Swan incandescent lamps," and "Ellen Terry."

Taking off her hat and getting pins out of her purse, Pamela tucked her hair in place, twisting the escaping tendrils. If Ellen had a surprise in mind for her, she wanted to look her best.

Raised voices were heard in the lobby, and the auditorium door flung open. A short, black man charged in. He wore a formal day coat, glasses, and a fez, like Ahmed. *Is this a sign a fez should be in one of my tarot cards?* A woman was on his heels, wearing an elaborate coat. It was the clothes, always the clothes, that spoke to her. They were actors, here for an audition.

The clerk from the lobby hectored alongside them as they started down the aisle. Pamela slunk in her seat.

Helen peered from onstage. "Miss Pardoe-Nash? Please do come and meet everyone."

The clerk turned on his heels and pivoted back to the lobby, giving Pamela a scowl on his way out.

The couple made their way down, his fez was bobbing like a cork in water. The embroidered back of the woman's coat was astonishing: a naked Adam with a fig leaf over his genitals next to a bare Eve, vines covering most of her. Her shoulders undulated with curling ivy, palm leaves, and split-open pomegranates dripping blood-red seeds. At the cuffs, yellow ovals glowed as vibrant as cats' eyes. All the images writhed into one another, the pomegranates bouncing up and down. The coat was a riot of color and motion as Adam and Eve conversed with one another, vines tripping and sliding up her sleeves.

Pamela sat up. A scent of violet, the taste of green. She had experienced this sensation before, an image becoming alive, beckoning her.

She walked down the steps, lured by the couple as they climbed the stage. Next to Helen was Miss Horniman, Golden Dawn chief. Helen guided the young women to the center and introduced Miss Beatrice Pardoe-Nash.

"Mrs. Carte, thanks so much," Beatrice said, "but I am Mrs. Pardoe-Ali now. I would like to present my husband, publisher, and Shakespearean actor, Duse Mohammed Ali."

Like a blown-out match, only a wisp of conversation was left hanging in the air.

Pamela sat in the front row to get a good look at that magical coat. Under the lime lights, the tapestry shimmered with golden threads. A slow movement in the fabric itself. Yes, there it was, on the cuffs—the cats' eyes blinked.

Where did I see this pattern before?

Then it came back. Her father's office in Manchester, a bolt of fabric with pomegranate was on display. Two men sat in chairs, laughing and talking. Her toy theatre was on the desk, the pomegranate fabric made up the little stage curtains.

Pamela suddenly blurted out, "Nicholas and Culshaw!"

The group onstage turned around to face the house. Beatrice swiveled and started laughing as soon as she recognized her.

❧

After Beatrice had managed to get her husband introduced to the ladies, she ran down the stairs and embraced her. They sat further back in the house. As she followed her, Pamela noticed Beatrice was much taller and about her age, twenty or so.

Settled in her chair, Beatrice began. "You look almost the same, Miss Smith. I knew it was you the moment I saw you. You remember, from my father's business trips to Manchester?"

"Yes, of course, at my father's office at Nicholas and Culshaw's. You were there when I showed my miniature theatre," Pamela answered. Beatrice scrutinized her. *Yes, Miss Pardoe-Ali, I'm either an old child or young crone.*

Pamela tried to keep her hands from tracing the pattern on Beatrice's cuffs while the cats' eyes blinked; they trained their luminous gaze on her. Pamela rubbed her eyes. Music played. The second sight was struggling to be heard.

"Miss Smith, I was in your house during one of your game nights," Beatrice said.

Pamela's parents had been the social heartbeat of Manchester when her father worked for the design firm of Nicholas and Culshaw, creators and purveyors of tapestry fabric, wallpaper, tile work and rug patterns. Her parents' "game night" was a regular rendezvous for not only Mr. Nicholas and Culshaw, but for all the artists in Manchester.

"I remember a girl my age there once, you recited a poem, yes?" Pamela asked. "It was the night I showed my miniature theatre I'd built. And I used this very fabric." She unclasped her hands and traced the yellow eyes in the pomegranates on the cuffs.

Beatrice seemed unfazed by Pamela touching her coat. "My father designed it."

"This was my favorite in all the sample books," Pamela replied. Roaring music filled her head as she took the pattern in. Pomegranates—she used them in almost everything she drew now. Vibrant yellow cats' eyes, dark red seeds, palm leaves. Heart thumping like a drum. Music overtaking everything.

Heart—slow down. Music—let go.

Beatrice softly said, "Are you alright, Miss Smith?"

"Yes. So many memories. I was so sad when we left Manchester."

"Where did you go?" Beatrice asked.

"We moved to Jamaica. Nicholas and Culshaw, they were so encouraging to me. . . ."

"Yes," Beatrice said, "so generous to my father. He became a 'made man' with their business. They visited us in Kingston-Upon-Hull."

"Where is that?" Pamela asked.

"On the eastern coast. It's where I met Mr. Ali. He was working in Hull as an actor and writer."

Pamela glanced up to see Duse regaling the ladies onstage. That Beatrice had met a black actor in Hull and agreed to marry him must have been the talk of the town. They were here in London, no doubt, looking for work.

"It will be hard for him," Pamela said, "to get roles that aren't fodder for crowd scenes."

"It was the role of the notorious Arab Osman Digna," Duse intoned loudly. "'You will end your days 'midst horrors of degradation, disease, and Arab licentiousness.' During my playing, the house hissed me endlessly."

Waves of polite laughter rewarded him. Beatrice sat up straight in her seat. "My husband is in his element right now."

"It must be difficult for him to find roles that are not demeaning," Pamela offered.

"You have no idea. So many roles are beneath him. So far, the British audiences have only known him as a reprobate and a misrepresentative of the Muslim faith."

"The evil sultan," Pamela supplied.

"That was one of his better roles. He just finished playing 'Nubian slave number one' in *Hypatia* at the Haymarket." Beatrice sighed.

"Damn."

Beatrice's head swiveled back to her, her beautiful eyes growing wide.

"You say you have family in Jamaica, Miss Smith?" Beatrice asked.

"Not any longer," Pamela answered.

A clamor offstage interrupted them. A chatter growing louder, dogs barking. Mussie and Fussie came trotting onstage, followed by their owners, Ellen and Henry. Between them they held up the frail Richard D'Oyly Carte.

Henry was wearing his "deacon's outfit" while Ellen wore a detested corset and a velvet dress in dark emerald, trimmed with white fur cuffs and collar. Something more than a casual lecture was happening if Ellen was wearing a corset.

Richard D'Oyly Carte was handsome with thick, dark hair. An esteemed producer, known for introducing Gilbert and Sullivan operas, he was old before his time. He had built the Savoy Hotel, another innovation but these endeavors had aged him and, at only fifty-six years old, he walked like an old man.

Helen left her group and rushed over to her husband, taking Richard's arm from Ellen. Her Scottish accent was more pronounced than ever.

"Now there, Richard, I've told you, we'll not be having any of this trotting out to socialize," she said.

"Darling Helen, get me over to those box seats," he answered. "Visitors want to see our new swan lamps in action,"

Henry took one of Richard's arms while Helen took the other, and they sat him in the box seats abutting the stage. They had been recently remodeled to be flush with the performance area so any attending royalty could be part of the show. Ellen sat down next to him when she spotted Pamela in the auditorium.

"Pixie, surprise!" she said, popping up and blowing kisses. "It's your friend from Hull, Beatrice!"

The lecture group jolted like startled animals at an ambushed waterhole and peered out from the stage. Even Fussie and Mussie stopped in their tracks.

Duse walked to the edge of the stage. "Mrs. Beatrice Pardoe-Ali has been most anxious to meet up with her childhood friend."

Pamela leaned over and whispered to Beatrice, "Mrs. Pardoe-Ali, I am a childhood friend?"

When she looked over at Beatrice, she saw tears standing in her eyes.

"Please, I have a confession to make. I sent a letter of introduction to Miss Terry." She turned in her seat to face Pamela. "And . . . I might have mentioned in the letter that we were best friends."

"You did what?" Pamela asked.

"Please excuse my forwardness; I know we didn't really become best of friends. It's just that we are desperate for work, and my father saw in a newspaper that a Miss Smith had illustrated tour brochures for the Lyceum Theatre. He knew it had to be you. So, I wrote to Miss Terry, asking to meet her. We hope the Lyceum Theatre will hire Duse as an actor this season. He's qualified. He's the Hull Shakespearean Society president."

Beatrice ran out of breath.

"I see," was all Pamela could manage to say.

"Please forgive me, Miss Smith," Beatrice twisted together. "I wish we were childhood friends. I could certainly do with one now."

Duse frantically gestured for Beatrice to join him onstage, but the woman's knees were shaking. Pamela stood and reached out her hand.

"Come, Beatrice, childhood friend. Introduce me to your Shakespearean Society president husband. And my name is Pamela to friends."

Both young women took the stage, and after Helen introduced her, Annie Horniman took Pamela aside. Where Florence

Farr from the Golden Dawn was breezy and casual, Miss Horniman had the manner of a meddling duchess, a stickler for rules and etiquette. She would not be attending a tour at the Savoy Theatre as a mere diversion.

She held Pamela at arm's distance and appraised her appearance. "I heard good progress is being made with the tarot cards, Miss Smith." She stepped closer and lifted up the red-stone necklace around Pamela's neck. "Caribbean coral?"

"Yes, Miss Horniman, from St. Andrews."

Annie did not adhere to the Quaker belief that the only personal jewelry allowed were wedding rings. She was known for her exotic and extensive jewelry collection, and she eyed her necklace with a determined glint. *I hope she isn't asking for my Nana's necklace.*

"Miss Horniman," Pamela continued, "the Magician and Fool cards are both complete. I am working on the third card, the High Priestess."

Miss Horniman subsidized the Golden Dawn for the last five years with her tea-fortune money and was known to all as "Hornibags." Her magical motto, "Bravely and Justly," had been invoked several times during the meetings to oust Aleister. Her refusal to include sexual activity on an astral plane was whispered was accredited to her prudishness not the morality of magic. Some men felt Aleister was justified in exploring the black arts for sexual techniques and polyfidelity. Recently, after a session of a name-calling ("prig," "prude," "pervert"), a faction of the Golden Dawn quit. She told them, "If you want a harem, go elsewhere, or I will be dipping my teabags elsewhere."

"Well, Miss Smith I am pleased with you," Miss Horniman answered. "These tarot cards will be excellent study guides for neophytes. Do let me know if you run into any resistance."

Pamela tried to keep a straight face. Tarot cards in her head popped up. *Ha! We are not study guides and there has already been plenty of "resistance."*

A commanding clap drew their attention to the box seats. Ellen was playing the role of the carefree actress, merrily entertaining Richard D'Oyly Carte. With her assistance, he grabbed the railing of the box seats and stood. He cleared his throat, commanding everyone's attention.

His tender glance trained on Ellen, he began: "Seventeen years ago, all three Terry sisters performed here at the Savoy Theatre in a benefit. First, Miss Florence Terry and Miss Marion Terry in *Broken Hearts*, then the piece de resistance, all three Terry girls in *Merchant of Venice*. Mr. Irving's Shylock in the courtroom finished us off. The talent in the theatre that evening has never been surpassed. It was a night to remember."

Henry nodded in agreement. "Yes, Mr. Carte, the Terry women have always had an effect on me."

Pamela heard several rapturous sighs from the ladies while Henry and Ellen looked at one another.

Helen gave an exasperated toss of her head. "Oh, but haven't I been hearing about the Terry girls all my life! I may be his wife, but it was Miss Kate Terry who was his first love. He composed some of his first music for her."

"Now, Mrs. Carte," Henry said, pressing his hand to his heart. "Don't tell me your husband hasn't written music for you."

"Thank you, no," she replied.

"In spite of all of my productions of Gilbert and Sullivan here," Mr. Carte chimed in, "I've learned my Helen prefers the tune of a well-balanced budget."

The electric lights in the house suddenly bumped up in intensity. The interior of the theatre glowed like a jewel box. A round of muted, gloved applause broke out onstage as the swan lights pulsed brightly without the hiss of gas or smell of whale oil. Ghostly orbs illuminated the balconies' undersides. The fanfare faded and the lobby door swung open to a group of noisy, chattering people, oblivious to anything other than their own conversation as they came down the aisle.

A stodgy man in an elegant frock coat was leading the way with his walking stick. "Mr. Richard D'Oyly Carte?"

"I'm up here, Your Highness."

Gasps escaped from the onstage group, and everyone bowed. Prince Edward made his way up the stairs to the stage.

Beatrice and Duse quivered with excitement, while the dogs yawned nervously. Pamela had never met royalty before. *Oh, if only my mother were here.*

When the prince made his way center stage, Mr. Carte walked over to him, unaided, and bowed his head. He then gestured to Helen's group, his voice taking on a new strength.

"Your Highness, may I introduce to you: my wife, Helen D'Oyly Carte. And, of course, you know Henry Irving and Ellen Terry."

The fifty-seven-year-old Prince Edward was portly, his girth magnified by his greatcoat. He took up a great deal of space, and his habit was to stand with his cane positioned in front. It kept most people at bay. That is where it remained as the prince introduced only one person from his group, "family friend" Alice Keppel. Beautiful Alice had a tiny waist, large bosom, and, it was said, an impoverished husband. She was thirty years old and a porcelain beauty. A mistress to the prince for a year, she was now allowed to socialize outside the "corridor creeping" at the country estates of the prince's friends.

"Without saying, pleasure to see you both," Prince Edward said. "And here is my family friend, Mrs. Keppel."

The assembled guests smiled as Alice daintily tossed her head. On cue, everyone bowed. Pamela's curtsy was more of a sideways teapot impersonation, but a curtsy, nonetheless.

Pleased with the smiles and curtsies to Alice, the prince addressed Mr. D'Oyly Carte. "Ah, Dick! I heard you were recovering from fortunes lost on *The Grand Duke*," he said, grinning.

"Your Highness, my recovery from that show will take time," Mr. Carte replied.

"Ach, between your Savoy Hotel and your next musical, I am sure you will soon be in fine form." The prince nodded to Ellen, and she gave him her hand. He kissed it, all the while taking in Ellen's neat waist. Next, he acknowledged Henry, standing next to her. "Henry Irving, excellent to see you again. Enjoyed your Lyceum show, as always. The Queen still talks of your performances."

"Thank you, Your Highness," Henry replied.

"Still playing the devil in *Faust*?" the prince said with a wink.

"When I can, sir, when I can. Speaking of playing devilishly hard roles, Your Highness, may I introduce to you Mr. Duse Mohammed Ali?"

Beatrice inhaled sharply next to Pamela. This was Ellen's doing? The prince turned and noticed Beatrice with a sharp snap of his head, like a dog seeing prey. It was hard to miss the beautiful young woman in the pomegranate-decorated coat. When the prince notice the short, black man in a fez standing next to her, Edward's gilded cane staked out further.

One did not start a conversation with the prince; one waited for the prince to converse with you. It was a delicate situation, trying to introduce someone new. It could backfire spectacularly. A black actor, even if he were the president of the Hull Shakespeare Society, was an unusual introduction. Henry was pressing his luck choosing a man instead of a fawning woman. The prince's foot began to tap.

"Mr. Ali is founder of the Hull Shakespearean Society and has recently found acclaim as 'The Young Egyptian Wonder Reciter of Shakespeare,'" Henry continued.

Duse shook hands with his Highness and bowed, the prince regarding him with a slight tilt of his head.

"Ah, Mr. Duse Ali," he said calmly, "glad to make your acquaintance. A 'Young Egyptian Wonder,' are you?"

"Yes, sir, I was born in Alexandria, Egypt," Duse answered. "At ten, I was sent to London to study at the Church of London England Cannon."

"Your parents are still living?" Edward asked.

Duse drew himself up proudly. "My father, General Abdul Salem Ali, was killed in the battle of Tel-el-Kabir."

Everyone froze. The battle of Tel-el-Kabir had led to the British cavalry securing Cairo and soon after that, the surrender of Arabi to British rule. For years, the stories of this early-morning battle had been legion: horses shot and killed under the riders, bayonets and rifles falling to the blood-soaked ground, the Black Watch of Scotland, in their kilts, charging over the hills as the cannons behind them roared. Many paintings depicted the riot of turbans, swords, and batons of fire that had killed so many Egyptian and English soldiers.

"Ah, yes," Edward answered. "What year was that?"

"1882, sir. My father was a fierce supporter of Arabi Pasha."

The name of one of the enemies to Britain echoed through the theatre. Eyes darted back and forth from the prince to Duse, from Henry to Mr. Carte.

"Well," Edward said. "I am pleased to meet a man whose father died fighting for his country." With that, the prince motioned to his mistress and Ellen. "Miss Terry, Miss Keppel, won't you charming ladies show me the new scenery backstage?"

Ellen and Alice entwined their arms with the prince's, and they promenaded past Mr. Carte.

"I hear the upcoming show is a revival," Edward shot at Mr. Carte as they passed. "Which one is it, Dick?"

"*Yeoman of the Guard*," Mr. Carte answered.

"Well, there we have it," Edward said as they disappeared backstage.

Pamela watched Henry give one of those looks she dreaded, the I'm-so-disappointed-in-you glares, to Duse and crossed over to Mr. Carte. Mrs. Carte and the ladies milled about in excitement. Duse approached the group with open palms, continuing the story of his father's battle. Only Miss Horniman appeared to give him any sympathy.

Pamela and Beatrice sat in the box seats, the dogs settling in at their feet. *What a morning!* Pamela let out a deep breath. Meeting royalty for the first time was trying for everyone.

Henry ambled over to Duse with a practiced grace. Placing a hand on Duse's shoulder, he said, "I've just been told by Dick Carte that you are a playwright, Mr. Duse. Please accompany me outside, where I might smoke and hear of some of your plays?"

Duse's face lit up. "Mr. Irving! Well, there is *The Jew's Revenge*," he said, "inspired by your Shylock. *A Daughter of Judah. A Cleopatra Night.* And I have started a musical revue, *A Lily of Bermuda.*"

Duse continued the recital of his creations as they went out through the auditorium. Pamela looked at Beatrice; she was pale as paper.

"If he had any chance of employment with Mr. Carte or Mr. Irving, he's ruined it," she said, resting her head in her hands.

Ambling in from backstage, the prince paused center stage, waiting for his straggling group to catch up with him. As Alice drew close to his side, he whispered in her ear. She smiled and nodded. When Ellen appeared near them, they broke off together, and the three talked quietly. Pamela and Beatrice glanced at one another as Ellen approached their box seats.

Pamela felt a pinprick in her stomach when Ellen leaned across the railing. Fussie began to whine while Mussie leaned up and licked his mistress's face.

"Now, listen to me," Ellen said in low tones, managing to settle Mussie down. "Mrs. Pardoe-Ali, I am going to bring you to the prince, but under no circumstances are you to leave with him or with anyone else of his party. Do you understand me?" Ellen touched the sleeve of Beatrice's coat. "And, if you hope to save your husband's career, it may cost you this lovely coat. Understand?"

Beatrice, flushed and confused, looked at Pamela.

"Do as she says," Pamela whispered.

Beatrice looked into Mussie's eyes—he barked at her.

"Understood," she whispered back to Ellen.

Ellen escorted her out of the box seat to the prince. Beatrice's coat floated in her wake like a painted flag of paradise. When she arrived next to him, the prince's eyes gleamed under the throbbing swan incandescent lights.

Beatrice and her Garden of Eden quivered before him.

An hour later, Duse sat in the theatre office with Mr. Richard D'Oyly Carte. Splayed on Carte's desk was a map of touring houses and fit-up towns, rundown cities with no theatres. Henry stood and listened as Richard talked of percentages. Duse penciled in benefits of deferred royalty fees.

Upstairs in the staircase overlooking the front of the theatre, Pamela and Beatrice looked out the second-story window. The royal party gaily tripped to their waiting carriages. The mistress's newly acquired pomegranate coat could be briefly seen in the back window of his Highness's carriage. A yellow cat's eye flashed from a sleeve; Adam and Eve shimmied.

Ellen's Unicorn Cabman approached the lineup. It was time to go. Pamela heard barking and, "Pixie? Shall we go?"

Beatrice, now wearing the simple black cape of the prince's mistress, sighed.

Pamela kissed Beatrice on the cheek and flew down the stairs. She tried not to show her disappointment when Miss Horniman also bundled into the cab.

❧

Later that week, Pamela finished her tarot card of the High Priestess at the British Museum artifacts office. The final rendition showed a young woman sitting on a throne between two pillars; a crescent moon lay at her feet and Hathor's cow horn crown perched on her head. A simple cross and the Torah scroll lay across her chest while a curtain with a pomegranate pattern hung behind her. She was perched between the two pillars, one black, one white.

Ahmed came in to lock up for the night but dawdled near her. He was trying to steal a glance of her artwork.

"Would you like to see my High Priestess?" she asked. She pushed all the papers covering the last sketch away from the edges.

"Yes," he said. When he saw it, he took a deep breath. "It is mystical and powerful. Your priestess looks like Miss Florence. Mr. Irving and Mr. Stoker will be told she is your next chosen muse, yes?"

"Yes, I've written them to let them know."

"Are you afraid for Miss Farr?" Ahmed asked.

"Should I be? I thought your priestess would protect her."

"She probably will unless her museum music starts to annoy her." Pamela laughed and Ahmed's eyes crinkled. He examined the drawing again. "The stars in her crown, the crescent moon, are all very good, but the pillars with the *B* and the *J*? There were no priestesses in King Solomon's Temple, you know."

"Yes, Mr. Kamal, but I am going to put in King Solomon's pillars anyway. *B* representing Boaz, for completion, and *J* for Jachin, as in beginnings. They are perfect anchors."

"I see. And good anchors for your pomegranate backcloth. The pomegranates are your apples in the Garden of Eden?"

"Yes, as symbols of temptation. Women may have been seen only as tempters, not allowed in temples, but my High Priestess will be seated in the temple. In fact, in front of the veil of temptation. She will be learned and the holder of secrets. Mr. Waite says she is the highest and the holiest of the Major Arcana," she said.

"Major Arcana?" Ahmed queried.

"Major Arcana, the first twenty-two major cards of the tarot deck. The Major Arcana is like twenty-two gods, or twenty-two royal mummies," Pamela answered.

"Your tarot deck will be like twenty-two royal mummies?" He began toward the door and turned back.

"You will need a lot more protection from the High Priestess."

CHAPTER SIX

Runaway Horses

F lorence Farr lifted her bicycle from the hallway, opened the door, and carried it down the steps of the house to the street. The late winter sky was gray and flat. In half an hour, she was meeting her fellow members of the Actress Franchise.

As she set off for Kensington Gardens, her bloomers allowed her to pedal without tangling her skirt in the spokes, but riding over cobblestones rattled her bones. In addition, there was the added danger of skidding if you rolled through one of the many mounds of horse manure scattering the road.

Living with her sister and brother-in-law in this middle-class neighborhood had been a comfort ever since Mr. Emory deserted her for America. She was free to come and go as she pleased, as long as she didn't bring gentlemen home, for it was known that she was an advocate of "free love" and had many admirers. Her sister's husband, Henry, had once asked her what her future plans were now that she was a divorcee.

"Temperance, with an occasional orgy," was her reply.

He never asked again.

Her bloomers whished as she cycled in the late morning light, the sporadic, disapproving glances from men on the street only fueling her legs to pump more determinedly. According to the ideas shared by the sisters of the Rational Dress Society, women should not wear more than seven pounds of clothing, which meant no corsets, petticoats, pantaloons, or other cumbersome layers of dress. Showing up at the Actress Franchise meeting in bloomers would be favorably received, a contrast to the reaction she was receiving now.

As she neared Pembridge Road, she saw a man wearing an advertising board, a London Boardman. On the front was a poster for Crowley's Family Ale, a black crow with a foaming glass. As he lurched down the sidewalk, a tiny girl in a plain, gray dress led him. Her dress was the outfit given to children in the workhouse. She could not have been more than seven years of age, but she seemed a practiced hand at supporting the teetering man. He appeared drunk, waving a handful of papers falling out of his grasp. As the man tottered near a group of men waiting for an omnibus, the rest of the handouts fell, fluttering into the street's muck of hay and manure.

Florence slowed her bicycle to a stop as a page flew near her, it was a flier extolling the virtues of Crowley Ale. The child propped the drunken sot against a tree, then stepped into the gutter to fetch the now filthy paper handouts.

"Zandra!"

"Runaway horse! Heads up, runaway horse!"

The child and Florence turned their heads in the direction of the shouts. A driverless hansom cab charged down the street, catapulted by a galloping brown horse. Sprinting alongside the cab, a man tried to grab the horse's reins.

"Ho! Whoa! Walk on, darling! Ho!"

The girl in the gutter looked up. The drunk reached out for her and fell into the street.

The man running alongside the horse grabbed hold of the hansom cab's front fender and lifted himself on the driver's seat. In one leap, he landed on the back of the runaway beast. The horse whined and reared, causing the cab to bump into the animal, frightening it even more.

The child and man were now in the direct path just feet away from the carriage. At the last second, the driver forced the panicked animal to the left. In a single blurred moment, the man reached down and grabbed the frozen girl from the pavement, while the carriage veered and ran the London Boardman over. The sounds of cracking poster board and the man's screams filled the air. The horse thundered on, and the rider threw the child's body across the horse's back like a sack of flour.

The men at the bus stop ran to the mound in the gutter.

"Gore, that's an ender!"

"Fetch the beadle!"

As the men tended to the man and looked for a police officer, Florence watched the runaway horse charge down the street toward Pembridge Bridge. The girl's body was now flopping across the man's legs. The child would never last while the horse was out of control.

Florence shook herself into action, fervently pedaling after them, some of the men running with her. The cab disappeared, turning up the block. They were running straight into the roundabout. The horse veered to the left branch, and continued on until it was in front of the Gate Theatre.

The cab teetered to one side and tilted, remaining in midair for a split second.

"There, now! Whoa. Steady girl, steady!" the rider called.

At the last minute, the cab righted itself mid-fall, and the horse was jerked into a halt.

Florence stopped her bike and threw it to the ground, running up to the horse and grabbing the bridle. Several whinnies later, the horse sighed and shook her coat, then stood still, panting, foam oozing from its mouth.

A short red-faced man ran up and grabbed the bridle out

of Florence's hands. He must be the missing cabbie. Florence watched as the wide-eyed beast stabilized under his croons.

"Ah, Zandra, how could you do that to me?" the cabbie cried, wiping down the animal's sodden jowls.

The rider on the horse handed the little girl to the men below and swung off. "You're lucky it wasn't raining, or she would have slipped and taken the cab down," the rider said, then, pointing to the scars on the horse's neck. "But I see you've got a lot to answer for."

The small child was crying in the sea of men surrounding her. Florence crouched down and took the girl into her arms, lifting her up. She looked at her chin to see where she was hurt. Her face was plastered with mud, her dark eyes filled with tears. But other than being spotted with mud and manure, she appeared unharmed.

The rider came over to Florence and cocked his head toward the little one. "Enjoy your pony ride?" he said as he patted her head.

A solemn shake of the head. "Not really," she replied tearily.

The crowd laughed.

"Me Da!" the child whimpered.

Florence took them both to her bicycle, sitting the child on the seat before walking the bike away from the crowd of men. She made for the street but was aware of footsteps running behind her.

"Here, now, I'd like to see where you are taking this little one," the horse rider said.

"She was with her father when she went in the street; I'm going to take her back to him now." She kept a steady grip on the girl and the bicycle. He walked backwards in front of them, keeping a faster pace.

"Ah. What's your name, darlin'?" he asked the girl.

"Daisy Ten."

"You're ten years old?"

"No, that's my name. I'm seven."

"Well, Daisy Ten, have you ever ridden a bicycle?"

"No."

He held the little girl's hands on the handlebars of the bike, and she attempted to steer as they entered Pembridge Road. For a moment the three of them laughed as Daisy steered the bike one way and then the other.

Ahead of them, Florence saw a small group of people gathered around a crumpled form of a man. His broken poster board sign lay next to him. Florence's heart clutched. As she picked up her pace, Daisy whooped for joy.

As they neared the crowd, the beadle standing over the body called out, "Ah, Mr. Terriss, I knew that horse rider had to be you."

Florence realized this was William Terriss, one of the matinee stars of the Lyceum Theatre. An impetuous and rash actor who was said to have rescued someone drowning at sea and whose wife was "unwell in the head." He was mostly known as an "action star."

Terriss dashed ahead and examined the man's body, then waved to Florence to avert the child's attention. But it was too late.

Daisy cried "Da, Da" over and over as Florence tried to hold her.

A street sparrow, one of the urchins paid to escort residents of refinement over the filth and straw in the streets, escorted a housemaid to the beadle. He reluctantly paid her for the bedsheets in her arms. As the maid unfolded the linen and draped it over the body, Daisy wiggled out of Florence's hold and dodged the beadle's clutches to throw herself next to her father's lifeless form. She pitched her cries higher and higher until she was picked up by two uniformed men. Kicking and screaming, she fought, her pathetic cries and her outstretched arms reaching for the white heap, wringing Florence's heart.

After Daisy escaped them, she ran to Florence, clutching her neck.

A wagon pulled up and a large woman with a matron's apron and a jangling set of keys climbed out.

"Good day, madam. I'm here to take the child."

"Excuse me, who are you?" Florence asked, feeling Daisy's hot breath and smelling her soiled clothes.

"We're the Temperance Ladies of Good Works. We've been talking with Daisy's father for a while. We promise to take Daisy to a cottage home and not back to the workhouse."

"Back to the workhouse?"

"Yes, he owes substantial debt, madam." She looked at the heap in the road. "Or owed."

Florence reached for the purse in her bloomers' pocket, but the woman lifted up a hand to stop her.

"Donchya be giving me coins for her here, madam. That's a matter for the bailiff to settle. If you want, come to the hearing next week."

Daisy howled as the matron pried her away from Florence and carried her to the wagon. It was all Florence could do to keep from snatching the child to her for safekeeping.

Daisy's sobs became fainter and fainter. Florence's throat closed up as she fought a crying fit.

Terriss stood next to her, tears in his eyes.

"If my wife, Isabel, wasn't overwhelmed with ours as it is, I would have taken her."

Florence shook her tears back to their spring and took a deep breath.

"Were you not tempted to take her?" he asked.

"Ah, but my situation is even more dire than yours," she said with such low volume that he had to step closer. "For you see, I have no wife to take care of the home while I do my business."

"I see. You've become Americanized."

Americanized. The popular term used for women who decided not to have children.

She turned and looked at him full on for the first time. He was a handsome man even with his suit mud-splattered, in his mid-thirties, and his blondish, brown hair hung in his face. His profile was classically Greek, with full lips stretched into a sad smile.

"I don't know who you are or why you feel compelled to speak to me in this frank way but, yes, some women are beginning to refuse motherhood. I do not see anything alarming in this. To me, it means that women will specialize in the future."

He wiped his hands together and extended one. "I just want to congratulate you on doing a kind thing. That is all."

With that, he shook her hand and walked away, toward the Notting Hill Gate stop. As Florence watched, she turned back to steady her bicycle, finding it difficult to focus.

"Americanized." Typical of men to try to define her. Like Mr. Shaw, claiming she wasn't fulfilling her destiny if not in service to his plays. But unlike the gangly George Bernard Shaw, Mr. Terriss certainly was a fine specimen of a man, one who embodied his reputation as a hale hearty and well-met chap. With a wife and many children in the bargain. Ah, what was forbidden could be so alluring.

> *Thank you for saving Daisy.*
> *Thank you for thinking I could nurture anyone.*
> *Thank you for walking away.*

Just then, the sparrow starvers, the children who tended the manure in the streets, appeared with their brooms and went to work. A carriage arrived and a tall, aristocratic young man got out, carefully making his way through the cleared path. Arriving at the cluster of people, he lifted the sheet, then dropped it. He picked up the advertising board lying on the ground next to the body. Tucking it under his arm, he went to the beadle. Owners from the nearby house came out to complain as the morgue carriage pulled up. Everyone gathered around the white sheet on the ground, shouting and yelling as the young man took out what looked to be a money pouch. All was quiet.

After he had paid the small circle around him, he looked up and saw Florence. Staring directly at her, he held up his hand, crumpling something before tossing it away, although nothing fell from his hand. It was one of the hand gestures used in the Golden Dawn binding spell—the one Florence had used to banish Aleister from the group.

She felt her hands tingle and tore off her gloves. No blackish fingernails; she was safe.

Looking back, Aleister Crowley was gone.

CHAPTER SEVEN

GOLDEN STAIRCASE

The haze of cigar smoke hit Ahmed in the face as he was ushered into Baron Battersea's drawing room at Surrey House. It was a Gents' Night, and fuming pipes, cigars, and cigarettes glowed from every guest. Ladies were banned for the evening. The host, Baron Cyril Flowers, was known to be uninterested in women unless they were in a painting, or so said his wife, Constance de Rothschild. It was a childless marriage between two rich, intelligent, politically active people with the same values. Lord Battersea was considered extremely handsome and Constance an excellent hostess. Especially when she absented herself during his Gents' Nights.

Chandeliers lit with candles hung from the ceiling, and chairs ringed the mahogany sideboards stacked with tiers of food. Footmen and butlers stationed against the walls were on call to refill drinks.

Ahmed looked across the room. There was Duse Moham-med Ali engaged in an animated conversation with William Lever, the industrialist. While Lever had no beard, he did have a shock of white hair that stood straight up, framing his pale face and bright blue eyes. Duse, with his red fez and dark skin from his Nubian mother, was an obvious foreigner.

Both Duse and Ahmed wore the red fez mandated by former Egyptian leader Muhammad Ali Pasha. They had been invited this evening with the firm directive to discuss Egyptian art, not politics. Duse's newly established newspaper had recently run a column about confiscated artwork from Cairo being held at the Customs Office, and in return for a halt on those stories, Duse had been granted an evening to rub elbows with William Lever, the soap king. And Ahmed, as Egyptian acquisitions director of the British Museum, had been promised an introduction to Lord Compton to discuss plans for the return of the statue of Sekhemka. It was said Lord Compton was hiding the two-and-a-half-foot stolen sandstone statue at his estate. Since the Lord couldn't display it for fear of having to answer for its provenance, Ahmed had hoped to give him the opportunity to share it with the museum rather than conceal it. And there was always the possibility of running into the elusive Earl Ashburham, who had yet to give up his mummies from Giza.

Ahmed watched Duse shake a finger at Lever. "That artwork belongs to Egypt, not to tomb raiders."

Tonight, he and Duse were already straining the limits of comfortable inclusion. Ahmed regretted Duse being invited.

"Your friend, Mr. Ali, is becoming agitated," a low voice purred beside him.

Ahmed turned and faced his attractive host, Baron Battersea.

In his late fifties, Lord Battersea was a dead ringer for both the son of Queen Victoria and Tsar Nicholas II of Russia, leading many to whisper of the inbreeding of the royal houses of Europe. At this gathering, the bearded gentlemen largely populated the drawing room, aping the style of royalty and aristocrats.

With him stood the notorious Englishman, Mr. Blunt, wearing a turban and a Middle Eastern tunic in a sea of formal evening wear.

"I know you want to have a conversation with Lord Compton," the Baron drawled, "but keep your friend in line, will you? We ask for civil conversation here." Then, as an afterthought, he made the introduction. "Mr. Blunt, meet Mr. Kamal."

He then bowed his head and walked away, leaving the two men to stare at one another.

Ahmed took in Blunt's outlandish outfit. Dressing like a sultan from *The Arabian Nights*, Blunt wore a red, embroidered, dalmatic tunic, and a white turban. Known to be pro-Ottoman and pro-home rule for Egypt and Ireland, he had spent many years in Egypt, fought bulls in Spain, lived in Athens, Paris, Lisbon, Buenos Aires, and raised Arabian horses on his farm near Cairo. He also currently had a "Bedouin wife," which led to the current petition for divorce by his wife, Lady Anne, granddaughter to Lord Byron.

Ahmed had recently corresponded with Mr. Blunt to donate some of his "travel finds" to the British Museum, unsuccessfully so far.

Blunt extended his hand from within the many folds of his robe. "How do you do, Mr. Kamal. Wilfrid Blunt."

"Mr. Blunt, pleasure to meet you," Ahmed said. "You are well-known to me and to my Egyptian community as a writer, especially for your support of Arabi Pasha. Your book, *The Future of Islam*, is much discussed."

Above the thrum of conversation, Ahmed could hear Duse's high voice sputtering in spirited response and saw Lever's face turn a deep red. He forced his concentration back to Blunt.

"Ah, you read my book, Mr. Kamal?" Blunt asked.

"I did. You claim the days of Egyptian rule are over. This has riled many of my military friends."

"Why is that?" Blunt asked, finding a cigar in his tunic.

"My friends do not trust an Englishman's calculation of Egyptian military power. Even a sympathetic Englishman," Ahmed answered.

Blunt waved a footman over to light his cigar. "I still regard Arabi Pasha's revolutionary struggle as a most noble and correct one. Even if my writing of your military's weaknesses led to me being banned from Egypt."

After the cigar was lit, a butler appeared and offered drinks; Blunt took a glass of scotch, Ahmed shook his head.

"You are a true practitioner of your faith, I see," Blunt said. "I'm sure tea can be brought for you."

Pamela had warned Ahmed that tea would not be on the menu at Gents' Night. He looked at Blunt's smiling face. He might be sympathetic to Egypt, but his outfit showed he was an actor, playing at being a Bedouin.

"Tea would be most excellent," Ahmed said to the butler.

Blunt surveyed the room. "So many agendas here tonight, Mr. Kamal. So many causes. Your friend, it seems, is determined to scold Mr. Lever for his business in Africa."

"I'm sure Mr. Ali is simply asking Mr. Lever to let the Africans decide the best way to develop African palm oil."

Blunt grunted. "Not going to be very popular in this room."

Ahmed's tea arrived and he accepted the fragile cup and saucer.

What an awkward way to drink tea, standing up instead of sitting down. And with no dates. He took a sip of the lukewarm liquid. *Undrinkable.*

Duse's voice was getting louder. Some of the men near him moved away.

Blunt sucked on his cigar as though it was a hookah. His fingernails were long and drew attention to his two scarab rings. Ahmed recognized them as possible artifacts from excavations at Giza, the first tomb Ahmed had inventoried. Were they worn to taunt him or as bait suggesting possible future donations?

Blunt saw him notice his rings. "Beauties, aren't they? Gifts from my Egyptian family. I'm curious about your friend, Duse Ali. He claims he is an expert on Egyptian affairs and that Arabi

Pasha once came to his house. Do you know, your Mr. Ali once spent an evening with me and claimed he was circumcised as a Mohammedan." Blunt, his eyes no longer smiling, held his scotch inches away from his lips. "Yet, when I went to recite the Fatha with him, Mr. Ali knew not a word in Arabic or Turkish. Strange for a Mohammedan, no? And are you familiar with his latest novel?"

There were rumors Duse's recent book was plagiarized.

"Very well researched, I understand," Ahmed said.

Blunt's eyes glittered. "Yes, Mr. Ali's *In the Land of Pharaohs* was a very good book on Egypt. Cribbed, nearly all of it, from myself."

Now was the time to change the subject. "Mr. Blunt, I would like to ask you if you are friends with Lord Compton."

Waving his bejeweled hand, he turned and faced him. "Before I answer that, Mr. Kamal, I would like to know if your expertise qualifies you to work in the acquisitions department at the British Museum. An Egyptian setting value on English artifacts?"

"My specialty is translating inscribed artifacts, some from Egyptian to Semitic languages and others from Arabic to French and English."

"Translating what precisely? Writing on coffins?"

"Egyptian hieroglyphs translated through Arabic rather than through Latin-based languages. I process artifact inventory from understanding of Egyptian history, not English value. Our history should be universal, not just for English spectators," Ahmed answered.

Blunt smiled. "You see by my dress, I am as Egyptian as an Englishman may be."

Duse's voice rang out. "Your British Empire is the piggery of the world!"

The men standing around Duse and Lever scattered. Mr. Lever raised his hands to subdue Duse.

"You dare try to censor me?" Duse shouted.

"The British Empire is the envy of the world!" Lever announced. "You will see, Mr. Ali, we will create prosperity for Africa, India, and Egypt,"

Duse drew himself up. "If it were only trade you were seeking, but England continues to pillage our resources and represses self-governing."

Lever took a step back. "It is because you cannot self-govern that our ruling is necessary. The Turks proved that long ago."

Duse took a swing at Lever's head. The room exploded in consternation as men grabbed Duse and escorted him out of the room, sliding him along the waxed wooden floors of the drawing room as he twisted and turned in their grasp.

"Using slaves to capture slaves won't work in Africa or Egypt!" he cried just before the door was shut. From the other side, his muffled voice carried into the drawing room. "Or India. Or anywhere else Britannia rules. Ahmed. Ahmed Kamal, use your magic on them!"

The room fell silent as all eyes turned to Ahmed and the turbaned Blunt.

Ahmed sipped his pale tea and tried to appear calm. Blunt still stood by his side, puffing away on his cigar.

Ahmed debated fleeing out the door himself as the actor William Terriss emerged from the crowd. They hadn't seen one another since the luncheon at the Savoy.

Terriss, in the evening dress of the Edwardian dandy, swilled his crystal glass of whiskey. "Mr. Kamal, a duel of magic? En garde," Terriss announced. He swung his glass of whisky near Ahmed's head, in a mock fight.

Ahmed playfully held up his teacup as a first line of defense. There were a few grins from those standing nearby.

"Mr. Terriss, could my magic save this fine English teacup from you?" Ahmed answered. "I think not."

Terriss clasped him on the shoulder. The room's pent-up energy relaxed and a hum of *basso profundo* rumblings resumed.

Terriss gestured to a man next to him. "Lord Compton, let me introduce you to Ahmed Pascal Kamal, Egyptian Acquisitions Director at the British Museum."

Blunt stepped in front of Ahmed before he could reply to Lord Compton; the ringed hand of Blunt extended to Terriss.

"Mr. Terriss, Wilfrid Blunt here," Blunt interjected. "Heard you wrangled a runaway horse the other day. You should come and check out my Arabian steeds at Crabbet Park. You, too, Mr. Kamal. We have the magnificent Mesaod, bred by Ali Pasha Sherif. Newly imported from Egypt. We hope that in the future, 90 percent of all pedigrees of Arabian horses will carry my Crabbet Park bloodstock."

"Mr. Blunt, I've heard of you also," Terriss replied. "You starve and neglect your horses."

Blunt tapped the ash from his cigar. "Well, Mr. Terriss, they are of Egyptian blood. You've heard of this desert tradition of horse rearing, haven't you, Mr. Kamal?"

Ahmed shuddered to be dragged into this conversation, especially in front of Lord Compton. Horses in his childhood were treated like royalty.

Terriss lifted his chin. "Didn't you just shoot seven of those beautiful beasts so you could keep them from your soon-to-be former wife, Lady Ann? You're a bloody monster."

Blunt regarded Terriss with a half-lidded gaze. "They're mine and it is of no business of yours how they are raised or destroyed."

Lord Compton shuddered and looked away from the quarreling men. Ahmed opened his mouth to deflect the conversation. Perhaps he could bring up Lord Compton's ownership of the statue Sekhemk? The words "Lord Compton" refused to be uttered, the word "lord" sticking in his throat. That title was for Osiris, Lord of the Underworld, and other royalty, not grave robbers. Lord Compton gave a nod of his head and wandered away.

Terriss leaned in and brushed away cigar ash from Blunt's tunic. "Cruelty to animals is always my concern, Mr. Blunt."

A yawn tugged at Blunt's mouth. "Stick to stage business."

Terriss stared at him for a moment, then tossed his drink in Blunt's face, the arc of liquid flying like a watery blade. After an instinctive jerk, Blunt's expression remained deadly calm, wiping his face with the long, loose sleeves of his tunic as his turban dripped whiskey.

As a surge of tuxedos lunged toward Terriss, Ahmed found himself jostled to the door as well. Somewhere, Ahmed's teacup fell. By the time he regained his balance, he and Terriss were deposited in the front hallway. The footman near the front door seemed unsure what to do.

As they were catching their breath, the door to the drawing room reopened and Baron Battersea stepped out. Putting both hands on his hips, he squared off before Terriss.

"Really, Mr. Terriss, quite unacceptable. I know Blunt is an outrage to our horse-loving community, but you cannot come and carry on as though you were in *Robin Hood*."

Terriss hung his head. "Baron Battersea, my most humble apologies. It's just when I think how he slaughtered your magnificent horse, Sapphire, it makes my blood boil."

Baron Battersea's hands dropped, and he looked up to the ceiling, tears in his eyes. "There isn't a day that goes by that I don't regret selling my horse to that man. But here's my dilemma now. This Duse Mohammed Ali is bound to write something about tonight in his Fleet Street rag. I can see it now, 'Brawling at Baron Battersea's.'" Battersea rested a hand on Terriss's shoulder. "Do what you must, but I cannot have his newspaper slandering me."

Terriss shifted his weight, gently shrugging off Battersea's hand. "I barely know Mr. Ali, Baron Battersea. Perhaps Mr. Kamal might have an idea of how to appeal to his friend."

Clearing his throat, Ahmed replied, "Baron Battersea, perhaps if there were paid advertisements for Mr. Lever's Pears soap in Mr. Ali's newspaper, then possible future articles could be dropped."

Battersea sniffed. "What is the name of his newspaper?"

"*The African Times and Orient Review*," Ahmed answered.

"A black newspaper? Would they even know what Pears soap is?" Battersea asked.

As Ahmed and Terriss stared at the Baron, he sputtered, "I only point out that his customers would have their own brands of soap. Pears soap adverts would mean nothing to them."

Ahmed fixed his gaze steadily on a spot at the center of Battersea's forehead. By concentrating on addressing Battersea's third eye, he could contain his own emotions.

After exhaling, he said, "Soap is soap, Baron. The bigger question is, will Mr. Duse Ali accept funds from Mr. Lever in exchange for editorial influence?"

"I suppose you are right, Mr. Kamal. After all, it seems you have heard of Pears soap, so perhaps Mr. Ali's subscribers have also heard of soap?"

Ahmed flinched, then nodded his head as the Baron guided them into a side room.

"Thank you for taking care of this issue, Mr. Kamal," Battersea continued. "In the future, I will be able to arrange a formal introduction to Lord Compton for you. Rest here for one last drink before I call my carriage for you."

Once safely ensconced in the side room, Ahmed took a deep breath. It was more art gallery than waiting room, paintings taking up every inch on the walls. How could the rich have an unused waiting room with priceless artwork only the privileged looked at?

"One last matter, Terriss," Battersea said. "Next month the Queen will be reviewing the troops heading out for the Boer War. It's been suggested we ride white charges alongside her carriage. Since the loss of Sapphire, I've no white horse left in my stables. Perhaps you would loan me Sorcerer?"

Ahmed saw a glint in Terriss's eye.

"Ah, Lord Battersea, that might be arranged," Terriss said. "I was wondering about your runaway stable horse I caught up with the other day on the street. The Lyceum's lost the stage horse for *King Arthur* this month. Perhaps we could use your stable horse instead of our autobus nag, which only responds to 'straight ahead bastard,' not exactly a medieval phrase."

Lord Battersea smiled. "Done. My carriage will take you both home." Battersea called to his butler in the hallway. "Get these gentlemen refreshments and see the carriage is called for."

He bowed to them, and throwing one last lingering glance to Terriss, he left. Laughter erupted from the drawing room upon his reentry. The two men smiled at one another as they overheard their names being mocked.

Terriss motioned to Ahmed to take a club chair facing the fireplace. "Sorry about the scene in there."

Ahmed shook his head. "Throwing your drink at Mr. Blunt was a very foolish thing to do."

"Yes, I have been told many times I am a fool, in addition to being immortalized by Miss Smith as such," Terriss replied.

"Is it true Blunt shot seven of his horses to spite his wife?" Ahmed asked.

"Yes. There is a court injunction against him for the assets of his Arabian stud farm. He is selling off his estate to support his drug dependency. He won't hand over his horses to sell, so he is slaughtering them."

Drug dependency. Ahmed now realized that was why Blunt was so prolific in his writing, traveling, and speaking engagements, not to mention the reason for his long fingernails. He was in thrall to the white powder's boost.

Looking at Terriss now, he saw the man's hands were marred with blisters and calluses, as well as a small wound on his right hand. It had reopened and was dripping blood. Ahmed gave over his handkerchief. Terriss dabbed the spots on his hand, trying to staunch the flow of blood. Stage fighting? Street fighting?

"Results from a boxing duel?" Ahmed asked.

"Wrangling a runaway horse yesterday," Terriss said. "The horse's stable belongs to Lord Compton. He heard of the incident and invited me to accompany him here tonight."

"Your dousing Mr. Blunt will have put an end to any further Gents' Nights."

"Compton, Battersea, and Lever all hate Blunt. Or rather, they hate what he is doing to pedigreed horses. Everyone knows my feelings. You mistreat horses, I'll find you, and let you know what."

It made sense. Ahmed could tell that Terriss was one of those men for whom the horse was his connection to wildness, to strength, to an unspoken intelligence and communication. To most of the men in the drawing room, horses were just an asset, something to bet on in a race, a necessary expense that needed grooms and animal doctors or the slaughterhouse when injured.

But it was a pity that one of the casualties of tonight was a proper introduction to Lord Compton. Before he could ask Terriss if he knew the lord, something in the large painting over the fireplace caught his eye. He stood up and walked to get a closer look.

"What? What is it, man?" Terriss demanded, trying to see what Ahmed saw.

"Look. It is Miss Florence Farr."

Ahmed pointed to a figure in the middle of Edward Burne-Jones's *The Golden Staircase*. Terriss was at his shoulder, peering at the painting. Eighteen, beautiful barefoot girls posed on a staircase. In a processional, they wore Renaissance type robes, some playing an instrument, some singing, making their way down a flight of stairs. En route to perform at a king's wedding, perhaps, Ahmed thought. Nearly identical, with differing hues of reddish or blondish hair, each girl had a calm, beatific face, united in a trance with her fellow dreamer. Except sharp-eyed Florence Farr on the steps with her harp, focused on an apparition in the distance. A Cassandra among the stupor.

Terriss breathed in quickly and pointed. "Ah, this Miss Farr here was at the scene of the runaway horse yesterday."

"She was a bystander?"

"Not a bystander. She jumped right in and tended to the endangered child."

They gazed at the painting while the fireplace's hearth glowed. The butler came in with a tray and delivered a whiskey to Terriss and a Turkish glass of tea to Ahmed—a proper cup, proving they'd had it all along.

As he studied the lovely Miss Farr, Ahmed sighed thinking of the day at the museum with her and Pamela.

As though he could hear his thoughts, Terriss mused, "If our Miss Smith were here, she could certainly hear these musicians' music, couldn't she?"

Ahmed smiled at the thought of Pamela seeing this painting. He had heard her criticize some Art Academy paintings as "more tinfoil nightgown than expression."

Within the painting itself, there was a flitting spasm of hands and heads moving.

Terriss stepped back, clutching his drink. "What is happening here? Did you see that?"

Movement shuddered within the canvas again as the young women shook themselves like sparrows flicking their wings in a dust bath. They turned and writhed, stretching as though waking. Florence, holding her harp, began to walk down the staircase, still fixated by something off to the left. The girls all turned to see what Florence was seeing, just out of sight.

Ahmed knew then that his long-silent gift had been reawakened. Not since he excavated the tomb at Giza had he experienced his gift. It came about when he witnessed the reanimation of mummy spirits, the masks of magicians breathing, heard sighs as bandages fell. It had faded these many years since Cairo. Or did it now come back as a curse, as the museum's art authenticator?

All pairs of eyes in the painting turned frontwards. When Florence reached the bottom of the stairs, she directed her intense gaze on the men, her blue-gray gown setting off her blazing eyes. Time slowed down, the noise from the drawing room dimmed, the material from Florence's dress rustled and billowed. Her long red hair became undone and spilled over her shoulders. She plucked a few strings from her harp and mouthed words to a song. They could hear and feel the instrument's vibration.

Ahmed saw Terriss back away to take in the whole scene. *Can Terriss see this?* The letters PCS throbbed in the actor's earlobe. *Ah, yes, Miss Smith's Fool has the gift too.*

A glow formed at the top of the painting, burning, crackling, as fine lines appeared. Within the brightness, the crown of Hathor materialized, a red orb framed by two prongs. The crown lowered, settling on Florence's head. She raised her finger, pointing at something behind Ahmed and Terriss.

"I see it," Terriss said, setting down his drink. "I know exactly what she is pointing at."

Ahmed stepped aside as Terriss jumped on the back of the sofa. "What?" Ahmed asked.

"The future! I jump into the void!" he declared, then executed a tumbler's vault, throwing himself off the couch, landing in front of Ahmed, holding his drink intact.

He clasped Ahmed's shoulder. "To taking risks!" he toasted and downed his drink.

A loud rapping at the front door jolted their attention to the hallway.

The footman went dashing by the door. Someone wasn't at their station. They heard the door open and shut, and then a stranger trotted into the receiving room.

"Hello there," said a young freckled man with red hair and a square face.

He beamed as the footman took his glossy top hat, walking stick, and opera coat. His starched wing collar and frock coat marked him as a young man of fashion; his walking stick and bejeweled watch chain as a dandy. After handing off his things, he gave a brief nod to Terriss and Ahmed, and not waiting for an introduction, exited.

From the opening of the drawing room, they heard the butler announce, "Mr. Winston Churchill."

The footman disappeared with Churchill's outerwear, and Ahmed and Terriss turned back to the painting. All of the painting's inhabitants were still. Florence was back at her original spot on the steps but now wore the crown of Hathor. The crown remained for a moment, then evaporated. Her expression remained like one of Cassandra, alarmed and all seeing.

Ahmed looked at Terriss. The initials PCS had returned on his earlobe, the letters glowing as though a fresh brand. He certainly was Pamela's Fool.

Ahmed felt strange, new blood flow through his veins.

What magic did Miss Farr activate?

CHAPTER EIGHT

POISON

~⁊⁓⁚~

Pamela entered the Lyceum Theatre's dressing room just as Edy draped fabric over her mother's right arm, creating a beautiful water-falling effect.

Ellen's star dressing room was the nicest in the theatre, even nicer than Henry's. A window overlooking the street, open this chilly afternoon, let in the outdoor sounds. A couch, tea tables, a pouf, a dressing table, a wardrobe, and chairs fanned out before a fireplace inset with a black iron stove. A teapot swung on a hook, tea at the ready.

Ellen saw Pamela in the dressing room mirror and started coughing. When she stood straight up, instead of looking like Hermione in Shakespeare's *The Winter's Tale*, she looked like a mummy.

Between hacks, Ellen cried, "Pixie! Thank the goddesses you are here. Edy is tormenting me with pleats."

Pamela set her hamper down as Mussie leapt all around her. She embraced Ellen and turned to greet her long-lost roommate with open arms. The younger, pale version of Ellen turned away and gathered up her belongings without looking either woman in the eye. Pamela felt a brick in the pit of her stomach. *No reunion tonight.*

"What can I do to help?" Pamela asked, watching the duo in the dressing room mirror.

"Stay out the way," Edy replied.

"Now I look like I'm in Ma's *Dracula*," Ellen said. "Darling, go! Go to your appointment; Pixie can help me get into this."

As her mother started to fuss with the gold cords around her waist, Edy lightly slapped her mother's hands away.

"Mother, when I designed this for you, I made sure you would be able to put this on by yourself in less than a minute."

"Pixie doesn't mind if I dress in five minutes," Ellen replied, focusing back on her reflection.

Pamela caught Edy's cool gaze in the mirror as she removed the straight pin cushion strapped to her arm. She stopped and handed it to Pamela.

Edy took her coat and purse off the coatrack and said, "Thank you for being here for Ellen. Please make sure she goes right home after the show and takes care of herself." Pausing at the door, she turned back. "And, Pixie, the cords tie in the back, or else she'll twirl them like a bored sentry."

As the steps of Edy faded away, Ellen made the motions of waving away bad fumes and Pamela started to laugh, opening her hamper. Mussie leapt up to pull the cloth off, and with a quick snap, grabbed the sausages inside. He darted down the hallway, toenails clicking at a furious pace.

Ellen and Pamela shouted after him as dressing rooms opened.

"Here, Mussie!"

"Here, boy!"

A door shut and the sounds of cooing reverberated. Chuckling, Pamela turned back to set the teapot to boil as Ellen was trying to untie the cords and stifle coughing.

"Oh well, they were his treat anyway. Let me fix that and you drink this," Pamela said, handing over a jar from her basket, an elixir with ginger threads and clouds of honey.

"How am I going to keep still in the statue scene?" Ellen asked between hacks.

The last scene of *The Winter's Tale* calls for the statue of Hermione to come back to life. The hair-raising effect worked only when the actress playing Hermione was stone-still beforehand. Henry, who played the jealous husband, was adamant that the audience shouldn't even see Ellen breathe during his proceeding monologue.

As Ellen drank her concoction, dabbing her running eyes, Uncle Brammie appeared in the open doorway. Something was amiss apart from Miss Terry's coughing, there was a stern and distant look.

"Pa," he said, using his nickname for Ellen. "Will you be able to make it through the last scene?"

"Ma," Ellen answered, using her private nickname for him back. She barked a rough cough and then cleared her throat. "I know that Henry will not forgive a coughing fit, Ma, no matter how involuntary."

Uncle Brammie offered, "Then let me summon Dr. Felkin for you. He will give you something to quell your cough."

Lena Ashwell, the young actress playing Perdita, Hermione's long-lost daughter, suddenly flew inside the dressing room. Panting, she stood before Bram and beat him on his chest with her fists. Pamela tried to grab one of her flailing hands, but Uncle Brammie motioned for her to leave it alone.

"That's not fair, Mr. Stoker! You said you would send Dr. Felkin to me! You promised he would come to me."

The towering bulk of Bram Stoker, former boxer and city clerk, didn't flinch as her fists pounded his chest. Lena was a spirited, young actress from America who had come over in William Gillette's *Sherlock Holmes*. She had recently been cast in the ingenue roles. Was she a younger, more beautiful version of Ellen? Pamela knew this was not said by Uncle Brammie or Henry but by the press. Youth. Beauty. The coinage of women.

Taking Lena's hands in his bearlike ones, he sat her in a chair. Meanwhile, Ellen crouched, putting her shawl around Lena's trembling shoulders.

"Lena, what's wrong, dear?"

"Miss Terry, Mr. Stoker's doctor gave me a drug for cough so I wouldn't be moving in the scene in *King Arthur*, but now he says I've had enough. But now, I need it—I need it in the worst way!"

Ellen stood up and looked Uncle Brammie in the eye. "What did the doctor give her?"

"Dr. Felkin has given this treatment many, many times with no ill effect."

"He has given this treatment to her many, many times? Do you hear yourself?" Ellen asked sharply. It was the first time Pamela ever heard her talk to Uncle Brammie that way.

Lovejoy, the stage manager, was coming down the hall, announcing in his cockney singsong, "Ten to places, ten to places."

Uncle Brammie lifted Lena out of the chair. Ushering her out of the room, he added, "Mr. Lovejoy and I will send for the doctor. He's attending the show tonight."

Pamela stared down the hall as he left. Where was Uncle Brammie's Irish accent? He had begun to sound like Henry Irving, all plummy vowels with the crunchy consonants chopping up the cadence.

She could hear Lena call out as she was carried away, "Don't let them do it to you, Miss Terry! My mind still isn't right. But I need it sore bad!"

Uncle Brammie called over his shoulder, "Don't worry about Miss Ashwell, we'll see to her."

Pamela and Ellen eyed one another in the mirror as they listened to Lena's pleas echo down the hallway. Ellen sipped her drink.

"Miss Terry, you're not coughing," Pamela noted.

"I think that scene may have cured me, Pixie," Ellen replied, applying rouge to her pale cheeks.

Once the curtain had rung down on the show, back in Ellen's dressing room, Dr. Felkin knocked on the door and entered without an invitation.

"Your stillness of Hermione in the last scene was astounding," Felkin said, fiddling with his monocle.

Pamela felt a frantic and dark energy from him as he fidgeted.

"This required onstage stillness has led to our Miss Lena's addiction to a medicine you have given her, Dr. Fenton."

"Bosh," Felkin replied, "only the imaginings of a delirious patient. But Miss Terry, we are still to escort you to my after-show party?"

Ellen asked, "Should I wait for Mr. Irving?"

Felkin gave a fish eye to Uncle Brammie, who appeared in the doorway. Uncle Brammie said, "Mr. Irving has had to bow out to learn lines for a new play."

What show would that be? The Unholy Trinity of Bram, Ellen, and Henry usually went together to late-hour soirees. But lately, Henry was nowhere to be seen after shows. It was decided that Ellen could attend only if Pamela went also and that they would walk. It was only twenty blocks to Blooms-bury Square.

Ellen's carriage would deliver Mussie home and come back to fetch them in two hours' time, Dr. Felkin announced. Pamela had rather that she was going home with the dog to work on her High Priestess or the book plate order from Watkins Books. She almost offered that she would accompany Mussie home, when Uncle Brammie pulled her aside.

"You must go with Miss Terry. I have urgent business to attend to, and I'll be there later. Please keep an eye on her at the peril of your life."

He left before Pamela could register a protest.

Ellen insisted the three of them promenade down the darkened cobblestones of Covent Garden. The unlikely trio linked arms, and Ellen, Dr. Felkin, and Pamela made their way through the empty market. The empty stands of the sellers echoed like tombs. Here and there lit barrels glowed with coal braziers. Wretched street people gathered around to warm themselves in the early spring air.

They passed a collection of ragged children, and a young girl reached out a hand to grab Ellen's silk dress trailing beneath her coat. Ellen stopped abruptly.

"Pity," the young girl murmured.

"What is that, darling child?" Ellen answered as she leaned over the ragamuffin. The little girl crouched further into the dirty street, her glassy eyes focused on Ellen's face.

It was after eleven o'clock at night, and not a parent or sibling was to be seen. Dr. Felkin tried to nudge Ellen along. Pamela felt a low thrum in her throat. All was not good.

"Dress so pity," the little one squeaked.

Dr. Felkin growled, "Ah yes, now we will be set upon by an army of pickpockets or supposed parents. I implore you, Miss Terry, shall we move on?"

The child released the dress and tilted her head. Her dark eyes were fringed in wet, gummy eyelashes, dirt smudged her mouth. When Pamela bent down next to her, the girl's dilated pupils followed the movement of her dangling onyx earrings.

"Stars!" the urchin cried.

Tapping his walking stick on the cobblestones in exasperation, the doctor sighed as Ellen straightened up and looked around.

Pamela peered into the darkened stalls, noting the many piles of debris thrown against the back wall: corn husks, burlap bags, and soiled muslin basket liners thrown every which way.

Pamela called out, "Hello? Hello? Is anyone there?"

Dr. Felkin grasped Ellen's wrist and pulled her to him at the sound of scuttling. Pamela realized the stacks of debris were bodies moving forward. Dr. Felkin quickly tried to get Ellen and Pamela out of the stall, but a mass of young men surrounded them like stealthy rats.

"Well, a haw-haw toff and a coupla petticoats. Whatchya down' with me sister?" the leader barked as he and five other cohorts stepped in front of them. The little girl was still seated on the ground and seemed as frightened of the boys as they did.

"What did ya do to her?" the young man demanded, hands on hips, now coming in closer. He was dressed in mismatched pants and a threadbare jacket. Hearing the anger in the voices, the young child started coughing, then, crying. She tried to crawl away to Pamela, but the young leader darted forward, startling her. She fell over in a heap.

"See there, ya did something!" he said as he squatted down next to her. "Persef, whatchya down' there, darlin'?"

Suddenly, the small girl vomited on his worn shoes. The boy howled and stood up, shaking his feet. As he did, the girl fell back. Foam appeared on her lips as she faced downwards, her small body shaking.

Dr. Felkin turned her over, commanding Ellen, "Hold her head still, Miss Ellen. Miss Smith, hold her legs! She mustn't bite her tongue."

Ellen held the little girl's head, her greasy, tousled hair flying everywhere, while Pamela held her thrashing legs. As Dr. Felkin pried the girl's mouth open and held his wooden walking stick against the child's teeth, the gang of young men gathered around. Her little body spasmed and writhed. In the street, a cart driver stopped his horse and jumped down, running over. Several others came up until the reassuring sight of a metropolitan policeman stepped forward. By this time, the little form lay motionless on the ground. Dr. Felkin opened her slack mouth. Keeping her jaw open with one hand, he felt her tongue with the other.

Ellen put her head next to the still little face and cried out, "She's not breathing!"

Dr. Felkin took off his monocle, blew in her face, and smelled her breath. "She's been drugged with cough syrup. She's asleep, not dead."

This doctor knows all the signs of being drugged. Pamela and Ellen saw the little chest rise and fall in tiny waves.

The policeman recognized Ellen and helped her to her feet. "Miss Terry, these thugs here takes these abandoned ones and gets 'em use to Mother's Little Helper so they don't cough when beggin'."

The young ringleader and his followers took off at a run, Dr. Felkin shouting after them, "I hope you're running to fetch the family, damned cowards!"

The driver from the horse cart, realizing his purse had been stolen, began patting his chest and hopping up and down in a rage. There were oaths not heard by Pamela or Ellen in all their time with the Lyceum backstage crew—sex acts with donkeys, thunder, lightning, old gods, and the power of smallpox. He swore at the policeman who showed no interest in chasing the cutpurses at midnight. Annoyed, the policeman threatened to lock him up for being a public nuisance.

He turned to Ellen.

"There, there, ma'am, these things happen. We'll drop the little one off at the alehouse down the street. Perhaps you could sponsor some neck oil for us to watch over her?"

"Neck oil?" Pamela asked.

"Beer, miss. Needed to watch over the child til the morning," he said flatly.

"Ah, I see," Ellen said, looking at the rolled-up little body on the ground. Ellen retrieved her coin purse from her coat's inner pocket while Dr. Felkin sniffed and looked off in the distance. Pamela realized they were all in on it, the gang, the cart driver; all performed expertly so the policeman would get his coin.

"Thank ye, ma'am. We'll take good care of her."

When they arrived at Dr. Felkin's house, the drawing room was full. Bursts of laughter, clinking glasses, and booming salutations greeted their entrance.

As Ellen was whisked away, Pamela looked for a place to sit. The overwhelming scent of flowers gave her a headache. Dr. Felkin was famous for his hothouse white gardenias, and they entwined every candlestick, in every flower arrangement.

She sat on the pouf before the fireplace just as Uncle Brammie entered. He gave Pamela his customary two-fingered salute.

He mimed drawing and mouthed, "Cards coming along?"

Pamela mouthed back "Yes" and gestured as though she were madly scribbling.

He nodded and turned to converse with Felkin, who was glued to Ellen's side.

Wearing a yellow bolero over a gold shift, Ellen swayed like a reed, her strawberry blonde hair adorned with lemon-colored rosettes. As Pamela watched Ellen perform greeting after greeting, the isolation of her pouf became oppressive. Pamela caught her own reflection in the mirror above the fireplace and let out a laugh. Short, squat, and wearing a dark green silk dress with black onyx jewelry, she looked like a frog on a lily pad. It took everything she had not to croak back at her image.

Dr. Felkin was recounting his time in Africa as personal physician to King M'tesa, who tried to kill him before hiring him, according to the story. Next to him was his wife, the hostess, Mary Felkin. Wearing gardenias in her hair and a blue-gemmed Worth gown with a sapphire moon pendant, her faraway expression was compounded as she listlessly opened and shut her white feathered fan. Pamela caught her eye as her husband's tale of a tiger hunt was coming to its climax. The hostess subtly pointed her fan at Pamela during the story's punchline, a gun's discharge.

Mrs. Felkin let her fan fall open on "bang." They smiled at one another. What was the meaning of it when a fan opened? Was it code for "wait for me" or "talk to me?"

The moment to join the hostess in conversation passed, as she joined the chorus of praises for the tiger's slaughter.

The image of the Covent Garden urchin preyed on her mind. Here they were, drinking, laughing, and telling ridiculous stories while others suffered mere blocks away.

She felt Ellen's hand on her shoulder and looked up. She saw tears in Ellen's eyes, unseemly at a party. Ellen brushed them away in a subtle move and sat with her. Dr. Felkin started another story.

Pamela whispered, "How can the good doctor be carrying on as though nothing just happened? That little one struggling to breathe while they drug her to behave."

Uncle Brammie brayed at Felkin's current joke, and she hated her adopted uncle just a little.

She turned back to Ellen. "And you know that Dr. Felkin takes his own version of the little girl's poison himself."

"Pixie! Dr. Felkin? Cough syrup?"

"Yes, I could feel it right away. Not cough syrup, though, one of the drugs the Golden Dawn chiefs take. Even Ma takes it."

"No, Pixie, you're mistaken. Ma would never take a drug."

"You know I'm right, Miss Terry. Why are there so many hallucinations in his *Dracula*? Or maybe it's laudanum?"

Ellen flinched but Pamela knew it was true. Bram had become so much more aggressive and controlling lately, not to mention he was always leaving for Golden Dawn meetings that no one knew anything about. Then, there were strange new cast members hired only for one show. And his constant reminders that Pamela should finish the tarot card deck. Why did he care so much? The chiefs of the Golden Dawn were her official patrons sponsored by Miss Horniman, but when she would ask him why the card's journey was so important to him, she was met with stony silence.

This evening's soiree, populated by middle-aged merchants, also included the strange new "doctor sect" that seemed to suddenly attend every arts gathering. At the theatre, there were usually two of these doctors on call, in the good house seats. Most of these men of science were unable to help anyone who stumbled or fainted in close quarters.

Pamela looked up as Ellen joined Uncle Brammie's circle, who waved her over. She shook herself and approached the huddle.

"Gentlemen, may I present Miss Smith," Uncle Brammie said. "Miss Smith, I was just telling my compatriots about vampires. More specifically, the vampires in Germany and Austria. But I wasn't able to remember your story of Jamaican vampires."

The performer in her woke up. She no longer included the stories of the *heg* in her one-woman show, it was too gruesome for ladies and young people, but at a soiree with inebriated doctors and lawyers it seemed just right. She registered the expectation on Uncle Brammie's face that she would perform. With a trace of a Jamaican accent, she introduced herself as Gelukiezanger and turned in a circle. She cast a piercing look into the eyes of every person standing around her, silently asking for help that these gifts not be used against her. Dr. Felkin motioned over two young men with identical curled mustaches and blasé expressions just arriving in the room.

"My stories have my accent; don't you be putting other's airs" rang in her head. It was Nana. From the corner of the room, she saw her former nanny's stern gaze, the one eye crinkled up in stern admonishment, her wagging finger. Nana disappeared before she could assure her. Pamela took a big breath and began.

"Well, then. I tell you the story of the soucouyan, called a 'heg' by the islanders. She is the sweet old lady that looks like every laundress or maid who helps out at the big house. But she has a house filled with shelves of human hair and cat skulls, playing cards, shells, and feathers. And all along the walls are tied bunches of herbs and leaves. She wears a blue dress with a big sash and all the peoples of the town know that when they see the heg, they know to give her the respectful eye.

"At night, though, she can leave her own skin, it fall right off her like a snake's in a heap on the floor. It wait there for her all night, for now she is a ball of fire that fly right out the window of her little house. It soar through the air, looking for the sweet blood of young children to feed on. And the heg got a bite, one that leaves a little purple mark on the neck. The next day, the baby maybe they die. Maybe not. Then, she fly through the air back to her house. She change right back to her skin before the sun come up and no one ever know she drink the blood of the children."

"How do you trap a heg?" Dr. Felkin interrupted, anchoring his monocle to peer closely at Pamela.

"Salt," Pamela answered.

"Salt?" he repeated. "Is that all?" he added, as though this were an impossibility.

"While the heg out on her terrible business, you find the skin she leave behind. You take the skin and salt it, inside and out, until it make the skin shrink and shrivel. When that first cock start crowing for the dawn, the heg come home and calls out, 'Skin, come to owner.' But no matter she tug it this way, she tug it that way, her skin no longer fit. She be in a fury but nothing she can do give her back her skin. She is just an empty ghost who can no longer drink the blood of the children because she have no body to use it."

After a loud explosion of laughter from the huddle of men surrounding Pamela, Ellen quietly sidled up next to her and squeezed her hand. Good, the performance was over.

Dr. Felkin's eyes reflected the walls' sconces of candlelight, yellow flames deep in brown orbs. He passed out drinks with a flourish.

"Allow me to play host to the two most beautiful and creative women. Here's to celebrating the devils' dinner hour with you!"

Pamela reluctantly took her glass and watched Ellen take a long sip. *Two of the most beautiful and creative women. That's a first. What a strange, metallic taste this drink has.*

"Let me introduce to you Miss Terry and Miss Smith," Dr. Felkin said as he pressed his hands together. "This is Jaime de Borbón and Earl Ashburnham."

Earl Ashburnham, the one who has provided mummies for Ahmed, according to Mr. Shaw. The earl immediately turned away from her to capture Ellen's attention while the shorter one gazed at her with half-lidded eyes.

"Miss Smith," he drawled, "a pleasure. What a scene you depict of those savage Caribbean islands."

"Mr. Borbón," Pamela replied, "I'm glad you enjoyed it. You know of the Caribbean?"

He looked at Ellen's back, "I know of it although I am more of a continental man myself."

Pamela's scalp began to burn. *Who is he?*

"You sound very English to my ears, Mr. Borbón."

"The effect of Beaumont College in Windsor, but I was born in Switzerland. And you, Miss Smith, where were you born? Cuba?"

Pamela's head jerked back. "I was born here in London to American parents."

He stood a little closer to her. "Ah, but you see I can tell that we have something in common. We are both pretenders."

"I assure you, sir, I am not."

He smiled, half-apologetically, "I only meant in the way that you are an actress when you pretend to be someone else."

Pamela relaxed her hand around her drink. "And what are you a pretender to?"

He leaned in and whispered, "Why, I am the pretender to the Spanish throne."

Pamela looked at him to see if he was joking, and seeing his large smile, she toasted him.

She tried to keep her bark of a laugh down. "You almost had me." He pointed at her as though he didn't quite believe her, and they laughed.

Pamela took another small sip of her awful drink. "I could say I am the pretender to the Fairy Kingdom."

A commotion at the door brought them out of their conversation, and several gentlemen in the foyer barked salutations. As they took off their coats, Pamela spotted Mr. Mathers, Dr. Westcott, and other Golden Dawn chiefs. Dr. Felkin took his two friends, the earl and the pretender, over to greet them. Ellen pivoted back to her.

"Your fan club has now—" Pamela stopped midsentence.

Aleister Crowley was wearing a great cloak, which fanned out around him as he twirled, he removed it and handed it off to the maid. Pamela's hand holding her glass jerked, sending a spray of wine flying.

Ellen looked at her, puzzled. Seeing Pamela's distress, she motioned to the houseboy to mop up the spilled wine.

"Get us out of here, now, please," she said, passing him a coin from the pocket of her bolero.

The houseboy quickly snatched the coin, and with a small wave of his wrist, motioned that they should follow him to the far door. From there, he ushered them down a short hallway to a magnificent pair of white French doors. On the other side was the stunning conservatory dome, its glass speckled with condensation. Against the night sky, the white outline of the dome's arches reached high above them.

The humid air of the open hothouse brought an even stronger scent of gardenias. As the ominous shadows of banana trees and ferns closed in on them, the houseboy shut the doors and moved ahead. As he forged a small path between the enormous palms and exotic plants, they followed him, dense leaves whistling against their faces like numb fingers.

Finally, they came to the conservatory's outer door. The young man fiddled with the lock, but the key refused to free the bolt. Felkin was calling Ellen's name behind them, from the other side of the dome. A door handle jiggled.

After making a sign for them to stay, the houseboy made his way back down the path where male voices grew louder.

Pamela grabbed Ellen's wrist, drew her near, and whispered, "My friend, a quick charm to keep us safe."

"A charm? Or magic?" Ellen asked. "Can you perform magic?"

Moving under a banana tree, Pamela brushed Ellen's eyes closed with her hand. She held Ellen's hands, closed her eyes, and channeled Obeah, her Nana in St. Andrews. At first, the spell tasted sour—the wine must have contained some magic or poison—but she pushed through the terrible taste. She looked up. There it was—the shadow of a big green lizard clinging to a branch above them. She nodded to the lizard. The lizard gave her a slow blink back. Just in time, as the men were making their way down the tiny path.

When Pamela looked down, she realized she couldn't see her own body. Nor Ellen's. Only the tips of four shoes peeking out from the floor of greenery. Two shoes were a sturdy brown boot, the other two, pale pink slippers. It was so dark the men would never see them. *How long can the magic hide us?* The wine's poison had surely prevented all the magic from working.

Felkin was just feet away from them. It felt exhilarating that they were disguised. Aleister was right at his elbow while Uncle Brammie stood in back.

"The ladies just wanted to see your flowers, sir. I didn't think it right to say no to them," the houseboy said.

"And you left them in here?" Felkin walked by them and tried to open the outside door. It remained locked.

"Yes, sir, they were in here just before you called. They must have gone back to the party."

Felkin snorted. Pamela could see Aleister scouring every black corner to see if he could see them. The pretender and the earl appeared next to him, looking. She felt Ellen hold her breath. Silence.

"Well, don't let anyone else come in here. Come, gentlemen, let us rejoin the party. It's too bad we didn't bring any salt with us to season a heg."

Aleister tried to move past Dr. Felkin to a spot on the pathway close to where Ellen and Pamela stood but Bram clasped his shoulder and pivoted him in the direction of the house. Even as a shadow, Pamela knew not to meet Aleister's glance or confront his energy. A small thrill coursed through her as she wiggled her toes and saw them pulse, even in the dim light.

As Aleister left, she heard him hiss. The lizard in the tree thrashed in response.

The door closed and men's voices began to fade, and Ellen's pink shoes began to fill in, then her dress. The lizard in the tree blinked and scuttled higher in the leaves. The shadow fell fully now and revealed Ellen's face, her mouth in a perfect 'o.'

Once they were both whole and apparent, Pamela pulled Ellen back to the brick path only to freeze at the sound of a door opening and quick footsteps. When the elephant ear plants parted, their hostess, Mary Felkin, was revealed. The houseboy and the maid were in tow with their coats.

Mrs. Felkin smiled at Ellen. "What a trial my husband is, Miss Terry. I am so sorry he has exhausted your good humor. I've heard you are trying your best to leave undetected. Let me be of assistance."

Key in her hand, she deftly moved to the outer door and unlocked it. After taking their coats and expressing their thanks, they left her and stepped into the cold night air.

It was a gorgeous winter garden. In the half-light from the house, they could see a pathway leading to an alley beyond the brick fence.

As they headed for their escape, Ellen stumbled on the uneven path, laughing, and coughed hard for a moment, almost falling. She took Pamela's hand and pressed it to her own face.

"Pixie, thank you for sharing your magic. I always knew you had it. Now, shall we flee from this hothouse of horrors?"

Pamela laughed and off they were, skipping and laughing as though they were two errant schoolgirls escaping a classroom. They had almost made it through the brick archway when Ellen tripped on the steps leading down to the alley and crumpled. Seeing her friend lying face down in the cold dirt shocked Pamela frozen. She ran back to her and knelt, cradling Ellen in her lap. Pamela didn't know where the soothing, chirping sounds came from as she swayed her back and forth. It was a long moment before Ellen's eyes flew open. She coughed.

With effort, Ellen whispered, "Poison. Fetch the Unicorn. Side street."

Pamela lowered her gently to the ground and ran as fast as her short, stocky legs allowed her.

CHAPTER NINE

High Priestess Muse

~~⧫~~

"Ladies, ladies, Golden Dawn business awaits," Miss Horniman called, waving her lady bell summoner, a brass statue of a medieval court lady. The lady bell's long legs under the skirt were the clangers, emitting a dull thud on ringing. A banging at the front door and Boudica's barking soon overtook any ineffectual bell tones.

"Adelaide, the door," the hostess called.

The maid scurried from the room. A few moments later, Pamela and Mussie appeared. Mussie ran up to Miss Horniman's Irish wolfhound, Boudica, while Pamela hung at the door mid-entry, her face flushed.

"Ellen's been poisoned!" Pamela rasped.

Edy ran to her side. Mussie picked up the energy and bayed. Boudica joined in and soon the two dogs were howling while the women moved in as one.

So much for me trying to tell Edy in calm way.

Pamela swallowed the lump in her throat, waiting for the moment when she could catch her breath.

Miss Horniman took her fingers and blasted a sharp whistle. Pamela felt her heart pound as she was brought to the front of the room, standing between Florence and Edy.

"First of all, is Miss Terry dead?" Miss Horniman asked.

"No, no!" Pamela replied. She reached over to hold Edy's hand, and she wasn't shaken off. "She was . . . she drank . . . we were . . ." Pamela felt Edy's eyes scour her face. *How could you? You promised.* Answering was impossible.

"Start from the beginning, Miss Smith. Is Miss Terry still alive?" Miss Horniman asked.

Edy sat down in Miss Horniman's throne-like chair near the fireplace.

"Yes, Dr. Mankers is now with her. He . . ." Pamela trailed off, seeing the looks between Florence and Edy.

The women crowded in closer. The room had become very hot. Edy was holding her head between her hands.

"Could we all please give Edy some room? And maybe some water?" Pamela asked, bending down to unbutton her friend's tight neck collar. Her own hands were shaking. It had been so long since she had been this close to Edy.

A glass of water was fetched. Edy's head lifted.

With an impatient swat at Pamela, Edy whispered, "Pixie, please, just tell what happened."

Most of the Golden Dawn ladies only knew Pamela as the artist who randomly showed up to take the required classes for Golden Dawn advancement. Concern in their eyes made facing the group difficult. Florence motioned for them to resettle in their chairs.

Her tongue felt thick, but she blinked and started.

"Last night, Miss Ellen and I were at Dr. Felkin's soiree. We drank some wine. I barely had a sip, but Miss Terry drank a whole glass. She collapsed a short while afterward."

Murmurs and whispers.

"We brought her home and Dr. Mankers is attending her," Pamela continued. "She was delirious, not recognizing anyone. We're hoping she doesn't fall into a coma."

Pamela's stomach clutched as she saw Edy twist in her chair.

"Who else is with her?" Edy asked, facing away from her.

"Aunt Alice, the maid, Mr. Irving, and Mr. Stoker."

Edy stood. "What does the doctor suspect?"

"He thinks it's an overdose of laudanum," Pamela replied. "Scotland Yard asked for the wine from Felkin's soiree to be tested. We are waiting for the Society of Apothecaries's report."

"Does Dr. Felkin know?" Florence asked as she paced in front of the fireplace.

"Scotland Yard went to his home this morning to confiscate his wine, so he knows something happened last night," Pamela replied.

"Who else was there?" Florence asked.

Pamela looked up at the ceiling. She saw them in her mind. "Dr. Felkin; his wife, Mary; Mr. Stoker; a Spaniard Jaime de Borbón; and Earl Ashburnham. Aleister Crowley arrived late with your husband, Moira."

Moira stood, her hands on her hips. A former Slade student, she wore her hair down, and with her sharp chin, had an elfish look. But Pamela knew despite her timorous voice and fragile frame, she had ambitions to rise through the ranks of the Golden Dawn.

Moira blanched. "Mr. Mathers only said that there was a small gathering last night. He didn't say anything about Mr. Crowley attending. And nothing was said about Miss Terry—"

"Your husband, Samuel Mathers, is currently contesting my presidency," Miss Horniman said, suddenly appearing next to Pamela. "And it was clearly stated there is to be no socializing with Aleister Crowley. He is banned from the Golden Dawn for crimes against members."

Moira sat down. Pamela felt a weight in her chest expand as Moira cast a sideways look at her. It was the look of a cat seeing prey move in a corner. Pamela forced herself to breathe. *Don't give her the power to see your worry.*

"Miss Smith," Miss Horniman asked, "what is Miss Terry's prognosis?"

"Dr. Mankers said most likely the result will be possible memory loss."

Possible memory loss. Miss Ellen Terry, the celebrity Shakespearean actress of the day, losing her memory. As the top repertory actress in England, her reputation was largely because of the many roles at her disposal. Sir Henry had memorized eight hundred roles, and he expected a high level of memorization in his company. Ellen was said to have at least four hundred in ready memory.

Edy stood in front of Pamela.

Thoughts streamed across her friend's pale face. Without her mother's income, a whole community surrounding her would collapse. She supported not only Edy and her brother, Gordon, but she also employed a retinue of artists, maids, housekeepers, and dressers.

She almost reached out to Edy, but then she heard a voice in the hall, followed by footsteps to the parlor. Adelaide handed a note to Miss Horniman, who read the cover and handed it to Edy. *From M. Stoker to M. Craig.*

Edy turned to Pamela, her hands shaking. The unopened letter quavered between them as she handed it to Pamela. She tore it open.

There was no making sense of it, the tears in her eyes making the letters dance.

Something shifted in the room. Gravity? Wind? A force unseen. Pamela tasted blue salt wind.

Florence was beside her and gently took the letter.

"Dear Miss Craig, I am here with Dr. Mankers. Your mother is now awake and talking of you. It is hoped almost all of her memory will come back. Bram."

The room erupted into applause. Pamela tried to embrace Edy, but Miss Horniman had already put a protective arm around her.

"I'm sure you want to get to your mother immediately. Do you need a carriage?" she asked as she escorted Edy out the door.

Pamela tried to wave to see if Edy wanted her to come with her but to no avail. She was gone.

Attendees helped themselves to refreshments. After a few minutes of chatter, Miss Horniman returned and Florence clapped her hands together, and the women turned their attention to her.

"Miss Horniman. I see you are serving wine this afternoon. Where did it come from?"

"It was a gift from Dr. Felkin."

"You must toss out every glass of wine from him. And every bottle in the larder, too."

At Miss Horniman's nod, Adelaide went around the room, collecting glasses on a tray.

"Until the authorities catch whoever might have poisoned Miss Terry, none of us are to drink anything at social events. No tea, no champagne, no coffee, no wine at social events. Not even water. If there is a madman out to poison friends of the Golden Dawn, we need to be alert."

Florence came up and put an arm around Pamela's waist. "Miss Smith, Mr. Stoker and I have a suspicion this attack on Miss Terry may have been aimed at you."

"Because of my tarot cards? Why?"

Florence held out a crumpled note for Pamela to read. "This note was delivered to the Golden Dawn headquarters last week. It was only discovered today."

Egyptian hieroglyphics were drawn at the top of the page.

Three figures and a feather were drawn on the wrinkled paper. Pamela felt vague stirrings of a memory. She was sitting on the boat deck with Sir Henry. A lesson in hieroglyphics with Edy.

"You know how to read this?" Miss Horniman asked.

Taking the note, Pamela studied it. "Here's is Anubis judging the Goddess and the Queen. And a feather. Oh! This is what it means: *The judging of your soul will find you wanting.*"

"Yes," Florence replied. "This threat features Anubis, the guide of the Underworld. He takes the heart of the newly dead and helps weigh it. If the deceased is found to be true through its trials, then it is weighed with a feather and found to be of equal weight. Only then will Anubis bring them to Osiris, to join them in immortality."

"Anubis? Osiris?" Miss Horniman asked, taking the note out of Florence's hand. "Moira, do you know anything about it?"

"I surely don't, and even though my husband speaks many languages, he has lamented his ignorance in Egyptian symbols," Moira answered.

How like an Art League model student she looked, with her long hair and demure expression. Pamela felt a coarse and heavy energy from her heartbeat.

"And if the heart is heavier than a feather?" asked Miss Horniman.

"The soul is damned to be restless for all eternity," a voice called out, its accent American. Pamela watched as a large, young woman in a red toga, impossibly high hair piled around a tiara and mounds of jewelry, made her way to the front of the room.

"Do I know you?" Pamela asked, a new hum at the back of her head.

"Susan Strong. We met last year at Ada Leverson's. I sang Venus from *Tannhauser,*" she said. "I know this Egyptian curse."

"From the world of opera?" Florence asked, her mouth pulled taut.

"From the world of a Mr. Aleister Crowley. He's been sending me profuse amounts of correspondence about it."

Pamela's mouth dropped open. The memory of the evening at Ada Leverson's came flooding back. Susan was the soiree's performer, and after her aria, Aleister had flattered the singer extravagantly. He was especially effusive when he learned she had just come into a substantial inheritance. That was the night he tried to paralyze Pamela after finding out she had been commissioned to create the tarot cards. The Golden Dawn chiefs in attendance were able to break Aleister's spell of black magic binding her. She knew then it would not be her last run-in with him.

Susan took her hand. "Our grandfathers both served as mayors of Brooklyn. Remember?"

Pamela Colman Smith and Susan Strong, granddaughters of mayors Cyrus P. Smith and Dennis Strong, embraced one another. Miss Horniman cleared her throat.

"This American reunion is touching, I'm sure, but we have a possible death threat for either Miss Smith or Miss Terry or the whole of the Golden Dawn to consider," she said, lighting another cigarette. "Miss Strong, what do you know about Mr. Crowley and Egyptian curses?"

"Only that he said he was working on a long-range plan to lead the Golden Dawn with magic," Miss Strong answered.

"Does he know you were here singing for us today?" Florence asked.

"Heavens, no." Susan laughed. "His relationship with me consists of fawning fan letters hoping to encourage his 'sex Magick' and boasting of having learned Egyptian curses." Susan looked at the crumpled paper again. "These symbols were usually in his letters. I never bothered to look them up."

Just the sort of remark to put off Miss Horniman's support for opera singers.

Sure enough, the maid was summoned, and Miss Strong was soon dismissed from the gathering.

Miss Horniman signaled everyone to sit in the chairs scattered around. It was the first time Pamela had a chance to take in the luxurious Portman Square apartment. Mussie was sleeping in the Irish wolfhound's lap before the fire next to the throne of Miss Horniman.

"I am calling an emergency meeting of the women of the Golden Dawn. Miss Farr, now is as good a time as any to discuss what we had planned."

Pamela sat in the front, and the hum in the back of her head vibrated stronger.

Florence motioned to Pamela. "You've completed the Magician along with the Fool card. What is the next tarot card?" Florence asked.

"The High Priestess," Pamela answered.

Should I tell her she is my muse for the card?

Florence crossed her arms. "Miss Smith, you are the only one here who has remained at level one of the Golden Dawn studies. Because of that lack of magical knowledge on your part, I would like to propose a spell to counter Mr. Crowley."

Moira asked, "A spell for what? How does Miss Smith deserve a magical spell from us?"

Florence replied, "If we study magic, what is the point if we do not practice it? We could conjure a spell of protection for Miss Terry, the innocent victim of Mr. Crowley's handiwork."

Florence didn't like Ellen and thought she was a spoiled star. Why would she ask this?

A log in the fireplace snapped, and a spark flew out from the hearth, knocking over the lady bell summoner with a clanging moan. Several startled cries rang out, and Moira rushed forward to brush the sparks away from the fine rug.

Miss Horniman inspected the singed spot and sighed. Florence motioned all the ladies to stand back.

"Let us begin," she said. "Stand apart from one another." As the women settled among themselves, Florence bowed to acknowledge the four corners of the room.

"From the four winds, I ask your guidance," Florence chanted in the sing-song voice that she used at the museum.

Lifting her arms, she intoned, "We ask for the knowledge and power to protect our own. May our magical intent carry out healing for Miss Terry. We surround her."

The group chanted back, "We surround her."

As Pamela watched, wisps of smoke curled in the air before settling around Florence's face. Fumes filled out a disc supported by two prongs, like a lunar headdress for the goddess Hathor, the Egyptian sky deity. Ahmed would be pleased to know that she recognized it.

Pamela stood next to Florence and reached up to touch the smoke snaking around Florence's head. Low musical tones tasted red on the back of her tongue. Tiny pomegranates cascaded from the ceiling. Did anyone else see this? From the looks of the Golden Dawn women, their faces upturned and radiant, they could see the fruit fall. Florence closed her eyes and also lifted her face. The fruit turned into golden yellow stars falling to the floor, then evaporated. Pamela kept her eyes wide open.

A club-like fist of smoke appeared from the fireplace, filled with blue flames. It traveled around the room as though it were hunting something or someone. Its fumes anointed every corner as a high-pitched cooing came from the hearth.

The sounds escalated until it was cawing, coming from the fire's blaze. A log writhed, twisting side to side. The noise escalated in pitch until it whistled and screeched, sounding like an eaglet urgently demanding food. As the strident chanting grew louder, the women covered their ears, trying to shut out the painful call. The din was about to overpower them. Pamela covered her ears. The noise stopped all at once. She saw it before anyone.

In the logs, a smoldering outline of a hawk's wings appeared. When the body became more substantial, the golden, green eyes fixed on the room and the fiery creature launched itself out from the grate. It swooped overhead, its claws grazing Florence's head. Screeching, it gracefully beat its huge wings and swooped in a circle around the room. After one arc, it floated back to the fireplace and vanished up the flue.

The heartbeat of every woman shared the same cadence. A breath escaped their lips at the exact same time. They were in sync for this one moment.

Pamela swayed back and forth in time as the heartbeat grew louder inside of her. There was a lake, filled with magical essence; it lapped at her feet. Deep, dark, dank. She dipped her hands down into the murky waters. Lifting her cupped hands to her lips, she drank. Powerful vibrations shook her throat. She felt herself say *My High Priestess*.

The sound of crackling wood brought her back to the room.

Florence stood in front of her. She touched her right ear. Throwing off her earring, a welt appeared on her earlobe.

PCS

The women gasped as they realized they had witnessed the crowning of the next tarot card.

Florence Farr, High Priestess.

The group clamored around Florence. Miss Horniman took Pamela aside. She tried to explain she had no power regarding how or when her initials earmarked someone. That once she drew the tarot card, the initials appeared on her muse on their own.

"Does Florence have any special powers now that she was branded High Priestess?" Miss Horniman asked.

"I don't know," Pamela answered. She remembered her promise to Uncle Brammie and Mr. Irving to tell them of the next muse. Somehow, it didn't feel right to discuss this promise with Miss Horniman just yet.

Miss Horniman watched Florence being admired for her earlobes' markings.

"I thought I would be your High Priestess since I hired you," Miss Horniman said, sitting in her throne, flicking the train of her dress for her dog to sit on.

So, it's not just Waite who wants to cast these cards.

Pamela sat cross-legged in front of Boudica and scratched the wolfhound's head as Mussie licked her hand.

"Well, I've been studying Miss Farr at the museum. She's not only a suffragette, but the mummy channeler of Mutemmenu, and a magician musician who teaches the highest level in the Golden Dawn. And she is learning skyring, flying outside the human body. Who better for the High Priestess?" Pamela persisted.

Miss Horniman, as generous as she was, did not study spells or practice magic. She only knew how to surround herself with magic by means of her money.

"There must be a Major Arcana card later in the deck you are saving for me," Miss Horniman said.

Pamela's eyes widened as she waited for an image to appear to her. Come on, muses, magic, be inspired by Miss Horniman. Where was the shutter's click, the torn canvas hole with the clear vision of the creation? But there was no click. No hole. Nothing. What was it that man at Dr. Felkin's had called her, a pretender? Was she only pretending she had the powers to create magic in her tarot cards? Did they have the power to create themselves without her?

"There must be a card for me," Miss Horniman repeated.

PART 2

RETALIATION RESOURCES

CHAPTER TEN

St. Mary Over the Water

~~~

Pamela was halfway across London Bridge when the cry of screeching gulls stopped her midstride, scattering her already fragmented thoughts. Clutching the railing, she looked upriver to the Southwark Bridge. Spring winds pushed faint clouds of smog from coal furnaces along with sails coursing up the Thames. Before her lay a crazy patchwork pattern of schooners, scows, and ferries stretched up to Hay's Wharf, the Larder of London. Bridges, thresholds where magic crossed under and over—crossroads. Didn't Terriss teasingly tell her to stay off bridges? He was joking, of course.

The scene two nights ago at Annie Horniman's had been playing over and over in Pamela's mind. The bird coming alive in the fireplace. Florence throwing off her earring. Florence, now incarnate of the High Priestess, was following in the footsteps of Terriss and Mr. Irving. When she had told Uncle Brammie and Mr. Irving the next day, they seemed unimpressed. She couldn't tell if it was because of her selection of muse or the believability of her story. When she showed Ahmed the completed High

Priestess card and told him Florence was the muse, he only pursed his lips.

His terse response was, "It's better than the Postumio's High Priestess."

The Postumio in the Sola Busca deck was uninspiring—it had been thought to be based on Saint Joan with its female warrior half-hidden by a shield. Waite had discouraged her from looking at the Tarot de Marseille. He felt, as a former Catholic, that the French deck's religious symbology was inaccurate for Golden Dawn purposes. According to him, outside the French Etteila tarot deck from a hundred years ago, there were no in-depth mass-produced tarot decks. Theirs would be unique. Why shouldn't they be the ones to corner the marketplace?

They're not just for the Golden Dawn. I'm creating something magical for the world.

But some of the women had reacted to the PCS initials on Florence's ear as if it were a party trick instead of a sacred bequest. It was not the reaction Pamela anticipated from the Golden Dawn women. One of the ladies even said she hoped tattoos would not be required of them, like sailors with their "HOLD FAST" tattoos. The women and Florence were relieved when the initials faded within an hour.

A large white seagull floated up, gliding on the breezy channels. The bird hovered at eye level, tilted its head, squawked, and dove back under London Bridge. Pamela laughed. Was this Florence practicing skyring?

It was something of a disappointment to see one of her muses come to life. Where did the power to manifest the magic come from? Was the bird the same bird she heard in the museum mummy casket chirping with Ahmed? She wasn't present when Henry or Terriss received their ear markings, but last night Florence seemed nonplussed. Pamela showed her the High Priestess card and told her she was the first female in her tarot deck. Florence only smiled.

Pamela gazed at the river, with its free-for-all of ships jockeying for docking rights—a dizzying spectacle. Lightermen shouted "Ease down!" and "Portside!" to passing watermen in their barges full of passengers. Scows full of hay and beer maneuvered near the buoys, their mournful ship bells clanging, while the more elegant schooners, piled high with barrels and crates, lined up to discharge their passengers. The brackish odor of the water, the acidic vinegar of pickle factories, and the tang of burning coal stung Pamela's eyes. On the Southwark docks, men clad in white shirts, dark vests, and hats lugged push-carts loaded with slat barrels. Forearms under rolled-up sleeves revealed blurry markings, but from this distance Pamela couldn't make them out.

HOLD FAST. The image of tattooed knuckles appeared to Pamela. It was a sailor's warning, meant to be seen on the backs of their hands as they grabbed a ship's rigging. Blackness swirled around in her brain. It was coming back—the reoccurring memory of the accident. Falling off the Waterloo Bridge. Black water. Inky currents buffeting her. Bubbles floating upwards. Follow the bubbles upwards. Her body greedy for that burst of air. Coughing, gasping, as a strong arm hooked her and hoisted her on his back. They had scrambled up a ladder and sat panting on the muddy ground. Her new coat was gone and one shoe missing.

"We're alive?" she asked him. He was breathing heavily.

"So alive!" William Terriss answered.

The memory of William Terriss saving her would come back to her any time she was on a bridge. How does one survive a fall from a bridge, much less the forty feet of Waterloo Bridge? A famous story in its day, now only remembered by her. Now a submerged dream inside her. Sometimes it would resurface, gasp for breath, and come alive. The memory of his words, "So alive," hummed within her. Who better to be her Fool than the man who had stepped off the bridge? Lately, her Fool had been edgy and preoccupied, his young actress daughter, Ellaline, had blurted out at rehearsal that her ill mother might be moved into a home. Maybe that was why Terriss disappeared after shows instead of letting Pamela ride his horse, Sorcerer, to the train station.

She peered down the great snake curve of the Thames past London Bridge and saw the river's tail curl under the bridges toward parliament: Southwark, Blackfriars, and somewhere out of sight, the magnificent Waterloo. She roused herself and started walking again to where the shoreline gave way to the shambled jumbles of pubs, warehouses, and storehouses on the water's edge. Ladders stretched down to the water, teeming with life.

A barge docked at the Southwark wharf was unloading marble slabs, a hoisted piece dangled over the dock like a heavy prey caught in a spider's web. On the other side, workmen steadied the load, while dockworkers readied themselves for the marble slab, jostling one another for space. The foreman gave a series of sharp whistles, prompting a young worker on the dock wearing a white shirt with longish blond hair to run and catch a rope tossed to him from the barge.

Afterward, he strutted on the dock like a peacock, white shirt billowing as the wind picked up. The men jeered him as he twirled the rope instead of lashing it to the piling.

How like the Fool. How like William Terriss.

"You mop-haired foozler, lash that up now!" the foreman bellowed.

"The wind be telling me what to do!" the man called back, laughing.

"Well, the tide is telling you to move your arse. Now!"

The mop-haired boy did a brief jig with the rope and lashed it to a piling before taking a bow. Pamela laughed. She had almost reached the first street exit when she saw a man, glaring at her from the end of the bridge.

Aleister Crowley.

He was wearing a hat slouched over one eye and an over-sized black wool coat. She looked around to see if there were others around her. Just a few straggling men fifty yards or so behind her. Her heart beat faster. Was this why she was remembering William Terriss? Because she was about to be thrown over? The words "Hold Fast; So Alive" flew by in her mind, yellow letters outlined in black.

As Aleister slowly approached her, Pamela resisted the urge to run.

"Miss Smith," he said, stopping a few feet in front of her.

"Mr. Crowley," she answered.

"You will stop conjuring incarnates. You don't know what you are doing," he said.

His dark eyes were blazing, and he was sweating profusely. But when he saw her grip the railing more tightly, he smiled.

"So now you have Florence Farr as High Priestess. Her powers have reversals that you will regret. You won't be able to handle her as you do your Magician and your Fool." As he took another step forward, his dark eyes turned golden, reminding her of Albert's, her childhood pet alligator. "I have no intention of hurting you, Pamela."

He paused; his yellow eyes scanned the dock.

Aleister took a step closer.

"But hurting those around someone is very effective," he said, pointing to the deck below.

A shout broke out as the slab of marble hoisted over the dock slid halfway out of the rope webbing, tilting the barge out of the water. The mop-haired boy ran and stationed himself below the wavering load and reached up to steady it, but the ropes on the bottom of the slab frayed, then disappeared as the marble cut through them.

The huge slab fell like a guillotine as the mop-haired young man tried to jump out of the way. Pamela screamed.

Cries rang out on the wharf and river. Like a pod of dolphins, the small boats jockeyed among one another to reach the ship's ladder. Shouts from ships to men on the docks echoed. Ropes snaked through the air to anchor the wobbly incoming vessels to posts. All the while, blood pooled around the boy lying next to the slab of granite. Pamela couldn't catch her breath. There were no bubbles of air here.

The top half of him was visible, his blond hair and white shirt outlined against the dock. His white shirt was changing color, red veins seeping up from his waist. The marble slab had landed like a tombstone in the middle of his body, and his blond head jerked from side to side as his arms jolted up in the air. As his arms fell to the ground, the slab fell over, cutting his body in half. Pamela doubled over, a howl coming from within. She stood and clung to the railing, panting.

Something was near.

Aleister.

"Desist, no-name child," Aleister growled. His forked tongue licked his lips, as he reached forward with a reptilian claw to take her face in his hands.

Fly. It was a woman's voice. Maud Gonne's.

She felt her body becoming lighter, her feet lifting her off the ground. Maud, her childhood idol and friend, had been there the first time she flew as a child. But the ability to fly had happened only one other time, when Aleister had threatened her Fool. She had not been able to command herself to fly again.

With one hand hanging on to the guardrail, she anchored herself. Was this skyring? Would she fall into the Thames?

Her body tilted backwards, her feet aiming at Aleister's face. Aleister dodged, then lunged to grab her boots. He started to float up as well, but as he neared her, she kicked him in the face, sending him sprawling on the pavement.

She told her legs to jump down, then, falling through the air to hit the ground. As soon as she did, she ran past Aleister's crumpled form, doing her best to keep herself from slipping on the slick stones. She had to reach the end of the bridge. There it was, the sign Exit by London Bridge and an opening to a stairwell.

She dashed down the stone steps, the dim light from above showing where to steady herself on the rough walls. It was a warehouse she was exiting by, dark and cramped.

At the bottom, she threw open an ancient, wooden door to reveal hovels and wretched three-story pubs. The Mayflower, The Mudlark, The Angel, The Courageous—one pub after another, men streaming out, heading for the disaster on the dock. Where was Aleister? Was he among the crowd?

Turning down one corner, then another, she met a dead end. The buildings fused together in the gathering darkness. Where was the dock? Did she even want to get to the dock to see the boy cut in half?

She could hear the cries from the greengrocer and pieman, and further away, shouts of sailors, but what street was this? She couldn't see Aleister behind her. Was he around the next corner?

Tears. She paused to catch her breath and found herself where she had started, at the bottom of the warehouse stairs. Now there was a cart with a hot-potato merchant dumping ashes from his fire bucket on the curb. Should she ask for help or would Aleister appear and kill him too?

She stood in front of the hot-potato man.

"A slab fell . . . black magician following . . . boy cut . . ."

He ignored her. *I'm just a madwoman prowling the streets.* Needing to keep moving, she ran down the side street she had taken earlier.

A large man with a bloody apron came out from a tiny butcher shop.

"Saw ya' runnin' by a bit ago. You're not from around here, are you, miss?"

"No, no," she panted. "An accident on the dock—"

The man wiped his hands and tilted his head. "Ach, that's what the hurly-burly's all about."

Trembling, Pamela took a step nearer. "I think I caused it."

The butcher grunted. "Don't be daft. You caused an accident on the dock? If you did, you can always ask for forgiveness." He turned to go back inside.

"Where? Where can you ask for forgiveness?" Pamela asked.

"Why, at the Mary Magdalen church, of course, miss," the man said. "Take this Clink Street to Dock Street, go away from the docks, the church is right there."

Checking the impulse to shake his bloody hand in thanks, Pamela ran, cocking an ear to hear if Aleister was following her.

There it was. The gothic spires rose before her. But instead of a sign saying Church of Mary Magdalen, a green sign in the front said Saint Saviour's. One of the heavy oaken doors was cracked open. Entering the vestibule, not a soul was about. She placed her hands in the fount near the entrance. Cool water to soothe her shaking. With her damp fingers, she touched her face, dotting her brow and lips. Breathe. Would Aleister enter a church? Maybe she was safe here.

Looking down the nave of St. Saviour's, she realized just how massive this church was. She forced her wobbly legs to enter and walk toward the dome at the back. Massive stone ribs lined the church from floor to ceiling, giving the framed interior the shape of an upside-down ship. The cold, cavernous space was muted and still, the scent of musky incense clinging to the air. At the rear of the church, a magnificent, triple stained-glass window filtered the last of the sunlight. A slash of blue light fell across Pamela from the cerulean center panel. The sun's rays settled on her uplifted face, warming her damp skin.

She stumbled up toward the altar.

Where could she ask for forgiveness for the dead boy? Was there a station for that? Halfway down the aisle, she turned around to take in the enormity of the place. Near the pulpit, a three-tiered chandelier shone weakly with two lit candles.

She stood underneath the chandelier and placed a hand over her heart. Her breath came back to an easy pace.

"Mary Magdalen, if you can hear me, I would like to ask for mercy," Pamela said out loud, her voice cracking on the word "mercy."

The light was falling quickly now, and she made her way to a side aisle. Walking alongside the polished oak pews, the sensation of looking for something stirred—ah, yes, her first-class train car on tour. Same low wooden door with the inset handle. Would Mary Magdalen be in a pew or in the pulpit?

The sound of the main door opening jolted her, and she stepped into the central aisle. It was a reverend, his clerical collar bright under his chin as he lifted his candle in the fading light. He clutched a stack of papers close, then walked toward her with small, mincing steps. With his fringe and perched glasses, he resembled more of a bug than a man.

"Oh, hallo! I didn't know anyone was in here. Can I help you?" the man asked.

"Yes, please. You see, I've just killed a man," Pamela replied.

As archdeacon at St. Saviour's, Reverend William Thompson could conduct confession on request, and he offered to hear hers. The story of Aleister, the guillotined boy, her flying, all of it came pouring out.

Reverend Thompson's eyebrows shot up several times during the course of Pamela's confession, and he crossed himself when she mentioned Aleister's forked tongue and his hissing.

"This confession was a courtesy for someone in need," the reverend said. "In exchange, I would ask that you consider being a part of our parish."

"I'm not forgiven?" Pamela asked. Her hands had stopped shaking and her legs were steadier, but her stomach still felt as though she had been punched.

"You're not guilty," the reverend answered. "You seem a perfectly fine young lady, but I doubt that you flew or that your friend . . . or, er, enemy, caused the death of that dockworker."

Pamela felt her blood curdle. Another nonbeliever in Aleister's magic.

"Now, we need to arrange for you to get home. This neighborhood after dark is not safe. One of the deacons in the rectory will hail a carriage. There should still be a few at the docks."

The word docks brought up the scene from the afternoon. As the reverend ambled to the main aisle, Pamela trailed behind him.

"Can Mary Magdalen forgive me?" Pamela asked.

"What? No. You already have forgiveness from our Saviour. Whatever gave you the idea Mary Magdalen could?" the reverend replied.

"Isn't this Mary Magdalen's Church?" Pamela asked.

"This church was dedicated to Mary Magdalen seven hundred years ago. It's now St. Saviour's Church. But a Mary did found the church in 1100 AD. She inherited a ferry that ran from Dock Street across the Thames," the reverend said, guiding her toward the church door.

"Someone named Mary founded this church?" Pamela stood in the center of the aisle, taking in the height of the ceiling.

"Well, to be precise, she founded a House of Sisters. The story goes like this: a miserly Mr. Audrey owned the current-day Southwark dock and ferry area in the Middle Ages. He fasted for forty days and nights, like our Lord in the desert. Then, to see if he would be missed, he feigned his own death. When his household began to celebrate that their master was finally dead, he sprang up from his supposed deathbed. In the struggle that ensued, Audrey was killed by his own apprentice. His daughter,

Mary Audrey, inherited the ferry business and decided to devote herself and her wealth to a House of Sisters. It was called St. Mary Overie, Mary Over the Water."

"Mary Over the Water? Not Mary Magdalen?"

"That's right, it was named after Mary, who had the ferry boat over the water. But when John Gower rebuilt this church after a fire in the 1200s, he renamed it St. Mary Magdalen's. That's what the locals still call it. I have to correct them frequently."

"John Gower, who rebuilt the church, is he here? Can I see his tomb?" Pamela asked.

The reverend sighed and pushed his glasses up his nose. "Yes, I suppose a quick hello to John Gower on the way out would not be out of line."

They walked to the other side of the church. Some of the ancient paving stones beneath her feet had writings etched in sweeping cursive letters, others had an owl or bull depicted in the middle of the stone.

"Are people buried beneath us?"

"Oh, yes, they are in subterranean tombs. Shakespeare's brother, Edmund, is buried here somewhere."

"Shakespeare had a brother?"

"Yes, a ne'er-do-well actor, probably played a third lord from the left in a history play. And Will Kemp, Shakespeare's fool."

What a day. To be walking over Shakespeare's fool after witnessing the death of a fool.

They approached John Gower's tomb. With its garish colors and gold accents, the tomb could have been onstage in Sir Henry's *King Arthur*. The statue wore a ruby-colored gown gilded with pomegranates, his head propped up by books and his hands folded across his chest. A panel in back of him featured three dancing angels. And pomegranates on his robe. Where had she seen that? Yes, on the coat of Beatrice Pardoe-Nash Ali, given to Prince Edward's mistress at the Savoy Theatre.

"This wooden figure on top is the likeness of John Gower? Is he buried here?"

"Yes, I can't vouch for the likeness, though," the reverend answered.

Pamela put her head on the chest of John Gower's statue to see if she could hear anything. She could sense fairies, spirits, voices from the other side calling to her. Maybe John Gower would tell her where Mary Magdalen was.

A shriveled chirping, like the sound of Mutemmenu at the British Museum, was barely audible. She felt warmth in her hands atop Gower's heart. A brief thought messaged its way into her brain: She was safe here. Aleister would not be allowed in. This felt so much better than the confession.

"Hello, Gower mummy," Pamela said, not looking up.

Reverend Thompson almost dropped his papers, fumbling with them to keep them from falling out of his arms. He lifted the stub of his candle, his fleshy turtle eyebrows rising up.

"A mummy! I should say not, Miss Smith. An effigy. An effigy of Mr. John Gower, who helped rebuild this church. You see three books under his wreathed head, a coat of arms at his side, a lion at his feet. You see the three dancing angels above him. Angels are not seen with mummies."

"If only Mr. Kamal and Miss Farr were here to see this," Pamela said, running her hand along the hem of John Gower's gown.

The reverend held out his hand to stop Pamela from exploring the rest of John Gower. "Please, Miss Smith. But if your friends would like to visit, bring them. We need supporters. The church is Gothic, you know. One of the few left in all of England. The locals certainly don't support us."

"I love it here, Reverend Thompson."

The door opened and shut, and a young boy ran down the center aisle.

"You're needed on the docks, Reverend Thompson," the boy said, barely getting the words out.

"What do they want?"

"Somebody killed in an accident. Family needs consoling."

"Well, I expect they tried a number of people before me. Miss Smith, I'll see to it that there is someone to escort you to a carriage."

"Thank you, Reverend Thompson. If it is alright with you, I'll wait for you here. Those last candles should hold." She wanted to be alone in this place just a few moments more.

The reverend nodded and then trotted off with the boy. His candle made a shadow play of a bobbing silhouette behind him.

Pamela heard the main doors slam shut. Its echo reverberated over the stone floors and up into the ribbed ceiling. In the flickering light of the last two candles, the ribs holding the roof looked like hands cradling the interior.

Now that the reverend was gone, she walked back to John Gower. She took her hands and placed them over his heart again. Both cool and hot from the red color, her hands itched. But now there was no sound, no cooing, no music, no whispers.

"Ah, well, next time, Mr. Gower. Thank you for protecting me from Aleister," Pamela said.

She stood and walked to the door to wait. Halfway down the aisle, she spied a side chapel. There was an altar holding a statue, a beautiful blue-robed Madonna. Or was it Mary Magdalen?

Pamela knelt on the pew before the statue. The Mary statue filled her with a blue peace. The blue of her High Priestess's robe. It bathed her as she sat. In the still air, a field of energy swirled beneath her feet. It was movement from the contents of the many tombs below her. From under the stones, there were sighs and moans from those in the midst of their eternal sleep.

"Sleep well, my mummies," Pamela said.

CHAPTER ELEVEN

Bomanji's at the Ritz

~◦⌇~⌇◦~

E ntering the Ritz Hotel's dining salon was a blinding experience. Six round tables with brilliant white tablecloths
reflected the white starched tuxedo shirts.

Think of it as snow.

Shaking her head to clear her thoughts, Pamela hardly
noticed the Parsi husbands in attendance. They could be mistaken for typical upper-class Englishmen. But their wives! Their
wives were small fantastical islands with shimmering saris and
headscarves nodding like bejeweled flowers.

The hosts, Lord and Lady Bomanji, greeted guests at the
doorway. Lady Bom, as she was known, wore a turquoise-col-
ored headscarf with actual turquoise stones. She was decorated
with jewels from head to toe, the thick strand of pearls at her
throat complementing her diamond earrings. They were both
in their early sixties; Lord Bomanji's distinguishing feature was
his curling mustache.

Pamela was ahead of Ellen and Henry in the line, who
had come together, a rare event. Ellen had insisted she attend,

especially since Lord and Lady Bom had recently bought some of Pamela's artwork, and Henry was recruited to escort them both. Truthfully, Pamela had been on edge ever since she witnessed the murder of the boy on the wharf, and an evening as Ellen's date would have been a relief. Ah, well. At least Ahmed would be here.

She felt the cold eye of Lady Bom. Guarding the entryway, she felt her appraise her jewelry—a homemade tiara fashioned out of sea-glass and coral. Ah, there it was, she was dismissed with a sharp nod and greetings to the next guest. Lord Bom opened his half-lidded eyes and barely moved his mustache as he mumbled an introduction. Moving further down the reception line, Pamela stopped when she reached Mehroo Bomanji, the hosts' daughter.

Mehroo was a living embodiment of Pamela's most recent painting—strange, given Pamela had never seen her before. But Mehroo's abalone-colored silk sari edged in real rubies was just as Pamela painted, her golden headscarf with diamond stars twinkling like a constellation. Pamela's painting featured her subject looking at the stars, and here were stars in the scarf, floating above Mehroo's head.

Lady Bom and a few members of the Parsi community had attended a recent art gallery displaying Pamela's work. Two pieces, *Sea Creatures*, a watercolor of sari-wearing mermaids, and *Prince Siddartha* sold for a good price. But it was the water-color of a sari-clad woman looking at the moon that fetched the highest price. That piece sold to Lady Bomanji. If only there were future commissions.

Mehroo kissed her on both cheeks. "Welcome, honored artist," she said, then projected her voice louder so her parents might hear. "I am so pleased to have Miss Pamela Colman Smith here at our Parsi Association Banquet," she said, then added, "Your artwork is so captivating."

"Ah, the painting of my daughter, that was your work?" Lady Bom asked, turning around and acting as though she were seeing Pamela for the first time.

"Yes, Lady Bomjani," Pamela answered. She could hardly keep her eyes off Mehroo, the shape of her nose, her full cheeks. Exactly as she painted.

"Fine work. Continue painting. You have talent," Lady Bom said before turning back to the next guest.

Pamela continued down the receiving line. This was one of the last get-togethers of the season before the "Glorious Twelfth" of August, when society retreated from town for grouse hunting. The nervous bows between eager Parsi and reserved upper-class English groups created green buzzing fields. The waitstaff's general confusion contributed to the melee; never had so many guests turned down so many drinks, tray after tray of drinks circling the room to no avail. Conversation between an English couple and a Parsi couple stalled in a stilted exchange. Between them, floating thorns undulated.

This was going to be a long supper. The luncheon at the Savoy with Henry and Ahmed had been a picnic compared to this.

Guests were encouraged to find their engraved place card and seat themselves. Pamela found her own, where she was listed as *Miss Pamela Smythe.* Thank the gods and fairies, she was next to Ahmed, who was already at his seat, and Dr. Westcott from the Golden Dawn. After being cool for weeks, Ahmed had finally warmed up to her in the last couple of days, helping her look up symbols. Looking around the room, it was obvious she'd been seated at the "arts and entertainers" table.

Ahmed was invited because he consulted on antiques for Lord and Lady Bom. Both Ahmed and Pamela had been warned by Henry that they should not expect the socially conscious Lady Bom to talk to them at supper, which honestly was a relief.

Interestingly, Miss Bomanji was seated on the other side of Ahmed, which gave Pamela a clear view of her. She was of marriageable age, mid-twenties, and a master of feminine gesture—a skill set lacking in most English young ladies. She excelled in slow eye blinks, the tilted head, the twisting of rings and jangling bracelets. Mehroo had not inherited her mother's prominent nose and eyebrows; hers were of a balanced proportion, her face round and smooth, and her smile, genuine and warm. No wonder her face had appeared to Pamela asking to be painted.

Ahmed turned back to her with a broad smile. It was a smile she had never seen from him before.

"Miss Bomanji, I believe you have met Miss Pamela Smith," Ahmed said, emphasizing her last name's pronunciation. Smith, not Smythe. "I have a cousin in Cairo named Mehroo. In our country, Mehroo means 'face of the moon,' although it can be said you have the face of the stars."

Pamela raised her eyebrows. It was the first time she had heard of a cousin in Cairo.

"We have just met tonight, although your painting would suggest we have met before," Mehroo said.

"Miss Bomanji, perhaps I have seen you during my astral travels," Pamela said. "Your face is very familiar to me."

They smiled at one another, and Mehroo murmured something in another language to Ahmed. Pamela tried to tap her feet on the ground to calm herself, but the chair was too tall. Seeing Miss Bomanji in person was disconcerting. There was no such thing as coincidences. Why had her face come to her?

"I was just telling Mr. Kamal how much I admire your beautiful headpiece, Miss Smith," Mehroo said.

So, the coral–sea glass tiara was not a total failure.

As Lord Bomanji settled into his chair across the table, he began to talk about the tradition of elephants at weddings, dividing his attention between Ellen on one side and Florence on the other. He must be partially deaf; his story was loud enough for the entire table. Florence patted her ears. She wore large enamel earrings. Were these to cover up the PCS initial on her earlobes?

Ellen waved her feather fan, grazing the air with her perfume. This evening was Ellen's first night out since her recovery, but her impaired memory was still a concern. She had made a pact with Pamela and Henry that if at any point in the evening she pointed at her temple, it was an indication that she "was up"—lingo for forgetting a line.

"Yes, the jewels in your headpiece cast a magical spell, Miss Smith. What are they?" Mehroo said, interrupting Pamela's observations of Ellen.

"Sea glass and coral," Pamela answered.

"Perhaps Mr. Kamal could tell us about magical spells. I understand he is an expert on Egyptian magicians," Mehroo said with a sidelong look at Ahmed.

And so obviously is under your spell.

"A magic expert? No. My wife, Fatima, says that I may know of Egyptian magicians but that I am not an expert," Ahmed answered, looking directly at Pamela. "Knowledge of magicians can be a dangerous thing."

"Do you know anything about magicians, Miss Bomanji?" Pamela asked. She could tell from the way the hostess swiveled slightly in her chair toward them that she had caught their conversation.

"I do know a little something about magicians," Mehroo said. "I know the first Egyptian magical spell begins with 'Abracadabra' and ends with 'Zoroastrianism,' the faith of my family."

The word Zoroastrianism swirled in Pamela's mouth. It was juicy. A melon. A moon.

"Yes," Ahmed said. "Our Egyptian magicians are fond of your faith's Zarathustra and his lord, Ahura Mazda, first mentioned as spell-makers."

Lady Bom noticed an empty seat and motioned a waiter to take the chair away just as its occupant appeared. Before he sat, the young man bowed to Lady Bom. Of average height, he was around twenty years old with a freckled, pug nose and red hair.

"Pardon my lateness, Lord Bomanji, Lady Bomanji," the young man said.

"Father, this is Mr. Winston Churchill," Mehroo said. "He's Lord and Lady Randolph Churchill's son. You met Lady Churchill last week?"

Churchill's father, Lord Randolph, had died four years earlier, but his widow, Lady Churchill, was a prominent member of society, and Jennie Churchill's sexual conquests were legendary. Ellen loved any and all talk of her.

Pamela's ears were burning. A buzzing sound from deep within her chest started to vibrate. The sea glass and coral in her tiara began to vibrate, making a high-pitched tune. It was annoying. Pamela tried to shake her head to stop it to no avail.

"Ah, Lady Churchill. Charming woman. Young Churchill, welcome," Lord Bomanji said, his mustache twitching.

"I am honored to join your table," Churchill said. Conversation had already picked up, and Winston's last remarks about running for office were barely heard. At least Pamela wasn't the only young, undistinguished guest. Her tiara's sea glass tune faded.

A line of waiters carrying silver domes entered the room. The subtle exclamations of appreciation following the unveiling of the first course faded as some of the diners discovered that ham was the entree. Lord and Lady Bom provided a typical English meal, much to the displeasure of the vegetarian Parsis. The grumbling did not please Lady Bom, who let the mango chutney be served only to herself and her husband.

Even though Pamela had been born in London, her childhood in Jamaica taught her to love mangos, not usually served on English tables. Mehroo saw Pamela eyeing the orange chutney and motioned the waiter to serve her a dollop. Her mouth watered as she inhaled its flowery fragrance. A moment of being on the beach in St. Andrews flooded back. Nana held a machete in one hand, cleaving mangos. Pamela sat in the sand gnawing on the discarded remains, scrapping sweet, silky fibers off juicy pits. But the memory disappeared when she tasted the chutney; it was made with Bombay mango, not the hairy mango she loved. She was further jolted back into the dinner party when she heard Ahmed say "magicians."

"Our faith of Zoroastrianism has nothing to do with magicians, Mr. Kamal," Mehroo said. "But our 'magi' may be mixed in with Greek lore, feeding into your Egyptian magic."

"I know only the basic tenants of your faith, Miss Bomanji," Ahmed answered. "I am being consulted on the furnishings for a Zoroastrian house in Kensington. Are you familiar with it?"

"What is Zoroastrianism?" Pamela asked. Ahmed and Mehroo turned to her in surprise. They had forgotten she was there. The buzzing in her chest picked up again. At least her tiara had stopped singing.

"Well, Miss Smith, we have good and evil, and a supreme being," Mehroo answered.

"Sounds like a universal formula and full of possibilities," inserted Dr. Westcott, leaning across Pamela.

Dr. William Wescott, Golden Dawn chief and coroner. Pamela had only met him once, at the Golden Dawn headquarters. It was still easy to identify him as a Golden Dawn man with his whiskers, elaborate grooming, and erudite air. Where were the others? Ah, yes there was Dr. Felkin with the earl and the Spanish man from Windsor college who had called her a pretender. Pamela ducked her head.

"Miss Bomanji, allow me to introduce Dr. Westcott, founding member of the Golden Dawn," Ahmed offered.

"Charmed, Miss Bomanji," Dr. Westcott said. "I am fascinated by the Oracles of Zoroaster. In fact, my book, *The Chaldean Oracles of Zoroaster*, has a chapter devoted to your faith's magician precepts. I am working on a recent translation from a Greek version."

Mehroo gave a polite smile while Pamela struggled not to smile. Of course, Dr. Westcott would bring up his book.

"Set in the Chaldean regime when it ruled Babylon last," Dr. Westcott added.

Ahmed looked at Pamela, and they exchanged a silent assent that Dr. Westcott was an ass.

Mehroo answered, "Congratulations, Dr. Wescott. Are you discussing both the Babylonian and Assyrian populations in the Chaldean Church?"

Dr. Westcott's face fell in dismay.

"There is quite a difference between one and the other, is there not?" Ahmed said quickly.

Dr. Westcott started to cut his ham with determined slices. "Not the focal point of my book, Mr. Kamal. Still designing the tarot cards for Miss Horniman, Miss Smith?" he asked.

"It remains a work in progress," Pamela answered. He would bring up Annie Horniman. "I'm sure you are sending only good thoughts for my project, Dr. Westcott."

"Good thoughts, good words, good deeds. Those are the three principles of our faith. I try to live by them every day," Mehroo said.

"Excellent principles," Ahmed answered.

At the table with Dr. Felkin, a turban-clad man rose, shouting, "That is all delusion and folly. You are ignorant of what man really is and do not understand anything!"

"Here is an example of my mother's least favorite part of entertaining," Mehroo said, leaning toward Ahmed and Pamela.

"Settling disputes?" Ahmed asked.

"Making sure the various factions from India do not come to blows. Mr. Ramanathan is a brilliant but boisterous Hindu who does not back away from conflict."

Lady Bom rose from her chair and marched over, taking the man aside. She motioned for her husband, who made his way over, grabbing the man's shoulders roughly. Playfully rough.

Pamela noticed the grim look on Dr. Felkin's face as the Bomanjis escorted Mr. Ramanathan back to the hosts' table.

"You will sit here, where my daughter can keep an ear on you and you will not be further misbehaving," Lady Bom said.

"I am sorry, Lady Bomanji. The woman at that table had views on religion which were intolerable."

"I gave all strict orders that religion and politics were forbidden topics at this dinner. Now I am going to leave you here to behave," Lady Bom said. "Mehroo, you are in charge. No religion. No politics. Only sparkling conversation and laughter. That is all."

With that, Lady Bom swept over to join the other table with her husband. A silence fell over their group. A new place setting appeared for the new guest. A vegetarian dinner was placed in front of him.

"Mr. Ponnambalam Ramanathan, welcome to our table," Mehroo said. "May I introduce Miss Florence Farr, Miss Ellen Terry, Mr. Henry Irving, Dr. William Westcott, Mr. Ahmed Kamal, Miss Pamela Colman Smith, and Mr. Winston Churchill."

Mr. Ramanathan nodded his head, unfolding his napkin without looking at any of them.

Ellen waved her fan. "I confess I am ignorant as to what a Parsi or Hindu is, Mr. Ramanathan. I only know that I admire your country greatly. It seems more and more I hear of various citizens of India being suggested for ranks of nobility."

Pamela saw Ellen's effect. Winston, Ahmed, and Mr. Westcott stared at her with dazed eyes, as though they were watching a baby rabbit eat a piece of lettuce, while Henry wore a smile expressing his pride in her feminine wiles. Even though Mr. Ramanathan folded his arms and continued to scowl, Pamela could see he was thawing by his twitching mouth.

"Yes, we have English Indian lords now," Churchill said.

Ramanathan jerked his head to take in Churchill before turning back to Ellen.

"Yes, Miss Terry. I was only just saying at that other table that we Parsi have been very useful to the British," Ramanathan said.

"How do you mean, sir?" Ellen asked.

"As Parsi, we do not have the same caste systems forbidding us from intermingling. The British have cleverly learned that raising Parsi to titled positions gives us both respectability and makes us obligated to the British Crown."

Churchill, his face beginning to match his red hair, put both hands on the table.

"Excuse me, Mr. Ramanathan, there is a guest here tonight who was the second Parsi to be elected to office and represents Bethnal Green. You do have representation."

Ramanathan lifted up both hands. "We have been forbidden to discuss these subjects by our hostess."

"Doesn't this election show the inclusion and rights of the Parsi?" Churchill asked.

"Mr. Churchill, I believe this talk is against my mother's wishes for conversation," Mehroo said.

Ramanathan puffed up his cheeks. "Whether I am a Hindu, a Mohammedan, Parsi, or Christian, I could be Indian. Or English. India is not a beetle to be crushed."

Ellen rapped Winston's wrist with her fan. "Speaking of beetles, Mr. Churchill, your mother's beetles were such a huge inspiration for me."

All conversation at the table stopped.

"Really? My mother's beetles were an inspiration to you? Tell me more," the young man said as he motioned for more wine.

Ellen placed her forefinger against her temple. Oh dear. She was up. What was it about the beetles that seized her brain?

Henry leaned in, interjecting, "Mr. Churchill, this inspiration came to her at one of our Beef Steak Room suppers at the Lyceum Theatre."

Ellen's head twitched. "Yes, it was your mother, Lady Randolph Churchill. She came to the supper wearing a dress with green beetles sewn into it. Glimmering like a ghostly apparition, she was unworldly! I knew I had to have the same effect when I played Lady Macbeth."

The infamous beetle dress of Lady Macbeth. Painted by Sargent, it had set the Academy alive with controversy. That had led to inspired ticket sales for *Macbeth*, the supposedly cursed show theatres put up when coffers were down.

"The beetles' wings were magic. Do you believe in magic, Mr. Churchill?" Ellen asked.

Winston stared at her. "I want to have my palm read. If any of that comes true, then I will believe."

"Ah, the prophecy of a handprint," Florence said.

"I'm sorry, you would be . . . ?" Winston asked.

"Miss Farr."

"You are an actress?" Winston queried.

Pamela saw Florence flinch.

Oh, to be asked this in front of Ellen.

"Our Miss Farr is not only an actress," Dr. Westcott said, "she is also a lecturer on Egyptian history, a harp player, a theatre producer, a Golden Dawn adept, and a suffragist. She also sings to a mummy at the British Museum. So many ideas for a woman."

Florence stared hard at the doctor. "Yes, Dr. Westcott, I'm full of ideas, questions, and answers."

"I've heard of you," Churchill said. "My friend, Mr. Shaw, says you are the New Woman."

Pamela tensed, remembering her time spent at the British Museum with Florence and George Bernard Shaw, the bully.

Florence laughed. "Oh, p'shaw. You are good friends?"

"Shaw recently sent me a telegram inviting me to one of his opening nights," Churchill said. "He wrote, 'I am enclosing two tickets to the first night of my new play; bring a friend . . . if you have one.'"

"Did you reply to that?" Florence asked.

"'Cannot possibly attend the first; will attend the second, if there is one,'" Churchill said with a grin.

With that, the table guests chuckled and eased into private conversation. The buzzing was now a humming in Pamela's head. Henry was beset by several fawning women, while Dr. Westcott continued listening to Churchill, who boasted of his upcoming assignment to Africa. Pamela was trying to recall what Mistress Quickly said in Henry IV. *Oh, what was the quote?*

As the ladies left Henry's side, he caught Pamela's eye, put his hand over his mouth, and whispered, "Swaggerer is the word you are looking for, Miss Smith."

How had he known what she was trying to remember? The lines Mistress Quickly says in *Henry IV, Part Two* to Doll Tearsheet. As her Magician, was he able to hear her thoughts? How much more could he read? They grinned at one another, and he went back to conversation with Dr. Westcott.

Mehroo continued to charm Ahmed. He was livelier than ever. How long had they worked side by side? Two months? No, going on three. And it seemed she didn't know him at all. Pamela tried to push her chair back, but her feet didn't reach the floor. A child shut out of grown-up interaction, watching others, she was back to feeling as though she were at her parents' game night.

As a new line of waiters cleared plates and delivered dishes of candied sweets, Henry sat up with a start. He was staring at Florence, who had taken off an earring, rubbing her pinched lobe. He took a finger and made the shape of a question mark. Without missing a beat, Florence nodded and then turned her attention back to Ramanathan, replacing the earring.

Henry had seen the initials on Florence's ear. High Priestess and Magician had met.

Ellen broke away from her conversation with Churchill, and unseen by the young man, slyly blew Henry a kiss. With the subtlest of movements, he mimed catching it and putting it in his vest pocket, patting it for safe keeping.

Even from where she was sitting, Pamela could hear the sweet thumping of Ellen's kiss in Henry's vest pocket. Her own heart writhed as fond looks traveled back and forth between Mehroo and Ahmed. Florence and Ramanathan. Odd woman out.

She felt a light tap on her shoulder. When she turned, a golden version of the Mary Magdalen glimmered before her. Blinking, the vision disappeared. It was Mehroo, her golden scarf undulating over her head like a halo. She smiled and extended her hand to Pamela.

"Miss Smith, please come visit a few of the other tables. Other guests are most anxious to meet you, our famous artist."

Pamela glanced around the table. Should she leave her assigned seat? She would have to walk by Felkin and his pretender friend. Ellen stopped her conversation to look at her and waggled her fingers, encouraging her to go.

Pamela's feet hit the floor and she stood.

The Empress commanded her. Tonight, she was no pretender.

CHAPTER TWELVE

GOLDEN DAWN PROTECTION

~⚬~

"Powerful magic is being channeled through my tarot cards," Pamela said from behind the podium. The Golden Dawn's tarot committee of doctors and chiefs seemed unimpressed. "And Mr. Crowley intends to harm those around me unless I stop creating them. He is behind Miss Terry's poisoning. I'm sure of it."

The quartet of doctors sat upright in their chairs as Florence and Miss Horniman leaned back in theirs.

"Poppycock!" snorted Dr. Felkin. "Miss Terry's memory loss is not from a poisoning. She had too much wine at my house, not uncommon among actresses. Scotland Yard suspects Miss Terry may have had a small stroke. I suppose you will say Aleister is to blame for that also."

"Mr. Crowley confronted me this week on London Bridge," Pamela answered. "He threatened me and demanded I stop finding incarnates. I witnessed a dockworker cut in half by a granite slab. And Aleister made it happen. This is a warning to all of us."

"You are overreacting," Dr. Felkin replied. "Mr. Crowley is reacting to his rejection from the Golden Dawn. He doesn't have the powers to harm anyone. He may be able to fly like a bug but that is all."

Dr. Felkin. So smooth. Shiny. Yellow puffs of air pulsed around him as he said one thing and meant another. He had the same glassy eyes as Aleister. Her heart beat faster.

Florence stood, peeling off her lemon-colored gloves and throwing them on her chair. "The evening when Mr. Crowley transformed into a demon here in the Vault was not a group hallucination, Dr. Felkin!" Florence said. "We saw him when he turned into the monster."

In the months since the occurrence, rumors had been rife among the Golden Dawn's three hundred members that Aleister would come back and kill them all. Another rumor was that Crowley could transform into a dragon and turn everyone into bats. Some whispered that Florence and Aleister had sex in the Vault, and at any moment she could appear as a Valkyrie with a goat's face. If you provoked her, she would *bah*.

Dr. Felkin rose, his glasses shining as he struck the pose of a deacon. "Come now, Mr. Crowley played a child's trick of mirage on us. Nothing more. All the more reason to follow my suggestion. I propose we seek international consultation on magic, and for that reason we have Mr. Ahmed Kamal of the British Museum in attendance with us today."

Ahmed bowed his head as the small group turned their attention to him. When Pamela first asked Ahmed if he would like to be part of this panel, his first question was whether Miss Horniman might donate some antiquities in return. His second was if Miss Farr was on the panel.

"Mr. Kamal is knowledgeable on the subject of Egyptian magic and symbols," Dr. Felkin continued. "He was a team member on important digs in Giza and will be our Egyptian consultant. We have just received word from the expert Swami

Madame Horos in Paris. She recommends we open a Paris Temple of the Golden Dawn. Between Mr. Kamal and Madame Horos, we will combine our resources to study Mr. Crowley's power of transformation."

The group murmured approval.

Waite cleared his throat. "I am happy we have these resources at our disposal."

By the look of his bloodshot eyes, Pamela knew he would be even more overbearing at their next work session.

"Oh, Mr. Waite, yes. We also look forward to your contributions," Dr. Felkin said.

Contributions. Permissions. Restrictions. She didn't know how her tarot magic worked, but it would not come about by committee.

Miss Horniman tilted her head back and half closed her eyes. Her low voice rumbled. "And who is going to pay for this Paris Temple of the Golden Dawn with this Madame Horos?"

"We would not ask you to pay for it, Miss Horniman," Dr. Felkin said. "We are very grateful you subsidize this headquarters. The Doctors' Association, a committee within the group, has decided to contribute funds to rent a Paris headquarters. Mr. Mathers, proficient in French, has offered to head up the French office. He will relocate there with his wife, Moira."

Moira's head popped up above her chair. So, she had been here the entire time.

Something's afoot.

Miss Horniman cocked her head. "And who is this Swami Horos? I've never heard of her."

"She is Swami Viva Ananda Horos," Dr. Westcott added. "She is daughter of the king of Bavaria and his mistress, dancer Lola Montez. She has earned much acclaim for her psychic powers. From a young age, she has shown an amazing ability to channel and voice the ancients."

A low gong rang out in the back of Pamela's head. Did anyone else hear? No, it seemed not.

Miss Horniman thoughtfully polished the silver snake bracelet around her wrist. "Why should we believe this illegitimate channeler when we have so many intuitive, gifted women here?"

Dr. Westcott turned in his seat to face her. "Swami Horos founded the Purity League at the Theocratic Unity Temple in Paris. She has amassed a large, prosperous following. I think it would behoove us to investigate and make an alliance."

Miss Horniman crossed her arms, the snake positioned to protect her. "Well, as long as it is understood I am not contributing funds to this Paris Temple. My project is Miss Smith's tarot cards. Guided, of course, by Mr. Waite."

Dr. Westcott grimaced. "Understood, Miss Hornibags. Sorry, Miss Horniman." He stood. "I move, then, that the Paris chapter of the Golden Dawn be officially approved. All those in favor, say aye."

A hearty round of 'ayes' filled the room.

"All those opposed, say nay," Dr. Westcott said.

Florence, Miss Horniman, and Pamela replied nay.

"A Paris Temple is our next project!" Dr. Westcott announced.

The men stood up, slapping one another on their backs while Samuel Mathers and Moira approached Dr. Felkin and Dr. Westcott to receive embraces. Waite cornered Ahmed to talk about private viewings at the museum.

Pamela stood apart, watching as the initials on Florence's earlobes lit up like a beacon.

Pamela hurried out of the headquarters and found her way to the Euston Square train. She knew she could go to the museum or the library for more research, but the thought of being there made her feel more claustrophobic. It had been almost a year

since she had returned to London, and she had only three completed cards and eighteen sketches. There had been the side
projects designing cards and posters, but that was only pocket
money and they distracted her from finishing the deck. And then
there were the canvases, all framed and primed, waiting to be
painted at the studio. *Will I ever get back to my artwork?* Time
was running faster and faster.

She had a few more hours of early autumn sunlight left.
After she exited the London Bridge Station, she walked quickly,
looking over her shoulder to make sure she wasn't followed.
She had been back to the church several times in the last month,
the last time the organ player had been practicing. It shook the
rafters and rattled the paving stones, a thrilling experience.

The Southwark neighborhood was familiar now, no longer
possessed of the terror she first felt going through the cobbled
streets. Arriving at the church, she found two carriages tethered
in front. Carnations were braided in the horses' bridles. Ladies
must be visiting—there would be no confession this time.

Entering the vestibule, Reverend Thompson was surrounded
by a group of well-dressed women. Rich benefactors here to
contribute to his stained glass window of Shakespeare, no doubt.
He led his group into the church; he swung a brazier of incense.
Pamela slipped into the church by another door and sat in the
last row. She was unseen as the group walked down the church's
middle aisle.

Reverend Thompson put on his best sermon warble.
"Although Shakespeare is not a typical subject for a church's
window, let us reflect on this verse from *Henry V*: 'God shall be
my hope, my stay, my guide, and lantern to my feet.'"

Breathing in the cool, calm air of the apse, she filled her
lungs with the sweet residue of incense. She barely remembered
going to Swedenborgian services in Manchester with her parents.
Sweet Frankincense always brought her back to that church.

As the incense dissipated and the stench from the nearby tannery and distillery drifted in, the reverend continued to drone. Some of the women held handkerchiefs to their noses. A few wandered away from Reverend Thompson to look at John Gower's mummy. Were they here to buy a crypt? Or subsidize a mummy, resting in peace? Did mummies need upkeep?

Pamela tapped the stone floor with her feet to feel the great thrum. A deep river of connective tissue hummed underneath the stones. A jumble of images danced in her mind, but she couldn't tell if they were her memories or someone else's. A naked woman standing in water, washing her hair with stars. A man driving a chariot with two sphinxes. A woman gently opening a lion's mouth. Perhaps they were moments of history torn away from its time. Whatever they were, this was sweet, letting the images wash over her, sitting where no one knew her. Here, no one expected her to be extraordinary.

A slight movement slithered to the side of her. It was a young ragamuffin, filthy and barefoot, barely ten-years-old, creeping up the aisle like a dog tracking meat. When he saw Pamela watching, he put his fingers to his lips, as though they were coconspirators.

Cooing sounds rose from the center aisle. A child of about three years in a greasy shift, sucking her thumb, walked toward the front. She stumbled. As she tumbled on the stone floor, wails echoed throughout the church.

Pamela hopped up from her seat to reach her, but two women from the group got to her first. Soon, a semicircle of clucking women surrounded her. The tallest scooped up the child as the church door opened and a bedraggled girl in her late teens ran to them.

"Sophie!" the girl cried. "We've been a-looking for you."

She took the crying child from the tall woman's arms. Loud clucking over the child resonated along the corridors. A shadow darted, running past the group. Before Pamela could call out, the boy bolted toward the main door.

Reverend Thompson's voice rang out from the opposite end of the church. "Stop! Stop, thief! Not in God's house!"

The women turned to one another as they discovered their pickpocketed items. Three purses in all. The young girl with the child had run to a side exit and was gone. Pamela, feeling her purse firmly in her skirt's deep pockets, consoled one of the distraught victims. Where was the mother to these cunning children?

❧

Pamela laid on her small bed back at Ellen's home, the gathering dark outside her window pressing in on her. How did the boy know she wouldn't expose him? Why didn't she expose him? Did he sense that she was becoming disillusioned of money being spent on stained glass windows, trips to Paris, and Ritz suppers? Were the children trained in the same way as the pickpockets at Covent Garden?

She nestled into her stack of pillows, almost knocking over her portfolio on the side table. A collection of studies for her tarot cards: the Magician and the Fool were in one pile next to sketches of Florence Farr, the High Priestess, in another. She picked up the completed High Priestess card. Yes, her High Priestess would impart wisdom and higher knowledge, using her half-seen Torah. She was the Triple Goddess: the male and female and the solar cross.

But what was the point to all this? There was so much suffering in the world—were her tarot cards going to make any difference? The Golden Dawn men certainly didn't believe in her gifts, although Waite, despite his claims that the cards were his creation alone, seemed sure they would create a sensation. Or were her cards just going to be a plaything for rich people?

With a dry mouth, she traced the still face on the card of her High Priestess. If only the card could touch back. There was no memory of a soft touch from Pamela's own mother, Corinne

Colman Smith. Her father always told her that her mother was a bon vivant and parlor actress. But it was Nana in Jamaica who'd held her. The hired maid, the below-the-stairs servant who brushed sand out of hair and sang to her, captivating her at bedtime with scary folktales that always began "In a long-before time," Nana had been the one to hold her hand as they stood over her mother's marbled crypt. Then Pamela was shipped back to the Brooklyn family and the Pratt school. It was over nine years since she had seen the sweet face of Nana. Was she even alive? Stories of Kings, Queens, Empresses.

The Empress.

Still no vision, no shutter click on what or who the Empress should be.

In her head, she knew the Empress should be a combination of all the women who had nurtured her. She would be a solace for unvoiced needs, unfulfilled yearnings. A true mother who would feed Pamela's hunger, listen to her, appreciate her, champion her. There would be water to swim in, air to fly in, earth to rest on.

Just as the looting children needed more mothering, the mother Empress would guide her, help her choose the rest of the Major Arcana. Her second-sight powers were inside the lines. In her sigil. Waite may claim that he owned the intent of the cards, but it was her secret signature that tied the muse to the card and the card to her own power.

Music filled her head, a Debussy symphony—what number was it? No, it was a Chopin. Celebrating the entrance of the Empress. The intent of the entire tarot deck would reveal itself, and the Empress would open the gates to her path.

Now she just had to wait for the shutter to click.

CHAPTER THIRTEEN

GELUKIEZANGER CASTS THE MUSE

B alancing a crown on her head, clutching a chalice in one hand and the satchel in the other, Pamela made her way up the steep stairs. She tried to catch her breath at the landing on the second floor, when she saw the studio door cracked open. Edy.

Her heart pounding, she opened the door. There sat Edy Craig on a couch next to the window, hunched over an expense book. Edy's glasses slid halfway down her nose.

"Pixie!" escaped her lips, along with a half-weary and half-delighted sigh. She inherited her father's Goodman profile and the Terrys' thin, cupid-shaped lips.

After fumbling to discard her coat, props, and bag, Pamela embraced her. Edy returned the hug with brevity. She had gotten thinner.

"Tea?" Edy asked, heading for the kettle hung in the fireplace.

"Yes, unless there is some Opal Hush left from our last 'Bohemian nights'?"

Edy shook her head and went to make tea. Everything about Edy was efficient, constrained, and neutral. Her plain linen shift, her hair in a tidy topknot, were so familiar as she clambered to set things out. So different from Pamela herself. Today, crow feathers were woven into her hair like a tiara, and she wore her favorite green velvet blouse, violet bloomers, and her seashell necklace.

Pamela sighed as she took in their studio, looking for traces of their last soiree. No bowls of cigarettes, the neat array of glasses on the buffet, wine bottles cleared from the piano. Edy had to have everything tidy when she worked. When was their last get-together? Two months? Three? She plopped down on the window seat, the velvet cushions from the Lyceum's *Vicar of Wakefield* emitting puffs of dust. Yes, it all was still here: the throw pillows with peacock feathers, the book of fabric patterns from her father's design firm, sketches for a fairy-tale book. She glanced up at the wall where Edy's costume designs were pinned next to set designs for her brother's play, long abandoned. Circling the window seat were a set of beautifully upholstered chairs, at least on the "downstage" side, the "upstage" side revealed coarse burlap and unvarnished finishes.

Yelping with joy, she discovered a book on the small table next to her. Flipping open the pages, she found the green inked squiggles and initials in the guest registry for their "Bohemian nights." Drawings for her *Green Sheaf* magazine. Sketches by Maud Gonne, calligraphy by Satish Monroe, poems from William Butler Yeats, Claude Debussy, Ellen Terry. The cartoon of Mussie attacking the bagpipe player mid-song. How he must be missing his brother, Fussie. A drawing of her spider, Annancy.

"Borrowing the crown and chalice for your tarot drawings?" Edy said, stabbing the fireplace's smoldering coals with a poker. The kettle rumbled to life.

"Yes, dear friend," Pamela said. "I need crowns, lanterns, and swords for the next card. I've such a lot of news to tell you."

"Yeth." Edy's lisp came and went, but the word "yes" was always difficult. "Hold on to your news until I get sorted with our tea. You're lucky you caught me here. I'm just sorting Mother's accounts for the fall tour."

"How is her memory? Still patchy?"

"You might say. Mr. Irving picked two shows with almost no lines for her."

"You won't miss me on tour, will you? Always trying to get me to the train stations on time," Pamela said.

No smile from Edy. The Lyceum tour, where they had first met, seemed eons ago, although in reality it was only two years since the last venue.

Edy set out teacups. "When you got the props at the theatre, was George gossiping about Mr. Shaw?"

"Yes, good old George! He told me Mr. Shaw had an interview recently trying to get Mr. Henry to option one of his plays while putting the mash on your mother."

"Chris thinks Shaw's going to cause real problems if Mr. Irving doesn't produce one of his plays soon."

Pamela shook her head, dislodging a crow feather.

"I see by your outfit, you just finished a performance of Gelukiezanger?"

"Yes, I was told to wear my 'savage' outfit for the Annancy stories. Today's recital was in Chelsea. Birthday party for eight girls. You can imagine the reaction when Death tracks the children up in the rafters and kills them."

"Yes, rounds of shrieking, your specialty. But, Pamela—" Edy stopped brewing the tea. "Is it true? Did you really perform your Annancy stories at your New York gallery opening?"

Pamela crossed her arms. "As I matter of fact, I did. I thought they would want to know who the artist was."

"You mean, mislead the public to who you are," Edy answered. "You're not Jamaican, despite your unruly hair. You think singsonging in a Jamaican accent is going to make your fortune? People are confused enough about who you are."

"It's going to make people aware I am capable of many things," Pamela said. "I don't have to be just one thing."

"That's why the Macbeth Gallery cleared out in ten minutes?" Edy asked, avoiding looking at Pamela's trembling lip, as she carried the tea tray.

"Who told you that? And why didn't you send a telegram? We always send a telegram on our openings," Pamela replied, trying to look into her eyes.

"Fees for transatlantic telegrams are outrageous," Edy said as she cleared a space for tea. She sat next to her. "But, why, Pamela? Why frighten would-be patrons with Jamaican horror stories when you're trying to get them to buy your artwork?"

Pamela crossed her feet under her. "It wasn't just the Annancy stories—I recited Yeats's *The Countess Cathleen*."

Edy rolled her eyes. "Oh, yes, much clearer content. How is having twenty-five careers, being storyteller, designer, painter, working out?" she asked, setting out the biscuits.

Pamela swiped two biscuits off before Edy noticed. "Same as you mending your mother's costumes, doing the accounting, and running a costume shop."

"Touché. And are your tarot cards coming along?" Edy asked, pouring the tea.

Edy's "coming along" sent little stabs into Pamela's heart. "Coming along" was Edy's nonanswer to all questions. How was the costume shop working out? *Coming along.* How was Martin Shaw doing since you'd broke off your engagement? *Coming along.* How was your new friendship with the man/woman Christopher St. John? *Coming along.*

"Yes, I've roughed out the Major Arcana," Pamela said. "Those are the first twenty-two cards. Just finished up with the High Priestess. She'll join the Magician and Fool."

"Crowley shown up again?"

"No, the incident at the bridge was the last."

Edy wrinkled her nose. "Worse poser than any stage villain."

"Listen to you, Edy, your lisp is almost gone," Pamela observed.

"Yes, Chris has been coaching me. Mother's ecstatic."

Pamela pulled the pouf closer to her. "I thought my initials on my muses were going to be a sigil, a gateway to call other magical help. That way, I could call my tarot muses when I needed them; we'd be a merry band of magic makers."

Edy replied, "Perhaps your initials are a warning for you to give up this tarot deck."

"Give up my tarot deck? Edy, this deck could change the way people channel spirits for guidance. Crowley knows that they could tap into a powerful vein of magic. He wants to be the only one who can channel their power."

"It's a limited quantity, this power of the symbols?" Edy asked, blowing on her tea.

"It may be. I don't know. But I do know from the art world, you sign it, you own it. The Golden Dawn wants the tarot deck to be used as a magical tool for their higher elite members."

"Oh, Pixie, why are you mixed up with these people? You're an artist, storyteller, and designer, not a witch. No, what is it you told Yeats? You're a 'goddaughter to a witch and a sister to a fairy.' Some of these people are just evil."

Pamela uncrossed her feet so she could reach more biscuits. "My second sight warns me when I'm in danger, even if my sigils don't."

Edy sipped her tea. The sigh, blinks, and pursed lips. *She is pulling away.*

"Oh, dear friend, you're such a killjoy. I've come by to tell you the most exciting news. I've chosen my next card. You know how I wait for the shutter click to reveal the incarnate? Like the last one, the High Priestess?"

"Oh, yes, who was it based on again?" Edy asked.

"Florence Farr is the High Priestess," Pamela replied, looking down at the cat.

"Good God. The mummy mumbler? Who's next?"

Pamela put her tea down on the pouf, taking Edy's hands in hers. "I promised Uncle Brammie and Mr. Irving I would let them know my next muse, but I thought I would tell you first. Your mother. Ellen Terry, the Empress."

Edy snatched her hands away. "Chris told me to watch out for this," Edy snapped. "Mother as Empress? No, Pamela, no. I won't hear of it. Subject is closed. Now, I've work to do."

She took up the expense book and opened it, sitting on the pouf near the stove. But Pamela stood up to be near her.

"Edy! Think of it! This will show that Ellen is no mere second-in-command to Henry Irving. Ellen will be seen as what she truly is—an Empress!"

"Ellen is adored by the public as the distracted heroine," Edy said, "the spirited and virtuous young woman who is wronged. Not nobility."

"But the Empress stands for all those women and more!"

Pamela fetched her satchel and took out her sketch pad, taking out her sketches. Edy dutifully put her glasses back on and sat down.

"Look, Ellen is wearing a crown of twelve stars, carrying the shield of Venus and a scepter. There will be a field of corn and a running waterfall, indicating the birth of a new idea or new way of life!"

"Mother is to advertise a new 'way of life'?" Edy asked, taking up her tea.

"No, no, not advertise. Ellen is always giving birth to new ideas, to creating new expressions, nurturing—"

"You think Ellen wants to be seen as a mother? I guarantee you, she does not."

"But she has encouraged and developed so many projects and people. Me, especially! She is the mother I never had. And now I can fix her memory loss with this Empress card."

"Stop! Just because you caused her memory loss doesn't mean you can fix it. Ellen is not your mother."

Pamela felt a brick pitch through her midsection. She felt nauseous and dizzy.

"Edy, you of all people." Pamela grabbed the crown and sketch pad, throwing them into her satchel.

Edy stood in front of the door and crossed her arms across her chest. "And what is this Golden Dawn? All I hear about are evil magicians poisoning Mother, sending astral attacks, and your muses marked with unwanted tattoos. You want Mother in their path? You're becoming just one more leech to pull off."

Pamela looked at Edy's angry mouth, twisted like barbed wire. Heavy gray wool in the air. Suffocating her. She was never really a part of the Terry family. A temporary pet, good for company only while touring. An exotic distraction, a humorous companion, a Pixie.

Pamela grabbed her coat and satchel, then clumsily picked up her props.

"Your accounting has major flaws," Pamela said, tears burning in her eyes.

She slammed the door behind her and clomped down the stairs, hanging on to the banister to keep from tumbling.

The sound of an account book thrown at the wall echoed from upstairs.

CHAPTER FOURTEEN

AWAY AT THE BOM'S

~~~

Pamela first saw Henry, a head taller than almost everyone else on the King's Cross train station, coming down the platform, reining in two white and caramel-colored Jack Russell terriers. Fussie and Mussie were brothers, the coloring almost an exact printing on each, except for the large clover print on Fussie's forehead. Henry jauntily carried his walking stick as the dogs led him, every inch the celebrity star manager.

The two dogs whimpered and barked, recognizing Ellen, even though Ellen's face was obscured behind an enormous bouquet of white roses. As she looked up from the blooms, she threw back her head and a delighted laugh floated through the air. How everyone tried to win those pearly sounds.

The bouquet was handed off to Pamela before Ellen crouched down to the dogs, who on reaching their mistress, licked her face with moans and yips. Henry had as much of a smile as he ever allowed himself, his eyes barely visible behind his glasses. Fussie had been Ellen's gift to Henry, while Mussie, the more subservient dog and younger sibling, was Ellen's dog. They were the only children Ellen and Henry would ever have together.

"Oh, my little pigs, how I have missed you! All the ham I have had while you've been with Henry!" Ellen exclaimed as Henry drew nearer. "So much ham! Oh, Pixie! Do you remember the stuffed boa constrictor? The one Henry brought on the train to scare my dogs?"

Henry's creased brow relaxed when he spotted Uncle Brammie leading porters to them with carts. "Madam, it was the size of your Saint Bernard I objected to on tour, not a decent, moderately sized dog like my Fussie."

"But was there a boa constrictor?" Pamela asked.

Henry's eyes twinkled. "I may have borrowed something like," he answered.

Pamela watched the troupe ready to board the train, Edy deep in conversation with Chris. Edy didn't look up or even acknowledge Henry and the dogs. Was Edy on the outs with Henry, too? Henry had been like a father to both of them in his day.

The dogs ran up to the company members standing near them, their leashes trailing after them. Mussie and Fussie were petted and fawned over as porters loaded the piles of luggage on the baggage car.

"Now boarding: Derby, Sheffield, Leeds!"

The train engine ahead of them belched sparks. Pamela's eye caught someone in back of the group walking with a large mastiff on a chain. Mussie and Fussie growled at the passing intruder before going back to belly rubs from the actors. The owner tugged the glowering beast away.

Uncle Brammie and Pamela had nicknamed this trip "Destination Memory." Ellen was under the impression that the Lyceum company was traveling to perform short scenes at the Bomanji estate, in actuality it was to be a cure visit. The visit was to the Bomanjis' personal doctor, in hopes of a cure for Ellen's memory.

Fellow travelers stared as Ahmed, Duse, and Satish, three "exotics", arrived. Satish, a Caribbean actor in the Lyceum troupe, wore a red, full-length coat and an earring; Duse Mohammed wore a red fez and formal black coat; and Ahmed Kamal wore his fez with an exquisitely tailored double-breasted coat. All three turned heads as they approached. Most North Country–bound passengers had never seen a black person from Egypt or India.

Henry crouched down to join Ellen in caressing the necks of the now sleepy-eyed dogs. Under Fussie's neck, his hands found hers. For a moment, all four creatures breathed together. Ellen and Henry looked everywhere but at one another.

"Now, Mussie, you mustn't follow the train the way you run after my carriage. We are all to travel together," Ellen muttered.

A sharp blast of the steam engine startled everyone, setting the dogs to barking. From across the platform, another train arrived, the ground shivering with vibration.

Suddenly, Pamela saw a dark blur racing down the platform. It was a moment before she could register what it was, then fur was flying everywhere. The large mastiff had grabbed Mussie around the neck and shook him like a rag doll.

The dog throttled Mussie while Fussie nipped at the black dog's haunches and Ellen shrieked. The large dog's chain was whipping around on the ground, keeping people from getting too close. Henry took his walking stick and tried to rap the beast on the back, missing with every stroke. Pamela rushed toward the snarling pair, stretching out to grab the whirling chain of the attacking beast. What was the phrase Nana had told her while fighting the duppie?

"Duppie, you no kin of mine, away!" Pamela shouted to the circling mass of dog and chain.

The panting black dog paused his frenzied shaking, the inert Mussie still in his mouth as drool dripped from his jowls. His crazed eyes focused on Pamela, and he lowered his head as though to charge her. She took advantage of the stillness to grab the chain rattling along the cement platform.

She gave it a jerk. The massive dog barely reacted.

Uncle Brammie rushed from the baggage cart. Just as the beast was ready to shake Mussie in his jowls again, Uncle Brammie's boot struck the dog's scrotum with an audible thud. The beast howled and dropped Mussie.

Fussie howled as he crawled over the bleeding body of his sibling, licking his face, his clover leaf mark bobbing up and down. Uncle Brammie examined Mussie's neck. The harness had kept the beast's teeth from biting more than once, but there was still a nasty puncture mark on the back of his neck.

Pamela chanted Nana's duppie phrase over and over to keep the other dog in check. The dog, lowered on all four haunches, trained on her as she circled him. She was still circling it when a tall man snatched the chain out of her hands.

It was Aleister Crowley.

Before he could say anything, the station master ran over, shouting at him for allowing his dog to run free on the platform.

The Lyceum group encircled Ellen, holding the whimpering Mussie in her arms. She kissed the trembling dog's whiskers over and over.

Edy marched up to Pamela and demanded, "Is that Crowley?"

With tears in her eyes, she nodded yes.

"What the hell did I tell you about these people? And now you're using black magic to fight a dog?" Edy asked.

"It's not black magic. It's Nana looking over me," Pamela answered, looking Edy square in the eyes.

Pale, Edy took Pamela by the arm and positioned her behind Chris.

"Well let's not have this madman have you in his sights any longer," Edy said in a flat tone.

Chris, in her usual man's suit, gruffly tucked Pamela under her shoulder so she was half-hidden. For once, Pamela was thankful for Edy's calm reaction to the hysterics of theatre life.

Pamela peeked out from Chris's side and watched a furious back-and-forth between the station master and Aleister, playing the role of the befuddled dog owner whose dog intended no harm. But on the other side of him stood Henry and Uncle Brammie, with Ahmed, Duse, and Satish standing a short distance away, poised for a fight.

A stylish young woman disembarked from the arriving train and approached Aleister and the dog, who cried out with a frenzy. The dog bayed as his mistress hugged him around his neck. The station master addressed the young lady and Aleister took out his billfold, handing pound notes to him. Aleister then offered some to Henry, which were batted away with Henry's walking stick. A few more inches taller than him, Henry said something that made Aleister's head snap up. He stormed away, tugging the dog along with him. The young woman jaunted to keep up.

When they reached the end of the platform, Aleister stopped and turned. He spotted Pamela behind Chris and gave a little wave with his hand. It was the two-fingered salute she used with Uncle Brammie, their private signal. Pamela's blood froze. Was that a sign Bram was next?

Ellen was too traumatized to leave both dogs, so it was decided Fussie would accompany her and Uncle Brammie and Henry would take Mussie to the stables to the animal doctor to be stitched up.

Instead of a boisterous and rowdy goodbye, the traumatized company took their seats on the train in silence. Pamela sat next to Ellen, holding Fussie on her lap. Across from them, Edy and Chris sternly looked at them both.

"Hello," Ellen said to her daughter. "Visiting family in the north?"

Edy stiffened. Pamela felt sorry for her that her own mother didn't recognize her. After everything she had been through to take care of her mother, to be forgettable.

"Pixie," Ellen whispered to Pamela, "maybe we should invite these nice ladies to our performance at the Bomanjis'."

"All aboard," the conductor shouted, and the train heaved forward. Fussie whimpered in Ellen's embrace.

"Away to the Bom's!" Ellen cried as they watched the platform slip away from view.

❧

Pineheath House was a forty-room mansion in Harrogate, Yorkshire, where Sir Dhunjibhoy and Lady Bomanji held residence during the autumn months. Harrogate was not an easy destination to get to, especially when subject to Ellen's objections along the way. She would have preferred to go to her own house, Smallhythe, in the opposite direction. What was the repertoire for this one? Who was cueing her? It was up to Edy, Pamela, and Chris to spin the tale of why they were staying at this country house instead of touring.

The Bomjanis had kindly sent enough transport for the dozen cast members from the train station when they arrived late at night. Pamela was shown to her room, down the hall from Ellen, not next door to her as Edy and Chris were. Pamela was glad to see a late supper already laid out on the desk, and after dining, fell into a deep sleep. In the morning she was shook out of sleep by a cacophony of birds, one of whom sounded like it was shrieking. Then, the knocking on Ellen's door echoed down the hallway, followed by Edy imploring for Ellen to open up. Ah, there it was—laughter followed by easy conversation. The doctor must be paying a visit. Perhaps Ellen's memory would be cured.

Later in the afternoon, Pamela came out of the house with her sketchbook. She was determined to work on her next card while Ellen and the rest of the company rehearsed the fictional production.

Ellen and Fussie cuddled on a chaise longue in the dappled sunlight of the Bomanji garden; books, teacups, and brilliantly colored leaves were splayed on tables beside her. The view of the steep hillside sweeping down before the house was full of ancient oaks and elms. Ahmed and Mehroo stood off to the side with glasses of tea, made to their liking.

Pamela crossed to Ellen's side and took her hand. She opened her eyes, gazing at the beautiful canopy of trees above her.

Pamela whispered, "How is my good fairy today?"

Still concentrating on the overhead branches, she answered, "My first role was Good Fairy Goldenstar, and later, Bad Dragonette. Story of my life—good to bad."

Mehroo walked over and leaned across her guest, tucking the cloak around Ellen in the chilly September air. Mehroo was a most attentive host, making sure everyone understood the troupe was there to rest, not perform. Fussie wagged his tail so hard it hit Ellen in the side.

Ellen closed her eyes and Mehroo motioned to the outdoor staff lurking by the door for a parasol. After the parasol was situated, more tea was poured for Ellen and a cup for Pamela. Mehroo crossed back to Ahmed, sitting at a bench overlooking the lawn.

The scent of ripening leaves in the air was delicious, their colors a riot. A happy hum started in the base of her skull; this was the weather she remembered from her childhood in Manchester, nothing like the hot beaches of Jamaica or the sweltering summers in Brooklyn. Asters, late-season roses, mums: all were at the height of their palette. This scent was England. A tingle of anticipation sparkled in her fingertips.

Pamela watched Ahmed and Mehroo stand close together. They looked like a fairy tale, Ahmed in his white tunic and Mehroo in her purple sari. No, not purple. Magenta. The vibrations of her floating silk dress reached out to Pamela. What would Ahmed's wife, Fatima, wear? Not a sari; perhaps a cotton gown from lilies grown along the Nile. Wasn't there a diaphanous material the French court imported from Egypt?

"Miss Smith?" Mehroo called out.

Pamela saw Ahmed blush and look down. She bounded over to him, the fallen leaves crunching beneath her feet, then wrapped both her arms around him, sketchbook still firmly in hand. He, as usual, rigidly accepted her gesture. She embraced Mehroo, who returned her embrace with an affectionate kiss on her cheek.

Mehroo asked, "Did you sleep well last night?"

"Ah, sleep. So brief and so many birds screaming at one another at the first sign of light," Pamela replied.

"Ah, yes our peacock likes to make himself heard very early," Mehroo said.

Ahmed offered Pamela a seat on the bench. "Miss Smith, Miss Bomanji asked me what the goals of the Golden Dawn are. I was at a loss to explain. Perhaps you could provide a definition?"

Pamela felt a lead lining coat her stomach. Even here, talk of the Golden Dawn. Why was Ahmed talking to Miss Bomanji about the Golden Dawn? Since Ahmed had been recruited by the Golden Dawn to be her "adviser," he liked talking about the purpose of her tarot cards, to her annoyance.

Just in time, Lady Bom's voice bellowed from the doorway to the house. "Mehroo, come at once; we need you."

Mehroo crossed the bricked patio to the doorway, her sari floating behind her like pulsing waves. As she held the doorway open, Edy and Christopher were in the process of coming out, carrying more tea supplies.

Edy, small and fey in her simple linen dress, the perfect demure dress of the day. But with her short hair, she looked more male than female as she cut through the gravel in her heavy boots. Chris followed, dressed in a three-piece wool men's suit, eating a scone from the tray she carried.

Ellen sat up. "Oh, Chris, you've dressed comfortably again, I see."

"Forgot my lawn dress, Miss Terry," Chris said. "I'll have to play croquet dressed as I am."

Pamela noticed Ahmed stretch his hands behind his back as Mehroo rejoined the group. A nervous tic of his, one she'd noticed at the museum. He usually did that when an estimate came in that was inflated or a workman tried to excuse an antiquity damaged in transport from Cairo. Seeing Chris dressed in men's clothing was unnerving Ahmed.

Mehroo passed the items from the tea tray to the small table next to Ellen. She handed Ahmed a cup, and he startled as though he had been zapped with an electrical cord from the theatre. Why, he was smitten. The only man among this wide assortment of women and he'd chosen Mehroo. Pamela thought Lady Bom did not strike her as someone who would welcome an Egyptian for her Indian daughter.

Pamela gave his forearm a friendly squeeze and walked to look over the garden.

"Mother, are you feeling better after your treatment?" Edy asked, picking up a scone. "Here, I promised you a scone afterward."

"Let us rehearse," Ellen said. "That's why we are here, isn't it? I know my lines. I don't know who any of you people are, though."

Edy sighed as Chris patted her arm.

Ellen sat up, dislodging Fussie, and wrapped her arms around her knees. "Except for Pixie, I know you, of course. You do look familiar, Edy, but I can't place you."

"Well, Pixie, why don't you read with her?" Edy asked, not looking at Pamela.

"Shall we rehearse *The Amber Heart*, Miss Terry?" Pamela answered.

The Amber Heart was the play Ellen and Sir Henry had first acted in. Next season a younger actress, Lena Ashwell, would be playing Ellen's roles.

"I'll read Ellaline," Pamela said, picking up a typed script from the pile on the chaise. Ah, the role of Ellaline, a role Terriss named his daughter after, it was that popular. It was a shame he had to stay to work with Uncle Brammie and Henry; he always livened things up. This was going to be deadly.

Ellen said, "Edy, you read Silvio. You have the first line, always a bonus."

"'Then you forgive me?'" Edy read in a dull, flat voice. At least there were no *s*'s in there.

Fussie, with a newly stolen scone crunching in his jaws, jumped back up on his mistress's lap. Distracted by the dog, Pamela looked to Ellen, who sat looking at Edy and Pamela.

Without a script, Ellen said, looking at the dog, "'There's nought, dear, to forgive—'"

Pamela picked up the passage in her script, "'There's nought, dear, to forgive. Now, go to her, for I would be alone. Yet, ere you go, I would you kissed me once.'"

"'With all my—'" Edy trailed off as Pamela gestured at her wildly.

Pamela stood still. Ellen, with both her eyes closed, was mouthing both roles.

"'Heart!'" Ellen exclaimed just in time with Edy's dialogue.

Pamela chimed in with the next line, "'Just once upon the—'"

"'Brow. 'Tis icy cold,'" Ellen finished.

Ellen's memory was coming back.

Ellen opened her eyes. She seemed far off, as if in a dream.

"'Now, get thee quick within,'" Ellen said. "'And tell her that I am happy she is loved. Go thou.'" Her sonorous, cello-like tones floated over the garden. She reached up in the air, as though calling a bird, and mimed as though it lit on her finger. "'I will sit here awhile and think. Do not heed me. I am happy. Get thee in.'"

A chatter started in the large tree above them, sending dust, leaves, and nuts cascading down on everyone. A squirrel jumped from branch to branch. Fussie barked furiously, trying to jump up to murder the intruder.

Ellen looked up and shook her fist. "Learn yer damn plays! That's the end of *Cyrano de Bergerac*, not *The Amber Heart*!"

Gales of laughter rang out.

Edy picked a large red leaf that had settled on Pamela's shoulder and placed it in Pamela's hair, positioning it as if it were a center stone in a tiara.

"Ah, the friends," Ellen said, coming over and draping her arms around both Pamela and Edy. After admiring the newly planted leaf in Pamela's hair, she planted another in Edy's. "Edy, I hope you keep our Pixie in the family, even if you have found a new friend in Chris."

Edy gulped and looked into mother's eyes, trying not to tear up. "Mother, I'm so glad you remember Pixie and now Chris."

"Remember?" Ellen retorted. "I just quoted lines from a play I have not said in fifteen years! Why wouldn't I remember my daughter's best friend and her new love?"

Chris shyly exchanged glances with Edy while Mehroo busied herself pouring more tea. Edy wouldn't meet Pamela's eyes. Maybe Ellen's entreaty that she be treated like family had fallen on deaf ears.

Ellen turned away from them, walking to the very edge of the hill, her brown cloak trailing behind her. Then, without a word, she pitched herself forward, rolling down the steep incline before anyone could catch her. As she spun, a collection of red and yellow leaves whirled around her.

Pamela threw down the script and ran to the hill's crest, Edy, Chris, and Fussie in immediate pursuit. As the three of them careened downward, Ellen stopped flailing and rolled to a halt. Fussie was the first to reach her, sniffing her outstretched hand.

The three women leaned over Ellen's body at the bottom of the gully. The smell of wood smoke, a pause in the birdsong, and a lump in her throat framed the moment.

Suddenly, handfuls of leaves flew up in Pamela's face as Ellen threw bursts of leaves at the trio. Then she laid back down, writhing in laughter.

Pamela burst out laughing, catching Edy's worried eye until her friend finally joined her. A full-on leaf fight began. Leaves drifted down like miniature floating stained glass windows. Pamela and Edy tossed leaves at Ellen. Chris picked up a handful and launched it at Pamela. And as Ellen shimmied in her brown cloak from side to side, the three merry maids threw the jeweled leaves at the convulsing treasure of the Lyceum Theatre. Fussie barked and jumped up to snatch remnants.

Grabbing Edy and Chris's hands, Pamela whooped and called out, remembering Nana's magical spells against the duppies, the witches of Jamaica.

CHAPTER FIFTEEN

VALENTINE'S EQUATIONS

Aleister turned over in bed to look at the sleeping Greta Valentine. She had one arm thrown over her face. Her only visible feature was her full, pretty lower lip, a feature often found in females of Portuguese descent. Even in her sleep, she pouted. Long, dark hair spilled over her pillow.

"Lady Sin," he said, nudging her.

Stretching her legs under the sheets, she barely opened her eyes as she arched her feet. He judged the chances of having another go-round as fifty-fifty.

"Yes, Lord Beer, what do you want?" she answered, curling up in a fetal position. The chances of round two were now plummeting.

"Did your father really attend the discovery of Jack the Ripper's first victim?"

As Greta sat up and leaned against the headboard of her canopied bed, Aleister helped himself to a cigarette from the nightstand. If he couldn't satisfy one desire, he could another.

Greta's room was a debutante's boudoir: flowers on the Baroque dressing table, a screen with a large cashmere shawl thrown over one end, and a matching set of rosewood wardrobes and chairs. Aleister's clothes were heaped on the floor on his side of the bed. There was a path of her clothes leading to the bed, ending with her chemise pooled near the mirror.

"Really, Mr. Beer, what a crass and ugly salutation after a lovely evening." Greta threw the sheets aside and took a dressing robe off the back of a chair. Opening her bedroom door, she called out, "Charity! Tea, please. And start a bath for me."

A dog barked from downstairs, its deep rumble echoing up the staircase. The clicking of paws running on wood was followed by whining. A great sigh echoed as the beast threw himself in front of his mistress.

"Goliath, hush," Greta cooed, scratching his head. "And stay."

The huge mastiff stretched out in the hallway as she closed the door.

Before she could fully turn back, Aleister jumped out of bed and knelt naked at her feet, offering her a cigarette, which she took.

"Goddess of Mathematics, divine one, I meant no offense." He kissed her feet and wrapped his arms around her legs.

Greta inhaled the tobacco. "Goddess of mathematics? Is this more of your sex Magick talk? Don't you know you didn't need to cast a spell for me to sleep with you last night?" She threw Aleister's trousers to him, handed him back the cigarette, and sat at her vanity table. "Charity only delivers tea to clothed guests."

With that, she took a white puff from a bowl of rose talc, opened her robe, and powdered her breasts. Aleister grinned, walking over to stub out his cigarette in the bowl of talc powder.

"Charity has experience with unclothed guests here at Hyde Park Crescent?" Aleister asked as he dressed. Greta watched him in the large mirror of the vanity.

"Only when Father and Mother have gone to Cornwall for a painting weekend. Speaking of which, you may stay another hour and then you must be gone." She began to comb and braid her hair.

After fastening his braces, he bent down to kiss the back of her neck. "Oh, my Goddess of Mathematics, I celebrate your many magical formulas. Your zeros and triangles and all your mystical equations."

As he began to fondle her under her robe, observing her in the mirror, she pulled the curtains open, flooding the room with morning light.

"I believe our calculations have come to an easy end," Greta said turning around to face him. "I hear Charity on the stair."

"As easy as that?" Aleister asked.

"As easy as that," Greta said, retying her robe more tightly.

"What if I want more?" he said, taking the end of her tie's sash out of her hand.

"There is no more to give," she said, tugging the sash back.

"That could mean trouble, as I need more."

"There is a difference between need and want, Mr. Crowley," Greta said, springing up to open the bedroom door just in time for Charity to enter. The dog in the doorway growled as he spotted Aleister.

Charity, a young red-haired girl in her proper maid's outfit, set down the breakfast tray. She didn't lift her eyes once to observe Aleister, still shirtless, just picked up her mistress's clothes and left. The dog followed her down the stairs.

"I see how well you train those around you," Aleister said, pouring tea into two cups before handing her one. "Here I am being of service to you."

"And what do you want in return before you depart?" she said, sipping her tea.

"Please, Goddess, just one tidbit about how your father was at the inquest for the Ripper's victim. Then I shall leave as you desire."

Greta sighed, standing to look out the window. "Why would you want such a gruesome story?"

"Just one of my curious interests."

"Very well. And then you'll leave. Twelve years ago, I think it was, I came down to breakfast and heard father talking to mother behind the door. He'd just returned from an early summons to attend the discovery of the remains of Catherine Eddowes. I'll never forget her name. She was found murdered and mutilated in Mitre Square, in Aldgate. Another doctor agreed with him that the girl had undergone the most brutal slaying ever witnessed. Torn rack from limb."

"Torn rack from limb," Aleister repeated.

Greta turned to face him. "Do you believe there is evil in this world?"

"Oh, yes. Great evil. That must be channeled for good."

"Well, I hope you find it." Greta picked up his shirt from the floor and handed it to him. "The good, not the evil."

Aleister put his hand over hers. "Are you dismissing me?"

"What more do you want?" She shook off his grip, tossing his shirt over his outstretched arm before returning to her vanity.

He began to button his shirt at a deliberately languorous pace, keeping his concentration on her.

"Well, I was hoping for a congenial friendship and an introduction to your father. In lieu of that, I will settle for a small list of items that only a doctor's daughter could procure."

"Condoms?"

Aleister sat on the bed to put on his shoes. "If you have some extra scumbags, those from last night were quite nice. However, that is not on my list." He reached into his trousers and handed over a note.

"'Chloroform, surgical knife, stitching twine, needles, a Deerslayer cloak.' You want my father's cloak? But he wears that on his watercolor painting trips. I can't just steal it from him to give to you. How do you even know he has a Deerslayer cloak?"

"From rumors of the appearance of the first doctor at the Ripper crime scene. They said he floated in wearing such a cloak.

What if I were to tell you I have discovered the map of the universe? And in order to decipher it, I need to perform exercises that require these items? But these exercises will work. Like magic." He tucked in his shirt, not taking his eyes off her.

"Bah. Magic. So why do you need my father's cloak?"

"For a costume ball next month. It's part of a formula that I will need to cast a spell from the seventeenth century, if you can believe it. But a surgeon's cloak would be a most excellent outfit. If you were unable to get it to me, just think how very disappointing it would be for your parents to hear how you are spending your time."

"I will loan you the cloak. But under no circumstances will I 'borrow' medical supplies from my father. Ask Freida Bluxom. I understand she's very generous with . . . supplies."

"What do you know about that?"

"I know that you are having relations with every doctor's daughter in our circle. Dr. Bluxom might not notice missing chloroform and knives, but I assure you my father would."

He crouched down and took her hands, placing them on either side of his face, moving in as though he were going to kiss her. Or bite her.

Instead, he yawned. Then, straightening, he crossed to the door.

"Do what thou wilt, Miss Valentine."

CHAPTER SIXTEEN

Tiaras and Handkerchiefs

At that evening's supper, Pamela sat between Duse Moham-med Ali and a sullen William Butler Yeats. Yeats was in a dark mood; Pamela couldn't tell whether it was from writing poetry or a hangover from his latest Golden Dawn spell. The last thing she felt like discussing with him was her recital of his poetry in New York. Why was he invited along on this "Destination Memory" tour in the first place?

Duse jerked his head in surprise when he saw her tiara of waxed leaves. She had taken care to weave large red oak leaves and yellow smaller leaves into her unruly hair.

"Very festive headpiece," Duse said, then looked around the table. Edy and Ellen were also wearing leaf tiaras. Pamela had taken great care that afternoon to weave the three tiaras together with a spell binding their love to one another.

"I love that tiaras are in fashion," Beatrice said loud enough for Pamela to hear. She gave a stern look to Duse.

Beatrice had been doing well since the prince's visit. She'd been given small roles with the Adelphi Theatre, and this evening was very popular with her table mates, although Pamela could tell she was nervous that her husband might not experience the same popularity. Pamela nodded her head to say that she would make sure he was included. Reassured, Beatrice went back to discussing wallpaper.

This evening's elaborate supper was in honor of William Hesketh Lever, First Viscount of Leverhulme, founder of Lever soaps. Pamela hadn't identified Lord Lever yet, as all the middle-aged gentry looked the same.

Several seats away, Ahmed and Mehroo were leaning toward one another, in the middle of an intense conversation. Ellen, wearing a golden shift, was gay and unperturbed, showing her leaf tiara to the infatuated man seated next to her. Despite what happened earlier, Ellen's memory was still cursed. She could not recognize Beatrice, even though she had been instrumental in helping the woman avoid the prince's seduction at the Savoy Theatre. Edy, sitting across from her mother, avoided Pamela's glances and moped over Chris' absence.

After refusing to promise Lady Bom that she would not discuss women's rights over supper, Chris had been excused. Chris was much happier up in her room anyway, smoking cigars and writing.

Pamela tried to feel the magical spell she wove into the leaf tiaras. The spell invoked the joy of dancing, wind carrying a wood smoke's aroma, and a comforting bird's song. She had hoped it might prolong the affection from this afternoon. But the euphoric feelings from rolling down the hill together had dissipated in just a few hours. How much longer would she be living with the Terry Family?

She turned back to Duse, hoping she could keep her promise to Beatrice. Pamela hoped Lady Bom wouldn't hear he had lost his temper at Lord Battersea's soiree and taken a swing at Lord Lever's head. Despite Duse's tendency to hog the conversation, he was one of the few men who talked about politics around her. And he positively beamed at his wife whenever he scored a point.

Pamela smiled at Satish, sitting across from them both, and he nodded back, his beautiful smile putting her at ease. Satish's long hair was swept back in tight curls and his mutton chops were closely trimmed. Ladies sat on either side of him and batted their eyes as Satish recounted his adventures. His beautiful blue-black face expressively recounted becoming an admiral, a warrior from Africa, or a member of parliament. Duse watched from across the table, ready at a moment's pause to add to the conversation.

"Mr. Ali, I understand in addition to your acting work, you publish a newspaper?" Pamela asked.

"Yes, articles the other Fleet Street newspapers won't cover," Duse said quietly, glancing to see Lady Bom occupied in talk. "The palm oil conflict has grown more intense, yet very few businesses want coverage in the newspapers they buy ads from. But how can I not cover the natives' pleas in India about enforced labor, homes burned, and land confiscated by Lever soap factory workers?"

Lady Bom's head pivoted in their direction.

"Which one is Lord Lever?" Pamela whispered. Duse pointed to the end of the table.

Lord Lever was placed next to Lady Bom, seated next to Satish. Lord Lever was handsome and polished, listening with great interest to Satish, who was in the middle of a story about West Indies pirates. Maybe Satish was more pirate than poet tonight.

Lord Lever asked Satish, "What is the capacity of the docks in the Virgin Islands?"

So much for pirates. Business not swashbuckling.

Pamela glanced at a fidgeting William Butler Yeats on the other side of her. A year ago, he had come to one of her Bohemian night soirees and fallen in love with Maud Gonne. He confided to Pamela that he was so shattered in love with her that he was going to ask her to marry him. Although he was part of the Golden Dawn, Pamela had yet to see him at a single meeting.

Pamela leaned toward Yeats and softly said, "*Quod tibi id aliis.*"

His brown eyes widened behind his glasses.

"Where is that from?" Yeats asked her.

"'What to yourself, that to others.' It's my motto that you helped me determine."

His distant mask fell away, and he turned his entire body to Pamela.

"Oh my God, I just remembered that night at your place," Yeats said. "When I met Miss Gonne. A Goddess. An angel. All other women fade in comparison."

At the mention of Maud Gonne, two Lords sharing spirited conversation about the Anglo-Ottoman Society stopped to scowl at Yeats. Pamela tried to see their place cards. It was a Lord Mowbray and Lord Lamington. Maud Gonne was a known agitator for Home Rule in Ireland and, therefore, a political enemy.

"Miss Gonne is an extreme supporter of the violent Home Rule movement. A very unpopular topic in this part of Yorkshire," Lord Mowbray said.

Lord Lamington added, "At least to this party of men in Yorkshire."

Ellen's voice floated over the men's hard tones. "Lord Lever, I was so flattered to see your Pears soap advert. I've been told numerous times the model in the poster looks just like me."

"Eh, what poster is that, Miss Terry?" Lord Lever asked, his eyebrows knit together.

"The poster of the Indian crystal gazer using a crystal ball to encourage a young lady to buy your soap," Ellen answered.

Lord Lever harrumphed into his soup.

Ellen continued, "Usually soap adverts show fat little children or muddy kittens. But the figure of an Indian man recommending Pears soap to an English young lady is so refreshing, is it not?"

Lady Bom looked mortified, while Sir Dhunjibhoy burst into laughter. He dabbed his mouth with his linen napkin.

"Ah, Miss Terry, that advert is for Pears soap, not Lord Lever's Sunlight soap. But do you know whose idea the crystal ball was? My own daughter, Miss Mehroo."

Mehroo blushed. "I am only friendly with a Pears soap artist. I asked him if he knew how to draw a turban, and he turned it into the advert."

"Well, Miss Bomanji, a clever idea even if it is for Sunlight soap's rival," Ellen said.

"Miss Terry, have you ever used Lord Lever's Sunlight soap?" Lady Bom asked. "Your complexion is famous for its clarity. Much better than my daughter's."

Pamela watched Mehroo's shoulders sink. How odd Lady Bom would compliment Ellen's skin over her own daughter's.

Ellen smiled at Lady Bom and turned to Lord Lever. "You are president of the Sunlight Soap Company, isn't that right? You built such a lovely village for your workers. Henry and I toured there once. When we played Wirral we called it "our perfect soap village.""

Soap village? Pamela looked to see if Edy was tracking this story. Yes, she was following along, her head nodding slightly.

Lord Lever lit up. "Yes, yes in Merseyside. Near the Coast. I built an excellent theatre there, and you and Mr. Irving played *Much Ado About Nothing* there."

"Ah, yes, I remember all those beautiful homes, hospitals, and schools you built," Ellen said. "How very clever and kind you are."

Lord Lever puffed up as Duse frowned.

"Mr. Duse," Ellen said, "you must tell us about playing Shakespeare at the Star Theatre in New York City. I hear you are a brilliant actor and orator."

Duse's face relaxed, as the corners of his eyes wrinkled behind his glasses. Beatrice beamed from across the table. Ellen knew how to get out a good story about everyone.

"I hardly know where to begin, Miss Terry," Duse said, his voice shaking. "The Hull Shakespeare Society, which I founded and Henry Irving endorses, is one of my proudest accomplishments. Yet, in spite of all the plays and musicals, I have yet to play the great Moor, Othello. It is said you played an excellent Desdemona with Mr. Irving and with the American actor, Edwin Booth."

"Yes, they switched the roles of Iago and Othello nightly. That I remember," Ellen replied, tapping her finger to her temple. The guests around her laughed.

The finger to her forehead stopped. Was this the signal? Pamela stretched her feet to reach the floor and steady herself in case she needed to help Ellen out. No, Edy shook her head. It was alright.

"Miss Terry, what was the difference between Booth and Irving's interpretations?" Lord Bomanji asked loudly.

Pamela saw Ellen take in all the guests turning to her. Like the professional actress she was, she leaned forward as though confiding a great secret.

"Well, Henry insisted on scrubbing up in a lot of dirt to look like the Moor, Othello," Ellen whispered loudly, "and I ended up wearing most of it. Whereas, the American actor used hardly any grease paint at all."

"A different technique from each," Lord Lever said, "traditional English versus classic American rebellion."

Ellen gestured to Satish with a flick of her hand. "Mr. Satish Monroe or Mr. Ali would make marvelous Othellos and Iagos, don't you think, Lord Lever?" Ellen asked.

Duse and Satish shifted in their seats to face one another. A grimace was exchanged.

Pamela looked at the Viscount, his black, glistening hair extending into dark bat-like waves. The blue of his eyes exploded. It hung in the air. Another manifestation only she could see.

The vision was droplets of blue, forming panels of men laboring. Scenes of a wharf. Workers carrying wheelbarrows to ships. The image was so sharp, it was like a lantern show at carnival. It disappeared.

Lord Lever lifted up his chin. "I'm not sure what your question is, Miss Terry?"

"Don't you think Mr. Monroe and Mr. Ali would make wonderful Moors and Iagos in *Othello*?" Ellen answered, her face smooth and guileless. "Two men of the islands doing what Mr. Irving and Mr. Booth did, rotating the two roles?"

Duse shook his head, saying, "An excellent idea, Miss Terry, but I was born in Egypt not the islands."

"Moors are Spanish, I believe," Lord Lever said, looking at Duse. "Iago is English."

"Mr. Kamal, is that right? Are Moors Spanish?" Ellen asked, leaning toward Ahmed.

Pamela saw her friend look down at his plate. When he lifted his head to answer, his brown eyes were unblinking.

"Yes, Miss Terry, Moors can be Spanish, Berber, or Arabic," Ahmed answered.

Lord Lever motioned for more wine, not looking at Ahmed. "Mr. Kamal, you are an Arab?"

"I was born in Egypt, but my family is originally from Turkey," Ahmed said. He turned slightly, catching sight of Mehroo, who tilted her head toward him.

Ahmed was born in Turkey? *What else don't I know about him?*

"Miss Terry, why do you feel an actor from the Islands or Egypt can play the great role of Othello?" Lord Bomanji asked.

"Othello's handkerchief was given to him by an Egyptian charmer," Ellen said. "A magician. So, you see, an Egyptian handkerchief starts all the problems in the play, and Othello could possibly be Egyptian. What do you think, Mr. Kamal?"

"I do not know *Othello*, sorry to say," he answered, his hand lifting up as if to erase the conversation.

"It has been conjectured that Othello's handkerchief was woven from the mummy's silkworms," Duse interjected, pushing his chair away from the table. "Or died in the embalming substance called mummy, which was black. But then, that would have meant Othello had a black handkerchief, which would be quite controversial." He stood. All conversation stopped. Duse began as though he were seeing a spider web in front of him.

"There's magic in the web of it
A sibyl that had number'd in the world
The sun to course two hundred compasses,
In her prophetic fury sew'd the work;
The worms were hallow'd that did breed the silk,
And it was dyed in mummy which the skillful
Conserved of maidens' hearts."

A polite round of applause lasted long enough for Duse to bow and sit down. Satish cleared his throat and lifted a glass to Duse.

"To an Egyptian Othello," Satish said, his Caribbean accent elongating the last 'o'. "May a mummy, made of maiden's hearts, give us all the magical powers to make others fall in love with us."

He lifted his wine higher to motion for a toast.

Cheers rang out, wine glasses emptied.

Guests settled down and paired off to private conversations. Ellen whispered something to her daughter and pulled a square piece of material from her sleeve and slid a silk handkerchief across the table.

Edy and Ellen stood, then bowed to the host and hostess, making their exit.

Passing Pamela, Edy threw the handkerchief into Pamela's lap, her hand brushing up against Pamela's leaf tiara. Feeling the edges of the leaves, Edy swatted them as though they were vermin. The tiara crumbled. Pieces of broken foliage fell on Pamela's plate, the table, the carpet.

Mother and daughter continued out of the room as more bits of red leaves fell from her hair onto the white tablecloth. She took Ellen's handkerchief and brushed away the leaf remains and tucked it up her sleeve. A handkerchief conserved of maiden hearts, according to Othello.

Maybe she wouldn't move out of Ellen's house just yet.

CHAPTER SEVENTEEN

SWORD OF ROBIN HOOD

~⚬~

Centerstage at the Lyceum Theatre, smoke rolled out from an open brazier.

Pamela tried not to cough as she held up her torch. Thanks to an emergency fund from an anonymous donor, the winter season at the Lyceum had been restored and the first show was in technical rehearsal. Watching three panels of the Temple of Diana fly overhead, Pamela watched transfixed as it landed at the top of a marble staircase lined by fluted columns.

This completed the set for the temple scene in *The Cup*. At the bottom of the steps sat a beautiful young boy. His inky blue-black hair fell across his face as he ate grapes from a dish. Wearing a loin cloth, his lute at his side, he looked like a creature out of a Caravaggio painting.

Ellen glided down the stairs in the role of Camma, priestess of the temple. Her flowing tunic billowed behind her as she led her maidens in sweeping gestures, their bare arms undulating in the mottled air.

The air became thicker with black smoke. *Oh, dear.* That was from their torches. She and Edy weren't holding them straight. She lightly nudged Edy with her foot to indicate their torches were tilting and Edy kicked her back. Her kick hurt.

Adding to the fumes from their torches was the smoke from limelight lamps rimming the stage and the incense drifting from a brazier. A small group of boys and girls, clutching baskets of flowers, cowered behind the columns. They held handkerchiefs over their mouths, trying not to cough.

Ellen beckoned the children to form a procession. They trotted out, strewing flowers as they clambered over to the boy, who mimed plucking a note on his lute. The violinist in the pit played the note as one of the seated children leaned in and tried to strum the lute strings. When he found there were no strings, he hummed a cheery version of the tune from the pit.

Uncle Brammie and Lovejoy came out from the wings. It was never a good thing when the managing director and the stage manager came out during a technical. It was eleven o'clock at night and the opening less than twenty-four hours away.

Ellen had recruited them to help out at this technical, as Uncle Brammie had been unable to hire his usual soldiers and policemen for extras. Children coughed and maidens swayed while Uncle Brammie went over the rules.

A single whistle rang out from above in the flies, signaling a set change in process.

More whistles followed, short and shrill, low and thready. Most of the fly crew had been sailors, communicating with their language of shrill tweets. Pamela recognized some of the whistle language from her transatlantic voyages. One of the whistles was definitely the signal for "grub." She felt the urge to whistle back but no one but the crew was allowed to whistle in the theatre. Whistling in the theatre by non-crew members was more than bad luck, it was dangerous, and Lovejoy would fine you if he heard you. A careless whistle could send a wrong signal to the fly men, careening a flat into harm's way, killing bystanders.

Pamela gasped as the door to the temple opened and fell off its hinges. Then it tumbled off the platform and crashed underneath. A collective moan went up.

In a shaft of light coming through the broken doorway, Henry emerged. Barely visible through the swirling layers of smoke, he struck a pose in profile made obscene by the fact his gold-plated armor had shifted at his sword, causing it to rise up. With his tiger skin cloak tied at his shoulders, the long red wig, pale make-up and crimson lips, Henry looked like a Roman fop. He tried to take his sword out of the scabbard, but his cloak got tangled. A momentary duel between sword and tiger skin began. Pamela bit the side of her cheek to keep from laughing.

The Cup was Tennyson's play, commissioned especially for Henry to play Synorix, the evil protagonist. Ellen was the loyal wife and William the hapless husband. Ellen poisons Henry's character by tainting their wedding chalice. Some said Henry picked this play as a subtle way of letting Ellen know that if he couldn't have her exclusively, no other manager could. Others said this was an acknowledgement that Ellen had been poisoned at Dr. Felkin's. Because of Ellen's limited ability to memorize, many of her lines for Camma had been cut.

The sword finally won over the tiger skin and Henry raced to the bottom step. Taking Ellen's hand with territorial vigor, he turned once again in profile, his favorite, the left side.

He gazed at Ellen. Children coughed. Pamela's and Edy's torches tilted.

Silence.

"Line, Lovejoy," Henry barked.

"'I am a life-long lover of the chase,'" Lovejoy shouted from the wings.

"'I am a life-long lover of the chase,'" Henry grunted, looked down and grimaced. "Lovejoy . . . what's next?"

The stage manager shouted again, "'And though a stranger fain . . .'"

"'And though a stranger fain . . .'" Henry repeated.

More spats of coughing from the children around the boy musician.

Henry's head jerked in their direction. "'Would be . . .' damn it, Lovejoy . . . what?"

"'Allowed to join the hunt.'"

Henry looked up in exasperation.

From backstage, a banging and thrashing was heard, followed by a shout, the sound of a barrel being kicked over, and swearing. Someone was running behind the legs, the black curtains separating the stage from the backstage area. Heads swirled, children and adults trying to pinpoint the source of the disruption. The moving curtain made its way along the back wall and burst open in the center.

A magnificent white horse bearing a toga-clad man galloped onstage, where it proceeded to run circles around the actors. Above them, the fly space and wings rang out with cheers and whistles. Children, shrieking, crying, and spilling their flower baskets, ran to huddle with maidens.

The horse rider made clucking noises, and eventually led the horse to a slow trot. The entire company stood spellbound, as he continued to ride around Ellen and Henry in the center of the group. Terriss lifted himself out of his saddle, and grabbing onto the pommel, dismounted, dropping straight in front of Henry. With one hand, he signaled his horse to do the same. The horse lowered himself, a white hoof sliding under Henry's uplifted chin.

"Are Sorcerer and I allowed to join the hunt?" Terriss asked, looking up from his bow.

The group held their collective breath. They never knew if the leader of the Lyceum Theatre would react as an outraged task master or benevolent employer.

When Henry threw back his head and exploded in a deep, rumbling laugh, the place burst into raucous shouts and cheers, clapping until they were all pounding the floor with their feet.

Pamela tried to clap while juggling the torch. She almost put her fingers in her mouth to whistle for Sorcerer, but the idea of paying a fine held her back. Sorcerer was one of Terriss's favorite horses. Once, Pamela had gotten to ride him back to the stables at Covent Garden. That was the day she knew he remembered her from her childhood. As he handed over the reins, he whispered, "So alive"—the very words he'd said after saving her from falling off the bridge.

Sorcerer rose from his bow, pink ears twitching. When the horse saw Pamela, he jerked his head. He recognized her.

As the theatre continued to erupt with mirth, the stage crew entered with sand buckets and took the torches from the girls, smothering the flames as they spurted to extinction. Pamela was glad to hand off the heavy prop and turned to commiserate with Edy, but she was already gone, off to chat with William Terriss.

Pamela hung back, delighted when Sorcerer ambled over to her and nuzzled her hand. Sorcerer was so like her pony in Jamaica, the clever tricks, the long eyelashes. A lump in her throat knotted at the memory of tearing along the roads in Jamaica in her little trap. Sorcerer gave her shoulders a little push with his great head. It was a message from her pony, sending his regards. Pamela laughed and kissed Sorcerer's nose.

Lovejoy and Uncle Brammie approached, Fussie running ahead of them to bark at the horse, which paid him no attention. Henry scooped up his dog, shaking his head at Terriss.

"Terriss, when you said you had an idea for the hunt, I should have known," he said.

"I take it that's a no on Sorcerer being in the scene?" Terriss smiled.

"A definite no."

"Well, let me unpack our cast supper then, for Sorcerer was told to earn his keep today."

Terriss unloaded two white sacks tied to the back of the saddle and threw them to the stage floor. A few of the children still cowered around the boy with the lute.

"You'd better unwrap these first," he called. "As you know, first come, first served."

The throng of children rushed forward and grabbed the sandwiches wrapped in butcher paper from the sacks. As Pamela edged closer, she saw there were biscuits, cured meats and roasted potatoes, too.

A clanging of pipes and footsteps on ladder rungs from the flies warned the booty had been spotted from above. The stage crew shouted and jeered as they made their way down from the rafters. Only the intervention of the women's chorus prevented them from snatching food out of the hands of the children.

Screeches of joy and teasing went through the company as they gathered around the sacks of food. Pamela ran backstage to grab fire blankets on the railing. A midnight supper picnic courtesy of their Breezy Bill! As she came back onstage she almost ran into Henry, who gave her a brief smile. He motioned to Uncle Brammie and Lovejoy, also bringing blankets onstage.

After a brief consultation with Henry, Lovejoy stepped forward to address the company. "Thirty minutes for supper break. Thirty minutes! And I don't want a crumb left on this stage. That goes for you too, Sorcerer!"

A group of smitten young girls and boys had gathered around Sorcerer, who was content to stand there and let his head be stroked by Terriss. As Pamela settled others down with food, she heard sobbing. As she turned around, she spotted Ellen comforting a young girl of about eight. The child's oval face was framed by long dark ringlets, her eyes rimmed with tears.

"So, you are partial to Mr. Terriss?" Ellen asked as she dabbed tears from the girl's cheeks.

"Oh, you can laugh," the girl solemnly answered, "but I wish I were hammered to him."

This set the entire crew off in snorts and mumbled obscenities.

Sorcerer was led away by a crew member who said between bites of sandwich, "That Terriss. 'E's a breath of fresh air, that one! This toga parade only comes to life when 'e's onstage."

Lovejoy grabbed him by the arm and whispered, "You want your job, son?"

The man stopped and gulped, "Yes, sir!"

"Then don't let the Guv'nor hear you say that!"

With that, Lovejoy swatted Sorcerer on the rump, sending the horse wrangler and horse galloping backstage.

Needing a new focus for their attention, the children gathered around Fussie as the fox terrier performed tricks for slices of ham. Dirt-smudged men approached women in white togas while Terriss held court with the young apprentices. Uncle Brammie handed Ellen and Edy sandwiches. Pamela watched as mother and daughter turned to one another in a private conversation.

Taking a seat on the faux marble steps, she unwrapped her food. If Sorcerer were here, she would share it with him, as currently, he was the only creature expressing any affection for her. She took a bite of her sandwich and looked to see if Edy was still talking to Ellen. There she was, walking offstage, probably going to sit in her mother's star dressing room.

The voice of Henry drifted from backstage. "And where do you suppose 'Breezy Bill' got roast beef sandwiches for fifty people?"

Uncle Brammie's voice answered, "Lord Tennyson?"

Pamela shook her head and smiled at the thought. The playwright Lord Tennyson was almost one hundred years old and too fragile to attend rehearsals.

"The poet laureate sent sandwiches for his bacchanal scene? Unlikely," Henry answered. "Send Terriss to my dressing room. And recast the guards holding the torches. They're a fire hazard."

Pamela peeked in between the gap of the stairs and the masking and saw Henry walking away. Uncle Brammie spotted her.

She held her breath. Was this the end of her employment with the Lyceum Theatre? No, he motioned with his two-fingered salute from his brow, their signal for "all clear." *Still on the boards.*

✺

Terriss sat sideways in Henry's dressing room throne. It was not a comfortable chair, being the former throne from *Henry VIII*, but it ensured guests would not stay long.

At the edge of the white-and-red woven rug, a gift from a patroness, sat Fussie's basket. Gaslights flickered next to the large mirror above the dressing room table. A simple wooden chair held Henry, his long legs stretched out. His valet, McClintoch, busied himself making tea at the sideboard on the other side of the room.

Smoke from their cigars curled around their fingers as the stogies glowed. Fussie groaned in his sleep.

"Ah, pig. Good pig. Go to sleep now," Henry said, looking down at him.

The dog settled down, stretching out across Henry's feet and falling into a deep sleep as McClintoch finished setting out the armor for Act II later that evening.

"McClintoch, can you bring the sword here, please?"

The bald man with the tidy bow tie dropped the laundry into a sack and picked up a scabbard on the prop table. He placed it across Henry's lap before softly shutting the door on his way out.

"Well, Guv'nor, are you beheading me or knighting me for disrupting rehearsal?" Terriss asked.

Henry drew on his cigar and half-closed his eyes. "Neither, Terriss." He picked up the sword. "You know the story of this sword?"

"I know it's not from the right era for *The Cup.*"

"Ah, Terriss, I can always count on you to tell me the truth. Yes, you are right, it isn't from the same time period as my Synorix."

"Or during the time of any toga town, my lord."

"Quite right." Henry put down the scabbard and picked up his tea. Terriss could see across the scabbard's front plate now, which read *Edmd Kean*. Terriss broke the cardinal backstage rule and whistled low and deep.

"Is that what I think it is, Guv'nor?" Terriss asked.

"Yes. This sword was given to me by Chippendale. You remember him?"

"Ah, yes, and what a run of ink he had! So many wives, so much drink, and what a run of shows! He lived a life!"

"Yes, he did. I knew him when I was first starting out. When I first organized a benefit night for myself," Henry answered. "It was *Hamlet*, in Manchester. My whole career depended on it. And you know who set the standard?"

"Kean," both men said.

Henry continued. "It just so happens our hard-living William Chippendale had done the show with Kean. And on the eve of my first performance as Hamlet, I traveled over-night in low-class seats to study with him in Birmingham. I wanted to know everything the old master did. Chippendale tutored me in Kean's every aside, every inflection and gesture. The success of my Hamlet provided the funds for me to come to London."

"And a lifetime of walk-on roles for Chippendale at the Lyceum. You were a soft touch for that sot. Mind half-shot, hands always shaking," Terriss said.

"At the opening night of *Richard III*, he gave me Edmund Kean's sword. Edmund Kean had given it to him. Or he won it from him in a card game, according to legend."

"A right proper bequeathing, I would say," Terriss said, exhaling a long stream of smoke.

"The heart of that man, to help me. Chippendale did more for me than any other person in my career. He kept Kean's legacy alive."

Terriss leaned in. "I still don't know if you're beheading me or firing me."

Henry smiled and reached for the handle of the long sword. The sword was three feet long and steel-clad, with etchings all along the side. The guard was rectangular, its brass plates riveted with ornate knobs. Three nicks on the right side were deeply etched, the grooves a dark hue. The ivory, spiral-shaped grip and brass pommel gleamed in the firelight.

As Henry held it midair, a scratching was heard at the door.

"Go away, McClintoch!" Henry shouted. "And neither, Terriss. I'm knighting you as the proper heir of this sword. You, more than anyone, are the knight of this company."

"Ah, Guv. Are you giving me this sword with the idea that I'll always stay? I'm getting pressure to have Isabel put in hospital, but the children and I want her cared for at home. That will take more than a Lyceum salary."

"I'm sorry, Terriss. This has been going on awhile."

"Longer than anyone knows. The cancer has had her three years. I can't stay here because of a sword."

"I'm giving you this because you challenge me to be a risk taker. A daredevil. A truth talker. Oh, Robin Hood, Giver of Sandwiches."

"A fool."

"And a fool."

Henry motioned Terriss to kneel. Grinning ear to ear, Terriss knelt as Henry held the sword with both hands, lightly tapping each shoulder.

"To my Robin Hood—because I know you took those sandwiches from the Savage Club's luncheon—I bequeath this sword. Pass this sword on to the next heart and talent."

The scratching at the door grew louder, and from the dog basket, Fussie roused himself and let out a long, low moan. After a few blinks, he farted.

Both men laughed. A black paw shot out from under the door and rattled the frame.

"Ah, it's that damn cat from your dressing room," Henry said, taking a handkerchief and wiping the merry tears away. The paw disappeared and the rattling stopped.

Henry handed off the sword to Terriss, refusing to look him in the eye.

Terriss looked at himself in the dressing room mirror, then, sword in hand. He made several swipes in the air, a low rush of air humming in its wake. Terriss twirled the sword in newfound patterns, figure eights, slashes, upcuts. Henry sat, puffing on his cigar as he watched the sword undulate back and forth in its new owner's hands.

A rush of air close to Terriss's head buzzed as the sword lightly clipped him on his ear. Terriss let out a loud yelp as Henry stood in concern. Taking his cupped hand away from his ear, he saw no blood.

The scratching at the door resumed as Fussie barked.

Henry motioned Terriss to bend toward him. He inspected his earlobe.

"I see the PCS of our Pixie's marking is still on you," Henry said.

Terriss peered into the dressing room mirror. "Yes, I seem to have had unbridled impulses since my ear tattoos appeared."

Henry gazed at his reflection in the mirror and turned his head to investigate his own ear. "You, Terriss, even more wild impulses? God help you," Henry laughed. "Diving off bridges, stopping runaway horses? What is next?"

"I don't know. Do you?" Terriss asked.

"Well, funny you should mention it. Recently, I seem to have the ability to know what someone is thinking," Henry said. "Doesn't happen all the time and only with those I know. Usually damn fools."

"Speaking of fools, I've seen the tarot card Miss Smith fashioned after me," Terriss said, sipping his tea.

"You look very fetching in your card. I look like a combination of Ellen's daughter and my oldest son, who is not yet twenty. Flattering to the point of being unrecognizable."

"Why do you suppose the Golden Dawn chose Pamela to create those damn cards?" Terriss asked.

"That cult senses a great war is on the horizon. They'll want to influence people along the way," Henry said, leaning down to stroke Fussie's head.

"To what advantage? Messages, guidance, entertainment? They're just flash cards used for guessing games."

"It's a mystery to me," Henry said. "I don't know what objective they aim for with these tarot cards. But Miss Smith definitely seems to be kicking over wasps' nests for the Golden Dawn. At least my valet believes that is what's at work with the tarot cards' commission."

"McClintoch believes in their magic?" Terriss asked.

"McClintoch has said when the show is going well, the initials on my earlobes illuminate. He calls them my 'magic barometers,'" Henry answered.

Terriss lay the sword back down on the prop table and sat down on the throne. The door rattled. Fussie whimpered from his basket. The door creaked as it was pushed open and a black theatre cat padded in. He stood in front of Terriss, his tail waving back and forth in midair.

"I'd like to take Hecate with me to the Adelphi Theatre when I go next season," Terriss said, stroking the cat's sleek ebony head.

"Ah, there it is. You are leaving me," Henry said.

"Opting out for just one show. *The Secret Service Man*. Miss Smith introduced me to her cousin, William Gillette, who wrote it for himself and needs to go back to America."

"Sounds dreadful," Henry answered, reaching over to pick up an open wine bottle from behind his makeup mirror. He poured wine into their teacups.

Terriss picked up Hecate. The golden-eyed cat rubbed its head against Terriss's chin and settled in on the arm of the throne.

"You know Hecate was female and this cat is male?" Henry said.

"This cat can play any role," Terriss replied.

"Really, I thought you were more of a dog person?"

"This cat is magic," Terriss said as the cat blinked and purred.

Both men lifted their teacups, pinkies held out.

"To magic," they toasted.

The dog whimpered as Hecate stared down at him.

CHAPTER EIGHTEEN

FIRE

~~~

Surely this young man knows Duse's father was killed fighting for Arabi Pasha, Ahmed thought.

But Winston Churchill continued his rant. "The Omdurman Battle was a true bloodbath, one of the last of the cavalry charges," he said, reclining further in his grand chair.

Ahmed studied his host, barely in his mid-twenties, so sure of himself. Any hope that he would meet guilty owners of ill-gotten antiquities dissipated. The other men in the drawing room, four dark-hued men from England's colonies, squirmed in red leather chairs. If Churchill knew Duse's father fought for the Egyptian cause, he didn't let on — even though Ahmed and Duse wore Egyptian tunics and fezzes, while the titled politicians, Lord Bomanji and Sir Bhownagree, donned white turbans of India.

Churchill continued, his watery blue eyes shining. "The dervishes swung their swords in wide circles, slashing cavalry horses. There were no attempts at civilized warfare."

Ahmed saw Duse take a deep breath and look up, as if asking for divine help. With great control his friend asked,

"And how did you think the Egyptian dervishes would fight, Mr. Churchill?"

Winston's high voice answered, "Oh, the dervishes fought manfully, alright. If you call pressing their muzzles up against the bodies of their opponents and slashing reins and stirrup-leathers conventional warfare."

"How long did the hand-to-hand fighting last?" Ahmed asked, eyeing the other guests in the room. The men from India were concentrating on the street traffic outside the tall drawing room windows. *He's asked us here to test our loyalty. Perhaps he thinks we all are spies.*

"Perhaps a minute, until the arrival of our new artillery, the machine gun," Churchill said. "And then our Lancers appeared, attacking them on three sides. Within a minute, every living foe was cleared in the dervish mass."

"Every living foe, Mr. Churchill?" Ahmed asked. He felt his face go hot and tried to still his hands, now quivering. "You do know our friend here, Mr. Duse Mohammed, suffered the loss of his father in this conflict."

Lord Bomanji and Sir Bhownagree blinked as Duse opened his mouth to say something and then checked himself.

Churchill leaned forward. "I know Mr. Ali was educated here in England and has started a Shakespeare Society in addition to running a newspaper. Since England has given him so many opportunities, I would expect him to be loyal to the crown. Would you say you are a patriot?" Churchill asked Duse.

"As a son of Egypt, I could never say I was pleased that tens of thousands of my countrymen were killed in a fight over the Suez Canal," Duse said.

Ahmed took a swallow of the pale excuse for tea that was sitting on the table next to him. *Wretched stuff.*

"Your countrymen. So, you consider yourself Egyptian, not English," Churchill pressed.

Duse stood and shook his head, taking a deep breath. "I

consider myself a man of the world, Mr. Churchill. I respect English law and custom, but I have the education and oversight to judge England's aggressions in their so-called territories."

Sir Bhownagree pulled Duse down back into his chair. "The question Mr. Churchill is asking you, Mr. Ali, is 'are you loyal to the crown.' There is only one answer. Of course, you are loyal, or you would not be here in London starting a business and currying favor, as we say."

"I believe in the fairness of the English people," Duse replied, his curled mustache twitching. "They have proven to be a fair-minded people once they know the facts. That is why my newspaper is of dire importance here, not only here in London, but to all of the British Empire."

"Well said, my friend," Ahmed whispered as he handed him his handkerchief to blot his perspiring face.

Churchill turned to the Indian politicians. "My good sirs, you have been elected to represent people in your precincts. Would you consider yourselves loyal?"

Lord Bomanji spoke in a measured tone. "We are loyal to the political process here in England. We have been able to win the trust of our neighbors and represent them. To that we are loyal."

The other man from India nodded.

"Ah. Good answer. Good answers," Churchill replied. The door opened and a large young woman entered. He beckoned to her.

"Christopher, could you retrieve the good cigars? The ones in the silver case," Winston said.

Christopher sighed and clomped over to the table holding the humidor. She was almost six feet tall and very odd looking to Ahmed. The femininity of her jacket's leg-of-mutton sleeves overpowered her simple skirt. Ahmed recalled her wearing the men's suit at the Bomanji weekend and was unsure whether this outfit was an improvement.

Lord Bomanji bent forward to Churchill. "A woman assistant?"

"Yes. I inherited her from my mother," Churchill said in a low voice.

Said well out of the woman's earshot, Ahmed noted.

"And you, Mr. Kamal," Churchill continued, "would you say that your first loyalties are to the crown or to Egypt?"

Ahmed smiled. *Ah, my turn.*

"Mr. Churchill, although I studied archeology and French in Egypt," Ahmed answered, "My family comes from Turkey. Like Mr. Ali, I consider myself a man of the world, although the antiquities in Egypt are more family to me than any idea of Egypt."

"Excellent!" Churchill cried out. "Men of the world, exactly the sort I wanted to talk with today. Chris, get a move on with the cigars, will you?"

Christopher approached languidly with the cigars.

As she stood in front of Ahmed, he remembered an afternoon when Christopher had come to the museum to meet with Pamela about a women's rights poster Pamela had designed which incorporated Egyptian hieroglyphics. Christopher thought it clever but worried that only Golden Dawn members would understand the symbols. In the discussion following, Ahmed voiced that he didn't understand why women needed to vote—they already had so many rights. Christopher snapped at him that until they had the right to vote, own property, and marry whom they wished, they had no rights. He knew Pamela had been disappointed when Christopher decided not to use her poster for their next march.

Ahmed saw the gentlemen's eyes widen as the scent of Chris's cigar tray went by.

"Yes, I brought these cigars back from Cuba four years ago," Churchill said. "They have just the right amount of curing."

Looking up, he saw the glowering giant lowering the tray to him, the pungent cigars snaking their overpowering scent.

Ugliest woman he'd ever seen. No, wait, Mother's aunt was uglier.

As if hearing him, Christopher looked right at him.

"Sir, shall I light for you?" she asked, her eyes flashing daggers.

"Sorry, sir — er, rather, ma'am. Yes, miss, no, thank you," Ahmed said, picking up a cigar. He took a deep breath. "We met at Lord Bomanji's weekend. You are a friend of Miss Pamela Smith?"

Christopher's gaze softened for a moment. Then her jawline hardened.

"Yes, Miss Pamela and Ellen Terry invited me to come along that weekend," Christopher replied. She moved to light Ahmed's cigar, but he waved her off, taking matches out of his pocket. She moved on to service Churchill.

Churchill picked his choice of cigar off the tray and sniffed it. As Christopher struck a match and held it to him, he gulped the end of the cigar as the flame held steady. She moved on to the other guests, lighting their cigars. Puffs of white gray smoke formed a cloud on the ceiling.

She sat at her desk against the wall and Churchill motioned to her with a flick of his hand.

"Chris take notes for me. This is just in case I say something pithy that I can use in my next speech," he said. "Being a former correspondent for the *Daily Graphic*, I learned the importance of good note-taking."

Christopher coughed and hunkered over her dictation pad.

Duse blew smoke over to the young man's face. "When you were a correspondent for the *Daily Graphic*, did you mention the killing of wounded men on the field after the Battle of Omdurman?"

Churchill waved the smoke away, keeping a blank expression. "I believe I did mention it."

"Your leader of this battle, Kitchener, did he approve the use of the new bullets that explode in a body?" Duse asked, jabbing the air with his cigar as though shooting bullets down.

Sir Bomanji rose from his chair and stood in back of Duse, patting him on the shoulder. "Now, now, Mr. Duse, this young writer is not to blame for the Omdurman slaughter. Yes, they are terrible things, these machine guns, but such is the nature of war." He tapped a finger on Duse's shoulder for emphasis.

Duse jumped up. He was a good deal shorter than Bomanji, but what he lacked in height he made up for in irritation. "Such is the nature of greed, Mr. Bomanji. This attack on my people has everything to do with the Suez Canal and nothing to do with governing our warring tribes! You wait until they get their hands on the diamonds in Africa or your palm oil in India. I've seen them in action. There is no stopping them!"

"Mr. Duse, I understand your concern—" Sir Bhownagree started.

"Concern? Concern, you call it?" Duse shouted. "Concern that the British army is invading and enslaving local populations to exploit their resources? The British will become very rich, making these slaves work for their profit, while my people and the people of the other nations can barely exist!"

Churchill crossed his legs. "This injustice is just what I am trying to bring to the public's attention. The British people will know about it from my article in the *Daily Graphic*."

"A newspaper I should be writing for!" Duse said. "Do you know how many times I have tried to write for the *Daily Graphic*? Or the *Morning Post*? But, no! They do not want a black man writing about what England is doing overseas. They do not want the perspective of the 'natives' or the 'kaffir'!"

Ahmed sighed. *Any hope that Churchill would be a liaison between aristocrats and the museum's antiquities department is fading fast. Political talk always kills art.*

Bomanji placed a firm hand on Duse's shoulder and pushed him back in his chair. "Mr. Duse, I understand your passion, but if you are thinking this is the way for Mr. Churchill to recommend you to publishers, you are mistaken."

Churchill leapt up, his red hair breaking free of the brilliantine. Ahmed noticed that when he stood up, he was even shorter than Duse.

The young man stood for a moment by the cigar box and lifted a secret panel. After selecting a choice stogie, he went to Duse, whose cigar had gone cold.

"May I?" Churchill asked, handing him the new cigar and taking away the old. He struck a flame and held it. Duse paused and then breathed the cigar to life.

A foot tapped on the polished marble floor. One by one, the men turned to discover the noise only to find Christopher absentmindedly striking the floor with her boot.

Winston smiled even wider. "Chris, would you care for a cigar?"

"Don't mind if I do," she answered, crossing to help herself to the secret panel of the box. Churchill winked at the men and walked to her, but for all his bravado, his hands were shaking as he held out the light for her. Christopher took his hand and steadied it. She drew deeply, her cigar flaming right away. She took a good long drag and blew her smoke upward. She returned to her desk and sat, ready for dictation.

"What these new modern women do is unthinkable," Lord Bomanji muttered.

"You see what I've inherited from my mother, gentlemen?" Churchill asked with a smile. "Now, I would like to address why I've called you here." He walked over to his grand piano.

"At last," Duse mumbled.

"I was asked by the powers that be to investigate potential contacts who could help us keep an ear to the ground for possible rebellions," he announced.

Duse snorted. "Spy, you mean?"

Sir Bhownagree nodded. "Yes, please explain yourself, Mr. Churchill. You must know we are loyal to the crown, but endangering our countrymen would not be in our self-interests."

Churchill leaned against the piano and looked out the large window. Out in the street, the clomp of horses' hooves struck the cobblestones with a percussive trilling. "This is the predicament, my friends. Scotland Yard has received information that a chain of revolutionaries is determined to undermine the British Throne through several of our jewel colonies."

Duse made a fist at the phrase "jewel colonies," only relaxing when Ahmed reached over and nudged him.

"There are always counter factions in every society," Sir Bomanji said. "The British cannot expect to quell them all."

"True," Churchill answered. "But there are several factions, as you call them, that are the most dangerous. These are currently training here in London. There are suspicions they are making their way through organized institutions for a massive strike."

Ahmed flicked the cigar ashes off his leg and cleared his throat. "You think there are Egyptian and Indian factions who would attack the Crown here?"

Churchill's pale blue eyes turned to Ahmed. They were dead flat.

"There may be, but right now our most dire threat is from the Carlists," he said.

"Carlists?" Ahmed asked. "I know of them—they were titled ones from Spain asking Egyptians to fight over Church rule." He remembered bishops from Rome visiting Cairo when he was young. They wore strange tunics and hats and asked the local interpreters to explain their cause to the populace for support. They stayed a week trying to recruit soldiers, to no avail.

"The Spanish Carlists are not plotting against the church here in England. They are protesting the legitimacy of royal succession in Spain," Churchill replied.

Sir Bhownagree laughed. "Spain? Scotland Yard is worried about spies from Spain? Who are these spies?"

"We know there are connections being made with Earl

Ashburnham and Jaime de Borbón, the pretender to the Spanish throne. We believe spies to be moving freely between the Golden Dawn and the British Museum."

Ahmed froze. *I'm suspected of harboring spies.*

Churchill cleared his throat. "I'm going to ask you gentlemen that you keep your ears open to any rumors of the earl. We suspect he's training Carlists at his country estate in order to place Jaime de Borbón on the Spanish throne. And all of you have had contact with these two Carlists at a recent Bomanji supper at the Savoy."

Lord Bomanji said, "The guest list was made up of society people my wife knows."

Sitting down on the piano bench, Churchill looked at his secretary. "Chris, be sure to write this down word for word. Lord Bomanji and Sir Bhownagree, I know you need help with your Parsi delegates in this upcoming election. My mother and her insatiable appetite for campaigning might be of service."

Duse grimaced. "And what is our reward for doing Scotland Yard's work?"

Churchill turned to him. "Mr. Ali, an introduction to my newspaper connections might be possible in exchange for your aide." Duse sat up straight, waving his hand in agreement.

Churchill then grinned at Ahmed. "And you, Mr. Kamal, I know of a statue, Sekemet, currently at Lord Compton's. You would be most curious to see this in exchange for confidences, am I right? Your British Museum with your imported mummies and the would-be magicians of the Golden Dawn is the perfect breeding ground for spies, wouldn't you say?"

Ahmed felt his throat close up.

Winston continued, "In addition to Carlists and magicians, you also know this young girl creating tarot cards."

"Miss Smith has nothing to do with Carlists," Ahmed replied.

"Perhaps so," Churchill said, "but she's absolute catnip to one of their most determined anarchists, and we need to watch her."

"We?" Ahmed asked.

"Mr. Kamal, you are either for the British Empire or against us. Now, what will it be?"

✑✒✎

By the time Ahmed left Churchill's house, the sun was slanting toward a murky horizon. That meant just a few more hours of natural light in the British Museum. The only rooms with electricity were the front hall, forecourt, and reading room. Using a candle in the back rooms was cause for immediate ejection, and the rooms he most frequented lost light many hours before the seven o'clock curfew.

When he unlocked the outer door to his office, he saw Pamela was not at her desk. It occurred to him that she had not asked him for artifacts to sketch in days. Her hours had always been erratic, but lately she came in early and left by two o'clock to visit a church or go to an art gallery, she said.

Entering his private chamber, he noticed a large package on his desk. He opened the note on top.

> *Let's let bygones be bygones. Here's to our next get together to discuss Egypt. ~W. Blunt*

It was from the mad Englishman who wore Egyptian robes and was assaulted by Terriss during the Gents' Night outing. Ahmed unwrapped the box; inside was an exquisite gold-plated hookah. *Ah, bribery for the foreigner.*

A sharp knock at the door almost made Ahmed jump out of his skin. Hoarsely he called out, "Come in."

Florence Farr entered, a shawl wrapped around her shoulders over her burgundy coat. Kashmir shawl from India, wool coat from France. Why do the English like everything from somewhere else?

"Mr. Kamal, hello. I'm looking for Miss Smith," Florence said. "Have you seen her lately?"

Ahmed couldn't look at her. Women at home had eyes rimmed with kohl and long hair simply plaited. Miss Farr wore all her hair on top of her head without any face painting.

"Miss Smith might have been in earlier," Ahmed replied, "but I have not seen her today. It seems a great many people are looking for her."

Florence replied, "Really?" and sat on the edge of his desk. She appraised the hookah.

"This looks expensive," she said.

"Yes, there is a great cost to this," he replied.

She nodded her head and looked at him closely.

"Has a Mr. Crowley come in looking for Pamela?" she asked in a low voice.

"No, not him," Ahmed answered.

"Who else is looking for her?" she asked.

Ahmed turned away to see the last of the light squeezing through the slats of the great gate.

"I'll only say . . . officials . . . are looking for her," he replied.

"Bastards," Florence said, taking off her gloves.

"Really, Miss Farr—"

"Mr. Kamal, you know they are. Is it that pipsqueak Churchill? He's always trying to score points for his base, prejudiced against artists or anyone who isn't landed gentry."

She stood up and Ahmed moved closer to the window. Her light eyes trained on him like a beacon.

"What can I do for you, Miss Farr?" Ahmed asked.

"I would like to see cupboard fifty-five," Florence said.

"Absolutely not," Ahmed answered. "You don't want to know what is in the secretum."

"Oh, but I do, Mr. Kamal. It is the Cabinet of Obscene Objects and you're just the person to show it to me."

Half an hour later, against his better judgement, in the fading light of the formerly walled up cupboard fifty-five, Ahmed let Florence into the secretum. The room was officially off-limits, available only to groups of ten men or less who had applied for visitation rights. Although a randy duke or two could waltz in and hold court there for hours, all under strict privacy.

It was a small, dark room with two divans against the wall and one small window. In center stood the gorgeous statue, *Bodhisattva Tara*. A gilded bronze statue of a goddess with ample hips, large breasts, and a small waist, she looked down from a pedestal, her right hand beckoning, her left hand in repose. A wedge of styled hair made her seem taller than she was. Her half-closed eyes and serene smile soothed any frazzled nerves Ahmed had.

"Oh," Florence cried, "Mutemmenu said she would be fantastic and she is!"

"Did Mutemmenu say anything about our Miss Smith?" Ahmed asked.

Florence looked up at him, and her smile dropped. "Only that Pamela is in danger. Great danger."

CHAPTER NINETEEN

Empress Incarnate

~~~~~~~~~

"Pounce."

"Pat."

"Pust."

Ever since the tainted wine at Dr. Felkin's, entire words had dropped out of Ellen's recall. Words she knew but could not say. Walking in her rose garden at Smallhythe, Ellen tried her hardest to remember the name of the young artist doing the Jamaican folktales and drawing. Her surrogate daughter. What was her name?

"Oh, come now. Picks."

Another loud laugh from the house and there it was.

"Pixie!"

As she sat on the bench, she noticed beetles crawling up the rose named for her, the Ellen Terry. It was a lovely cream rose with a slight blush in the bloom's center. The scent was a very light, almost powdery aroma. Even though there were many things she couldn't remember, she was sure June had never seen so many roses. The bluebells and larkspur in the flowerbeds stood in contrast against the ancient timbers of her sixteenth-century house. It was now filled to the gills with guests. Just as in the days of the Lyceum Theatre tour breaks. It was a happier house now—the timbers seemed to sag a little less.

And what a motley group had traveled here. Christopher St. John, Annie Horniman, Ahmed Pascal Kamal, Florence Farr, Yoshio Markino, and William Butler Yeats. A terrific smash of people, as they would say, who had come down on the train the day before yesterday. William Terriss and his new leading lady from the Adelphi Theatre, Jessie Milliward. But Jessie was not his wife. Ah, well. Ellen had been in a relationship like that with Henry. But he was not in attendance. Neither was Ma. Was Bram back planning the repertoire at the Lyceum? One thing she did know is that after the disaster of *Peter the Great*, written by Henry's youngest son, Ellen wouldn't have a job.

The two girls came out of the door together, the skinny, sour-looking one and the short, happy one. The happy one wore a kitchen towel as a turban and carried a feather duster as a scepter; the grouse carried the tray. Mussie trotted under foot. Oh, he was getting fatter by the day.

The turbaned girl performed a spastic, meandering waltz around the other one.

In a Jamaican accent, she crooned, "Oh, the Henry Irving Waltz, like Henry, has no schmalz, just a big boss, and a big name, running the show on his big, big fame." She waved her feather duster scepter wildly.

Ellen burst out laughing, hearing the lyrics written about Henry. He would be so cross if he heard it.

Oh, lemonade and biscuits! She reached for a biscuit and the singing girl tickled her hand with the feather duster.

"Pixie!"

Thank the gods, the name for this one had come back. The girl knelt and hugged her around the waist. The towel fell off her head, and her hair stood at all angles.

Definitely not a Terry. Not her daughter. Who was she again?

The sour-looking one crossed her arms and sat next to her, glaring at the dancing girl. "Pamela, would you mind giving Mother and I a moment to talk alone?"

Ah, yes, this one. She was the daughter. Edy.

❧

Pamela went back into the cool, dark kitchen where hanging baskets of herbs and drying flowers dotted the ceiling. Scents of lavender, mint, and thyme wafted through the air. Mussie's nails clicked on the red tile as he followed her. Upon reaching his oval rag rug, he threw himself down and farted.

The local cook poked out from the pantry.

Pamela asked, "What time is supper?"

The woman snapped back, "Supper is always late here. That's why there's afternoon trays," before disappearing once again.

Other people's kitchens, other people's dinner hours. When she and Edy had lived together, they would eat at all hours. This was Pamela's second trip to Smallhythe and the first where she was feeling like a guest and less like a family member.

Hearing the cook move about, Pamela tossed the feather duster and towel onto a wicker chair and hurried into the dining room. The white wall framed with ancient timbers looked like the inside of a ship. Where else had she seen that? Oh, yes, the Mary Magdalen church. She couldn't bring herself to call it St. Saviour's.

Mismatched chairs sat in front of the great open hearth, pushed back as though their occupants had just left. Pamela cocked her ear to see if she could hear anyone else in the house. If they were still upstairs, they were either reading or sleeping. The wide Tudor plankboards would creak at the slightest movement. Even the spirits of the house were still.

The grandfather clock against the wall maintained its steady beat. Pamela's heart slowed to its rhythm as she sat in one of the big, tufted chairs. She looked out the leaded glass window. Edy and Ellen, side by side in the falling light, cast a beautiful image among the flowers of the gazebo.

Pamela's heart caught in her throat. Her own mother had been lively but remote. Maud Gonne was her childhood love but had been off fighting for the Irish cause; her sister fairy had not written her in almost two years. Before that, Pamela received letters from Paris or Dublin at least on her birthday. There hadn't been a sign of her since the night she returned to England as she floated next to the carriage.

And then there was her third love, her Nana. Her dark apple-cheeked guardian, storyteller, rustler, and witch who cared for her all those years ago in St. Andrews. In Jamaica, Nana was the one who truly looked at her, into her very self. She was the one who challenged her, coddled her, made her perform the Annancy stories. Her crinkly eyes would slit if she substituted a word or pronounced something wrong. "If you be tellin' my stories, I wanna hear the real Jamaican sounds, not the English la-di-das of your mother."

But Ellen came the closest to being a real mother. When they were on tour with the Lyceum, it was Ellen who inquired after her artwork, her showings, her latest news. Ellen who brought her to parties and private homes, introduced her to people as her "Pixie," and teased her about how so many of Pamela's fingers were in so many pies. Ellen encouraged focusing on her artwork and tarot cards.

Her tarot cards would be like stained glass windows, filtering the magic of symbols through the vibrations of color. The images called to her, flew to her day and night, clamoring to be part of this deck. She would make her name with them. Would she be condemning her friends to Aleister's vindictive magic in the process?

She didn't pick Henry Irving as the Magician or William Terriss as her Fool. They just appeared in her artwork, and her initials showed up on their earlobes soon afterward. Florence becoming the High Priestess was not a choice either. Ellen was the first tarot muse she selected, and now Ellen was suffering.

Ellen's beautiful mind, beautiful memories, and beautiful laugh were now tainted. "Mental problems," it was whispered in theatre corners. Time and again, Ellen paused, drawing a blank look when she saw Pamela.

Edy was holding her to blame, she could feel it, as Ellen had lost several acting jobs outside the Lyceum Theatre. No one was sure if her mental problems were only temporary.

Now, as she watched Edy and Ellen lean toward one another in the fading sun, she was struck with a burning sensation, like a bolt of lightning. She may have lost them both. Hot tears streamed down her face.

Hoping the glass might soothe her cheeks, she leaned her head against the window. A lamb strolled into view, helping itself to the windowsill's box of flowers. Its tongue darted out of its mouth to taste the flowers, and it hurriedly chewed as many petunias as it could. Lambs. So sweet. So cuddly. Like living dolls.

A story Henry had once told came back to her. She had tried to embrace Henry one time, in thanks for the hieroglyphic lessons. When he repelled her hug, she asked him why he hated being touched. He told her his parents had abandoned him in the care of relatives who showed him no affection. No pets nor friends, he was often lonely. On the cliffs next to their house was a flock of sheep. One day as he sat reading his book on the rocks, a young lamb came and sat next to him. He reached out to pet it and was bitten severely in the face. He asked Pamela, in light of that, could she restrain herself? She answered she would warn him if she was going to try to hug him again. A slight grin was his response.

Three ewes strolled up to the windowsill to join in, their necks stretching up to reach the flower box full of petunias. All four animals stopped mid-chew. And all at once, all of them screamed at her. She fell off her chair. The lambs' collective scream was the most humanlike screech Pamela had ever heard.

❧

Later in the afternoon, Pamela saw Ellen greet the last arrivals in the garden and was relieved to hear Florence assigned to one of the prized bedrooms. Pamela then bustled to help set out the late tea on the far side of the lawn. Earlier she had arranged the stones in a circle before the assembly of chairs, some already occupied. A late October breeze rustled as the sun dipped toward the hollow. Tonight, the veil between the two worlds would be at its thinnest. Birds began their end-of-day arias in the fruit grove. The light conversation stopped as a strange chanting came from the second story, Florence stopping mid-stride, concentrating on the sound. Heads swiveled toward the house, and Florence lifted her arms as though receiving the chanting to her own self.

Ahmed was completing his evening prayers from his guest bedroom. For most, this was the first time they had heard of salah. Pamela had prepared a few before the trip down, but none of them had actually heard someone practice the prayers before. The murmur of his prayers floated over the garden.

He had been distant ever since the Bomanji weekend. They'd had a curt conversation over symbols from the Egyptian cultures in the Sola Busca tarot exhibit and he'd asked her how her Empress was coming along, but other than that, nothing. She had asked after his wife and if they had children, and he curtly told her that subject was off-limits. Their easy back-and-forth about the origin of ideas and provenance of art was gone. Now she didn't know how to explain why her ideas were inspired by many places. Pamela knew that her Empress should be the great Earth mother, from the Romans and the Greeks. Or from India. From talking with Mehroo Bomanji, she learned about the seven chakras. That should be part of the Empress, too. Pamela had asked Ahmed if Mehroo would like to come down for the weekend, but he quickly replied he was sure she had other plans.

As the dusk began to fold in, the partygoers went back to their polite chatter. As rounds of conversation started up again, Ahmed's Maghreb prayer rose and fell.

The midges came out and bounced through the last light, a shimmering column of dancing specks. Then the small, twittering squeak of bats began, their tiny bodies diving from their roost in the barn. A small gathering of deer startled at the edges of the grove. A brave rabbit ran from there to the garden, making for a sporadic dance between earth and sky.

William Terriss rose from his chair, clenching his pipe between his teeth, and helped Pamela light a small bonfire in a pit before them. Terriss's new leading lady at the Adelphi Theatre, Jessie Milliward, beamed at him from her seat. Pamela noticed she was a shorter, younger version of his sick wife, Isabel. The smoke smoldered and Terriss fanned it to chase the twilight insects away. Ahmed came out and bowed to the group, making his way to a chair behind Florence.

Ellen sauntered from the house, the glow of her costume, made of a thousand jeweled beetle wings, shimmered. The infamous Lady Macbeth court dress caught the last eye of twilight. The dress had a ragged hem, and some of the beetle wings were broken off. As she walked, the wings undulated like the buds of dew on a spider's web. Because Ellen often turned up late for the half hour call at the theatre, the dress was distressed from her careless haste in dressing at top speed.

But even with some of the wings gone, Ellen glowed, more apparition than human. On her head, a wreath of Queen Anne's lace bobbed. Her elaborate dress contrasted with her bare, white feet gliding between the blades of grass.

As she neared, Terriss's small fire in the pit burst into flame. The long, wavering notes of a robin and liquid warbling of the nightingale pulsed.

Florence rose from her seat and brought Ellen to the center of the seated circle. Pamela was so pleased that Florence had offered to do this twilight blessing with Ellen.

In the diffused light, Ellen took in all her guests. Pamela watched the deep breath she took, the closed eyes, the tilted head. As Ellen exhaled, Pamela saw a burst of blooms swarm around her. The itching inside Pamela's head started, a sign that more sensations were about to start. And, sure enough, there it was: a sweet, clean scent of lilacs and the pungency of the peonies puffing in purple clouds. William's pipe and the fire smoke added a layer of greenish scent, deep and primal, the smells themselves becoming layers of color.

Florence held her lute with one hand and used the other to motion for Pamela to join with Ellen in front of the group. The three of them stood together. Florence played a simple tune on her lute. Pamela lifted her arms to embrace the colors racing past her fingertips in a silken rush, while the wind grew stronger. It was the night exhalation of Mother Earth. Leaves roiled and grasses swayed. The audience's heads turned from side to side, catching the motion of debris in flight.

The rustle grew as the wind picked up even more. Bats, birds, and dust twirled in columns. Twisting sheets of flower petals, leaves, and pollen began to rain down on them. Ellen took a few steps off the stones and walked toward the lawn, covering her eyes. Pamela gasped as she saw Ellen covered by a cone of swirling jeweled beetles.

Pamela stepped closer to Florence while the rest of the guests rose and swatted away the insects. The sun blinked its last golden ray and sank beneath the rim of earth.

Ellen's outstretched arms were ringed with twirling legions of black jeweled creatures, her face upturned to the last reaches of the twilight. Each tiny, whirling insect took a turn flying around her head.

Above the din, Pamela heard Ellen chanting random words:

". . . Pixie . . . If I am condemned upon surmises . . . 22 Barkston Gardens, Earls Court . . . Gosterwood Common . . . Alice Carr."

These were recollections that had failed Ellen recently. Pamela recognized her nickname, Ellen's line as Hermione from *The Winter's Tale*, and Ellen's address in Kensington. But Pamela didn't know what Gosterwood Common was. Alice Carr was the costume designer for the Lady Macbeth dress. What else was Ellen remembering?

Pamela heard a voice inside her head, the voice that had told her to fly.

Tell the beetles what to do, Pamela.

A pond formed in the middle of the gathering. Not the lake that appeared when Florence became her High Priestess; this one was still and fragrant. And much smaller. A pond. A tarn in the mountains. Pamela's hands were sticky, and the blood slowed in her veins.

From the calm and still faces watching from the chairs, Pamela could tell they couldn't see her pond. She crouched down and dipped her hands. Cool. Clear. The water was cerulean blue. Standing, she splashed her face with water.

"Mend her memory," Pamela cried.

The beetles continued to swarm Ellen. She tilted her head and let the whirring iridescent wings envelope her. She was a writhing mummy. Pamela stepped closer, suddenly fearful they were eating her. But the beetles were crawling into the fabric of the dress, discarding their bejeweled wings, dropping into the grass, and crawling away.

They were filling up the holes of Ellen's memory. Scarabs who brought transformation and resurrection were now protecting her. . . .

". . . Account number 547, Charing Cross Road . . . Buller-Lytton . . . Imperial Theatre Trust bond . . ."

Ellen's face emerged from the crawling mass. As soon as her mouth was visible, she laughed. The wind died down as the last of the hued sky became a light gray slate. The beetles no longer covered her but were a moving river of antlers and shells making for the woods beyond. The bats swooped and pounced on the hapless insects from above, picking off the moving river.

Pamela wasn't afraid of bats, even after reading Uncle Brammie's *Dracula*. Much to his annoyance, she called them "sky puppies." But these creatures were different. Bigger. And their shrill cries to one another made the flesh on her arms rise.

Edy ran to her mother's side. Ellen turned and motioned for Pamela to come to her.

"Pixie, you have the handkerchief?" Ellen asked.

The handkerchief Ellen had given to her at the Bomanjis' had been tucked in Pamela's dress ever since the trip. Pamela gently wiped the handkerchief over Ellen's face. The white veined initials PCS throbbed on Ellen's earlobes. The Empress incarnate process was complete.

Ellen took Pamela's hand holding the handkerchief and kissed it. She looked into Pamela's eyes. "Fabulous!"

"Mother, not fabulous. Bugs!" Edy replied, flicking away beetle carcasses from her mother's shoulder.

"Don't you see? These beetles, they've fixed my memory!" Ellen said as she ran away from both of them. Looking up at the sky, she began to twirl, holding her train. As she spun, she laughed the Terry laugh. Soon, fat little Mussie joined in, adding excited yips.

Terriss and Jessie ran up and joined hands with Ellen, making a merry ring while Christopher and Edy soothed those confused over what they had just witnessed. Only Ahmed stayed seated in the rear row of chairs, watching everyone with a calm countenance.

Pamela was on her way to him when a bat dove down right in front of her, almost hitting her. The winged blurs fluttered and dove, emitting high-pitched squeaks. As they gobbled up the beetles, some tried to escape, limply airborne for a few seconds. Some of the ladies in the group squealed, repulsed. Florence took two long strides toward the carpet of beetles and lifted her arms into the darkening sky.

"Begone!" Florence intoned.

A column of bats swirled into a traveling cyclone. It trailed upwards until it receded, becoming smaller and smaller.

Pamela ran up to Florence.

"How did you do that? What were they?" she asked.

Florence looked down at her. "The beetles were Aleister's minions—his magic could make them appear here. My guess is that they have been around Ellen the entire time of the spell. Luckily, our familiars can end his curse."

Pamela looked back at the guests, still thronging around Ellen. Turning back to Florence, she asked, "You know how to command bats?"

Florence laughed and chucked Pamela under her chin. "Since I've become your High Priestess, I've commanded all sorts of creatures," she said.

"Bats are our friends and familiars, then?" Pamela asked, scouring the sky for the twisting cloud of creatures.

"Bats, cats, horses, and dogs at my call. Just don't ask me to command a man—that still seems beyond my reach," she said, resting a hand on Pamela's shoulder as they looked up together. The full moon was ascending above them. A small army of creatures flew across the moon's pearlescent face.

Pamela softly said, "Uncle Brammie's bats."

Florence patted her on the back. "Don't call too much attention to this; we don't want our guests to know magic has been afoot."

Mussie was jumping up and down on the darkening lawn, barking and biting at the sky.

Ellen twirled away from the writhing circle of dancers and breathlessly encircled Pamela and Florence. The train of her dress was full of flowers, buds, and grass; she carried a bouquet of flowers like a scepter. Her disheveled hair spilled over her shoulders as Ellen took Pamela's hand and squeezed it.

"My Empress," Pamela whispered.

"I know you, my Pixie," Ellen replied. She spotted the handkerchief sticking out of Pamela's sleeve. "My magical handkerchief I used in *Othello*."

"You gave it to me at the Bomanjis'," Pamela said.

Ellen laughed. "Yes, I was going to say an Empress never forgets, but we know that's not true. Keep the handkerchief close, it has powerful magic. I have a feeling you will need it again." Ellen took Florence's hand. "Thank you for saving my minions. To be the Empress of beetles is an honor I dreamed not of."

"As you say, Empress of Scarabs," Florence replied before walking away to Ahmed, who was standing at the edge of the lawn.

Ellen whispered in Pamela's ear, "Will there be retribution for breaking the beetle's spell?"

Pamela looked up to the sky to see the twelve stars in the Empress's crown, the shield of Venus, looking down on the restored daughter, with her scepter of power and pomegranates.

"Let him do what he can, my magic belongs to me."

PART 3

BATTLE OF THE CARDS

CHAPTER TWENTY

Carlist Threats

~⟋◡⟍~

Annie Horniman mailed engraved invitations to the
Golden Dawn chiefs to answer the complaint by one
of their members of "harassment by a rogue magician."
Attendance at the meeting would be mandatory.

After her trip to Smallhythe, Pamela told Waite she was
reluctant to continue with the cards if Aleister could appear
anywhere with his magical beetles or marble slabs. Waite, stung
that he was not invited along to the weekend trip, refused to
register the complaint with the Golden Dawn. He believed
Pamela's "nerves" were working overtime rather than in the
visitation of a jealous Aleister Crowley. It had fallen to Mrs.
Horniman to hold a formal hearing.

All the male Golden Dawn chiefs sat in the front row
before Pamela at the Headquarters. Seeing their folded arms
and stern expressions, Pamela felt a gray clanking rattling her
heart. This felt more like a trial than a hearing. If she hoped to
solicit protective spells, she would have to prove that a former
member was using Golden Dawn magic for evil.

The conversation in the room increased as Uncle Brammie
escorted Miss Horniman to sit next to Pamela onstage. Florence

followed, every man's head turning as she settled in the adjoining chair. Pamela saw Dr. Felkin sneer at her "Votes for Women" pin.

Miss Horniman's hat, on the other hand, earned a different reaction. Several Golden Dawn chiefs smiled when they saw it. An enormous platter-shaped chapeau with a feather tableau featuring an egg—it reminded Pamela of the hat in the Savoy restaurant where the dove attacked her. Miss Horniman sat on the other side of her.

Dr. Felkin walked up the steps to the stage, clapping his hands together.

"Good afternoon, ladies and gentlemen of the Golden Dawn," he boomed. "Our first order of business today is a matter of complaint against one of our former members. Miss Smith, thank you for being present."

Dr. Felkin motioned to the little table with her four tarot cards splayed out next to her.

"Miss Smith is commissioned to create tarot cards for our group. But her complaint states that magic, possibly developed by a Golden Dawn magician, has been used to harm civilians. This harm has been executed by threats via shape-shifting, a supposed recent death of a dockworker, and an alleged poisoning in my own home."

Pamela opened her mouth to dispute that the poisoning was alleged but she stopped. Ellen's poisoning had been dismissed by Scotland Yard due to lack of evidence. Dr. Felkin denied that Aleister had ever been to his house.

Picking up the Magician card, Dr. Felkin continued. "These are the four tarot cards you've created so far?"

"Yes, Dr. Felkin, in collaboration with Mr. Waite," Pamela answered.

Waite's arm shot up, locating him in the third row. There would have been hell to pay if she didn't acknowledge him.

Dr. Felkin held up all the cards. The audience looked at them; her chest tightened even more. The images squirmed on the cardstock. No one else could see their discomforted twitches. Who were these men of science and country clubs to judge? Florence gave her a sidelong glance in sympathy.

"We would like to get to the bottom of these rumors about Aleister Crowley," Dr. Felkin continued. "You say he threatened you numerous times?"

"Yes," Pamela replied.

"And you claim during an incident on a bridge," Dr. Felkin read from a paper, "that Mr. Crowley had contact with you."

"He threatened me in an astral display."

Dr. Felkin inhaled. "Ah, an astral display. Please explain."

Pamela felt icy needles in her hands. "He accosted me and then levitated. His face turned into the devil."

"The devil! Well, at last we'll know what he looks like! What does the devil look like?" Dr. Felkin asked, stroking his beard.

Miss Horniman interjected, "Dr. Felkin, I would ask that you remain cordial to Miss Smith. She will not respond to snide remarks."

Pamela took a deep breath. "His eyes were golden like an alligator's, he had a forked tongue, and when he reached out to grab me, I saw he had a claw."

"When you say levitating," Dr. Westcott cut in, "how far off the ground was he levitating?"

Pamela was relieved Dr. Westcott had asked a question. While he never seemed to like her, at least he wasn't as hostile.

"He must have floated up two feet before I kicked him in the face," Pamela answered.

Titters from the audience.

"So, he threatened you with words and then you kicked him in the face? Was this when you were both floating?" Dr. Felkin asked.

She saw what he was trying to do, prompt her into saying that she attacked him first. Her heart raced and little yellow splotches appeared outside of her head. "Yes, he threatened me, saying he would hurt those around me if I didn't stop creating the tarot deck."

"And then?" Dr. Westcott asked.

"He killed the man on the dock to show he could hurt those around me."

"Really, Miss Smith? The police found it was negligence on the part of the shipping company," Dr. Westcott said, eyebrows raised.

Pamela looked at him with a steady gaze, "Dr. Westcott, Aleister Crowley threatened my loved ones and when I refused to stop the tarot cards, I saw on the dock below, he astrally cut the ropes holding a marble slab. The marble fell on a man on the dock, cutting him in half. It was on cue."

"I'm afraid your theatrical life has led you to make huge leaps of imagination in the real world, Miss Smith," Dr. Felkin replied. "Just because there was a group hallucination here at the headquarters in the Vault, does not mean Mr. Crowley has the means to cut ropes from a distance. Were there any witnesses at the bridge?"

Dr. Westcott chimed in. "Perhaps you are too high-strung to finish this tarot deck, Miss Smith. Besides, who would he harm?"

"My muses, the four people who—"

Florence's hand on Pamela's arm stopped her. Pamela noticed Florence's clip-on earrings. She wore them the night of the Bomanji dinner. Outside of the enamel earrings, a few white veins were snaking and throbbing. Her initials had been activated.

Waite stood up, his tremulous voice shaking. "Excuse me, fellow Dawn Chiefs, but as cocreator of this tarot deck, I must have it understood that these first four cards have been executed by Miss Smith according to my instructions. They are the first of twenty-two tarot cards of the Major Arcana. Now, she has responded very well to my research and ideas on the composition of each card, but I am the master charting each card's step in the hero's journey."

Dr. Westcott leaned back in his chair. His disdain dripping in a mocking tone, he answered, "Well, have you been threatened or approached by Aleister Crowley over these tarot cards, Mr. Waite?"

The typewriter key sound started, Waite's annoying musical tone that infected her brain. *Tap tap tappity tap tap.*

Waite's bushy mustache twisted. "No, I have not. Not yet, that is."

Miss Horniman asked, "Mr. Waite, is it fair to say that Mr. Crowley sees potential in the magic of these tarot cards?"

Waite lit up at Miss Horniman's address. "Yes, it is fair to say. I have no talent for drawing or perspective—obviously, she brings those gifts. What I bring are ideas! Research! She has not been a devoted student to the outer levels of the Golden Dawn, but Miss Smith is a most imaginative and abnormally psychic artist. However, she makes no attempt to understand the subsurface consequences of these cards. Aleister Crowley does understand them and wants to own their magic."

Pamela grabbed Florence's hand.

"How does Crowley even know her progress with the cards? Has she been bragging about it to her friends? Or just to fairies?" Dr. Felkin sniffed.

In trying to stifle the growl forming in her throat, it came out as a croak. *Bragging!* What did Dr. Felkin or Waite know what she had been through?

William Butler Yeats popped up from his seat in the back, his hair falling over his forehead, his glasses gleaming. "Miss Smith has a natural talent for understanding symbols and ideologies," he said loudly in his Irish accent. "She actually can see the fairies, but you wouldn't know as they won't present themselves to braggarts."

Pamela hadn't talked with him since the Bomanji supper. When they passed one another at the Golden Dawn headquarters, he avoided her studiously.

Yeats continued, "Crowley is obsessed with creating his own following. A known Carlist rumored to be investigated by the Queen's intelligence, who are also now looking into our group, thanks to him."

Carlists. The word she first heard at Felkin's soiree where she met the Spanish pretender.

Miss Horniman's gloved hand pounded the arm of her chair. "Really now, Mr. Yeats. Why on earth would the British Secret Service investigate the Golden Dawn? No one here has anything to do with revolutions or the Carlists."

Pamela whispered to Florence, "What's a Carlist?"

"Later," Florence said, barely moving her lips.

Yeats replied, "It is rumored that the Golden Dawn chief Mathers received a shipment of explosives and machine guns for the Carlists in Paris. What sort of magician needs explosives? Or politics?"

Dr. Westcott answered, "The Paris chapter is none of your business, Yeats. The new outer-and-inner level chiefs are taking care of it."

Shouts exploded in the lecture hall. So much for championing for official magical protection from the chiefs.

Tap tap tap tap.

As the voices in the room got louder, Pamela noticed her four tarot cards on the table. They were trembling. A low buzzing in the back of her head grew to a chalky roar. The taste of each card started to form on the back of her throat: the lemon of the Fool, sandalwood of the Magician, incense of the Priestess, and lavender of the Empress. One by one, the cards started to move in a circle, jostling one another, then settling in their upside-down reversed position. They understood there would be no magical protection from this group. Her tarot spirits were on strike.

Pamela stood and the squabbling paused.

"My cards are telling me to stop creating magic here. You'll need to convince them, not me, that they will be used for good in the world. And that you will stand up to Mr. Crowley."

Pamela looked to Florence, motioning with her head that she was leaving. As she grabbed her satchel and the cards, Florence followed. Uncle Brammie held the door open at the top of the stairs, and they escaped.

❧

Early fall rain fell at a steady pace as they entered the Thatched House Chambers, the men's club next door to Mark Mason's Hall, the Golden Dawn headquarters.

In the doorway, Pamela asked, "Women are allowed?"

"I am welcome to bring 'discreet' guests to the private dining room," Uncle Brammie answered, "as long as they are not actresses."

Florence snorted. "According to your employer, Henry Irving, I'm not an actress as he has never hired me."

Bram's jaw tightened. As long as Miss Terry was the leading lady at the Lyceum Theatre, no others were necessary, unless they were understudies.

As they followed Uncle Brammie to the private dining room, she noticed how his chin jutted out defensively. He must feel pressure to take care of everyone. Even her. At least the job of creating these tarot cards had given her some independence away from the theatre payroll. Especially since she was told that her aspiration to be on the creative staff for the Lyceum Theatre was "against the rules," as they didn't hire women set designers.

The dining room was almost empty, populated only by two older gentlemen lingering over their lunch. The alcove where they sat was snug, and the French doors were left open to the common room. A glass of Scotch was immediately placed at Bram's elbow and two glasses of wine for the ladies. *How often has he been coming here to have this standing order?* As Florence took out her cigarettes, a small card fell on the table. Pamela picked it up. On the back was tacked a small piece of silk painted with a butterfly. Florence tugged the fabric off the card and gave it to Pamela.

"Do you collect cigarette silks, Miss Smith?" Florence asked.

It was not big enough for a handkerchief and too square for a ribbon. The butterfly was exquisitely painted.

"I will now," Pamela answered, taking the silk.

She folded it in half so both wings were visible and tucked it into her hair. She felt them beat against her head. Had Florence given her a familiar, a spirit to watch over her? Or was this Pamela's own magic? She couldn't tell, but it was comforting.

Uncle Brammie lit Florence's cigarette.

Pamela relaxed and took a drink of her wine. Now that Uncle Brammie wasn't being badgered for a job, it was nice to see him bring some of his Irish charm to Florence.

As she exhaled smoke, Florence said, "Well, that meeting was a right-up collie shangles, wasn't it?"

"The chiefs are unlikely to cast a spell of protection for the cards just yet," Uncle Brammie replied. "They'll want to see proof the cards have magic first."

Pamela drew a deep breath. "The chiefs will ignore my complaint because Aleister is with the Carlists? And what is a Carlist? Does this mean that Aleister is working for the Secret Service? Who is he?"

Florence replied, "One question at a time, Miss Smith."

"Ah, Pixie," Uncle Brammie said, "Mr. Crowley's identities are a dog's lunch."

Florence grimaced. "Yes, he claims to be many things: Trinity University graduate, an officer of the Crown in the Cadet Corps, lead rebel against religion, Alan Bennett's magician, and ceremonial master of Templar Knights."

"How do you know so much about him?" Uncle Brammie asked and then downed the last of his drink.

"You forget, Mr. Stoker," Florence said, "I was on the committee to interview Mr. Crowley for his Golden Dawn membership. But he didn't disclose then that he was a Carlist."

"What is a Carlist?" Pamela asked. "What were the explosives Yeats was talking about?" She touched the butterfly wings throbbing against her head.

Florence looked up at the ceiling as though recalling a history lesson. "The current duke of Madrid claims he should be king of Spain. To most he is called the pretender to the throne. But his uncle, Don Carlos, has supporters, these Carlists, who are forming assassination squads to ensure his seat."

"Don Carlos would kill to have his nephew on the throne?" Pamela asked. "Who is this nephew?"

"Jaime de Borbón," Uncle Brammie answered.

The pretender to the Spanish throne at Felkin's party.

Pamela's mouth dropped open. "I met him at Dr. Felkin's, the pretender to the throne. Who are they going to kill?"

Florence answered, "Carlists don't believe women should be on the throne anywhere. Not even Queen Victoria. They want to set an example of purging. These explosives are part of Lord Bertram's plot to assassinate her, it is said."

"Assassinate the Queen?" Pamela asked in a hoarse whisper. "Who is Lord Bertram?"

Florence tilted her head and looked at Bram, who averted his gaze out the window. "Pamela, Lord Bertram is Earl Ashburnham."

Earl Ashburnham. The patron who was donating the mummies to Ahmed. The man with the pretender to the throne.

"How is killing Queen Victoria going to procure the pretender's Spanish throne?" Pamela asked.

Uncle Brammie cleared his throat, making sure no one was near the private dining room. "Carlists believe the recent queen, Maria Christina, regent while her son was underage, destroyed the Spanish empire. Others feel Queen Victoria in her dotage is on the same course to give away the British Empire. Last year, to end the Spanish–American war, Maria Christina signed the Treaty of Paris, giving up Spain's claims to Puerto Rico, Guam, and Cuba."

Were you born in Cuba? The question Borbón had asked her at Felkin's. He couldn't tell the difference between Jamaica and Cuba. This continental man had obviously never been to either Caribbean country.

"So, Carlists don't believe women should rule?" Pamela asked.

"That's an understatement," Florence said.

Uncle Brammie leaned across the table. "After that night at Felkin's when I saw de Borbón and Lord Bertram talking with you, I had to find out their connection to Mr. Crowley. Carlist recruits are training in military maneuvers at Betram's estate in Wales. Crowley is one of them. Black magic and machine guns, a terrible combination."

The waiter swaggered up to the table. Uncle Brammie made a circle with his hand to indicate drinks needed to be refreshed. "Three kidney pies," he ordered.

Once the waiter left, Pamela asked, "But why would Aleister be in with the pretender to the Spanish Throne?"

"To recruit a following to get rid of Queen Victoria," Uncle Brammie answered.

"And Prince Edward would be king?" Pamela asked.

"There is talk of placing Prince Rupprecht, son of Maria Theresa of Austria, on the throne. He is rumored to be a Carlist and would reward those who would crown him," Bram finished.

"Aleister is part of a plot to kill the Queen? Is this why he wants my tarot cards?" Pamela whispered as the butterfly silk rustled.

"We believe he is," Florence answered. "The question is, Miss Smith, what do your tarot cards do that would help him?"

"I don't know," Pamela said, her palms itching.

Uncle Brammie stared across the table at Florence's earrings.

"Since becoming her High Priestess, Miss Farr, have you felt any special powers?"

He had been told Florence was the High Priestess right after the evening at Miss Horniman's. But like Edy, he would be furious if he knew Ellen Terry was the Empress. Pamela would get around to telling him that later.

Florence half-closed her eyes. "Mr. Stoker, have you discussed the power of being a muse with Mr. Irving or Mr. Terriss? Or am I special?"

The stillness between them was broken as the waiter came and placed steaming pies in front of them, closing the doors as he left.

"Eat, please," Uncle Brammie said.

Pamela shivered and felt her satchel next to her vibrate. Now her cards were responding. She took the four cards out of her bag. Maybe they just wanted to join the trio for lunch. She laid them out on the table in order: Fool, Magician, High Priestess, and Empress. An ultramarine violet mist boiled underneath the surface of the cards. The cards began to rotate on their own.

She watched the cards spin until they were upside-down.

Uncle Brammie and Florence ate, watching her nonchalantly.

Florence asked, "What are you seeing?"

"Reverse positions."

Uncle Brammie put his fork down. "What does that mean?"

"They don't want their powers to be used for a cause," she said.

"Any cause? Or they don't like Aleister being in with the Carlists?" Uncle Brammie asked.

"I don't know. Reversals take a lot into consideration," Pamela answered, her voice edging higher.

"Pamela, you do see we are talking about a plot to kill the Queen," Uncle Brammie said.

She picked up her cards and put them back in the satchel. Turning to Florence, she said, "Instead of pledging to protect me from Aleister's magic, the only thing the Golden Dawn chiefs did was insult me."

Uncle Brammie sputtered, "Pixie, we know some are—"

Pamela gathered her coat and satchel and stood. "If the Golden Dawn chiefs won't protect me from Aleister, my cards will. They are telling me that they will not be used for the Golden Dawn's war or the Carlists' killing."

Uncle Brammie reached out to hold her hand. "We'll protect you, Pixie. It's what we've pledged to do."

"But Aleister killed that man on the dock, and the Golden Dawn does nothing!"

The heads of the two men at the other table in the other room heard them and turned their way. Pamela lowered her voice and tried to steady herself, one hand on the table.

"Aleister was behind Dr. Felkin poisoning Ellen, and I don't know what he could do to the both of you. Even if I wanted to give you readings on the Carlists or Aleister, my cards are refusing to cooperate."

Florence smoothed a stray curl around Pamela's pinned butterfly. "What can we do to help?"

"Tell the Golden Dawn chiefs to do their job protecting their members. And tell Miss Horniman I expect additional hazard pay to continue," Pamela said as she struggled with her coat. Uncle Brammie stood, taking the coat and holding it out. She backed up and jerked her arms through the sleeves.

She turned to the table. "The cards' power belongs to me and my muses. Not to men playing king maker."

Pamela swung her satchel over her arm, the butterfly silk fluttering in her hair as she strode out.

CHAPTER TWENTY-ONE

Skyring Spies

A s the newly elected president, Florence had vowed to learn all the magic that had been previously denied to her in the Golden Dawn. Yet she couldn't help but feel nervous as she and Yeats arrived at Annie Horniman's family home, a stately pile of bricks with few windows.

Florence shifted her heavy satchel to one hand and with the other lifted the doorknocker shaped as a large, reptilian claw. As it hit against the door, a small panel slid open, causing a green speckled eye to pop out and roll into the gnarled claw's center. It glared at Florence and Yeats.

"Not the warmest welcome," Florence said to Yeats, who lowered his glasses, the lenses frosting in the chilly autumn air. He was shorter than William Terriss but taller than Ahmed, a superficial quality she couldn't help but be attracted to.

"Agate's stone," he said, smoothing his mustache.

A maid opened the door and ushered them inside. Florence saw from the foyer that the hallway was chock-full of side tables, bureaus, and curiosity cabinets. Every surface was crowded with grouped artifacts. How could anyone live in all this clutter, antique or not?

"I'm Florence Farr, this is Mr. Yeats. Is Miss Horniman at home?" Florence asked.

"Miss Horniman doesn't live at Surrey Mount anymore. She left instructions for your access to the basement. I'll show you the way," the maid answered, turning to lead the way.

"This is no longer Miss Horniman's home?" Florence asked the scurrying back of the maid.

"No, miss," she replied, not stopping. "They're turning this into a museum."

"Ah, short trip—" Florence said to herself.

"Miss Horniman said there is . . . a piece of furniture down-stairs for us?" Yeats interrupted.

"Yes, there is a 'thing' down there. She said I was to keep away from you while you were using it," the maid said, squeez-ing by an oversized table almost blocking the hallway.

Several crowded corridors later, they reached an incon-spicuous door set into the floor. Opening it, they smelled a dank odor coming up from dark stairs. After peering into a hamper on the top stair, the maid picked up two candles, lit them, and handed one to Florence. Then they started down the wooden stairs.

As Florence trailed the maid, she noticed the young girl trembled. At the bottom of the steps, they reached a damp, close room haunted by the faint odors of coal, rotting vegetables, and sulfur. Squinting into the corners, Florence made out stacks of chairs, rugs, and settees haphazardly against the wall.

In the middle of the dirt floor stood the six-foot-tall wooden Vault from the Golden Dawn Headquarters. Its black varnish glimmering in the candlelight. Seven walls were cov-ered in symbols: Egyptian letters, an eagle's head, snakes, two trapezoids, tattva cards, Hindu symbols. When Florence patted the side of the structure, a thunking echo answered. The maid made the sign of the cross, cupped her candle, and raced back up the stairs.

Setting her candle on the ground, Florence then stripped off her gloves. "We'll see if we can't protect Pamela from here."

Yeats wrapped his scarf tighter around his neck. "Does Miss Smith know we'll be communicating through astral travel, not skyring?"

When skyring, one was limited to only seeing an image in a different location. There was no interaction with the location's inhabitants. In astral travel, the adept's body could transform into the parallel dimension. You could touch objects, travel at will, perform ceremonies, and interact with other astral entities.

"The idea is to use the tattva cards to astral travel," Florence replied.

Astral travel was essential today. The Golden Dawn was divided into two groups: the French faction with Mathers and the doctors, and the London base with Yeats and Waite. Rumors of Carlists and assassination plots within the group had to be cleared up. If today's attempt was successful, she and Yeats would be able to astral travel and interact anywhere.

"Mr. Yeats," Florence continued, "our promise to guard Miss Smith is the only reason she is continuing with the tarot cards. You can hardly blame her."

Yeats blinked and coughed—not the most robust specimen of mankind. Her attraction to him dipped. Florence took out a battered old book and a stack of cards.

"Smells like cat piss in here," Yeats spat.

They approached the Vault and looked up. The door seam was flush with the sides and hard to make out—only a skilled magician would know how to open it.

The Vault had been moved from headquarters and reassembled here in Forest Hill after Aleister had transformed into the beast, Baphomet. There was much discussion as to whether he'd used the Vault as a portal to fly away that evening of the confrontation. And on the bridge when he met Pamela, was that astral travel or something else? Where did he find the magical resources to perform that neat trick? One thing Florence knew, Aleister would do anything to find this Vault again.

She slid a hand along the underside, finding the hidden bolt. It snapped the main panel open. Inside, there was barely enough room for two people to sit.

"Mr. Yeats, shall we start?" Florence asked, opening *The Flying Rolls.* It was the most coveted of the Golden Dawn's grimoires, the ultimate medieval book of spells. This book was only available to the six chiefs who had completed the top levels of study.

Yeats stood close to her and put his face inches away from her.

"My consciousness and desire are one," Yeats said, brushing back his floppy hair away from his face.

"Excellent," Florence said, trying not to smile. His words were borrowed from a spell in *The Flying Rolls.*

Yeats moved nearer, his breath forming clouds in the cold air, and took her hands. Florence's body felt an electric shock go through her, to her surprise.

"Despite and also because of the stench here," Yeats said, "I look forward to astral travel."

Florence gently shook off his hands. How could she be drawn to this womanish Irish poet? He certainly didn't have the virility of Ahmed or the dynamic appeal of the actor William Terriss.

She and Yeats had both experienced skyring as part of their Golden Dawn studies. Florence's last skyring session took her to the inner sanctum of the British Museum to visit Mutemmenu, where the mummy spirit teased her that Ahmed was becoming very fond of her. Across the centuries, the tormenting others over lovers remains the same.

Florence heard the rumors that Yeats's skyring had led him to Paris, where he'd observed the beautiful Maud Gonne at the cemetery in Samois-sur-Seine. Unfortunately, this trip happened when Maud was seducing her current lover next to her baby son's coffin. Yeats could only be a helpless spectator. He watched her make love to the Frenchman as she was trying to reincarnate her dead son. When he told this tale to Florence it made her wonder if he was trying to learn how to astral travel to protect Pamela or to spy on Maud again.

Florence stepped inside the Vault, put the candle in front of her, and spread the stack of tattva cards on the floor. The tattva cards were designed to break down the Hindu concept of Solar Prana, the electrical current from the creation of the universe.

Once they were splayed out to her satisfaction, Florence sat cross-legged and adjusted *The Flying Rolls* in her lap. Yeats plopped down across from her. The squiggles on the tattva cards were barely visible in the dim light. Yeats leaned over to study them as Florence began to read the spell out loud.

"Consciousness of being is the name we give to—" Florence couldn't make out the next word.

Yeats glanced at the book, "I remember when we first used these tattva cards to skyr. Do you think they have the power for the next level of astral travel?" He picked up a crescent moon tattva card.

"Yes," Florence answered, spreading her skirt out to sit more comfortably. "They've been a good jumping-off point for transporting ourselves. If we use all five elements in the next spell, we should be able to interact once we arrive."

"I've found these cards basic and limited in what they access," Yeats replied.

"True, they pale in comparison to what Miss Smith's tarot cards will do once her deck is complete. But she meets with Waite today, and I promised we would be present to protect her."

"Protect her from Waite's incompetence or Crowley's wrath?" Yeats asked.

"Both," Florence answered. "If I only knew how Crowley finds her."

"Her fear calls him," Yeats said. "He senses her fear and is able to track her from her vibrations."

Florence's mouth dropped open. Of course. Why hadn't she thought of that?

"Which is why we need to keep her from being afraid," Florence said.

"Agreed," Yeats said. "What's our first step?"

"Our first step should be to interact with the forces around Pamela. But without them having the knowledge that we are in their environment." She scooped up the tattva cards and began to shuffle them.

Yeats smiled. "Silent skrying, then."

Florence held out the deck of cards and Yeats drew a card. The moon card.

Yeats dropped his smile. "Och. The moon card. All that is submerged. This device surely conjures up strong magic."

"Place the card in front of you," Florence replied. "We must own our magic by participating in other's lives for good, not for our own means. Crowley and the Carlists want to steal the tarot cards' magic, but they don't know their power."

"What do you think her cards' powers will be?"

"They will open up a portal for transformation and comprehension, creating a compulsion to belong, to obey. The Carlists could use this compulsion to dominate."

Yeats's mouth twisted. "Crowley's cult won't be able to steal Pamela's magic. Only she knows how to get to the pools of magic to create them. They won't know her language. And you can't create a cult without a special language."

"True. What is your card?" Yeats asked.

Florence set down the open book of spells and reached for a card in the pile. "Ah, Vayu, the air card."

She felt her stomach lurch. Both had spent the early hours of the day fasting for this ritual in the Vault. Adrenaline shot through her like icy fire.

Pointing out a line, Florence murmured, "We concentrate on our essence, fused in the still of the mind—"

Yeats began to hum. He lifted his head and looked at her with lowered lids. He began to croon:

"Come near, come near, come near—ah, leave me still

A little space for the rose-breath to fill!"

A sweet puff of rose scent enveloped her. Ah, he was using his magic to lure her. It would have to wait for another time. Placing her hand on his arm, she said, "William, try to focus. If we are to graduate from skyring, it will take absolute concentration."

Yeats shook his head. "I can't focus. I am distracted."

"To focus," Florence read, "thought has to be the same effect as sunlight. In this fire, a master raises his consciousness until it separates from his gross body."

A deep inhalation from Yeats resounded as he threw the moon card away. "This moon card is useless."

"Pick another," Florence said.

Blinking, he reached into the pile of cards. Akasha, the black egg, the spirit card, appeared in his hand. He smiled.

Florence laughed. Of course. Fertility and death in the same card. She called Akasha the tattva sex card.

Yeats blushed. "You see why I cannot focus. You are mesmerizing."

It would take so little to seduce him now. *Back to business.*

"Concentrate on astral travel," she said. "One must visualize the head as a globelike center, from which rays of thought radiate."

Closing her eyes, she filled her lungs with breath. Darkness sank inside her head, making her mind heavy. A blue orb began to form. Sideways inside her head, slices of light peaked in and pulsed. Even with her eyes closed, she could feel the panels of light seeping out of her brain.

"Now let us open our eyes and use the tattva to bring us to a state of energy," she said, opening her eyes. Waves of blue washed over her; the color felt cool. Blue, the color of her tattva card, spooling out, spilling inside her skull. A flash stilled the color.

Yeats grunted. "Ah, yes. I feel it, the black flash of my egg card. I'm ready."

Florence chanted, "See the symbol as a doorway. See the shape call to you as you visualize floating into the parallel dimension."

A blue circle throbbed on the floor between them until it was crawling up the side of the Vault, ebbing in and out. It dissolved from a compact, deep blue to a light, airy hue. Florence slowed her breathing to keep time with the beats of the orb's pulsing.

"We are a glowing ball of compacted force," Florence chanted. "Project outwards!" Florence shouted, closing her eyes as a rushing sound took over.

Vapor was drifting from the top of her head, a trail circling over to William. More vapors streamed out of the Vault's wall, the rushing sound becoming a roar. With a blast, the Vault blew wide open, extinguishing the candle. Sound and color dissipated.

The Vault was gone. A coil of smoke remained, oozing through space until it wrapped around Florence and Yeats and jerked them forward in the dank basement. They were hurled up the chimney. Off they went, up out of the room, traveling up out into the heavens.

Everything went black. She was outside, freezing. Why had she taken off her coat? Yeats was not there. *Off reciting poetry to Maud no doubt.*

She floated down the street to Mark Mason Hall on the corner. She drifted inside and down the headquarters' hallways until she found the library.

Ah, there they were, Pamela and Edward Waite at a table. She hovered over Waite, sitting across from Pamela. He shivered and looked up. She drifted higher to the ceiling. Waite followed her every move but said nothing.

She remained a ghostlike shadow, softly floating upwards.

❧

Would Waite never get to his point?

Pamela slumped over a drawing desk, chin in her hand. These weekly meetings were maddening. It was as though she were a maid, receiving her list of chores. All these damn rules. Rules ruined art school, her parent's church, and her future as a Lyceum Theatre designer.

Waite was droning on about the placement of the Fool card in other decks when Pamela felt a cooling hand on her neck. She sat straight up. Florence. She'd said she would be here. Was she here as an astral projection?

Waite's head jerked back and forth; he was also sensing something unfamiliar in the room.

Seeing Waite's alarm, she decided to distract him. "Mr. Waite, why do you insist on all these symbols? Aren't there too many?"

She peeked around to see if she could see Florence in the reflection of the bookcases' glass. Nothing. Perhaps Florence's appearance only meant a tactile presence.

Pamela continued, "Astrology, astronomy, hieroglyphs? Are our cards a curated heap of Judaic, Islamic, Hindi, and Christian symbols? Most people don't know anything about these different cultures and religions. How are regular people supposed to read these?" she asked, rubbing her cold neck.

"Really, Miss Smith, if you want the respect of the Golden Dawn, you must apply yourself to the first studies. To understand international symbols is paramount," Waite said, standing in front of her.

He was every history teacher she ever had. Their version of interpreting the past was the only view. The past that belonged to them, the men of classical studies.

As he droned on, she sighed and stretched, extending her feet in front of her and wiggling them. One foot was sound asleep, but now electric currents raced up her leg. She tried to reach down to the floor to knead it away. Blast it, these chairs were always too high.

"So, excuse me, Mr. Waite . . . ow, ow, ow. My foot. Wake up!" She playfully hit her foot, Waite looking on with dour exasperation.

She heard a soft, feminine laugh above her. She scanned the ceiling, seeing nothing unusual.

"You want people to study these tarot symbols, but they won't understand or recognize them," Pamela said. "I thought the directive was that each card was to have simple symbols, accessible across cultures. Oh! This foot! How will the common person recognize Egyptian symbols, Roman letters, Hebrew phrases? Not everyone has had a classical education."

Waite blew air out through his lips. "It is no concern to us if the common people do not recognize our symbols. The elite people of learning will. There is a group I am part of outside the Golden Dawn who may be able to introduce them worldwide."

Florence floated down near Pamela's ear and whispered, "Carlists?"

Pamela was ready for Florence's voice and didn't flinch. "But won't the cards become a tower of Babel?" she asked.

"Not to those of us who study them. There is a great need for the language of these cards."

"But who will need them, Mr. Waite? The Carlists?" Pamela cried.

Waite sat down next to Pamela—too close, but then he was never good at personal space boundaries. Pamela could smell alcohol on his breath. *Tap tap tap.* That tiresome sound. A cobbler pounding nails? Boot nobs hitting pavement?

"Ah, Miss Smith, you've heard about the Carlists. Can you imagine the loyalties these images might inspire? If we were to understand them, we would have access to all the languages in the world." He took Pamela's hands in his. "Miss Smith, our

symbols will have a common root and a common end—a path
to the divine illumination."

Pamela removed his gummy hands. "And what happens
with this illumination?"

"We can determine who should rightfully guide and rule,"
Waite answered, his shabby mustache twitching.

"So, our cards will allow people to become superhuman,
godlike persons?"

Waite stood and paced. "Let us just imagine, Miss Smith,
that an unformed person encounters the Magician or the High
Priestess. What would you say happens?"

Pamela looked up and finally saw Florence floating on the
ceiling. Florence held a finger to her lips, drifting lazily in the
air, her linen skirt edged by her lace petticoat.

Pamela tucked her head down. "Well, if they encounter the
High Priestess, they must answer for their actions if they want
to be led past her veiled curtain," Pamela answered.

"You see magic as a test?" Waite asked.

Pamela sighed. She had body magic, not this schooling of
formulas and math angles.

Waite stood before her. "You know, Miss Smith, I am not
so different from you."

"How is that, Mr. Waite?"

"Well, I, too, come from American parents. I was born in
Brooklyn; I know your grandfather was the mayor there."

"Yes, but you only want to be English. You are the most
English person I have ever known."

As he stared at her, she saw it then, a burst, an image, a
mirage. Her second sight: Waite's mother thrown out of the
family house, an unmarried mother. Two children, a missing
paper. Marriage license? Death certificate? The vision burned
bright and then disappeared. Now she understood why this man
burned to be in charge. His dark, brown eyes trained on her as
he ran a hand through his gray flyaway hair.

"I ask—is there one myth assigned for each person? A single tale tailored for each of us," Waite said. "Would a singular myth for all of us make us understand one another?"

She looked up. Florence was reclining in a pose as though she were laying on a couch. The tapping sound stopped. A moan.

In front of Pamela's desk, a small whirlwind of dark dust picked up. It twirled low to the floor, a miniature storm. It gathered in strength around her left foot, making it tingle. She shot straight up in her chair as the tingle turned into a sharp pain.

In one quick move, Pamela was upside down in the air, hanging by her left foot. Waite's watery blue eyes widened behind his glasses, his mouth open as he looked up. She was in the hangman's pose, hanging from the chandelier. It was the pose in her sketchbook on the desk.

The moaning sounds grew louder, then slowed to a stop. Pamela was released from her upside-down pose and fell, landing in a heap on her head. Waite helped her stand up as the dust tunnel continued to spiral. On the back of Pamela's head, she could feel a bump forming.

The whirlwind swirled up from the floor to overtake Florence, still floating near the ceiling. Once it covered her, she was thrown from wall to wall. The moan grew louder with every collision. Pamela flinched each time Florence hit the wall, and she tried to jump up to shoo away the dust storm, unable to make any difference.

Waite climbed on the nearest chair, feeling the rushing energy with both hands. "Stop, desist, you spirit, I command you!"

A black egg appeared on the ceiling, following Florence as she was catapulted about. It planted itself on the side wall, just before Florence's translucent body was thrown against it. Pamela watched as Florence grabbed the egg and held on to it. The egg floated to the chandelier, towing Florence behind it. As they stabilized, the black egg disappeared. Florence panted as she held onto the chandelier. Yeats materialized next to her.

Pamela looked at Waite; he was tracking the diminishing swirls of dust, unable to see either of them.

A strong scent filled the room: burning steel, cat urine, and an acrid herb melded together. The last time Aleister had made an appearance in the Vault, that smell appeared first. Pamela tried to keep her hands from shaking.

The flying dust mass slowed midair, twisting into a towering stack of back motes. It stilled and dropped into a huge charcoal statue that formed two feet above Pamela and Waite in the air.

It was Baphomet, the horned goat devil. Two golden goat eyes glowed, and its claws motioned, snapping something in half. The sound of a dog's yelps filled the room.

Aleister's face appeared in the darkened mist, goat eyes glowing, a cruel mix of boyish beauty and beast. Waite clutched his heart. So, he could see the beast.

"Miss Smith," Aleister said, "your ecstatic Fool is ridiculous. The Fool is a divine madman."

Waite opened his mouth to speak.

Aleister's mouth opened, and his green twisted teeth formed a sneer. "Not one word, Waite. You await instructions, not give opinions."

Waite screeched as his hand flew to his mouth. His lips were blistering as though burnt.

Aleister's face distorted in waves. "My warnings have no effect. The magic you purloin is not yours for the taking. We all must make sacrifices."

With a rush, Florence and Yeats streaked down from the chandelier and put their hands into the spiral. A roar like a railway engine erupted. Aleister twisted around, whirling in between the desks and chairs. Pamela stood in front of Waite, holding her hand out as though she could fend Aleister off. She felt Florence and Waite shielding them from flying debris.

The goat devil fell apart inside the dust cyclone, a few strands swirled and then disappeared. When Pamela was able to move, her feet felt as though they were stabbed with a hundred needles. Waite stood next to her, bug-eyed, pale, and swaying.

Florence and Yeats were nowhere to be seen. The sound of a dog's bark, then a whimper. A man crying out. No, not a man, Henry Irving, her Magician. The dog's moaning ebbed away.

"Fussie!" Pamela cried.

CHAPTER TWENTY-TWO

THE LAST HAM

~⟋⟍~

Pamela's legs felt wooden and slow as she tried to run to Grafton, where she knew Mr. Irving had his local apartment. As she waded past Piccadilly, the impossible traffic of electric cars, buggies, carriages, and wagons made crossing the street of frozen mud a nightmare.

This is a bloody nightmare. Where are the street sparrows?

Just then, a ragamuffin of a boy, smudged with dirt and holding the newspapers for the day, approached her.

"Cross the street, miss? A farthing to cross?"

She fumbled in her coin purse, then held the farthing out for the anxious hand. Once secured, a sheet of newspaper was draped across the boy's arm, and he motioned for Pamela to place her hand on the paper. They ventured out into the stream of traffic.

The boy's soft voice turned into an enormous Cockney roar.

"Watch it there, mister, I've a real lady here! Crossing! Crossing, no doubt about it. Hey! Hold your horses, we're down here!"

Oaths and curses railed down on the pair from coaches and buses as they weaved between them. Some wagons slowed down, other riders sped up, and one carriage with passengers sitting on top seemed to topple right on them. The sounds of Fussie's whimpering in her ear, Pamela screamed in terror as a horse reared up right in front of them. Only the boy's persistent grasp kept the two of them together, dodging vehicles right and left.

Once they made it to the other side, the boy took an already blackened rag from his pocket, found the one with a clean spot left, and wiped the newspaper ink off of Pamela's begrimed hand.

"There ya go, miss. Watch yourself."

And with that, the boy threw himself back into the sea of blasting horns, whistles, and shouts, disappearing into the powdery air.

She ran on, the heaviness of her coat and the wool skirt weighing her down.

Please let the vision be a mistake!

On Grafton street, she found Uncle Brammie, her red-haired giant, standing outside Henry's apartment with Ellen holding Mussie in her arms. The dog was looking up at his mistress with a concerned expression, his head tilted, one ear bent.

"Is he dead? Did Fussie die?" Pamela asked.

"Yes, Henry's devastated. Pixie, how did you know?" Ellen said.

Pamela grabbed on to Mussie's sweet muzzle, smelling the wonderful scent, half Ellen's perfume, half luncheon meat. Tears sprang in Pamela's eyes. "How did it happen? Who did it?"

Uncle Brammie took Pamela's hand. "It was an accident at the theatre. A stagehand left his lunch in a coat next to an open trap door to the pit. Wouldn't you know there was a ham sandwich—and, you know Fussie and ham. He nudged it along the stage until he fell into the pit."

"Oh! No! Who was the stagehand? Did you know him?" Pamela cried.

"It was just one of the crew," Uncle Brammie said, fumbling in his pocket.

It was Aleister. He warned me he would hurt those around me.

"Henry brought Fussie's body back here," Uncle Brammie said.

Ellen blinked back tears. "He doesn't believe Fussie's dead."

The front door was unlocked, and the two women clutched one another as they followed Uncle Brammie to the second-floor landing, Mussie panting behind them. A soft murmuring was heard inside.

Uncle Brammie knocked softly. "Henry, it's Bram here. We've come to check on you." He turned the key in the lock and opened the door. Mussie bolted forward and charged into the room.

Henry was seated at his table; in front of him his preshow dinner sat half-eaten. On the fur rug in front of the fireplace, Fussie's body was curled in what could have been a sleeping pose, the large clover print on his forehead motionless.

Mussie's tail drooped as he slowly approached Fussie's body. Once he was next to him, he frantically began sniffing him from head to tail.

"I was just explaining to Fussie here that he has had his share of meats today and that he won't be having any of cook's excellent beef tonight," Henry said, reaching for his wine.

Nor nevermore, thought Pamela.

Ellen took off her coat and threw it on a chair. She sat on the rug next to both dogs. Mussie curled up beside her, while the still form of the other dog lay before her as an altar. Gently, Ellen began to pet the prone creature.

"Oh, that's a good boy, Fussie. Are you tired? Did you have a long day?"

Henry, downing some of his wine, added, "I should say he did. Always into trouble, this one. Thank goodness he has common sense and knows when to come to his master."

Uncle Brammie and Pamela were still standing near the doorway, blinking. Uncle Brammie moved slowly toward the fireplace, looked into the small fire, and sighed, while Pamela sat on the other side of Fussie's body. Keeping one hand on Fussie, she petted Mussie with the other, who was whining quietly.

Touching the white fur of both dogs, one living and one dead, she felt the difference in energy between them. One restless dog and one stilled. Ah, the little brown mark around Mussie's eye, his head now resting in her hand, nervously licking his chops. What spoiled and clever dogs they both were. In the late hours of rehearsal, when the cast would be onstage at three or four in the morning, the management would call for a tea break "by means of Fussie." The little dog with the cloverleaf mark on his face would run onstage with the handle of the tea bell firmly in his mouth, bell ringing as he ran. Joyously jumbling at every stop he made. Making his rounds from person to person, he would take their glee seeing him as his own triumph. A common grumble amongst the company was to wish for "Fussie Hour."

Mussie stopped whining, let out a large sigh, and rolled on his back, his paws touching the side of his departed brother. It was quiet in the room as creatures and humans alike paused.

Images of Pamela's pony, her baby alligator, and theatre cat flashed before her. She had never really had a pet of her own, except Albert, who died young and was stuffed when she was twelve. And now, Fussie, the white dog leaping up next to the Fool in her very first tarot card, was dead. The white spirit that would come out of nowhere to take chances. The adventurous companion leaping into the void. A gift to Henry from Ellen, all those years ago when it seemed that she and Henry were off to live separate lives.

Ellen was very still murmuring quiet endearments to the silent dog.

Uncle Brammie walked over to sit in the other chair at the table. "Mr. Irving, why do you think that Fussie loves ham so? Is it as Lovejoy says, from listening to your Hamlet all these years?"

Ellen looked up from the rug, smiling off her tears. "Why, surely not, Ma!"

Pamela looked at Henry, still cradling his wine as Ellen continued to stroke Fussie's face.

Henry grunted. "No . . . no . . . he was our little ham because of Lovejoy's pronunciation. Ah, Fussie. He was a glory fest reveling in his own dogginess. He had no interest in being a good company member, he was an amateur. Or as Lovejoy says—"

"An 'am," the trio responded.

Mussie's head snapped straight up. Henry stopped eating, rose, and positioned himself to sit among the two women and dogs, petting his still dog's head, while the other dog's tail beat a cautious rhythm.

Henry's voice was now very deep and resonant as he lowered himself to sit next to Fussie.

"Yes, Ham. Our little piggy one."

There was silence as they watched his long, slender fingers caress the silky dog ears and stroke the whiskers around his nose. Henry took off his glasses as tears began to slide off his beautiful hawk nose. Large, silent tears, dripping onto the fur beneath his hands.

"Poor pig. Poor greedy one. Never enough ham, was there?"

Pamela and Ellen held their breath as they watched his eyes move toward the fireplace, a small flame wavering in the hearth. Only Pamela could see the dip of her initials—PCS—on Henry's lower earlobe.

Henry laid down, one hand caressing Mussie's twitching ears, the other patting the body of Fussie.

Aleister did this, open trap door or not.

"Fussie. What's the fuss all about?" Henry murmured.

Keep my Magician safe. Keep his tools his own.

Mussie crawled over to Henry's side on all fours, as though he were a penitent before a king. Gently Mussie began to lick the salty tears off Henry's hands. The calm sounds of licking, his coarse tongue scouring off tears, filled the room.

Pamela would have to unite her tarot muses as soon as possible.

That night the repertoire at the Lyceum was *Peter the Great.* Would Henry be in his dressing room for his typical one-hour makeup and preshow rituals? Everyone, from Gilbert, guarding the backstage door, to Lovejoy, the stage manager, was anxious. Would Henry arrive? Usually, the clicking of Fussie's nails along the backstage entry hall was the first sign warning wardrobe that Henry was there.

Ellen got flowers for his dressing room, or rather her new secretary, Christopher, bought the flowers. Pamela rearranged them and handed them to Ellen to place inside his dressing room. Uncle Brammie and the three women hid around the corner to monitor his arrival.

The silent stage door to the street opened, and the tall, gangly form of Henry Irving made his way down hallways and then upstairs to Walter, his dresser. Pamela stepped out into the hallway and peered through the partially opened door.

Henry entered his dressing room and stopped in front of Fussie's elaborate dog bed still next to the dressing table. Wouldn't you know they had forgotten to remove it, and Walter hadn't seen it either.

Before Walter could remove it, a squat shadow streaked under Pamela's feet and flew down the hallway. It stopped at Henry's door and padded into the room. It was the fat wardrobe cat, Tybalt. He was a huge ginger cat with a black fur patch over his left eye. Tybalt had never before dared to enter the great man's inner sanctum. But now, Pamela spied the pudgy cat leap up into the dog bed, sniff the soft blanket, turn in three circles, and throw himself down into a plump furry circle.

Walter held his breath. Pamela looked back at Ellen, Uncle Brammie and Christopher plastered against the hallway trying to see in. Their expressions would have been hilarious if the circumstances weren't so tragic. Pamela turned back to see Henry hold out his hand. Tybalt's purr, like a hundred complacent bees, starting humming, and could be heard even by Pamela, as long swathes of the cat's tongue bathed Henry's hand.

Henry caught Walter's eye, turned away quickly, and gruffly ordered, "Well, you'd better go out and get this cat some meat."

Once Walter was outside in the hallway, Ellen, Uncle Brammie, and Pamela scampered down the hall. Walter mimed wiping his brow in relief as he passed them silently huddled in Ellen's dressing room door. Uncle Brammie and Christopher followed Walter down the hall, and Ellen shut herself in with Pamela.

"It's one thing when they try to poison me; it's another when our pets are targeted," Ellen said.

Pamela looked up and saw that beneath the woven edges of her wig, Ellen's earlobes were visible: PCS faintly appeared in white veinlike lines.

Ellen's light eyes no longer sparkled. "Your black magician targeted Fussie, didn't he?"

Pamela held both of Ellen's hands. "Yes, but I will make a spell to protect everyone."

CHAPTER TWENTY-THREE

QUEEN NOT EMPRESS

~~❧~~

Aleister looked out over the Thames as the sailing yacht floated up against the Pelican Stairs landing. He could barely make out the *Firefly*'s gold lettering sparkling on the bow in the dimming light. Golden Dawn Chief Samuel Mathers stood up in the prow and waved a white handkerchief; Aleister waved back from the deck high alongside the riverbank.

From the upper street level of Wapping Wall, the sight of the handkerchief brought a burst of applause from men gathered around the Prospect of Whitby pub. Oaths and joking reverberated as they jostled down the stairway, but with a whistled reprimand from Mathers, they lined up quietly at the landing. A bucket brigade of boxes started from the yacht, and the boxes made their way up the steep steps to the pub's storeroom.

As the shipment unloaded, Aleister mingled with a well-dressed Frenchmen and an older, austere-looking Spaniard near the pub's entrance.

"Is the earl of Glenstrae coming with us?" the Frenchmen asked.

"Who is earl of Glenstrae?" Aleister asked.

Francoise gestured to the boat.

"Mathers told you he was an earl?" Aleister snorted. "In his mind only. He's a clerk."

"But this owner of the *Firefly* is an earl?" Francoise asked.

"Bertram es un conde?" the Spaniard asked.

"Bertram?" Aleister answered, "Yes, Earl Ashburnham is Bertram, a real earl. Not to fear, Don Carlos, your nephew is safely in keeping with the earl."

Francoise translated for Don Carlos, who watched Aleister's face closely.

Aleister turned away from them and rested against the railing to observe the dockmen. "I'm wondering, Don Carlos, does your nephew outrank Bertram, our Earl Ashburnham? How do they compare?"

Francoise translated and added, "You know, Mr. Crowley, we have no earls in France."

The Spaniard answered, "No. Duque, marqués, conde, vizconde, barón, señor."

Francoise replied, "Si, prince, duke, count, baron, knight. It seems here in England, only a duke matters."

Aleister slapped his leg, laughing, "True, that. Any member of the peer can be a lord, but a duke has it in spades. I would settle for marquess any day, though."

"I see," Francoise answered, "your earl is our count. The unloved middle child."

The Spaniard started to speak very rapidly, and Aleister put his hands up.

"Francoise, you'll have to interpret for me."

"Mr. Crowley, you don't speak Spanish?" Francoise asked, his eyes opening wide. "You said you spoke all continental languages."

"Never got around to Spanish, too popular to learn. But you can ask me anything in Latin, Greek, or German."

Francoise said, "Don Carlos just said, 'What good are these titles of nobility when Salic law is disregarded?'"

"True," Aleister said, watching the bobbing packages passing up the ladder. "Our inheritance of thrones, fiefs, and kingdoms passing into the hands of women is destroying civilization. And corrupting our waiting princes."

Don Carlos and Francoise smirked. At least Don Carlos understood that.

"Your prince is proof—such a very fat and useless prince," Francoise said.

"Yes, the prince is a spoiled lapdog of the Queen. The Queen, who at eighty years of age, refuses to die. Edward is only good at eating and fucking," Aleister said. "A cautionary tale."

Don Carlos threw his hands up, saying, "La reina Victoria es Emperatriz de la India. Australia. Neuva Zelanda. Sudamerica. Africa. Canadá."

"Yes, I understand you. She's an Empress everywhere in the world, but here she is only Queen. A soft, invisible Queen refusing her heir to appear at royal events, lest they start to follow him."

"We thought your Queen was going to die several times. There have been how many—eight—assassination attempts?" Francoise asked.

"We thought she gave up the ghost when her prince consort died, but now it seems the old cow keeps living. Without Prince Edward learning a damn thing as future king." Aleister crushed the remains of his cigarette under his boot. "We've waited long enough. We've surrounded the prince with enough men of influence to save the British Empire from the prime minister. And there are other candidates to save us from our Queen's bad decisions."

Francoise grinned. "You think your Queen has more power than your prime minister, Lord Salisbury? She isn't the one sending your troops to Africa."

"She influences the middle class, providing the young men as cannon fodder, not Lord Salisbury in parliament," Aleister said. "Her recent pronouncement, 'All our smart, idle men can miss a season and rough it out with troops,' has only made recruitment go up."

Francoise whispered, "Since the opening of your parliament is postponed again, is there any chance she would open it later?"

"No. She hasn't opened parliament in years, and she's cancelled all this week's public events," Aleister said, moving away from the workmen.

Aleister motioned the two men closer to him.

"When will she appear next then? We can't hide the earl's 'mummies' forever," Francoise said softly, stamping out his cigarette. "We were lucky enough to sail from Wales without incident."

"She'll be reviewing the Boer War troops at Windsor in a few days. Translate, Francoise," Aleister said.

As Francoise explained to Don Carlos, Aleister mulled over the last time the Queen was trotted out at Windsor Castle. Christmas season, inspecting the troops, she handed out some tins of chocolate from her carriage. All in exchange for a future loss of an arm or a leg.

Don Carlos spewed a lengthy tirade as Aleister tilted his head to listen.

"What's that all about?" Aleister asked Francoise.

"Estoy orgulloso de ser Carlist!" Don Carlos said.

Before Francoise could interpret, Aleister thumped the Spaniard on the chest. "Shut the hell up! Eyes and ears are everywhere."

Don Carlos puffed up, putting his fists up to box while Francoise held him back. Don Carlos spit on the ground.

"Not another word," Aleister said, waving the agitated man away and moving back to the railing.

Watching the men lugging boxes on the deck below, Aleister imagined them working for him. Coarse worker bees who knew nothing about magic or real power. But they could be part of the new order, helping him set people free. He just needed to get rid of those who would limit him. Just last week, one of his tributaries of magic dried up, thanks to that ignorant tarot child. Killing the dog took much more magic than he thought it would. If he were to take over, he would need much more. The pungent odors of the tide reached him. How he hated the Thames, such a dirty, ugly tribute of water.

He looked back at his two compatriots.

"Be patient. Tell your men in three days they'll be assigned to lodgings next to Spitals Barrack."

"Where is that?" Francoise asked.

"Windsor."

CHAPTER TWENTY-FOUR

Grave Confrontation

E llen paused, put her hands on her hips, jutted her chin out, and dipped lowly to the ground in the pose of her character in Sardou's *Madame Sans Gene*, that afternoon's play. Pamela sat sketching on the staircase of Miss Horniman's foyer. If she could just quickly sketch Ellen's great comedy moment. Such a relief to draw a human figure, no secret symbols, only a moment caught in time.

Ellen was playing Catherine, a washerwoman who becomes Madame Rejane and is made a Duchess. During a dancing lesson, the dancing tutor coaches her with admonishes of "Dip! Duck! Swanlike, so." Ellen had created a bit of clever stage business in this scene that had become famous. She gathered up the train of her costume, squeezed it out as though it were a wet piece of heavy clothing, and draped it over her arm, treating it like damp laundry. The working-class audience recognized this moment as a washerwoman's instinct, and it always brought down the house.

Miss Horniman, Uncle Brammie, and Waite gave Ellen a nice round of applause at the end of the stage business, and Ellen prepared to leave. Ellen had arranged for her carriage to come back for her after the matinee and this was one pity carriage ride Pamela was glad to take. The trip from Horniman estate to Barkston Gardens would have been a good two hours on the train.

"Break a leg, Pa," Uncle Brammie said as he kissed her on the cheek.

"Not only will I break a leg, Ma," Ellen answered as she gathered the train of her coat, "I will wring out every laugh." With that, she twisted the train and tossed her head and left.

Miss Horniman and Uncle Brammie chuckled and motioned to Pamela to make her way to the parlor. Waite trailed behind. Pamela had asked that all four of her muses be here for an incantation of protection, but she was informed they were too busy: Henry with Lyceum business, Terriss training yet another horse for a show at the Adelphi, and Florence skrying with Yeats.

They don't take Aleister's threats seriously after all this.

Pamela sat down in front of the flagstone fireplace. She sorted the four tarot cards on the floor while Miss Horniman perched in her throne. Magician, Fool, High Priestess, Empress all looked up at her. Waite loitered near the fireplace, and Uncle Brammie squeezed into a chair near Miss Horniman, swirling his drink.

Miss Horniman began. "Miss Smith, a letter was delivered here this morning with the spell you requested from Miss Farr. I believe it is from the Golden Dawn grimoire."

She handed Pamela the letter, tattvas in a row, and underneath was a sequence of Hebrew words written unintelligibly.

"I don't know this spell or language," Pamela said.

"Well, you should have studied harder in your curriculum of the first degree," Miss Horniman snapped.

Pamela's face burned.

"We will solicit the co-committee to translate for you, it may take some time," Miss Horniman said, softening her features. "Meantime, let us discuss the overall progress of this tarot deck. Mr. Waite, you said your deck's first five cards would be:

Fool, Magician, High Priestess, Empress, and Emperor. What is different from the French Marseille deck?"

Pamela chimed in, "Mr. Waite says we will have no Popess, Miss Horniman."

Miss Horniman smiled. "Well, it seems you did study some subjects."

Waite leaned against the mantlepiece, taking out his pipe. "The oldest complete deck of the seventy-eight cards of the Sola Busca. That will be our imprint. The most important cards are the first six: Mateo, the Fool, Panfillio, Magician, Postumio, Popess, Lenpio, Empress, Mario, the Emperor, and finally, Catalo, the High Priestess."

Annie leaned down to look at the tarot cards. Good, now Miss Horniman would see for herself that Waite was instructing her to mine the Sola Busca and Marseille tarot deck instead of coming up with new images.

Miss Horniman asked, "And why are you imitating the Sola Busca's first six cards, Mr. Waite?"

"The six chiefs, leaders of the Golden Dawn's new order, insist on it," Waite replied.

Pamela watched Waite clench and unclench his pipe. Florence, as the new Golden Dawn president, would not like the elimination of the Popess. What chiefs was he talking about? The new order from Paris or Florence's?

"You see, Miss Horniman, these images channel archetype associations, providing a language between those who understand their meaning," Waite continued. "The Popess has no current cultural meaning."

Uncle Brammie choked on his drink. "Archetypal associations? I have a university degree, and I don't know what the hell you're talking about. Italian commedia d'arte figures? French tapestry figures?"

Miss Horniman patted Uncle Brammie's knee. "Now, now, Mr. Stoker, give Mr. Waite a chance." She stood and approached him at the fireplace. "The Sola Busca, the Marseille, and the Visconti-Sforza decks all seem to have been a playing card guessing game, nothing more. How does your tarot deck contain magic?"

Waite shuffled right up next to her, looping his thumbs through his vest. *Ah, would he never learn that he stands too close?*

"This is where my deck shall be different! I am injecting magic with my awareness," he said.

Pamela felt a twinge in her left eye. Did her cards on the floor just titter? *Injection indeed.*

He continued, "The deck will be comprised of true symbolism. The Golden Dawn will cull symbols from cultures throughout time, and I will install them in a manner so that they tap into powerful magic, although the manifestations will only be accessed through the most skilled magicians."

Miss Horniman's metallic threaded dress sparkled in the firelight. The tune surfaced—that odd hum when something was off. She heard a door open and shut. There were no sounds of the maid coming in to announce someone. She tasted the yellow of her cards floating up to her. Her brain was crosshatching again. The scent of sage. Or was it cedar? What door opened? Was Florence astral traveling to send a message?

"You're not answering my question, Mr. Waite. What prompts magic through these cards?" Miss Horniman asked. "Is it the cards themselves or the magical symbols in them? I want to know what is leading the process."

"Oh," Waite answered, "the querent will be led to the magic by the secret language inherent in these cards. There is a new order coming that will know how to channel them."

"New order? You mean the Carlists, Mr. Waite? Or a new order as in something after a war?" Uncle Brammie asked.

"There is always a war coming, Mr. Stoker. But I mean a new order of consciousness, which the Carlists represent," Waite replied.

"Even after reports that they are threatening us, you are a Carlist?" Pamela asked.

Waite laughed, his face turning red. "Me, a Carlist? No! I don't care about illegitimate claims to thrones, but I see they may be coming into power. My interest in the new world order is a position to enlighten people. Miss Smith may be drawing the tarot cards for the Golden Dawn, but she has no real magic. We've seen that in her ineffectual response to Mr. Crowley."

"Who is this 'we,' Mr. Waite?" Uncle Brammie asked, one eyebrow drawn down.

"Why, the newly elected Golden Dawn chiefs: Mathers, Felkin, Westcott, Yeats, Richard Archer Prince, Farr."

Uncle Brammie was not elected Golden Dawn chief.

Florence had said they both would protect her, but what if he wasn't a chief?

"The chiefs will be using the cards that yourself and Miss Smith have researched? This is my project. How are the Carlists aligned with us?" Miss Horniman asked.

"Miss Smith merely takes the dictation of my research," Waite continued. "These cards will be part of the Golden Dawn's new order and their teaching techniques. The deck will be known as the Rider-Waite deck."

"Wait, who is Rider?" Uncle Brammie asked.

"The publisher of the deck, Rider and Sons," Waite replied.

Pamela stood, blood pounding in her temple. The yellow tasted sour in her mouth. Her name would be nowhere on her published cards. Cards to be used by magicians who didn't understand them. Uncle Brammie took her hand and squeezed it.

"You've selected a publisher?" Miss Horniman asked. "As patron of this project, I was to choose."

"Yes, Watkins Books has expressed interest in publishing these cards," Uncle Brammie said, motioning Pamela to retake her seat. "Why have you gone with Rider?"

Waite looked at Bram and smiled. "Rider published my first two books and offered to print my third. They can spot quality writing."

That was meant to sting. He must have known Uncle Brammie's failure in having *Dracula* published.

"When Miss Smith has the Empress card ready, I'll take the completed cards to Rider Publications and see what the first run will cost," Waite said. "They are offering a very good distribution for us. And we don't want this to be a small, in-house, vanity printing, do we?"

"Mr. Waite, since I am underwriting this project, you will see to the cards being published when I tell you they are ready," Miss Horniman said.

Waite stretched his arms and cracked his knuckles.

"That would be agreeable. Well, I really must go, my wife waits supper for me. Miss Horniman, Mr. Stoker, Miss Smith. We've made very good progress, very good."

Waite hustled out the door, and Uncle Brammie and Miss Horniman followed. Pamela noticed the fire dying and threw a small log onto it, where it smoked immediately. It must have been green. Her eyes smarted, although whether it was from smoke or the news that her name wouldn't be on the tarot cards, she couldn't tell.

Even the magic in my cards doesn't belong to me.

She centered herself before the fire and picked up the tattva note from Florence. Trying to decipher the letters made her eyes cross. This must be from *The Flying Rolls* spell book.

The tread of someone coming in the parlor caught her ear. She turned to complain to Miss Horniman and Uncle Brammie. Only it wasn't them. Four people stood in front of her. At least, she thought they were people at first. They wavered and undulated in the smoke.

William Terriss, Henry Irving, Ellen Terry, and Florence Farr. Each was dressed as on her tarot cards. They silently hung in the air. Pamela's initials, PCS, glowed from their earlobes.

She watched as Ellen as the High Priestess lifted a finger to her lips as though to shush her. What was that smell? Oil paint. Turpentine, castor oil, vinegar. The odor overwhelmed her. Her ghostly friends suspended in midair began to bubble and blister, as though made of burning pigment. As they started to turn into white-gold flames, a shot behind her turned her around.

Aleister was standing in the middle of the fire, jaunty in his university robe. His dark eyes glowed in his pale face, his head enlarging until it became two giant orbs. An insect. Then a beast, writhing in flames. Finally, a bearlike creature with eagle claws. The monster twisted its slash of a mouth from side to side. A reverberating moan pulsated in the room.

The strong odor of paint soured, turning into noxious fumes of sulfur.

Pamela ran to the door, but the knob had disappeared. The room began to shrink, the walls closing in. Dirt fell from the ceiling, sprayed out from the walls, pushed up from the floor. A river of dirt was swallowing up the room.

She fell down a hole, into a grave. She was being buried alive. She pressed her hands to her face to keep dirt out, but it kept coming, piling over her from every side. Spitting out a mouthful of dirt, she looked up. The fireplace light danced on the ceiling. Heaving for breath, she paddled her hands against her sides. How to keep from being surrounded? Screams. Tears turning to mud. Panic, a black syrup, anchored her to the pit. She was being carved into a coffin.

"Help! Help! For the love of all that is good, help me!"

The parlor door flew open. The coffin, the dirt, all disappeared. The room was restored. She stood alone in front of the flickering fireplace, holding on to the mantelpiece.

The scent of violets lingered in the air. The perfume from Pamela's childhood. Maud Gonne's perfume.

The scent that reminded her to be brave, to soldier on. Her friends wouldn't burn. She wouldn't be buried. Fears won't stop her.

She shook her fists. "I have a right to my magic!"

CHAPTER TWENTY-FIVE

OLD FAMILIARS

L ater that day, the steep stairs to her studio seemed twice as long to climb. Rather than go back to Ellen's, she needed time to herself. The day's hallucination came back full force as she caught her breath at the landing. Miss Horniman was sympathetic, Uncle Brammie distant when she told them of the nightmare of being buried alive. Both told her to be patient; Florence was working on protecting her now that she was "the official Golden Dawn president." So far, Florence's title had done little good. Pamela had now experienced four manifestations of Aleister's threats, and they were escalating in terror.

Her wet coat, umbrella, and art supplies were heavy and cumbersome. No door ajar today, it was locked tight. Edy was off with Chris no doubt. The last meeting here clawed at Pamela's heart. To be called a leech and have Florence called a "mummy mumbler" still hurt. At least she still had her four muses—perhaps their magic would keep her inspired.

But just today she was informed that William Terriss was leaving the Lyceum Theatre. Since the death of his beloved dog,

Mr. Irving had been dismissive to her overtures of friendship. When Pamela last addressed him as "Henry," he flinched. Ellen was busy with her theatre and society schedule. And just today Uncle Brammie warned her not to let her second sight get the better of her. She was speechless. How was she to do that?

As she worked the key in the sticky lock, the first of their Bohemian nights came flooding back. She and Edy were the latest thing in London's artistic set, and there was a line of people at their salon door. Even now as Pamela swung the door open, there sat the table where people signed the guest book in green ink. There was the worktable where the *Green Sheaf* magazine came to life. And behind that curtain, guests dressed in their costumes for *tableau vivant*, the silent guessing game. Edy had torn down all the costume renderings on the wall. They were repinned at her new costume shop in Covent Garden. Not that commissioned costumes nor the *Green Sheaf* ever earned them enough to keep going.

The chilly room had none of the flourishes during flush times: flowers, bottles of wine, bowls of fruit, and newly bought books. Pamela's first payment from Annie Horniman was down to the last five pounds. Pamela would need to finish the High Priestess and Empress cards before asking for the next installment. Her other work designing wallpaper, bookplates, and book covers had dried up. Their studio was in the process of being sublet to the Women's Suffragette Atelier. Florence had worked out the details with the atelier group, highlighting the fact that Pamela's studio was in the heart of the up-and-coming artistic Chelsea area. Time to clear out her things and make room for the new tenants.

Chairs and poufs were turned every which way, in the last position from the Bohemian night months ago. In a corner was a pile of half burned candles and Albert, her stuffed baby alligator. The memory of performing the Jamaican folktales with him here caused a little pinprick in her heart. A knock at the door startled her.

"Come in," Pamela called.

Beatrice Pardoe-Nash Ali entered, even more beautiful than before. Wearing a respectable, small porkpie hat over coifed hair and a tailored dove-gray coat with matching gloves, she was elegance itself.

"Pamela, so pleased to see you," she said, kissing Pamela on the cheek. "I'm on the committee for the Women's Suffragette Atelier now." Peering over Pamela's shoulder, she noticed the room's disarray. "Heavens, there must have been quite the party here."

Wearily, Pamela showed her in. Such a feminine creature, much more so than herself. So much more in keeping with what Henry, Uncle Brammie, or Ahmed responded to. Ahmed. Where the hell was he these days when she needed him?

"Miss Farr told you it would be ten shillings a month to share our workspace, and the char woman comes in once a week?" she asked.

Beatrice didn't respond, just stood still, fixing her lipid eyes on her. The porcelain complexion started to shift and move, becoming mottled and scaly, the whiteness flaking off into rose petals, falling on the messy floor.

Something unworldly was happening.

The air became thick, the wallpaper began to drip.

Beatrice's gloves split open and terrible claws sliced their way out of the fingers. Her porkpie hat slid down her back and the coils of her beautiful hair began to writhe as a mass of snakes. Her eyes were the same yellow-green eyes of Aleister's on the bridge.

A long tongue slithered out of her mouth, flickering.

Pamela let out a scream and stepped away. Beatrice's clothes were shredded, slipping to the floor in heaps; skirt and bodice breathed together like discarded lumps of glowing coals. Beatrice's nude body began to elongate into the smooth, shiny belly of an alligator. She shimmied up and spread her arms upwards. As she towered over Pamela, green, jeweled scales began to cover the naked body.

"Aleister, leave me!" Pamela croaked, covering her eyes, preparing for a blow.

A low laugh followed by a thump filled the room. A rustle. Bags being dragged across the floor? What was it? She removed her hands from her eyes and looked up.

A huge scaly creature stood before her. It tilted its head and examined her, its huge tail beating like a happy dog.

"Ah, Miss Pamela, dontchya recognize me now?" the beast said.

Pamela stood from her crouched position and took a small step forward. The rumbly dinosaur roar, a *chumpf*, filled the room.

"No . . ."

"I'm the gift from your Nana. You called me Albert."

Pamela sputtered, gazing at the apparition. It was. It was a huge version of Albert. "Albert? I had you stuffed years ago!"

"I know, child. You also called me Albert though I be a girl. You think a boy gator would be lookin' after you?"

The Jamaican accent. The stubby front legs gesturing. Pamela burst into a loud, long laugh, holding her sides, and sat down on the floor.

"Albertina," she said when she could talk again, "what are you doing here?"

The large reptile staggered around the room, taking in the clutter, emitting a series of the *chumpfs* in a row, her crooked mouth hanging open. There they were, the enormous hundreds of front teeth and oversized pin teeth on the side. *Be careful of her teeth!* her mother had always said. *She's a wild deranged animal.*

The curious, large head tilted slightly, froglike eyes on top blinking. Albertina stopped in front of Pamela's artwork pinned to the wall, her stubby claws touching paper. It was Pamela's painting of Annancy, the spider.

"Child, there's a war comin', dontchya know. I been following you for a while now. At the museum, Florence card night, and Ellen bug party. I called to you."

"The chirping at the museum was you! I thought it was a mummy!"

"Hawks, eagles, gators, all hear baby egg calls. But I come to help you with something else. You be needing to breathe under the water. You need how to fight the firestorms."

Water began cascading down the dripping red of the wallpaper, spilling onto the floor. *For the love of Horos, first dirt at Miss Horniman's, now water at the studio?* Water spewed from the walls. Albertina rumbled a terrible growl. Her claws reached out and grabbed Pamela around the waist, dragging her down into the water, now up to her knees.

It was the brink of the horizon under a Jamaican ocean, a blue-green sky overhead. Albertina was swimming under her. One stubby leg kicked Pamela up on her back. She climbed on top of her scaly back, a vague memory of riding her pony telling her how to hold on. The brackish blue water was cold but not freezing.

Albertina writhed, making their way through choppy waves. The reptile's face disappeared beneath the surface just long enough to submerge her snout. A torrent of bubbles streamed from its sides, up to the surface. Pamela laughed and Albertina gave her backside a twist as a slight slap of her tail propelled them. Albertina dove deep into the water, the bubbles swirling around Pamela's submerged face.

"You breathe, child. Mouth still, lungs fill."

❧

When Pamela woke up, Beatrice was standing in front of her with a cup of tea in a chipped teacup, her kind green eyes blinking at her. Pamela slowly pulled herself up in the armchair and looked around. The afternoon light was barely leaking into the front windows, the fog already starting to throttle the sun's rays. Several candles were lit, and the sound of horse's hooves on the cobblestone echoed down the street. There was the stuffed body of Albert—no, Albertina—propped up on the piano. How had she gotten there?

"Horniman's tea is supposed to be very good for the nerves. This will soon set you right, Miss Smith."

"What happened? Who are you?"

Beatrice placed her own teacup and saucer on the side table, serenely settling back.

"Miss Smith, you know me; I'm Beatrice. I'm here to make the arrangements to take over the lease on your studio here for the atelier group. You just fainted. You seemed quite overcome."

Beatrice's face betrayed nothing out of the ordinary; it was as if she were recounting the notes from a meeting. Pamela watched her very intensely, unsure if she should trust her or not.

"You did call out, though, almost as though you were drowning. I had quite the time getting you here to this chair, let me tell you."

The sound of people climbing the stairs to the studio came from the landing, followed by a sharp rap at the door.

"Enter," Beatrice answered.

The door opened to Duse Mohammed Ali, who stood there, grinning wildly. He bowed low before presenting a bottle of wine.

Beatrice laughed and ran to greet him, turning to Pamela to declare, "Oh, Miss Smith, I hope you don't mind. I asked my husband to join us to celebrate the shared lease."

Duse stepped forward. "Miss Smith, I have been most anxious to speak with you since the Bomanji outing."

More footsteps were heard in the stairwell. She blinked back tears. Who else would be intruding here? Where was Albertina?

From the landing entered a tall, stately apparition wearing a veil and in black velvet. She reached out her arms to Pamela, whispering in her throaty voice.

"Oh, Pamela, I've missed you so much."

She was swept up in a crushing embrace. Tears clutched at her throat as the scent of violets overwhelmed her.

Maud Gonne, childhood sister of a fairy, had arrived.

CHAPTER TWENTY-SIX

Reviewing the Troops

"Gentlemen, I am pleased to present to His Royal Highness our enlisted members of the Carlist cause," Earl Ashburnham said to the dozen men at the table.

Aleister watched the next Spanish king, Don Jaime, duke of Madrid, choose to whisper to Earl Ashburnham rather than stand and address his followers. "Don Jamie" to his continental friends, "Jaime de Borbón" to the Carlist devotees, and "pretender to the throne" to the rest. The duke of Madrid fell silent and squirmed in his chair.

The earl cleared his throat. "The duke of Madrid is concerned over how much of a war our new order will require."

Yes, what are the rest of us willing to sacrifice for the duke to rule in Spain? Aleister wondered.

The earl clasped the duke's shoulder. "Your Royal Highness, gentlemen, there will not be a real war. Eh, perhaps a little fighting here and there. Not to worry. Over in a month."

The duke slunk down in his chair, and Aleister clutched his fists. All this preparation to seize the day, and it was apparent this ally, this future king of Spain, was no Henry the Fifth. The pretender's formal evening wear paired with a sash heavy with medals made him look a dilettante, not a king. The night Aleister met him at Felkin's, at least he had worn a uniform.

Aleister leaned over to Dr. Felkin and whispered, "How did the earl come to know the future king of Spain?"

Dr. Felkin answered, "The duke of Madrid attended Jesuit school here in Windsor, as did the Ashburnham family."

Ah, that was it. *Aristos planning cannon fodder for their own ascension.* What would they think if they found out his own fortune came from Crowley Ale, not inherited splendor? He looked at the assembled members. This secret committee of the Carlists was made up of disgruntled peers and ambitious politicians, some doctors, some men of science.

Aleister watched Mathers twist in his chair, desperate to be nearer the duke's uncle, Don Carlos, who was speaking very quickly in Spanish to the would-be king. Mathers began to interpret for those around him.

Only last month Aleister earned his first Carlist medal, training at the Earl's country house in Wales. Now promoted to captain of the first order, it would only be a matter of time before he worked his way up the ranks. No magical assistance was used during this phase. He promised his spirit guide his magic would be rationed—only using it in battle—in order to keep the magical pools from depleting.

He caught the end of Mather's translating, " — Our beloved king serving in the army, ready for the day of liberation."

"The pretender to the throne is in the Spanish army?" Aleister asked the doctor near him.

Dr. Westcott snorted, "He'd be killed in a day by the Spanish monarchists if he were. His Royal Highness is currently in the Russian army, stationed in Warsaw, learning military maneuvers."

A Spanish revolution headed by an aristocrat born in Switzerland, brought up in Paris, educated in England and now in the Russian army. The success of this Carlist insurrection was looking less and less likely.

"Is the duke popular in Spain?" Aleister asked Wescott.

"Let us say, right now he is more popular than the four-teen-year-old King Alfonso," Westcott answered. "That king child can't rule, so his regent mother, Maria Christina of Austria, bungles everything—from the Spanish Caribbean holdings to Guam. She has given everything to the rapacious United States in exchange for nothing."

Earl Ashburnham lifted his chin to call the men to attention. "We will motivate all monarchists to rally to our legitimist claims of the Carlist that the duke of Madrid is the rightful Spanish king. Now is the time for us to set a determined fight."

Ashburnham had tricked the officials in Paris into seizing the wrong load on his ship, the *Firefly*. After a detour to his estate in Wales where he held military maneuver training for young Carlists, the guns now sat in the upstairs storeroom of The Prospect of Whitby pub. Enough gunpowder, cartridges, and rifles to take the old Queen out at her review in two days' time.

The duke of Madrid lifted his limp hands up at the end of Ashburnham's "set a determined fight" as though to rally the troops. It was mistaken as a sign to rise and toast the future king, resulting in a weak response of mumbled "here, here's."

The earl signaled to Mathers.

"Mr. Mathers, what is the final arrangement?" the earl asked quietly.

Mathers kept his gaze on the future king. "Our connections will arrange the bomb in the Queen's carriage before she heads out to Spitals Barracks for the troop review."

Dr. Westcott asked, "Where will Prince Edward be?"

Mathers answered, "Safe and unaware in London."

Good. Once the old Queen was gone, the male heir would take her place. Although Edward was not especially progressive, he was permissive. And Aleister had a chance to rise up through the ranks of society with him in charge rather than the restrictive Queen.

The thought of that old, black silk spider on the throne revolted him. Castrating men of ambition, thwarting men of science and ideas, all because of her repressive, middle-class ideas of morality. She was like his mother, the religiously obsessed crone who beat him and called him "beast six-six-six" as a child. Women should be subjugated to serve, not rule.

The duke of Madrid, future king of Spain, lifted his glass. "To the rights of men!"

A hearty resounding echoed, "To the rights of men!"

Dr. Westcott and Dr. Felkin smiled at Aleister. The doctors were chafing under Mrs. Horniman's rules. Florence Farr as president was bungling the use of the Vault. Scotland Yard was poking around for Carlists. It was time to hand the magician's enclave back to the doctors and professional men. And restore the tarot project to Aleister himself.

None of the other magicians knew Pamela Colman Smith was draining the sources of magic. The Golden Dawn had theories about the magic, but it was Aleister's spirit who had shown him the pools of Risk, Enchantment, Transformation, and Enhancement. Each with a spell tapped by secret words, sigils, and trances. But the pools were receding, the waters of Risk had already been drained by the Fool incarnation of Miss Smith's tarot. The perfume of flowers and herbs in the last trio of ponds was fading.

These magical pools, once vast and seemingly bottomless, had fed all his magical spells. But in the past year they began to diminish, ever since the Smith child began siphoning them off for her tarot cards. The pond of Transformation was half full, and the pool of Enhancement was almost gone. That this uneducated child could tap into the ponds he needed was maddening. Their potency was limited, and he didn't know how he could replenish their source. He needed to drink all of the waters, absorb them to process their magic. They had to be deep enough to swim in. At that thought, he shuddered. It didn't help that he had a lifelong horror of being underwater.

He would arrange for the child and her muses to be there at the Queen's review during the attack. No reason to bother the Carlists or the Golden Dawn with this fact. Time to live up to his magical motto.

Do what thou wilt shall be the whole of the law.

CHAPTER TWENTY-SEVEN

Magician, Fool, High Priestess, Empress

⌘

It took an hour for Beatrice and Duse to clear out, but eventually Pamela and Maud were left to themselves. It was dark outside, and the rain had turned to wet dissolving snow.

Maud's head, with her enormous cascade of dark curls swirled into a beehive type cluster, nodded as she took in every sketch spread out on the table before them. Pamela turned to check her own hair in a mirror—it was sticking out half a foot from her head. She should have at least used a brush since coming back from Miss Horniman's. Or after swimming with Albertina.

Maud pushed the rough sketches away and gestured to see the tarot cards in Pamela's hand. Pamela's throat tightened. Would they be seen as trivial and silly? She placed the four cards in front of her.

Maud looked down at the card nearest her. "You start off with the Fool, the innocent on his journey?"

"Yes, he has the holy spirit or animal guide, the white dog is by his side, and the mountain is the scene of his jumping off point."

Maud murmured a low "mmm," petting the illustrated dog on the card.

"Now, this Magician, with the number one at the top, he endows the gifts?" Maud asked.

"He shows where the gifts might be from, either from what is in his hand or on the table. The tools he bequeaths are: wand, star, cup, and sword."

"The Fool is going on a journey and needs the tools of the Magician," Maud said. "I don't know who the fool is based on."

"William Terriss, the actor," Pamela replied.

"Ah, yes, now I see it," Maud said, "Breezy Bill. The High Priestess, tell me about her. Why do the pillars behind her have a *J* and *B* on them?"

"The High Priestess has magic over the Magician, understands the higher order of things, but she also has the knowledge of Eve."

"What does that mean? She has sex like Eve?" Maud asked.

Pamela blushed. "Yes, she is worldly in the way of carnal knowledge. See the palm leaves and pomegranates, in the tapestry behind her? The pomegranates are the apple in the garden of Eden. The *J* and *B* on the two pillars stand for Jachin and Boaz, two pillars from the Temple of Solomon."

"So," Maud answered, "the *J* and *B* mean the pillars themselves were called Jachin and Boaz?"

"Yes," Pamela replied. "The left pillar, Jachin, symbolizes 'It is strength' and the right pillar, Boaz, signifies 'It will establish.'"

"Pamela, why did you put Egyptian pillars in your third tarot card?" Maud asked sitting down on the settee.

"Ahmed, my . . . associate at the British Museum, has been helping me understand universal symbols. Since an Egyptian woman created one of the first libraries, I wanted the High Priestess to be the next step, the knowledge that women pass on during the Fool's journey. The High Priestess has the strength to establish decisions."

"And who is this muse modeled after?" Maud asked.

"Florence Farr, I thought she was perfect for the High Priestess, symbol of intellect and scholarly knowledge."

"I see. And next, the Empress on the couch, of course, is Ellen Terry. What of her?"

"The Empress is intuition and motherly love," Pamela said, her heart racing. Was Maud thinking that Ellen supplanted her? Maud was her first childhood attachment, first supporter and muse.

"The Empress's robe is so loose; she is pregnant?"

"Pregnant with possibilities," Pamela replied. She thought of Ellen's fans, all the young assistants clamoring to be the theatre star's next secretary. Yes, very much pregnant. "You see the Empress's pomegranates from the Garden of Eden on her robe and twelve astrological houses in her crown."

A low whistle hummed from the side table—the stack of rough drawings of the court cards: Kings, Queens, Knights, Pages. Pamela shuffled through the stack and found all the Queens. Her first sketches, with pencil shapes of queens on thrones—there were only a few sections colored in red and blue. She placed the Queens face up, and they began to vibrate as though being shaken by fierce tiny hands. The four figures of the Queens—Wands, Swords, Cups, and Pentacles—became a specter of blurry faces.

The cards stilled.

All four faces of the Queens turned, their eyes coming to rest on Pamela.

Maud caught her breath.

Pamela bent forward over her Queens. "Yes. I'm here. What is it?"

Their mouths moved in unison. A faint chanting.

British Empire won by water.

The color of the cards faded in intensity. They were only drawings once again.

Pamela started laughing. "Well, that was useless, wasn't it?"

Maud put both hands on the table as though she were drawing up strength and took a deep breath.

"Tell me everything about your muses."

Pamela poured out their stories. William Terriss saving her as a child when she fell from the Waterloo Bridge and becoming the Robin Hood of the day. Henry Irving using real magic instead of stage magic on the Lyceum Theatre stage. Florence Farr, elected Golden Dawn president and Woman's Suffrage leader. And Ellen, performing the magical ritual on Smallhythe lawn to rule the beetles and bats. The PCS initials etched on each muse's earlobe.

Pamela's vision narrowed like the lens of a camera. Aleister as the devil, stalking her. Her mouth felt dry, her heart raced. "Aleister claims all my muses will be killed by his black magic. He hates me."

"Why?"

"It must be because I'm creating the cards."

Maud paced back and forth before the window, hands clasped behind her back, and said, "Tell me everything Mr. Crowley done."

Pamela looked at Maud's black velvet bodice. Amber stars orbited its nipped waist—as Maud paced, the stars spun. Pamela started with the story of how Aleister transformed into a flying devil in the Golden Dawn's Vault; floated above a bonfire on a London street; cut a man in two with a marble slab; buried her alive in Mrs. Horniman's parlor. Killed Fussie.

It all came tumbling out. And before she knew it, she was in Maud's lap, crying into the dancing stars of her skirt. Maud's calming hand soothed the back of her head. As half-breaths and small sobs subsided, Maud began to hum.

"You've been through a lot. When you flew as a young girl, I knew you were part of the invisible world."

Maud stroked her hair. No one had touched her hair in a long time.

"I'm glad to see your hair is still a wild garden," Maud said.

Pamela sat up and smiled for the first time in a while. "And yours is still a manicured lawn."

Maud helped Pamela stand. "First things first," she said. "Tell me why you are designing these tarot cards. And don't tell me it was just a job."

"It was . . . it *is* . . . for the secret language they will hold," Pamela answered. "When Mr. Irving taught Egyptian symbols on tour, it was like our secret language. I drew our symbols on the sets we built at the theatre. In the props, on shields, in embroidered handkerchiefs, costumes. They are our symbols of good and evil."

"Like the PCS on your muses' earlobes," Maud said. "So you have your Mr. Irving as King Arthur and William Terriss as Lancelot, Ellen as Guinevere, and Florence as your Lady of the Lake. Where will you go from here?"

"I'm not sure. After the twenty-two cards of the major cards, I want to make the minor deck its own mystical journey."

"Not following you, Pamela."

Pamela found her sketch of all seventy-eight cards.

"The first twenty-two cards are the Major Arcana, just as they are in other decks." She picked up the Magician card. "The minor suits will be the Magician's tools on the table: Swords, Wands, Cups, and Stars."

A light blinded Pamela as a camera lens shuttered her eyes. She opened them. It was a bright vision: Mr. Irving, kneeling. A sword swung around his head. "Mr. Irving is to be knighted! The first actor as Sir. He'll be so pleased."

"I'm sure he will be. Now, back to business." Maud walked back to the table, picking up the Empress card. "What card is after Empress?"

"Emperor, then Hierophant," Pamela said, touching the dancing yellow stars in Maud's jacket.

"What is it in drawing the deck that infuriates Mr. Crowley?" Maud asked.

"There must be power in the completion of the deck. He wants it channeled into this group he is part of. He wants to rule."

"Bloody unlikely, that," Maud said. Her eyes turned to steel. "Have your four tarot incarnates met one another?"

"Florence and William haven't met, I don't think. Everyone else knows the others from the Lyceum."

Maud turned Pamela to her and held her by the shoulders.

"There is a great war coming, Pamela, and cults will fuel hate. The hate that will power and populate this war. Your calling is to put this tarot card journey together. They will encourage people to ask for guidance within themselves instead of looking outside themselves. The blind symbols of crowns and flags stir people into mindless acts."

"What should I do next, Maud?"

"You need help from the other side to protect you. Aleister has mastered fire, air, and earth in his torments. But his magic lacks the element of water. Where do you feel most safe these days?"

Pamela looked out the window and tried to remember a time or place she felt protected and secure. In her studio window looking out onto the street, a small inset of stained glass glistened in the setting sun. It was a Celtic cross of green and gold.

"The Mary Magdalene church, Mary Over the Water, St. Saviour's!"

"Are those three churches or one?" Maud asked.

"One, just one," Pamela answered.

Maud gathered her cloak and purse and marched to the door.

"Come, Fairy Sister, time for help from the waters."

CHAPTER TWENTY-EIGHT

Fool Challenges Magician

~⌐⌐~

Henry sat at his dressing room table wiping off bright red makeup. The role of Mephistopheles in *Faust* was one of his favorites, but the makeup required elaborate removal. Walter stood holding a steaming bowl of hot water and towels. Removing the goatee was taking its toll, the spirit gum chaffing his sensitive skin. Tybalt, his newly adopted ginger cat, noisily murdered his bowl of chicken livers on the floor.

Taking a towel, Henry asked, "Walter, have I become more thin-skinned with age?"

The valet bowed his head. "Sensitivity is a privilege of age, Guv'nor."

"Yes, but can I survive it?" Henry asked.

The orange cat stopped eating and lifted his head as though seeing something midair. He darted under the daybed, disappearing except for his tail, which whipped back and forth. A small shrieking sound pierced the air, followed by sounds of thrashing and Tybalt reappeared. His mouth clutched a large dead rat. Trotting over to Henry, he threw it down in front of him.

"More livers, Walter. Or we are next."

The offending rat was scraped up with a towel and taken out by Walter. A few minutes later, more chicken livers appeared in an elaborate chalice from *Henry VIII*.

The elderly wardrobe woman knocked softly as she entered and hung a freshly starched shirt on the back of the door. When she bent over for the laundry basket, she faltered slightly, and Henry held a hand out to help her steady herself. As she smiled a toothless grin on her way out, Bram entered. He presented the daily reviews and the nightly box office tally. Lovejoy was right behind him, with the walk-ons check-in list. Time was running out to dress for the postshow reception at the Savage Club.

"All one hundred and thirty witches accounted for in tonight's witches' kitchen scene," Lovejoy said.

"It helped there was a rumor that real witches were in it," Bram said, chuckling. "Standing room only."

Henry scribbled his initials on the roll call. "We need to be SRO since each witch now costs us three shillings if they break legs."

The black curtains hung to conceal the backstage area from the audience were an innovation of Henry's, and the crew's term for them, "legs," led to the coining of the phrase "break a leg." One was only paid when they got to "break a leg," so it was a term of endearment amongst the actors.

"What's the verdict in tonight's rag? I hope it wasn't Shaw on assignment," Henry said, getting into his shirt.

"Not Shaw," Bram answered and opened the newspaper. "'The climax of Walpurgisnacht revels on Broken Mountain is stupendous. The special effects are overwhelming: organ music, mists rolling in, cannon balls for the thunder. The show was a technical wonder. But *Faust* was not produced to showcase the acting talent, but for Henry Irving's management and cutting-edge stage effects. Still, even if Irving's Mephistopheles is deservedly the talk of the town, William Terriss is the new matinee lover.'"

The buttoning of Henry's shirt came to a halt. In *Faust*, Terriss had the role of Charles, lover to Ellen's heroine. In real life, Terriss was currently involved with a young actress while his wife was in her final days of illness at home. The mistress was willing to wait out the situation in the hopes she and Terriss would move to Australia. At least that was the gossip Henry had heard.

And Henry certainly knew about complicated marriages. Ever since his wife had demeaned his profession after his first great triumph onstage, he'd refused to be in her presence. But he provided for her and the boys, and Mrs. Henry Irving enjoyed coming to the shows, if only to make fun of him from box seats. She sneered at his Romeo, declaring him too old at forty-four to be playing to Ellen's Juliet. Still, if Henry wanted to maintain the Victorian standards of the mores of the time, he knew that a divorce was out of the question. Especially if there was ever the hope that he would be the first actor knighted.

But Terriss being singled out in any review as the new, younger matinee lover was not a good sign. Bram saw Henry's stalled dressing and motioned to Lovejoy.

"We'll catch up with the other reviews at another time," Bram said and motioned everyone to leave.

There was another quick knock on the door.

Henry barked, "Laundry's collected."

The door swung open. It was Terriss, jauntily leaning against the frame. "Ah, Guv'nor, if only all of our dirty laundry could be so easily dealt with."

"Terriss, my Fool, come sit and have a drink with me!"

"A quick one, my Magician."

Brandy was poured and both men admired Tybalt, licking the remains of bloody livers from his paws. The cat stopped and stared as though he were seeing a phantom floating above him.

"That's right, cat, it's the ghost of your father," Terriss said. "Is this cat Hamlet?"

"He's Tybalt, named for rat-catching abilities, not for his brooding."

"Ah, good call. Guv'nor, I have some news," Terriss said, setting his drink down. "You know I've been hired short term by the Adelphi Theatre for *The Secret Service*. Now they want to extend it to full-time employment for next season. I'll be taking my leave at the end of this schedule."

Henry drew in a sharp breath. The cat stopped moving momentarily, squinted a golden eye at Henry, and resumed cleaning with renewed vigor.

"Terriss, I can't afford to pay you more."

"It's not about money; it's about the roles. If I take other jobs, Jessie could be in it with me," Terriss replied.

"Ah, yes, your friend, Jessie Milford," Henry answered. "I currently employ a score of women to understudy Ellen, and they will never go on as leading lady. Lena Ashwell is next in line for the ingénue roles."

Terriss sat up straight in his chair. "The thing is, Jessie's a great little comedienne. She wouldn't be right for *The Corsican Brothers* or *The Lyons Mall* but a walk-on comic in *Olivia* would fit her gifts."

Henry slowly stood and finished dressing. "Terriss, it's not only that there are no roles for Jessie, I can't risk the situation."

Terriss took a quick swig of his drink. "I know, sir. It wouldn't please the Queen to know that her intended knight had employed an adulterer."

Henry saw Terriss bite his lip. It must have taken great self-control not to mention Henry's long-standing affair with Ellen.

Henry struggled with his cuff links. "What could I do, outside of a pay raise, to get you to stay?"

Terriss stood and helped Henry close his shirt cuffs. "Henry, for the love of God, mount a new play! The repertoire here is beyond creaky. Fellows like Shaw, Ibsen, and the rest are doing new-idea shows. You're falling behind, doing the same old thing. At least let Ellen play Rosalind in *As You Like It*, and I'll play Orlando. Get some new blood! I need to take some new risks or I'll drown!"

Henry's thin lips pursed as he extended his hand. "Goodbye, Terriss, my Fool. I shall miss you more than I can say. I hope that Pixie's initials will not be the only thing that binds us."

Terriss executed his bow from *The Corsican Brothers*' dueling scene—one foot forward, right hand over the heart, left hand shooting straight up. When he straightened, he took Henry's hand and pumped it.

"I'll say this about having that tattoo on my ear," Terriss replied. "Ever since that thing appeared, I feel if there are any risks in life I haven't taken, now is the time to take them. It's a lucky talisman, I know it." He started for the door, but at the last moment, turned and looked back. "I'll leave the door open, Guv'nor."

Clumping boots echoed down the hallway as Henry picked up Tybalt. He rubbed the purring head and felt the cat's tongue lick his earlobes.

"Are they a lucky talisman, Tybalt? Or a plague on both our houses?"

CHAPTER TWENTY-NINE

THOMAS THE FERRYMAN

~~~

Pamela realized Reverend Thompson was cross when he didn't respond to her requests to visit. After the pickpocketing incident at Saint Saviour's, the church was open by appointment only. An engraved note from Ellen Terry was sent to him, confirming the actress's participation in the dedication of his Shakespeare stained glass window, and it was soon followed by an invitation to call. Waiting for Maud outside the French consulate, Pamela breathed in the chilly September air, steadying herself for the trip to Saint Saviour's. With Maud at her side, she would contact Thomas the ferryman in the crypt.

The South Kensington area was pretty, but there were no pots of geraniums on the stoops as there were in Ellen's Barkston Gardens neighborhood. Here lived daughters of wealthy families who commissioned her artwork, Lyceum Theatre patrons, and sponsors for Ellen Terry's pet projects. Next door to the consulate was the townhouse of Mrs. Charlotte Robinson, the society widow who read palms. Pamela remembered an evening when she performed there as Gelukiezanger.

Mrs. Robinson's door opened, and a young man wearing a top hat, silken cravat, and greatcoat skipped down the stairs. Fancy clothes for so early in the morning. Unless he had stayed the night and had no other.

"Miss Smith! So glad to see you again."

Pamela stared at the swaggerer. Not a clue.

"We met at the Bomanji Ritz supper a few months ago," he said, taking off his hat to reveal disheveled red hair.

Yes, the red-headed politician from the supper. "Yes, Mr. Churchill, we meet again," Pamela said. "I've been hearing about you from Chris St. John."

What she had heard was that Chris detested working for him, taking dictation and lighting cigars.

"Chris, my secretary?" he asked.

Winston's heavily lidded eyes opened wider, and he let out a laugh that was more bark than mirth.

"Ah, yes, she's a very enterprising young . . . woman. Very mannish." He eyed Pamela's outfit—purple skirt, orange scarf, and wrapped headdress.

"Mannish?" Pamela asked. "Because she wears suits and writes speeches?"

"Writes speeches?" Winston asked. "She's just an assistant."

"Christopher St. John is currently secretary and writer for Ellen Terry at the Lyceum Theatre."

"Ah, speaking of the theatre, you don't by any chance happen to know the beautiful Miss Ethel Barrymore?" Winston asked. "I have been trying my best to contact her before I ship out, but her whereabouts are being kept tighter than a state secret."

"Sorry, I don't know Miss Barrymore. Are you shipping out to India?"

"No, Miss Smith, I'm off to Africa to be a correspondent for the *Morning Post*. I'll cover the Boer uprising. Just had my palm read and was told there's a remarkable career for me. Who knows if palms can foretell the future."

She looked at this unlikely candidate for a remarkable future and wondered what Mrs. Robinson saw.

Pamela felt a rush of wind and heard from far off the sounds of men shouting. Black lines streaked her sight; she closed her eyes as the taste of blood blossomed in her mouth. The moans of falling bodies from charging horses filled her ears. But here was red-headed Winston, running, leaping up to grab something. Then he fell a great distance. Now he was hiding in a small box, no, a railway car. Sounds of rifles being fired. Breathe, force the air in her lungs, sweep out the carnage. When she opened her eyes, she was sitting on Mrs. Robinson's stoop. Winston's arm was around her, and his pale freckled face showed genuine concern.

"Are you alright? Is there someone I should call? You had a right faint there."

Pamela realized his accent was very different.

"You're Irish!" she said.

Winston looked down and blushed, the red color a deeper shade than his hair.

"Went to school in Dublin when my father was stationed there, but not Irish," Winston said.

"I love the Irish," Pamela said, trying to shake the last of the vision out of her brain.

"Well, Miss Smith, I am not lovable in most aspects, but I will take credit for being loveably Irish."

"You will be in great danger, Mr. Churchill. I just saw it. You were falling and being chased by men with rifles."

"That's what I'm hoping! It will be how I make my career!"

"By being reckless?" Pamela asked.

"By being lucky!" Winston replied.

"Is this the great war that is coming?" Pamela asked.

Winston stood back from her, hands on hips. "What do you know about a great war?"

Pamela felt a chill. Why did Ahmed's face just appear to her, a finger to his lips?

"One of my interests is art history," Pamela said. "In most classical art there are scenes of a great war. Or a war between worlds. A World War."

"A world war, what an idea," Winston answered. "No, my trip is to cover local African resistance to British rights. I try to cover the underside of things. Speaking of which, Miss Smith, I have recently heard interesting things about you."

"What did you hear?" Pamela asked, crossing her arms.

"You've had interactions with a Mr. Crowley, is that right?"

Pamela looked at his pink, freckled cheeks. He was half piglet, half bulldog.

"Why would you, a newspaper man and a would-be politician, care about my interactions with Mr. Crowley?" Pamela asked.

"There is a belief that he is part of a dangerous group."

"The Carlists?" Pamela asked.

"No, this Golden Dawn group you're a part of," Winston answered.

Seeing the suspicion in his eyes, she said slowly, "As a member of the Golden Dawn, I can only tell you that we are artists interested in the world of magic. But it doesn't take a magician to realize a great war is coming."

"You are no Cassandra, Miss Smith—men in the know are aware of the clouds of war on the horizon. But it is a matter of foreign policy to resolve, not card artists or magicians. As long as the sun never sets on our British Empire, all will be right with the world."

Nana in Jamaica knew the boasts of the British Empire and their never-ending sun. At her knee, Pamela heard the stories: mountain people sabotaging British slave traders, women in the hills who tricked the British officers so they lost the trail of hidden rebels, the sunken treasures in the Jamaican harbor. This boy-man knew nothing of the real world, or what his British Empire did.

"Did you play solider as a boy, Mr. Churchill?"

"Yes, I did, I must say. From them I learned strategy and defense."

"And in remembering strategy, did the palm reader tell you to jump up?"

"Pardon? How do you know what the fortune teller told me?"

"I do know you will have to jump up to save your life, Mr. Churchill."

"Well, I'll keep that in mind, Miss Smith."

A feminine voice rang out.

"Pamela?"

Maud came behind Winston, who almost toppled over at the sight of her—her night with her French lover had made her even more luminous.

Bending down to help Pamela up, Maud's scent of lilacs wafted in the breeze. Winston was immediately by Maud's side; he barely came up to her shoulder.

"Pamela? What is going on?" she asked.

"I had a slight spell, but Mr. Churchill helped me collect myself."

Winston gazed up at Maud. Between her high-heeled boots, mass of coiled hair, and a tall hat shaped like a Roman shield, she seemed eight feet tall.

"Miss Gonne, a pleasure to meet you," Winston said. "Your work on behalf of Irish home rule is notorious, of course, but having lived in Ireland, I am in full agreement."

"I will take you at your word," Maud replied. "Come, Pamela, we have a full day's schedule. Good day, Mr. Churchill." She took Pamela by the arm and spirited her down the sidewalk.

Taking a quick glance backwards, Pamela saw that Winston had taken a cigar from his coat pocket. He sucked on it in a most obscene way as he stood staring at them.

Maud tucked Pamela's arm under hers, whispering, "Mr.

Mathers has arrived from the Golden Dawn's Paris office. We have a lot to discuss on the way to your St. Saviour's."

ᐫᏛᏗ

The clergy house at St. Saviour's was a well-appointed, two-story brick home adjunct to the church. Reverend Thompson was pleased to see them. He was just readying his oratory warm-up. Perhaps they would like to hear it? As Pamela took in his longish hair, owlish glasses, and elaborate collar, a tune from a Gilbert and Sullivan opera started to wind up in her head. She batted the tune away.

"Mr. Thompson," Pamela said, refusing the chair he offered, "I've brought Miss Gonne to see your exquisite taste in religious artifacts."

"Miss Gonne, I am so honored to have you here at our humble clergy. A small cordial before we get started?" he asked, staring at Maud.

"No, thank you, Reverend Thompson," Maud replied. "We are here to enjoy your expertise on Saint Saviour's history. It started out as St. Mary Over the Water nunnery, I believe?"

"Ah, yes, the legend," he answered, plopping down into a chair, then rising to signal them both to sit. They sat. "In 1106 it is said a ferry landing right outside our church property was home to a successful ferry business. But Thomas the ferryman, unsure who was loyal to him, feigned his own death to witness his funeral. When he discovered an ungrateful apprentice rejoicing his death, not grieving it, he killed him. His daughter, Mary, inherited the land and fortune. With her inherited money, she established a House of Sisters, named in honor of the Saxon Saint Audrey or Etheldreda of Ely."

"The church was built to celebrate a nunnery here, then, Reverend Thompson?" Pamela asked. *Will we ever get inside the church?*

"No, not a nunnery, it was built for the Virgin Mary," Reverend Thompson said. "'Saint Mary Overie' or 'Saint Mary Over the Rie,' 'over the water,' was the church's first name. It was not built as a tribute to the ferryman's daughter or nuns, contrary to the rumors. Later, ladies called it the Mary Magdalene church, but we finally got the name right with Saint Saviour's. But, enough of the women's stories. Let's talk about who is buried here. We have the poet John Gower, as well as Shakespeare's brother and a number of other notables."

"Shakespeare's brother?" Maud asked.

"Yes! I raised the funds for a stained glass window commemorating William Shakespeare. The dedication is next month. Ellen Terry will be laying the wreath at the ceremony. Shakespeare worshipped here as his theatre was quite nearby."

Maud gave a toss of her head.

"I was unaware that Shakespeare claimed to be a Catholic," she said.

"Oh, very quietly known. Very quietly known," Reverend Thompson said. "We ourselves have just announced to be pro-Catholic in the hopes that we will be a cathedral very soon." He stood. "May I show you the Shakespeare window? You won't be able to see the full effect by this afternoon's light, but still, you must come and see!"

Maud and Pamela exchanged a glance and were ushered into the apse.

Pamela caught her breath as they stood before the newly installed triplet window. In the dim light of the reverend's lamp, three figures were silhouetted in gold light with a dove on top. In the stained glass itself, the dove ruffled its feathers. *Why do the birds always make themselves known first?* In the left panel, in the corner of her eye, Pamela caught a quick movement. Propped up on Shakespeare's left hip was a book, its pages shuffling. As the book's pages continued to flutter, Pamela looked at Maud and the reverend. They were concentrating on the brass plaque dedication.

"'To the glory of God, in gratitude for his good gift to men in the genius of William Shakespeare,'" Reverend Thompson read.

In the right panel, Pamela spotted the figure of Spencer, wearing an enormous ruff shrug. He winked at Pamela, and the book he was holding closed. In the center panel, the Muse of Poetry twitched as he scratched away at a page with a quill, the sound echoing in the church. The three panels continued their almost imperceptible movements.

A tableau vivant for me.

The reverend's voice broke her train of thought.

"This window, designed by Charles Eamer Kempe, celebrates Shakespeare as loyal, ardently loyal, to Christian themes and values . . . good, bad, redemption, punishment. It's all there in his plays! Christian through and through!"

A banging on the front entrance of the church rang out, and Reverend Thompson's church brother appeared. Out of breath, he announced the reverend was needed in the clergy house to receive an unexpected party.

"So sorry, it may be patrons. I will return." He handed the lamp to Pamela and left with the brother.

As soon as he was gone, Pamela hurried up the center aisle, holding the lamp ahead of her. From behind her she heard Maud call out.

"Is it this one?"

Pamela turned, seeing Maud crouch next to the garish effigy of John Gower.

"No," Pamela answered moving ahead.

Pamela walked by a crypt with a black tablet before it, gold letters glimmering in the dim lamplight.

As Maud came up to it, she read out, "'Here under lyeth the body of William Emerson, departed out of this life the twenty-seventh of June, 1575, in the year of his age ninety-two.'"

"That's not him, Maud," Pamela answered, standing in the cross section of aisles.

She heard a faint murmur from under her feet and knew it was nearby.

Crossing to the east side of the north transept, she spotted it. The effigy lay on the floor. It was a molten, blackened form, covered up in winding sheets. Inset into the floor itself, there were no plaques to identify it. Maud gasped when she came to it, and Pamela knelt next to it.

"Listen!" Pamela said softly.

Maud knelt next to her.

"I hear nothing."

"Be very still."

It was a small chirp, a bird calling. A mouse squeaking. Albertina in the egg, unhatched.

"Maud, this is Thomas, the ferryman. I need to visit him privately."

Maud stood.

"I'll stand guard at the Shakespeare window." She took the lamp and left, the only light becoming fainter and fainter.

Sitting cross-legged in near blackness, Pamela cleared her mind and asked for guidance. There she was—ten years old, on her first transatlantic voyage with her parents. The sounds of the ship had frightened her at first. The cacophony of moans of twisting ropes, the sound of slaps of water against the bow, and the rattle of chains distressed Pamela. The jangles, slaps, and hisses were a constant thrum. But she learned to love their cozy hold, a private berth with ten-foot-tall ceilings framed with dark beams. Her parents hung her paintings on the cream-colored walls, making their room more country cottage than ship hold. Her father told her to imagine the kerosene lamp was their fireplace back home in Manchester. Or Aladdin's lamp, whatever she pleased.

She was on the floor sketching as her parents lay in the bed, the only lamp smoking. The rolling of the ship made it hard to draw straight lines. Pamela could see her mother put one arm dramatically over her head as she lay among the quilts; the other hand held a damp cloth to her eyes. Her father sat next to her, reading a book about Japanese art. The boat heaved upwards and came down with a thud. Pamela's stomach hung midair, the ropes groaned like an elephant's guttural growl. The lamp slid across the floor, and Pamela caught it just in time as she heard a snarled throb from the underside of the twisting ship. She looked to her father, whose dark eyes appeared above his lurching book only to give a slow blink and a finger to his lips for silence.

She was back on the floor, no longer kneeling but laying down looking up, one arm overhead like her mother's. A jade cloud formed above her in the duskiness. From below, the ribs of the church looked like the ribs of a ship. Something was forming in the jade cloud. Stubby paws swimming, an extended snout swinging side to side. It was Albertina, writhing midair in all her beautiful green iridescent splendor. Other figures swam next to her. Mermaids, sirens wearing saris from India, starfish, mermen, and water sprites.

A round of hissing and groaning enveloped her, swirling in the half light. A river channel flowed next to her. A flat boat on the surface appeared in the distance.

As the boat floated to her, a hooded man manning the oar became visible. When he came close enough, he stretched out his hand to her. As she held it, her hands shook slightly.

"For the protection of the waters, what will you give?" he asked.

"The Six of Swords," Pamela answered, the answer flowing naturally from her.

"You will dedicate it to Thomas, the ferryman, father to Mary Overie," his deep voice rumbled.

She tried to see into his darkened hood. There was no face.

"You will protect all my muses?" she asked.

"All those who are loyal to one another and remain loyal," he said. "One is already gone."

Their hands unclasped, the buzzing stopped, and everything evaporated.

Pamela took a moment to breathe and got up. Maud was at the Shakespeare window holding the lantern high.

"Did he promise to protect you?" Maud asked.

"Yes, in exchange for a ferryman tarot card. But he said one was already gone. I don't know what that means."

Pamela looked up at the stained glass window. A light shone from the top of the center panel, lighting up the central figure. Who did this Muse of Poetry look like? Yes, it was her Fool, William Terriss—he had the same beamish smile. The dove from the top of the panel lit up and flew down in the glass, disappearing. Three letters etched themselves in the Muse of Poetry's shoulder.

PCS.

Just as the *S* was finally etched in place, the entire Muse of Poetry panel turned black, leaving only the three initials.

A voice from the crypt of Thomas croaked.

Run!

When Reverend Thompson came back to his living quarters, three men stood in the entryway.

A distinguished, bearded man stuck out his hand. "Reverend Thompson, Dr. Westcott. This is Dr. Felkin and Samuel Mathers, from Paris. There's been an accident, and we need to fetch Miss Smith, who we believe is here."

CHAPTER THIRTY

THE FOOL

~~~

Aleister willed himself to astral travel to the pools. The torches along the cave's walls barely lit his path. The air smelled rank, and moss no longer clung to his boots as he found his way to the sacred chamber. A ring of twenty-two pools lined the interior hall. The first pool was a gaping black hole, only a thin film of water coated the bottom; the second basin was halfway emptied. He walked quickly to the next two. They had lower water levels as well. The rest glimmered like watery, black opals. It was only a matter of time before they were all used up. The fonts of magical nutrients were siphoned off just when he needed them all. That idiot child must have been communing with an ancient to deplete so much of the feeding waters. Or was it her tarot incarnates stealing from the magical fonts?

He took a torch off the wall and knelt down to look into the dregs of water of the first pool. In the reflection of the water came a vision: a man diving off a bridge, a runaway horse almost knocking the same man down in the street, a food hamper opening to reaching hands. So much magic flowing through this man. Was he even aware of it? His jumping, his leaps of faith, his love of the people and by the people. *All this should be mine.* He who lives by the air should not be bold to breathe the water.

The throb and thrum of his blood raced.

Do what thou wilt shall be the whole of the Law.

As William Terriss jumped down from his cab at the corner of Maiden Lane, he spotted the cluster of fans already waiting for him at the Adelphi Theatre's backstage door. It wasn't a secret where the actors came in, but few knew Terriss had his own entryway, and he preferred to keep it that way. He would have work to do to dispel them before he could enter.

He turned back to pay the driver the fare and felt a playful punch on his shoulder. Turning, he met the smiling face of Harry Groves, box office manager, who put his fists up as if to box.

"Ah, man, no worries for you, you've still got it," Harry said. "Look at all the maidens on Maiden Lane, waiting for *The Secret Service* hero."

"Yes," Terriss answered quietly as he walked toward them. "All the maidens in a row. Too bad the true meaning of Maiden Lane is manure lane."

Harry laughed as girls held out photographs for Terriss to sign, which he did. He was top dog here at the Adelphi, and of course, it kept him closer to Jessie Millward. Jessie was the perfect ingénue for him: lively, devoted, and totally understanding of his responsibility toward his terminally ill wife. They had become a sensation as a stage couple in a short time.

Harry nudged the fans away, and Terriss headed toward the door. Motion in the upstairs window caught his eye—Hecate, the black theatre cat. Irving had let him take the creature from the Lyceum, and now it was his dressing room cat. It settled against the window just above the royal crest. Nothing like having your own entryway with the royal crest, proclaiming royals had the right to use the doorway at all times. Prince Edward was known to show up every once in a while; perhaps he would catch the matinee today? Jessie appeared in the window with the cat, picked it up, and waved to him.

Where are my keys? He searched his pockets for the separate chain. There it was. As he pulled it out, a hansom cab pulled up, and a mustached man in an inverness cape got out and walked toward him. He was probably a walk-on signing in early. When did this lock get so sticky?

Terriss looked up to see the black cat place one paw on the window. Terriss laughed and lifted one hand in response. Jessie laughed as she held the cat closer to the pane.

As he tried once more to turn the key, a flash distracted him. The man in the cape leapt forward right next to him. In the dimming light of the early evening, a shiny metal object pierced Terriss's shoulder, driving him to his knees. Quickly, another blow hit his back.

Terriss screamed. Down the street, the last stragglers of fans turned and shrieked. As they saw their idol crumple to the ground, the attacker raised his arm high, the hunting knife dripping blood, and dealt one last blow. The knife was dropped next to Terriss's prone body, and the attacker ran to the still-waiting cab. In stunned confusion, the crowd only knew to cry out from a distance, their screams prompting the escaping horse to bolt.

Blood was everywhere. Harry ran and knelt next to his convulsing friend. Jessie threw open the door, screaming.

"I saw it all!" she sobbed.

The door was still open to the fans now crowding the entryway.

"For God's sake, get him inside," she shouted.

They set him down in the hallway, Jessie taking his limp hands, smoothing his curly hair. From the holes in the coat, small rills of blood dripped onto the floor. His beautiful blue eyes trained on hers.

He mouthed, "My God, I am stabbed!"

Two shudders, and then the light left his light blue eyes. A strange pulsing appeared around three letters tattooed on his earlobe and vanished.

Howls from the fans outside mounted to a hysterical roar.

Hecate blinked his golden eyes and positioned himself against the windowsill, watching the crowd.

Ellen sat at her dressing room mirror, wearing a wrap-around gown, signing whatever correspondence Chris handed to her to sign. There were stacks of autograph requests, speaking engagement contracts, recommendations for actors, university referrals, emergency funds benefits. Chris had verified that every piece of correspondence was to help a young woman, as Ellen Terry was the *only* possible liaison for advancement.

An unsigned photograph fell to floor where Fussie lay on his carpet. He sniffed it and went back to sleep. It was a cabinet card—a photograph of Terriss and her in *King Arthur*, she as Guinevere, he as Lancelot. Ah, Terriss, Breezy Bill. Men never asked favors of her, at least not the kind of favors sitting on her dressing room table. Men wanted friendship, distraction, whimsy. Women wanted introductions, opinions, assistance. The dog whimpered and licked his mistress's face as she bent low to pick up the photograph, her hand touching her earlobe, white veins of letters pounding to life.

Henry's orange cat, Tybalt, came bounding in, leaping onto the dressing room table and scattering the heaps of correspondence. Chris swore, Ellen laughed, and Henry entered, his face drawn and alarmed.

Chris left the room on Henry's signal, and as he closed the dressing room door, Ellen quieted Fussie. She turned to see Henry, sitting in her chair, head in his hands. He looked up.

Tears streamed down his face. Both their ears glowed with the white embossed letters: PCS.

"Something's wrong," Ellen whispered.

"Yes, but if you are safe, then all is not lost," he answered, standing to take Ellen in his arms.

"What has happened?" Ellen asked. He breathed in spasms. She untangled herself.

Henry took her by the shoulders. "William Terriss has been murdered."

CHAPTER THIRTY-ONE

BATTLE ON THE DOCK

Maud and Pamela ran down the main aisle of Saint Saviour's, out the front door, and down to Montague Close. Between two ancient buildings, they spotted a narrow passageway. Ducking inside, they plastered themselves against the alley walls, holding their breath as three men sprinted by. Once they were sure they'd gone, the two women crept down the next block and headed toward Hibernia Wharf. When they got there, the huge beauty of London Bridge stood before them, five massive stone arches framing an empty slip at the waterside.

Pamela stopped in her tracks. She heard the clink of coins, the smell of a fresh, green field. She saw stars washing over the dark sky. When the sensations cleared, London Bridge had disappeared; there was only a small group of travelers at the river's edge. They wore cloaks, heavy boots, feathered hats, and stood in a line to pay at a primitive tollhouse. Further off, people clambered down wood stairs to a boat. Where was Thomas the ferryman? The vision began to fall apart, images disappearing on the ground like falling soot.

She felt Maud's hand on her shoulder.

"Prepare," Maud said. "Remember Aleister's weak element is water."

On the word "water," Maud fractured into a thousand pieces, turning into feathers of dark charcoal floating down the dock to the water. The world was back, London Bridge was in its place, and Hibernia Wharf was crawling with dockmen and ships.

Pamela ran down to the pier's edge, churning water slapping the boards. Those sounds again. The sounds from the ship with her parents. Slaps, moans, thuds. Looking east, she saw a cluster of boats sailing toward the dock. It was a flotilla of lightermen, the workers of the Thames. The boats jockeyed between one another, and in the middle of the swarm, a racing yacht snapped its sails.

Her stomach felt cold and heavy. *Is this fear or another gift appearing?* She reached into her coat pocket and found Ellen's handkerchief and Florence's butterfly silk. Quickly, she tied the handkerchief around her neck and tucked the silk in her bodice. Looking into the Thames, she saw a lurking form surface about twenty yards away, then submerge and graze the wharf, darting underneath the pier.

Pamela held out a hand. Words Nana taught her on a Jamaican beach came rushing back. "Sacred Stream, my Provider, my Boundary, my Protector, help me to battle the veil that wishes to extinguish me."

She felt the words "jump up" inside. Willing herself to jump up, her body became a breeze. She felt her weightlessness take her midair and her breath held inside her like a balloon. Floating, jumping, skyring—it was all the same thing. On that thought, her body became a stone, and she plunged into darkening water. Cold. Black. Everything churning around her. Frantic hands trying to settle herself, she almost hit the muddy bottom near the shore. Her foot hit coins, Viking helmets, and Caesar's jade axe. A dark form floated above her, blocking any light from above. Fighting to get back to the surface of the water, she grabbed it.

Albertina.

Rising up on the webbed carpet of Albertina's back, they broke through to the surface. Pamela sputtered water, gasped for breath, and a rumble vibrated through her body.

Chumpf, Chumpf, Chumpf.

Albertina rumbled across the waves. Her gigantic head swaying side to side.

Pamela answered back, "*Chuff, chuff, chuff!*"

The alligator's eyes rolled back, her tail thrashing back and forth in the black water. They neared the wharf, and her tail rotated with such force that her entire body corkscrewed up out of the water, launching Pamela onto the bricked pavement.

The lightermen escorting the yacht were almost at the Hibernia Wharf. It came close enough for Pamela to see the name *Firefly* on the side. Further down at the end of the wharf, deck hands and sailors streaming out of the warehouses stopped to see what was happening. From behind her, a sudden horn blasted, piercing the air so loudly that she jumped straight up in the air. A ferry was coming in. And so was the fog.

Phantoms stood at the helm in the rolling carpet of the fog—Henry, with Ellen by his side, and Florence in back. Her Magician, Empress, and High Priestess. A shot of adrenaline coursed through Pamela's body. They were too far away for her to shout. She began to run to the ferry's dock. Dodging the obstacles of workers, trolleys, and cargo, her course was a zigzag of confusion.

As the ferry docked, a sailor threw the rope to anchor it, and the trio made their way to the gangway. On the wharf from the other direction, the Golden Dawn doctors hustled to meet it.

Pamela tried one more burst of energy to run as fast as she could when someone grabbed her and bundled her against a load of cargo. It was Maud, holding her fast with a finger to her lips. They huddled against the load, spying on the slip.

"Heads up!" a dock hand yelled as the flotilla arrived.

The *Firefly* glided in, the sailors whistling cues to one

another to drop lines and pull ropes. Rippled orange and yellow lights reflected on the roiling surface of the water as the ferry and the *Firefly* churned up waves. Pamela's second sense started sparking. Light-headedness hit her as the setting sun gave way to nocturnal dusk. The gas lamps on the wharf were scaled by lamplighters, igniting glowing jeweled touchstones.

From the elegant deck of the sailing yacht rang out tinkling laughter, and then a heartier laugh. As it settled against the pier, floating ghosts streamed down to the deck. No, not ghosts, lanterns carried by crew. On the deck, Ahmed appeared, alongside the dainty Mehroo, her beautiful head in a wrap. Maud wrapped her arms around Pamela tighter. Her heart sunk when she recognized the other passengers visible on the yacht's deck: Yeats, Uncle Brammie, and Edy. So many Aleister could hurt.

Pamela jerked forward to go after them, but Maud held her back, hissing, "Not yet."

For the first time, she felt it. A faint initial throb in her own earlobe. PCS was now etched in her own ears. Scanning the ferry to locate her muses, she saw Henry, Florence, Ellen—Magician, High Priestess, Empress—preparing to come ashore. But where was her Fool? Where was Terriss?

She turned to Maud, whose eyes were filled with tears.

It hit her. That's what she felt in the church. Terriss dying. She tried not to let out a howl.

Maud held her fast, half to keep her from making too much noise, half to keep her hidden.

"My Fool is dead," Pamela moaned.

The first muse and incarnate, irrepressible Terriss, gone. Her limbs felt loose, and tears ran down her face.

With a whoosh, the dainty feed of fire of the lamplights burst into towering flames.

Maud whispered, "Heads up!"

Between two buildings on the dock, Aleister walked casually toward them, carrying a torch. His disheveled hair hung over his long face; he seemed to be smiling. Following him was a man in a Deerslayer cloak.

Aleister stopped a short distance away from them and raised his torch high over his head. Pamela began to move to him, but Aleister took his torch and held it to his leg. The flames ran up his body, eating at his clothes, until he began to rise up in the yellow fog. He became a fume of fire, half demon, half goat, crystalizing in the sky. Cries of astonishment from the dock workers rang out. *They see what I am seeing!* But as she turned to see the dockworkers, she saw it was the flames from the gas lamps on the dock that had their attention.

Pamela stood directly below the floating Aleister.

He floated over her like the smoke from burning embers, his eyes yellow and lizardlike. His mouth didn't move, but Pamela heard him all the same.

"You are willing to risk all your theatricals, No Name?"

Pamela placed herself underneath him. "I own my magic!"

Aleister opened his mouth, all pointed teeth and forked tongue. Between them, a gas lantern exploded into flames and a pillar of fire roared up into the sky. Balls of fire appeared in his claws, and he lobbed them at her. Some skidded along the pavement to her, others bounced over to boats tethered at the shore. Flames were lobbed in every direction. One caught the old timbers of the ferry's gangplank on fire. The Golden Dawn chiefs were now standing with Henry, Ellen, and Florence on the second deck. Over at the *Firefly*, Pamela could barely make out Uncle Brammie and Ahmed. Between the fog and smoke, they were almost invisible. There was a glimpse of Edy and Mehroo scuttling to the far side of the ship.

All the gas lamps on the wharf were now ablaze. Cries of "Fire!" rang out as Aleister continued to throw balls from ruptured gas lamps. A fireboat tug, tooting its horn, approached the mayhem, but with all the noise and chaos, it could only circle, trying to dock. Men tried to get near the sputtering flames of the lamps' gas line with calls to form a bucket brigade, Maud getting in line to help. None of them were looking up. The men couldn't see Aleister floating above the fiery gas lanterns, lobbing fireballs from midair.

Bells from St. Saviour's Church began to toll, and along the serpentine curve of the Thames, lightermen swiveled their flat-bottomed barges. They raced one another to the pier as the London Fire Brigade tugboats chugged through the monster soup.

Above her, Aleister continued to bat fire every which way. The heat was terrible.

From the side, a large comet hit her. Yellow and blue fire caught ahold of her clothes. Her body burst into fire, she was sulphur, iron, slag. Toxic fumes filled her nose.

She was enveloped by toxic magic once before on the streets of Kingston—a duppie, the local witch, attacking her. Nana across the street, shouting, "Don't wanna kill her, but you kill fire with fire!"

Pamela shook off the flames and floated up into the night sky. Swinging up until she was directly across from Aleister, she faced him as he shook himself. He was an even larger demon in the sky. She drew a circle of flames around him, caging him. He clawed at the wall of fire as her eye caught sight of the ferry's gangplank fully ablaze. Henry, Ellen, Florence—where were they? A pillar of fire spiraled next to her. She reached over to it and cast a handful of fire as hard as she could. It landed on the gangplank, devouring the approaching fire. The hull of the ferry was safe.

The Golden Dawn chiefs tried to rush down the remains of the plank, but Pamela threw a lasso of flames to keep them on the prow. They lifted up their hands in protest as they were held prisoner to Pamela's flames.

Pamela motioned to the river, and with a great *whoosh*, Albertina rose up out of the darkness. In a moment, she was flying to her mistress's side, tail balancing her to keep her upright. Pamela climbed aboard and pointed toward the many flames on the wharf. For a moment, Albertina wobbled, her great snout sniffing. With a great *chumpf*, she opened her jaws and unleashed a swirling river. It gushed from her belly to the wharf, the fires sputtering and extinguishing. A river of water surged between Pamela and Aleister, still imprisoned in flames. Or so she thought.

In the middle of the swirling water, Pamela felt herself being pulled off Albertina and into Aleister's claws. She fought against the current.

Albertina's voice resounded in her head. "Go under, go deep, and keep still."

She slowed her panic. Propelling upright to face the monster's claws, she was confronted not with Aleister but with her Fool. The one who had saved her years ago from the waters of the Thames. Now William Terriss was before her—a watery ghost. His mane of hair undulated like a watery halo, his eyes bright, and he extended his hand.

"Swim!"

The tunnel of water they were in was far above everyone; swimming meant thrashing through a floating river above the dock. As they swam, circling the flames, Albertina joined them. They sped faster and faster, the flames of the lamplights becoming smaller and smaller until they were snuffed out like puny candles. From afar, Aleister tried to lob more fiery balls at them behind his fire pen, but his flames drowned on contact. Terriss and Pamela swam to the far edge of the floating river, safe behind the swirling wall of water.

Aleister took a ball of fire, setting his own confines ablaze and forming a great green ball of fire. It flew like a projectile, lurching toward Pamela. When he was just behind the wall of water in front of her, he stuck his head through. His jaded-colored, writhing face was inches away from hers.

"Magic is finite and only for the entitled. Burn, child, burn."

He reached down into his chest and formed a green ball of flames. Winding up, he threw it directly at her.

From behind, the wound-up tail of Albertina smacked Aleister from his airborne perch into the dark, muddy Thames. He sailed like a malignant comet and *thunked* as he sank into the surface of the water.

Ellen's handkerchief around her neck slipped off as the silk from Florence took flight as a butterfly, the two fabrics joining midair as a canopy. Pamela jumped up and held fast to her floating keepsakes. The butterfly set her down on the pavement. She tied Ellen's handkerchief around her wrist, and she stashed the butterfly silk in her bodice, where its wing beat a faint rhythm. Standing in the middle of a charred circle on the ground, there was no monster goat, no Aleister. Only black markings at her feet, peeking out underneath a carpet of fog.

She looked around. The floating river of water was gone, Terriss with it. Albertina floated above her.

The creature blinked her eyes and flew straight down, making baby alligator chirping sounds.

Leaning her head close for caresses, Albertina pressed against her mistress's breast. To the sounds of her squealing and squeaking, Pamela stroked her between the eyes. In the distance, Pamela saw a small scourge of flames, some smoldering lampposts and outbursts still separating the ferry from the dock. She pointed to the flames.

Albertina soared up and danced about in the air, casually spewing water from her jaw, dousing one hot spot after another. She squirted some water right next to Pamela, startling her. Pamela waved her finger to tell her to behave and Albertina positioned her head back and spit at the charcoal circle, dissolving it.

"*Chuff, chuff, chuff,*" Pamela cooed.

Albertina lifted her head back and sprayed an entire group of workers fifty yards away. There were no surprised cries, which made Pamela's heart thud with disappointment. They could not see her—Albertina was in her other-time place.

With a great groan and snap, Albertina floated up high over the warehouses, then pivoted, flying over the Thames. Circling above London Bridge, she splayed her stubby legs and dove like a missile into the river, just missing a mail carrier tug coming in. The shouts of excited men aboard erupted on seeing the splash. On the docks, she saw Maud in conversation with a circle of men. Scotland Yard? Secret Service? And now a charge of reporters was racing down Hibernia Wharf from the street.

Pamela walked to her and saw Churchill leading bobbies to the *Firefly*.

Maud waved to her and then called out, "Mr. Churchill, over here, please."

As Churchill's group neared, Pamela saw Henry's group from the ferry make their way to them. Looking around, she saw no signs of the chiefs except Yeats. Florence and Ellen were there to embrace her. Reporters were soon on them, circling with shouts of "What happened?" "What did you see?" and "Where did it start?"

Ellen untied the handkerchief around Pamela's wrist and wiped the soot and ash off her face with it. When she was finished, she handed it back to Pamela, who tucked it into her bodice next to Ellen's cigarette silk.

No one talked about witnessing what she just performed. There were no questions, no shocked reactions to her floating in the air, battling Aleister, swimming with Terriss. Florence motioned to Ellen and Henry, and they linked arms with her and the four of them walked to where Pamela landed. Henry squinted at the circle left behind by Albertina. Florence pointed to the symbols—an eye, a squiggle, a box.

"As your High Priestess, Pamela, I can tell that you have won this battle, but there are major skirmishes ahead. Your High Priestess is warning you that Aleister has become one with Taphthartharath, the spirit of Mercury. And he will execute as many as he sees necessary to rule."

"Aleister didn't drown? I saw Albertina . . ." Pamela asked. If they didn't see the battle, how was she to explain it?

"No, Pamela." Florence pointed toward the dark Thames riverbank.

A man in the water was being pulled up into a scow by a man in a Deerslayer cloak. The small boat bobbed at the ferry's side, and four other men already in the boat reached out to steady him. Aleister was rescued by Golden Dawn chiefs. And who was the Deerslayer man? Before Pamela could say anything, the men in the boat rowed furiously downstream, and they disappeared from sight.

Pamela cried out, "Are they gone? Or just invisible?"

Florence grimaced as she peered into the darkness. "I don't know. They could be skyring, but how they managed to make the boat disappear is—well, that's a different spell level altogether."

Pamela felt the intense gaze of Henry staring at her.

"Is William Terriss really dead?" she asked him.

Henry answered, "Yes, killed by a madman, Richard Archer Prince. Disgruntled actor and Golden Dawn member."

Tears filled Pamela's eyes. "Aleister hired him to punish me?"

Florence touched her cheek; the butterfly silk beat faster inside her blouse. "We believe he enlisted him to stop you. But you have your Magician, High Priestess, and Empress to protect you. It will be up to you to cast and incarnate the rest of your deck. This power Mr. Crowley so desperately wants to use must be very strong."

Pamela turned to Florence. "If I activate each tarot card, I will be asking for my muses' death!"

She was surrounded by kind faces with tight smiles and loving looks in soft eyes, her initials beaming on the earlobes of each of them. Her clan, her family, calling out to one another. The color yellow washed across her eyes.

Ellen wrapped her arm around Pamela's waist; Florence took her hand.

Florence said, "There are rituals in the Golden Dawn that will help protect you on your journey. I will teach you."

Pamela asked, "Are you my earth, Miss Farr?"

Florence looked off in the distance. "I am not here as a single element, Pamela. I am here to lead you to the essential vibration at the heart of all things."

"What is that? Love? God?" Pamela asked.

Florence gently took Pamela's hands in hers. "You. The essence of you."

Ellen lifted their joined hands. "And, Pixie, I pledge to nurture your artistic path. I have no Golden Dawn spells to give you, only the comfort of a home."

The three women turned to Mr. Irving, who had been staring at the ground. Irving, tutor of hieroglyphs, took his foot and followed the outline of the symbols.

"I see that fire consumes and erases all in its path," Mr. Irving said. "You have found water from your Fool. You will also need air and earth as your allies."

His hands were warm as they cupped hers. Mr. Henry Irving, who was bitten by a lamb and never wanted contact, held them for a long minute.

"I will be your air, Miss Smith," Mr. Irving said.

"I thank you, Henry."

"And I go by Mr. Irving, Miss Smith," Henry said, his eyes lowering. Pamela felt a little sting but nodded in agreement.

Uncle Brammie walked up with Maud and Yeats. In a low voice he said, "They found explosives and guns in the *Firefly*. Scotland Yard believes the Carlists were going to assassinate the Queen at Windsor."

Churchill came chugging up behind him, inserting himself in the middle of the group. "I was to be at the reviewing of the troops tomorrow! Barely escaped with my life, I tell you."

Duse, the newspaper man, ran up, barely ahead of the mob of reporters trailing him. "If you don't want to be quoted in tomorrow's papers, I suggest you leave now."

Uncle Brammie started toward the stairs to the street. "We'll hail cabs on the bridge."

The group quickly started for London Bridge, Mr. Irving holding out his arm for Ellen, and Florence trotted down the cobblestone, trailed by Yeats. Where was Maud? Gone again for another eon, no doubt. Reporters surged toward them, and Pamela quickened her pace.

As Pamela hurried along, her boots felt a strange vibration coming up from the cobblestones. No, it wasn't a vibration, it was a wave of voices. Singing, from the pavement itself. From the site of the first nunnery, from the wharf itself. The memory of ancient ship-going songs in the Jamaican port of Saint Andrews echoed with them. Pamela slowed and realized she was standing where the tollhouse had manifested.

A deep voice murmured from the stones, "Thomas the ferryman bids you to find the scepters."

Pamela wavered on the humming cobblestones, her legs still aching from being astride Albertina during the battle. "Scepters?" she whispered. "Who would have scepters?"

"Those who lead the undead," the voice replied.

The vibrations from the cobblestones stopped. Who would lead the undead? Pamela looked ahead at Florence and Ellen, both standing at the base of the stairway to the street. Florence motioned with her lit cigarette for the group to start climbing as Ellen turned back to Pamela, still unmoving on the Embankment.

"Pixie," Ellen cried out, "catch up!"

Pamela could feel the talismans in her bodice, Ellen's handkerchief and Florence's cigarette silk, thump in unison. Like two heartbeats singing in harmony, they urged her on. She commanded her aching legs to run to their beat as she sprinted to the steps.

Her High Priestess and Empress would guide her through this next challenge.

Acknowledgments

First, I would like to thank Andrea Robinson, my intrepid editor, who helped me shape *High Priestess and Empress*, this second book in the Arcana Oracle Series. We worked together during the awful days of January through March in 2020, when COVID was in high gear and our emails veered between edit notes and notes about keeping our families safe.

Next, I express gratitude for my trusted group of readers for this novel: Mary Micari, Joel Jones, Kent Meredith, Karen McKendrick, Christina Burz, and Ryan Brown. Thank you for your insights, notes and suggestions.

My writing group—Barbara Lucas, Catherine Siemann, Gro Flatebo, Finola Austin, and Laura Schofer—helped with fine tuning, grammar and hearing Pamela's voice. Thank you for your notes, rewrite suggestions and ideas.

Many thanks are due to Derek and Kim Notman, the descendants of Pamela Colman Smith, who so generously shared their family stories of her and allowed me to view the artwork that remains in the family.

And I feel special gratitude for Nikki Sanders, the generous soul in England who reached out to share the stories of her grandmother, Rosa Baille, who was Pamela's best friend. I also learned of John Baille, Rosa's brother, who exhibited some of

Pamela's artwork in London. I will cherish the artwork Nikki Sanders inherited from her grandmother, created by Pamela, for all of my days.

A special mention of Stuart R. Kaplan is necessary, for I am so grateful for his generosity in sharing his collection of Pamela's printings, letters, diaries, and artwork with me. And a big thank-you to him also for publishing the definitive collection on her, his book *Pamela Colman Smith: The Untold Story*. I hope Stuart and Pixie are having a fine glass of Opal Hush together in the Great Beyond.

Thanks to everyone at U.S. Games Systems, especially Lynn Araujo for her support and cheer.

At SparkPress, my special thanks goes to Shannon Green, my editor on this book and the previous book *Magician and Fool*. Thank you for your patience, sharp eye, and kind words. SparkPress also has the keen talents of Crystal Patriarche, Lauren Wise, and Addison Gallegos. Thank you for all your hard work, insights, and dedication. And for the leader at SparkPress, Brooke Warner, thank you for your trailblazing efforts into the world of publishing, where you have created opportunities for so many of us women authors.

As for my darling twin sister, Cynthia Wands, thank you for all your prompts, suggestions, rewrites, ideas, and insights on how to make better beginnings and endings. Your writing talents, along with your ability to read my mind, are much appreciated.

And Robert Petkoff, thank you for lending your ear, eye, and perspective on my writing and for all you do to help me write and publish. I am lucky beyond measure for your love and support.

ABOUT THE AUTHOR

Susan Wands is a writer, tarot reader, and actor. A graduate from the University of Washington, she has acted professionally across the United States and on Broadway, has written plays, screenplays, and skits, and has produced several indie films. As a cochair of the NYC Chapter of the Historical Novel Society, she helps produce monthly online book launches and author panels. Wands's writings have appeared in *Art in Fiction, Kindred Spirits* magazine, and The Irving Society journal *First Knight*. She lives in NYC with her husband, actor Robert Petkoff, and two cats, Flora and Flynn. The third book of the Arcana Oracle Series, *Emperor and Hierophant*, is currently in the works.

Author photo © Robert Petkoff

SELECTED TITLES FROM SPARKPRESS

SparkPress is an independent boutique publisher
delivering high-quality, entertaining, and engaging
content that enhances readers' lives, with a special focus
on female-driven work. www.gosparkpress.com

Magician and Fool: Book One, Arcana Oracle Series, by Susan Wands. $17.95, 978-1-684631-86-5. Hired by the Golden Dawn to illustrate a deck of tarot cards, Pamela, a London-born empath with second sight, wants to keep the power of her creation out of the hands of her nemesis, magician Aleister Crowley, who desires to use her cards for his evil purposes.

Sky of Water: Book Three of the Equal Night Trilogy, Stacey L. Tucker. $16.95, 978-1-68463-040-0. Having emerged triumphant from her trials in the Underworld, Skylar Southmartin is stronger and gutsier, and can handle anything that comes her way. In the gripping climax of the Equal Night Trilogy, she uncovers one last secret no one saw coming—one that Vivienne, the Great Mother of Water, hoped would stay buried for another 13,000 years.

The Goddess Twins: A Novel, Yodassa Williams. $16.95, 978-1-68463-032-5. Days before their eighteenth birthday, Arden and Aurora's mother goes missing and they discover they belong to a family of Caribbean deities. Can these goddess twins uncover their evil grandfather's plot in time to save their mother, themselves, and the free world?

The Thorn Queen: A Novel, Elise Holland. $16.95, 978-1-943006-79-3. Twelve-year-old Meylyne longs to impress her brilliant, sorceress mother—but when she accidentally breaks one of Glendoch's First Rules, she accomplishes the opposite of that. Forced to flee, the only way she may return home is with a cure for Glendoch's diseased prince.

The Blue Witch: The Witches of Orkney, Book One, Alane Adams. $12.95, 978-1-943006-77-9. Nine-year-old Abigail Tarkana has a problem: her witch magic has finally come in, but it's different—and being different is a problem at the Tarkana Witch Academy. Together with her scientist-friend Hugo, she face off against sneevils, shreeks, and vikens in a race to discover the secrets about her mysterious magic.